Afterlove

Afterlove

TANYA BYRNE

HODDER CHILDREN'S BOOKS

First published in Great Britain in 2021 by Hodder Children's Books

10

A CIP catalogue record for this book is available from the British Library.

ISBN 978 1 444 95595 8

Typeset in Adobe Caslon by Avon DataSet Ltd, Alcester, Warwickshire

Printed and bound in Great Britain by Clays Ltd, Elcograf S.p.A.

The paper and board used in this book
are made from wood from responsible sources.

Hodder Children's Books
An imprint of Hachette Children's Group
Part of Hodder and Stoughton
Carmelite House
50 Victoria Embankment
London EC4Y 0DZ

An Hachette UK Company
www.hachette.co.uk

www.hachettechildrens.co.uk

*There's a field somewhere
beyond all doubt and wrong doing.
I'll meet you there.*

– Rumi

For my mother and everyone else who got on the boat.
I hope you're where you want to be.

Alice Anderson is exactly where Deborah said she would be, on the cliff in Saltdean looking out at the sea. Not that I could have missed her in that hot-pink fur coat she's wearing. It's the sort of thing I'd make a beeline for in a shop, but never be brave enough to buy. I'd try it on, take a selfie, then put it back in favour of something more sensible. Something black that I could wear to school without getting detention.

That's one of the hardest things about this, how hopelessly normal they are. Alice could be from my year or the girl behind me in the queue at Primark, waiting for the changing rooms. Someone I could have passed in the street and never noticed until tonight.

It's hard to tell in the dark, but from here she looks my age – sixteen, maybe seventeen – with a froth of blonde curls that the wind lifts up and away from her face so I can see her profile. I can't see the colour of her eyes, but I can make out the sweep of her jaw and her neat button nose, her lipstick the same colour as her coat.

Judging by her knee-length dress and heels, she's been out tonight. It's far too cold for bare legs, but maybe she thought she'd be OK because she was getting a cab home, then lost her purse and had to walk instead. Or maybe she had a row with

3

her boyfriend and told him to stop the car here, insisting that she'd make her own way home.

I don't know why I do this, why I make up stories about them. That will pass, I suppose. Maybe in a few months when I've done this enough times that I won't even remember their names any more.

Until then, I can't help but ask myself why they're there.

Why them?

The sea is rough tonight, the waves a rolling boil that will snatch you clean off your feet and drag you in if you get too close. Not that I ever do. I've always been scared of open water and nights like this remind me why. The waves are so loud that Alice doesn't hear me approach, but I keep my distance because I can see that she's shaking.

There's something about that moment, when you're stuck in that woozy midpoint between being here and not, when you feel everything at once – fear, joy, hope. It's not so much a rush as a flood and it's like you're drowning, like someone is holding your head under water and if you can just find your way back to the surface, you'll be OK.

That's what's so cruel about it. There's a split second when you're sure that you got away with it and the relief is dizzying. It's kind of like that moment right after you kiss someone for the first time and you feel untethered, like you could float up and touch the sky. That's where I come in, to make sure you don't.

I give Alice a minute to steady herself, watch as she closes her eyes and sucks in a breath. Her whole body shudders and I wonder if it's then that she knows that there's nothing there.

Finally, Alice turns, her blonde curls swirling in the wind, and when she sees me, she takes a step back.

I wait a beat, then another.

'Alice Anderson?'

The crease between her fair eyebrows deepens. 'How do you know my name?'

'I'm Ash.'

She stares at me so I nod at her. It takes her a moment, but when she realises that I'm gesturing at her to look over the cliff, she does, then lets out a wail that sends the seagulls scattering in every direction. She staggers back from the edge and covers her mouth with both hands. When she spins round to face me again, I have to fight the urge to turn and run because what if she wants me to say something?

This is what she'll want me to say: everything is going to be OK.

This is what I can't say: everything is going to be OK.

She doesn't say anything, though, and I'm glad that she doesn't ask me how or why or any of those impossible questions I can't answer. Maybe she'll want to know when. I can tell her that. If there's one thing I've learnt doing this, it's that in that moment, when all the years you thought you had ahead of you dissolve into a few seconds, why doesn't matter. What matters is who you'll leave behind and I get that more than anyone, believe me.

Like I said, there's something about that moment. Everything – all those things you did and didn't do and said and didn't say – falls away and you see everything with absolute, startling clarity. People go their whole lives waiting for that moment.

They climb mountains and swim seas and read books hoping to find it. A lucky few do, but most of us – people like me and Alice Anderson and all the ones who went before us and all the ones that will follow – don't until it's too late and, God, it's cruel, isn't it? How, when there's no time left, you suddenly know exactly what you should have done with it.

When Alice lifts her chin to look me in the eye for the first time since she found me standing here, I wait and wonder if this is it. She knows and it will come out in a rush. All the things she should have done. The lies she told and secrets she kept. She can't take it with her, so she'll leave it with me. Everything she wished for when she blew out her birthday candles. I'm there and this is it, her last chance to say *I'm sorry* or *I love you* or *Forgive me.*

All the times she should have jumped and didn't. All the people she should have kissed and didn't. All that time she wasted being too careful or too polite or too scared when, in the end, nothing is as scary as watching your whole life narrow to a single moment that's about to pass, whether you're ready for it to or not.

Maybe I'll see it then – the regret – burning off her, right through her clothes, and she'll never look so alive. She'll laugh and cry and scream, exhaust every emotion until there's nothing left and it will be like watching a light bulb flare then burn out.

Alice doesn't do any of that, though. She doesn't tell me her secrets, doesn't tell me about her dog, Chester, who sleeps at the bottom of her bed at night. Or about the lipstick she stole from Boots last year, the red one that wouldn't come off, even when she scrubbed it so hard her mouth felt bruised for days.

I should be OK with that because it means that I don't need to explain, we can just go. But I want to. I want Alice to ask me who I am. If she did, I'd tell her that I'm Ashana Persaud and that I'm sixteen. I'd tell her that my favourite song is 'Rock Steady' because it always gets my parents on the dance floor at weddings and my favourite film is *Dilwale Dulhania Le Jayenge*, even though I tell everyone it's *The Shining* because it's easier. I'd show her the scar on my chin that I got falling off a slide when I was six and tell her about the tattoo I was going to get on my eighteenth birthday. I'd tell her that I'm scared of open water and clowns and being puked on and that from here, you can see where I had my last kiss, a couple of weeks ago, right there on the beach. And most of all, I'd tell her that it's not fair.

It's not fair that she gets to go, when I have to stay here and do this.

She doesn't ask, though, so we just stand there, on the edge of the cliff, the moon watching over us and the sea beckoning beneath until finally she says, 'The moon looked so pretty. I just wanted to take a photo of it. I didn't realise I was so close to the edge and then it just . . .' she stops to look up at the moon, '. . . wasn't there any more.'

When I see her smudged eyeliner, a mascara-coloured tear skidding down her cheek, I realise that her eyes are brown, like mine, but the light behind them has gone and I wonder what they were like before. Before I got here. And I wonder who's waiting for her at home. If her parents are up, pretending to be engrossed in *Newsnight* so it doesn't look like they've been waiting up for her. Her mother swaddled in a thick dressing gown, phone in hand, while her father listens out for the

7

curmudgeonly creak of the gate, followed by Alice's careful footsteps as she navigates the gravel path in her heels.

But she isn't going home, is she? The thought makes me want to turn and run into the sea, let it pull me under, carry me to wherever it is that I'm supposed to be. But I can't. I can't leave her. So I walk over to where she's standing and peer over the edge. It's dark, but I can see her – Alice Anderson – on the path, her limbs at unnaturally odd angles on the concrete, a halo of fresh blood beneath her head.

We stand there for a while, my hands in the pockets of my jacket and Alice's in the pockets of her hot-pink coat. Eventually, she tilts her cheek towards me. 'Are you an angel?' I try not to laugh. 'If you're not an angel, what are you, then?' She looks me up and down and I let her. Let her take in that I'm in black, from my DMs and jeans to my hoodie and leather jacket. Her gaze narrows when she sees my silver scythe necklace.

With that, her pale skin becomes almost see-through against the dark sky, her edges blurred, like she's already disappearing. A whisper of moths gathers, settling in her curls as she watches me look over the cliff again then does the same. When she sees the sharp shadow of Charon on the beach below, the moonlight picking out his wooden boat as it bobs gently on the suddenly still sea, she turns to me with a curious frown.

'Is he here for me?'

I nod.

'Where am I going?'

I hold out my hand. 'You'll see.'

ONE

As school trips go, visiting a wind farm to learn about the importance of renewable energy isn't much to get excited about. We don't even get to go on a coach because we're only going to the Marina so Mr Moreno makes us walk there, saying that the exercise will do us good.

It's chaos, of course, all of us spilling out of the school gates at once in a roar of laughter and chatter that you must be able to hear halfway down the street. We Whitehawk kids have a bad enough reputation as it is, but when we're travelling en masse like this, it's enough to make people shake their heads and tut as they cross the road to avoid us.

By the time we get on to Manor Hill, Mr Moreno is clearly regretting his decision to make us walk as he runs back and forth, frantically doing a head count to make sure none of us have wandered off while his TA urges those of us lagging behind to hurry up or we'll miss the boat.

I'm one of them.

'It won't be that bad,' Adara tells me, offering me a cheese and onion crisp, which I refuse with a surly scowl as I stuff my hands into the pockets of my leather jacket. She's right, of course. After all, it's quite a hot afternoon for late September, the sun high and bright in the sky, and I'm missing double chemistry, which is never a bad thing. Besides, it's Friday and Mr Moreno says that we'll be done by two thirty, so I should be thrilled that we're finishing early, even if it means hanging out at a wind farm for a few hours.

My reluctance, however, is less to do with *where* we're going, rather, *how* we're getting there.

'Listen, yeah,' Adara says, stopping to reach for another crisp and pointing it at me. 'I know you don't like open water, babe, but it'll be fine. I promise. We'll sail to the wind farm, look at the turbines, marvel in the energy of the future and sail back.' I obviously don't look convinced because she adds, 'What's the worst that can happen?'

That question is answered as soon as we arrive at the Marina and Dan McCarthy runs up behind me. He must have overheard us talking because he picks me up and threatens to throw me into the sea. I shriek, telling him to let go of me as I try to kick him, but he just laughs and asks me if I want to go for a swim. I'm aware of Adara shouting at him, but that just makes him laugh harder as he holds me over the sea wall, the waves so close it's as though they're reaching up to lick the soles of my DMs.

Mercifully, Mr Moreno intervenes, marching over to where he has me dangling. 'Daniel McCarthy! Put Ashana down *right now!*' Mr Moreno never raises his voice, which I almost admire, given that he has to keep a classful of sixteen year olds engaged through double chemistry on a Friday afternoon when our only concern is what we're doing at the weekend. It works, though, because Dan lifts me back over the edge of the sea wall and puts me down.

Mr Moreno's cheeks go from pink to red. 'What were you doing, Daniel?'

'We were just mucking around, Sir.'

We? I'm tempted to interject, but Year Eleven solidarity dictates that I never grass on a fellow classmate, even if they're as annoying as Dan.

'It didn't seem like Ashana was in on the joke, though.' Mr Moreno crosses his arms, waiting for me to agree. When I don't, he gives up with a sharp sigh. 'Apologise to Ashana. *Now.*'

'Sorry,' he says, trying to swallow back a laugh and failing.

Mr Moreno, clearly unimpressed with Dan's lack of remorse, uncrosses his arms to raise his finger. 'We'll discuss this on Monday, Daniel. I want to see you in my office at eight o'clock, do you understand?' I can tell Dan wants to object – eight o'clock on a Monday morning! – but he thinks better of it and nods instead. 'Now try to behave yourself for the rest of the afternoon. Do you think you can manage that?'

Dan grunts something I assume is yes then runs off to join his mates.

'Prick,' I mutter, adjusting my leather jacket. I didn't think I'd said it loud enough for Mr Moreno to hear, but he turns to me with a fierce frown that lets me know that he doesn't think it's a proportional response. Now it's my turn to apologise, which is deeply unfair given that I nearly just died. I mutter one anyway, which he acknowledges with a nod before ushering my classmates who gathered to see what's going on towards the gangway that leads to the boat.

'You OK?' Adara asks as we follow, albeit with less enthusiasm.

I nod and she knows me well enough to leave it at that.

My legs are still shaking as we walk over to where everyone is gathered in a horseshoe around Mr Moreno at the foot of the gangway, his face back to its normal colour. He must have been waiting for us, because when Adara and I stop, lingering at the back, he holds his hands up. 'I know we're all excited to learn about the marvel of renewable energy.' There's a collective groan, which he ignores. 'But you're representing Whitehawk High School this afternoon, so please try to remember that, OK?'

He tilts his head and raises his eyebrows at Dan McCarthy, who looks back at me and laughs.

'Ignore him,' Adara tells me as Mr Moreno claps his hands and turns to lead the way up the narrow gangway towards the waiting boat. 'You know what Dan's like.'

'He's kind of hard to ignore when he's trying to throw me in the sea, Ad.'

'I know, but he only does this stuff because he fancies you. You know what boys are like. That's how they show their affection.'

'He's not my type,' I remind her with a sour smile.

She laughs. 'He doesn't know that, though, does he?'

'First of all.' I stop to smooth the palms of my hands over my scalp, trying to tame the fine hair that has escaped from my ponytail thanks to Dan's grand romantic gesture. 'He doesn't fancy me, he's an asshole. And even if he did, we're *sixteen*, Ad. Aren't we beyond boys pulling our pigtails in the playground?'

She goes quiet and when the skin between her precisely

drawn eyebrows pinches, I know that she's asking herself whether all the boys who teased us over the years, who tried to pull off her hijab and told us that we smelt like curry, were just 'showing their affection' or if they were assholes, like Dan.

I'm about to tell her not to worry about it when there's a bristle of excitement. I wonder what Dan's done now as Mr Moreno marches down the gangway towards us, reminding Adara and I that they're holding up the boat because we're late as he corrals us on. It's then that we discover what all the excitement is about: we're not alone. There, on the other side of the deck, is a huddle of girls who look as horrified to see us as we are to see them.

'Who are *they*?' Adara asks, blinking so furiously the wings of her eyeliner look set to take flight.

'The Whitehawk kids and the Roedean girls.' I smirk. 'This should be interesting.'

There's a tense moment of silence as we stare across the deck at one another. To their credit, they don't recoil, rather push their shoulders back and lift their chins as if to say, *We're not scared of you.* Some even cross their arms and while it does nothing to deflect the stares they're getting, when I see them in their neat navy uniforms, it's enough to make me want to lick my thumb and bend down to wipe away the scuff on the toe of my DM.

When I turn back to Adara, she's fussing over her hijab and I follow her gaze across the deck to a girl with the sort of hair I've only ever seen in shampoo adverts – long and blonde and practically *glowing* in the late September sun – who is staring shamelessly at us.

15

'What's the matter?' I ask her, crossing my arms. 'Never seen brown people before?'

The girl immediately flushes, then turns to her friend to whisper something. I'm about to tell Adara to ignore her, but I don't need to as she looks at me and rolls her eyes.

'Right. Everyone keep to the left, please,' Mr Moreno tells us as the teacher from Roedean tells them to keep to the right, as though we're warring football supporters who might charge at one another.

The boat engine starts and as soon as I feel the reluctant rumble of it beneath my feet, I remember where I am and reach for the railing to steady myself as my legs threaten to give way. I'll give them that – the Roedean girls are a welcome distraction from the sea encircling us, but as the boat begins to pull away from the dock, I'm lashed in the face with the cloying smell of fuel and feel the milk from the cereal my mother made me have before I left home curdling in my stomach.

'Deep breaths,' Adara coos, rubbing my back with her hand, but I can't – the heady smell combined with the smoke chugging from the engine is so strong, I can taste it coating my tongue.

I cover my mouth and nose with my hand, but it doesn't help. Sit down, but it doesn't help. Close my eyes, but it doesn't help. The seagulls aren't helping, either, hovering uncomfortably close to the boat like vultures circling a fresh kill. Eventually, one breaks away from the others, swooping down to snatch a crisp out of Dan's hand and carrying it away in its beak. The response is swift, this sudden roar of shrieks and laughs, which makes the seagulls even more hysterical as I cling on to the railing, sure that I can feel the boat tipping from side to side as everyone runs back and forth across the deck.

I can hear Mr Moreno and the teacher from Roedean telling everyone to calm down as I tighten my grip on the railing and cover my eyes with my other hand. And I can hear Adara asking if I'm OK and focus on the familiar sound of her voice. I can't speak, everything blurry and out of reach, the deck no longer solid, more like sloshing water beneath my feet as I try not to give into it and let it pull me under.

I find my voice and ask Adara to give me a minute. I retreat to the other end of the boat to put as much distance between me and the engine as possible. It doesn't help and just as I realise that I won't be able to swallow back the wave of nausea rushing up my chest much longer, I remember Mr Moreno telling us before we left that seasickness is your brain struggling to understand why it feels like everything is moving while you're still. Apparently, if you look at the horizon, your brain notes the movement and resets your internal equilibrium. I'm willing to try anything at this point, so I lift my head and focus on Shoreham Power Station.

I hold on to the railing and wait for my brain to do its thing as I watch the shoreline recede in the distance. Nothing happens, though. I still feel wretched, so I reach into the back pocket of my jeans for my phone, half tempted to call my mother and beg her to come get me when, to my surprise, I realise that it's working. I feel better. Kind of. I still feel like I'm about to chunder, but it's nowhere near as bad and, after a few minutes, I stop shivering. After a few more, I've

17

stopped sweating and my breathing has settled enough that I feel able to stand up straight.

That's better. My legs feel a little steadier, the breeze cooling my hot cheeks as I suck in a breath and let it out with a relieved sigh. Just as I feel able to loosen my grip on the railing, I'm aware of someone next to me and flinch so suddenly I almost drop my phone into the sea, sure that it's Dan come to succeed in throwing me in this time.

But it's not Dan, it's one of the Roedean girls.

'Does it make you want to jump?'

I'm too startled to answer as she looks at me with a slow smile. All I can see is her hair. I don't know what they feed them at Roedean, but they all have such good hair. It's in a ponytail, which is a lot neater than mine, and it's red. Not just red, but *red* red. The colour of the sari my mother wore on her wedding day. A rich rust red with threads of gold that, when the sun hits it, makes it look like it's on fire.

I know I'm staring because all I can think about is whether her eyelashes are the same colour under the layers of mascara. If she notices, though, she has the grace not to say anything, she just keeps smiling. I almost smile back but I catch myself, suspicious of why she's there. Perhaps she saw my leather jacket and DMs and thinks she can ponce a cigarette from me that she'll smoke with great flourish. A tiny display of defiance to show her friends how cool she is. Or perhaps she wants to ask me where I'm from so she can tell me about that time she went to India.

Whatever the reason, when I look at her Roedean uniform and her full cheeks, pinched pink by the wind, I can think of no good reason why a girl like her wants to talk to a girl like me. I mean, side by side, we make no sense. Her, immaculate, the sunlight settling in two moons on the toes of her saddle shoes, and me, greasy and crumpled, a thin layer of sweat drying on my top lip.

'Does it make you want to jump?' she asks again before I can ask her what she wants. 'Like when you're on a bridge or on a platform and you can hear the train coming and think, *I could jump.*'

Yes, I almost say, but stop myself again.

She shrugs, tucking her hands into the pockets of her blazer. 'You're not the only one.'

Really? I thought there was something wrong with me.

'Some say it's healthy.'

Healthy?

'It's called high place phenomenon,' she continues, clearly unfazed by the fact that I haven't said anything yet. 'A scientist called Jennifer Hames interviewed a group of students at Florida State University and found that, for the most part anyway, thinking stuff like that is pretty normal.'

How is that normal?

'It means that you have a healthy will to live.'

'How does thinking about jumping off a bridge mean you have a healthy will to live?' I say at last.

Her eyes brighten at the challenge.

'Cognitive dissonance.' I like the way she says it, like she doesn't assume I don't know what it means. 'When you're standing on a bridge you're not actually in any danger, are you? Not unless someone comes along and pushes you,

19

which isn't likely, is it?'

I think of Dan then and quickly conclude that I wouldn't like to be alone on a bridge with him.

'It's all in your head.' She takes her hand out of her pocket and taps her temple with her finger. 'When you're on a bridge, your brain sees the edge and tells you that you're in danger. So you get scared, but you shouldn't be scared because you weren't in any danger, were you?'

I nod, fingers tightening around my phone as the boat jerks suddenly.

'So later, when you're trying to rationalise why you were scared, you conclude that it must have been because you *wanted* to jump, even though you had no desire to.' She puts her hand back in her pocket and shrugs again. 'It just means that you're sensitive to internal cues of danger, which reaffirms your will to live.'

I have no idea what she's on about, but I like listening to her. She doesn't talk like anyone I know. She's not scared if there are a few beats of silence. She just leaves them there.

'You don't want to jump. It's just your brain playing tricks on you. Like now.' She nods at the sea. 'Being on this boat is making you think that you're going to throw up when you don't actually want to.'

'I still might.'

She throws her head back and laughs and it's the most beautiful thing I've ever heard. This delicate shiver, like the sound my grandmother's gold bangles make when she's clapping roti, that grows and grows until it's so loud – I can feel it in my bones.

I don't want her to stop, and try to think of something else to say to make her do it again, but then her chin drops and when she looks at me, smiling at me in that same slow way she did when she asked me if I wanted to jump, it's as though she's struck a match and set me alight.

We're talking so much that we miss the discussion about the wonders of renewable energy which means that I will almost certainly fail next week's test, but I'm struggling to give even *half* a shit because I want to ask her everything. I know that her name is Poppy Morgan and she's sixteen, like me, and she's just started at Roedean after being kicked out of another super-posh boarding school called Wycombe Abbey. I know that she likes to twist her ponytail around her hand when she talks, that she presses her lips together when she's thinking and that she's OK with open water, but she doesn't like heights.

It's not enough, though. I want to know if she has any brothers or sisters and what her favourite song is so I can go home and listen to it on repeat, but it's all so perfect. It feels like she and I are encased in a soap bubble that will pop if I am foolish enough to do anything to disturb it.

So I don't say a word, painfully aware that a clock is ticking somewhere as the shoreline gets closer and closer, and it's like I'm floating, like I've left my body and I'm looking down at us, standing on the deck on the boat and God, it's perfect. The sky so big that I want to see every corner of it. I tell myself – beg myself, actually – not to overthink it. To just enjoy these last few moments, but the clock is tick, tick, ticking and the shoreline is getting closer and closer and I'm waiting.

Waiting for the bubble to burst, because it always does.

She's so near that I feel the heat of her next to me, and I warn myself not to make it more than it is. I haven't done this often, but I've done it enough to know how this ends. All the girls in the rainbow T-shirts who kiss girls to impress boys but would die if anyone called them a dyke. The girls with the careless smiles and thirsty hearts who draw lines only they can see and move goalposts when I'm not looking. All those things said and unsaid, never to be spoken of again. All the times I said, 'OK' when I really wanted to say, 'I don't want to be friends.'

The ghost girls who are there, then not there, who let themselves give into that itch of curiosity, just for a moment, and make me feel something, only to conclude that it isn't for them. The ones who are bored or scared or both, who'd rather tell me that they were drunk than let me know that they felt something as well because all they want is a quiet life. Someone they can love without it being brave. Someone they can invite over for Sunday lunch and go with to prom.

I am the first and last and nothing inbetween. The mad one. The wild one. The one who sees things that aren't there. I am to be unloaded on, to be bled on and cried all over. I am the one they experiment with. The one they can let go with because I'll never tell. I am the one they have saved in their phone as Alfie or Harry or Luke. The keeper of secrets and soother of guilt. But I am never the one.

I am not to be loved. Not out loud, anyway. Maybe, one day, if I'm lucky, I'll be a *what if?*. Or worse, the one before the one. The one that made them realise that it wasn't just a phase.

But, for the most part, I will barely be a footnote in the book of that quiet life they want so much and as I stand beside Poppy, looking out at the wide, wild sea, I wait. Wait for her to move away when one of the Roedean girls approaches or to suddenly mention a boyfriend like this is nothing, like she's just talking. Like that's all this is, just talking. After all, even fear becomes a habit after a while, doesn't it?

We're approaching the Marina and this is it, I know. The moment has passed. The pain in my chest is so keen that it brings tears to my eyes as I make myself look down at the water so Poppy doesn't see as the boat pulls in. When I do, I notice that the water is a different colour here. A colour I've only seen in postcards from other people. Poppy must notice as well, because she says that we could be in the Côte d'Azur. She says it with a dreamy sigh and when she closes her eyes, she suddenly feels very far away, even though she's standing right next to me.

The nearest I've ever been to the French Riviera – or France in general – is a croissant from the Real Patisserie, and it's as close as I'm ever likely to get. But for whatever reason, our paths crossed today – call it luck or fate or good old-fashioned magic – and they're about to part, never to cross again. I mean, it's not like I'm going to bump into her at Lidl or waiting for the 1A, is it? This is it, I know, as the boat docks. She'll just be that girl I think about sometimes when I look out at the wind farm or when I eat a croissant.

'Here.' Poppy takes my phone out of my hand so suddenly, I don't have a chance to object. When she gives it back, I look at the screen to find that she's added her number to my contacts.

'If you ever feel like jumping,' she says, the corners of her mouth twitching mischievously when I look up again. 'Or a coffee.'

My chest hurts for a different reason this time because I want to see her again – I really want to see her again – and she wants to see me and that never happens. I don't know what to say, so I just smile back as she winks at me. I watch her turn and walk away, her hips swinging and her hair ablaze, and I wonder if there are words for how this feels but I don't know what they are yet.

TWO

Now I feel woozy for an entirely different reason as I make my way off the boat to look for Adara. My phone is still in my hand and as I look down at it, it's all I can do not to message Poppy immediately. I don't know how I stop myself, because every thought in my head has been burned away and replaced with her. Every thought, every sound. The seagulls squeal her name while the waves pull back and forth, back and forth, whispering it in that careful, hushed tone Adara and I use when we're in the library. Even my heart, which is throbbing so furiously I can hear it in my ears, seems to be saying it in the space between heartbeats.

Poppy.

Beat.

Poppy.

Beat.

Poppy.

When I find Adara on the dock, she grins and hugs me tightly.

'You OK?' she asks when she steps back. 'Happy to be back on dry land?'

I should laugh, but I wonder if she saw me talking to Poppy, which is why she hasn't checked on me until now. I want to grab her by the shoulders and tell her everything, let it all spill out of me in a crazed rush that makes my hands shake and the back of my neck burn. But I know what she'll say. She'll tell me to calm down, to be careful, that I don't even know this girl. So I don't say anything, just smile back at her, because I want to relish this moment of hope a little longer, savour it while whatever happens next still holds all the promise of a fresh notebook.

Adara must have seen us talking, though. She's going to ask me about Poppy, so I'm grateful when a couple of girls from our class approach to ask if we're going into town. They've obviously decided to take advantage of finishing early as well so tag along as we head to the bus stop.

I don't remember waiting for the bus or even getting on it, just that I'm there, on the top deck, listening to them complain about how boring the trip was. I can hear Adara reminding them that the world is burning, but they're more concerned about how they're going to get booze for Mo's party tonight. Adara's right, as always, but then so are they – visiting a wind farm isn't how most sixteen year olds want to spend a Friday afternoon. I mean, meeting Poppy there is hardly a story for the grandkids, is it?

There I go again, getting ahead of myself. I can't help it, though. This feels different. I know I say that every time, but it really does.

This could be something.

We could be something.

I unlock my phone to check that Poppy's number is still there and not something my brain conjured in an attempt to give us a happy ending. I bite down on my bottom lip to stop myself from smiling when I see that it is and I fix my gaze on it, as though if I look away, it may disappear and be gone for ever. The thought makes me want to message her even more as I stare at it so hard the numbers eventually melt together and for one terrible moment, I think it really has disappeared. I can hear my heart in my ears again as I blink furiously – once, twice, three times, four – until finally the screen refocuses and her number is back.

'What you grinning at? Are you thinking about that girl you were talking to before?' I hear Adara ask, as we stand up to get off. Before I can respond, I hear someone say my name as we step off the bus and turn to find a woman in a green Extinction Rebellion T-shirt smiling at me.

I'm about to tell her that I don't have any money on me, assuming that she's going to ask for a donation, when she says, 'You don't remember me, do you, Ash?'

Shit.

This never ends well.

'I'm Gillian,' she says when I don't say anything, just stare at her. 'I work with your mum in A&E.'

'Oh, hi,' I say in a way I hope doesn't betray the fact that I don't remember her at all.

'How's it going? How's school?'

'Good. We went to Rampion Wind Farm this afternoon.'

'That's brilliant!' She beams. 'I'm so glad they're teaching you about stuff like that. It's so important.'

'Yeah.' I nod, tucking my phone into the back pocket of my jeans. 'I guess.'

'Who's this?' She nods at Adara who is next to me, scrolling through her phone, and when Gillian's smile gets a little tighter, I feel each of the muscles in my shoulders clench at once.

'This?' It's a moment too long before I can catch my breath to finish the thought as I turn to Adara, who is looking up now, gaze narrowing at her – this Gillian – and I wonder if she's thinking the same thing. If Gillian knows. If my mother told her, and now she's going to tell my mother that she saw me in town with a girl.

'Adara,' Adara says with an equally tight smile.

'Yes, Adara. This is Adara. This is my friend Adara. We've been friends since infant school.'

I have to stop saying Adara, but I don't want Gillian to forget her name so when she tells my mother that she saw me in town with a girl, my mother will just say, *Oh her. They've been friends for years.*

Adara must be thinking the same thing because when Gillian excuses herself, saying that she needs to pick her son up from school, Adara waits until she's across the road before turning to me with a scowl.

'Do you think she knows?'

I shrug. 'If she does, I can't believe that my mother told her.'

'No way.' Adara shakes her head. 'She can't have. You don't even know if she's told your dad that you're, you know.' She raises her eyebrows up and down. 'Why would she tell some random woman at work?'

'She wouldn't.'

Would she?

'She wouldn't, Ash. Don't worry about it.'

I am worried, though, so when she turns to me with an eager smile, I'm a little startled. 'What?'

'Come on then?'

'Come on *what?*'

'The Roedean girl? What's her name?'

'Oh.' I try not to smile, but fail miserably. 'Poppy. Poppy Morgan.'

'Of course she's called Poppy.'

'What's that supposed to mean?'

'Does she have a brother called Hugo?' Adara chuckles sourly as we cross the road and head towards Churchill Square. When I don't take the bait, she changes tack. 'How old is she?'

'Our age.'

'What did you guys talk about?'

I daren't tell her about the jumping off the bridge thing, so I say, 'All sorts.'

'And you know that she's definitely . . .' She raises her eyebrows up and down again.

'Of course not!' I scoff. 'Do I ever?'

'Well, you need to find out sooner rather than later this time.'

'How, though?' I shrug. 'I can't just *ask* her, can I? It's rude.'

'And stringing you along so you torture yourself for weeks, wondering if she likes you, for her to tell you that she's just *super flirty* with her friends and she's sorry if she gave you the wrong idea, isn't rude?'

Wow. Way to sum up every relationship I've ever been in, Adara.

'Thanks for that,' I mutter, stuffing my hands into the pockets of my leather jacket.

She stops walking so suddenly, a woman pushing a buggy almost goes into the back of us. 'I'm not trying to upset you, Ash.' Her whole face softens. 'I just want you to be careful, yeah?'

I stop as well, avoiding eye contact as I let out a sullen sigh. 'I will be careful, Ad.'

'Just don't rush it, OK? I don't want you getting hurt again.'

'I won't.'

She doesn't seem convinced, but lets it go and starts walking again. 'So how did you guys leave it?'

'She gave me her number.'

She turns to look at me, her light brown eyes suddenly dark. 'You haven't WhatsApped her yet, have you?'

'Of course not,' I tell her as we head into H&M.

'Did you find her Insta?'

'Of course.' What am I? An amateur? 'It's locked.'

'Good. You have to wait three days.'

I turn to blink at her. '*Three days?*'

She nods. 'I watched this thing on Netflix about the psychology of dating. If you WhatsApp her straight away, you'll seem desperate, but if you leave it longer than three days she'll think you're not interested.'

'I hate this bit,' I mutter as I stop to reach for a yellow tartan scarf so I don't have to look at her.

I'm ready *now*, but Adara's right, it's too soon. I only met Poppy a few hours ago. I suppose I should be pleased that I'm the one in control, for once. Usually I'm the one waiting.

The one who messages too soon and answers too quickly and is left on read for days until I get a *Sorry, babe. Been busy* response.

This is the best and the worst bit.

The best because the promise of it is *dizzying*. I've never actually been on a first date, which is tragic, I know. Most of the girls I've dated – if you can even call it *dating* – have been messy hook-ups at parties after too much vodka and not enough self-control that I've tried – and failed – to turn into something more. The thought of going on one with Poppy, deciding what to wear and sharing a pizza and wondering if she's going to kiss me, makes me feel light-headed. It shouldn't – I'm not twelve, after all – but I just want to know what that's like.

Just once.

It's also the worst because I have to navigate my next move with the sort of care usually reserved for disarming a bomb. I have to be cool, but not cold. Flirty, but not creepy. Then, if I don't manage to fuck up somehow and we go out, I have to worry if she's going to turn up and if she does, if she's going to come with some mates, assuming it's a group thing, and if she does turn up alone, I have to spend the entirety of the date wondering if this is a friend thing or a more than friend thing. Even if she kisses me, I have to ask myself if it's because she likes me or if it's because she's had too much cider and wants to see what it's like to kiss a girl.

It's exhausting.

'Three days,' Adara reminds me.

Three days.

THREE

As soon as I put my key in the front door, I hear my mother calling to me from the kitchen.

'Hey, Mama,' I call back. The whole flat smells of ginger and garlic – of home – and something in me realigns as I kick the front door shut behind me and bend down to unlace my DMs.

'Ashana?' she says again as I toe them off and drop my backpack to the floor. 'Is that you?'

'No, it's an axe murderer.' I shrug off my leather jacket and hang it up. 'I'm just over-affectionate.'

She pokes her head out of the kitchen holding a cutlass, her gaze narrowing, which I think is more of a threat to me than a potential axe murderer. I should probably be intimidated, but given that my mother is now shorter than both my little sister and me, it's hard to be. So I smile sweetly at her and she mutters something I probably don't want to hear, then heads back into the kitchen with a huff.

'You hungry?' she asks as I follow her in. She doesn't wait for me to respond, just puts down the cutlass and plucks the fresh roti from the tawa on the stove with her fingers. She folds it in half and in half again then goes over to the sink and starts clapping it furiously between her hands until it begins to fluff up.

I don't know how she does it. I tried it once and the roti was so hot that I screamed and dropped it into the sink. My Aunty Lalita thought it was hilarious, laughing for a good minute before berating my mother for not teaching me how do it sooner, saying that I'll never find a husband if I can't clap roti. I didn't dare tell her that I'm not bothered about either of those things.

I'm guessing my mother just got out of the shower, because her hair's still damp and beginning to dry in a fluffy halo around her hairline. It's the same colour as mine, but threaded with grey now, which she used to hate, but has now given into, not bothering to dye it any more – not after she got some on the bathroom tiles last year and couldn't get it out.

She's wearing a pair of my father's tracksuit bottoms and an old T-shirt of mine that says, *OVER IT* and is swamped in both, the cuffs of the tracksuit bottoms pooling over her red velvet slippers. She'd be mortified if anyone called round now and saw her like this, but I like it.

She looks like she does in those photographs of her and my father as teenagers.

'Here,' she says when she's satisfied with the roti, putting it on a plate.

'Oh yes!' I grin, rubbing my hands together as she holds it out to me.

Everyone thinks their mother makes the best roti, but they're wrong because *my* mother makes the best roti. They're light and fluffy and crispy, all at once. I once told her that if I ever found myself on death row, her roti and chicken curry would be my last meal. That or her pumpkin and bake.

33

We decided in that scenario I could have both.

'Thanks, Mama,' I say, making actual heart eyes at the steaming roti on the plate in front of me, but when I reach for it, she pulls her hand back and nods at the sink.

'Wash your hands.'

I do as I'm told with a theatrical groan.

'Don't be so dramatic, Ashana,' she tells me, watching as I head over to the sink. 'Do you know how many germs you've come into contact with today? You may as well eat this off the pavement. Come.'

I hold my hands out to her and, content that they're clean, she finally hands over the plate and pads back to the stove.

'What's for dinner?' I ask.

It's Friday so I already know what it is; pulling a face when she says, 'Fish curry.'

'Yum!' I say, tearing off a piece of the roti and popping it into my mouth.

'It's good for you.'

We used to have fish and chips on a Friday night. It was the one indulgence my mother allowed herself, but then my father had to stop working at the hospital so now it's fish curry.

'How was your day?' I ask, watching as she holds her palm over the tawa. 'Did you get any sleep?'

'Not really. That bloody dog next door has been barking its head off all day.'

She sighs and she sounds tired – really tired – and I feel bad for being an ungrateful brat about the fish curry, which she's probably been making for hours while Adara and I have been trying on lipstick.

34

'I'm sorry,' I say, watching as she takes another ball of dough from under the damp kitchen towel next to the stove and rolls it into a circle using the thin wooden belna that used to belong to my grandmother.

'Between him and that cat two doors down . . .'

'Dorito?' I ask with a frown. 'What did he ever do to you?'

'He hates me. He always hisses at me when I walk past.'

'Cats can sense evil, can't they?'

'It's a shame they don't sense disrespectful daughters.'

She arches an eyebrow at me and it's quite a feat given that her eyebrows have all but disappeared after years of over-plucking, but she manages to make her point.

'You're just jealous because he likes me, but he doesn't like you,' I tell her with a smug smile.

'He only likes you because you stroke him every time you go past. Why do you think I got you to wash your hands as soon as you got in?' she says, pointing the belna at me.

She's right, of course. I did tickle him between the ears as I passed him on Miss Larson's doormat.

I don't tell her that, though. 'He just likes me because I fixed his boiler.'

'When did you fix Miss Larson's boiler?'

'*Ages* ago. Remember in the new year when it snowed?' I remind her and she nods to herself as she puts the rolled roti dough on the tawa, pressing it down with a spatula when it starts to puff up. 'Miss Larson knocked for Dad to see if he could help, but he was at work, so I had a look at it.'

'So you're a plumber now, are you?'

''Course not.' I shrug, tearing off another chunk of roti. 'But

35

it was doing that thing ours did last year. You know, when it was losing pressure?' She nods, flipping the roti and brushing it with oil. 'So I turned the lever thing and it came back on. Dorito was very pleased. Cats get cold, you know?'

'Do they now?'

'That's why he only sits on the doormat when it's sunny,' I tell her, popping the piece of roti into my mouth. 'You'll see. As soon as the weather turns you won't see him again.'

'When the weather turns do you think I won't hear that dog again?' she says, then softens. 'It's not the dog's fault,' she admits, shaking her head. 'It's not fair to keep it cooped up in a flat all day.'

'I know, but Mr Cameron can't walk that far since his hip operation. And even if he could, where's he going to go? It's been three weeks and the lift's *still* broken. How is he supposed to go up and down six flights of stairs?' I point out and my mother nods. 'I don't know. He needs help, doesn't he? It's just him since his wife died. Maybe Rosh and me should go around there after dinner and offer to walk the dog for him.'

My mother turns to look at me, her eyebrows raised. 'Yeah right,' she scoffs, turning the roti and brushing the other side with oil as well. 'I'd like to see you picking up dog poo!'

'Rosh can do that part.'

That makes her laugh and she comes over to kiss me on the cheek. 'You're a good girl, really.'

I beam at the compliment, choosing to ignore the *really*.

'What time is it, by the way?' she asks.

I take my phone out of the back pocket of my jeans and check. 'Four forty-one.'

'Already? I need to leave soon for work soon.'

'How come?'

'I have to go in early for a meeting about diversity in the NHS, or something.'

'The patients need that more than you guys.'

'True,' she agrees with a snort, as I pop another piece of roti in my mouth. 'But if they don't want me to treat them because I'm brown, then it's less work for me to do, isn't it?'

She shrugs, but it's got to hurt, being spat at and told to go back to where you came from when you were born here. Especially when all you're trying to do is help. I honestly don't know why she bothers.

I'd tell the patient to *Die then* and get myself fired halfway through my first shift.

'Are you at least getting paid for going in early, Mum?'

'Of course not.'

'Don't go. Stay here and have dinner with us. Daddy will be home soon.'

'I'd love to, baby girl.' She sighs wistfully and I believe her. 'But I can't miss this meeting. They've deliberately scheduled it between shifts so everyone will be there. They'll notice if I'm not.'

I remember Gillian then and for one mad moment, I consider not telling her so we don't have to have this conversation. But if they see each other at this meeting and Gillian tells her that she saw me in town, my mother will be even more pissed off. I'd better tell her now before Gillian grasses me up.

'I saw your friend today,' I say carefully.

'Which friend?'

'Gillian.'

'Gillian Lawrence?'

'I don't know her surname. She said she works with you in A&E.'

'Gillian Woźniak?' My mother turns to me with a frown. 'Where did you see her?'

'In town.' I hold my breath and it's like I've lit the touch paper and now I'm waiting for the *BOOM*.

Her whole face changes. 'When were you in town?'

'Just now. With Adara.' I say it with a shrug, like it's no big deal, and I'm hoping she agrees.

'Why weren't you at school?'

'I was, but my trip finished early and—'

'Trip?' she interrupts and I'm grateful because I haven't thought of an excuse to be in town yet.

'To Rampion Wind Farm, remember?'

She huffs, letting me know that she does. 'You should have come straight home.'

'Ad needed something so I tagged along.'

'What did she need?'

My brain scrambles for something. I can't say lipstick, obviously, and I can't say a book from the library because if Gillian tells her that she saw us at the Clock Tower, the library is nowhere near.

'She had to return something to Marks & Spencer for her mother,' I say with a triumphant smile.

I don't know where it comes from, but if I could kiss my brain, I would.

'Such a good girl,' she murmurs, turning the roti with her fingers to check the other side.

I don't know how she manages to compliment Adara and insult me at the same time.

She's quite skilled, my mother.

'Ashana, what's the time now?'

'Four fifty-two.'

She mutters something in Guyanese, scurrying over to the sink to clap the roti. I stuff the last piece of mine into my mouth, hoping it's for me, but she puts it on another plate.

'Roshaan!' she calls out to my little sister as she washes her hands then goes back to the stove to check the gas is off. 'OK. The roti's done. It should still be warm by the time Daddy gets home.' She points at the oven then at the saucepans on the stove. 'So all you have to do is reheat the curry, dhal, rice and bora.'

'I think I can manage that.'

'Roshaan!' she calls out again, then mutters something about needing to get ready for work. As she passes me, she stops suddenly and glares at me, her eyes wide. 'Ashana!' she spits, grabbing my ponytail with her hand and yanking it towards her so she can smell it. When she lets go of it, she looks so angry that my heart jumps up into my mouth and cowers on my tongue. 'Have you been smoking, Ashana?'

'Of course not!' I sniff my ponytail. 'It's the smoke from the boat engine.'

I wait for her to warn me that I'd better not start smoking, but she's even more angry. 'What boat?'

'The one to the wind farm.'

'You were on a *boat*?' She goes from zero to furiously making the sign of the cross in about three seconds, as though I've just told her that Mr Moreno took us base jumping off Beachy Head.

'The wind farm's in the middle of the sea. How did you think we were getting there? Teleportation?'

'Why didn't you tell me, Ashana?'

I try not to roll my eyes as she makes the sign of the cross again, thanking God for keeping me safe.

And *I'm* the dramatic one?

'Ashana! Do you know what your grandmother would say if she knew that I'd let you go on a boat?'

I dread to think.

'You're my daughter! Don't I have to give my consent for you to go on a boat?'

'Daddy signed the permission slip.'

'You know he doesn't read those things.'

'I asked you first, but you *told me* to ask him to sign it.'

'No boats, Ashana.' She holds a finger up to me. 'You could fall off and die. I've seen it happen.'

'You've *seen* people falling off boats?'

'*Yes.* In A&E. Those that made it to A&E, anyway.' When I hear her voice go from sharp to high, I stop pulling a face at her as I realise that she isn't actually angry with me, she's *concerned*. 'The floor of the sea is littered with the bodies of foolish teenage girls who didn't listen to their mothers and went on boats.'

Nice.

Super-glad we didn't have this conversation *before* I got on the boat this morning. But then that's one of the joys of having a mother who is also an A&E nurse – she always thinks of the worst case scenario.

'No boats, Ashana,' she says again. 'You can't even swim. What were you thinking?'

I shrug. 'That I don't want to fail chemistry.'

She shakes her head with a heavy sigh then heads out of the kitchen, calling out to Rosh again as she goes. I wash my plate and by the time I'm done, Rosh still hasn't emerged from our room so I'm tempted to eat her roti. She obviously doesn't want it and it would be a shame to let it go to waste.

'That's for your sister,' my mother says as I reach for the plate, suddenly in the kitchen doorway again, this time in her nurse's uniform, her thick curls contained into a neatish bun.

'It's going cold, though.' I pout.

'Go get Rosh and tell her that it's there, then.'

'I'd rather just eat it.'

'Go get your sister, please.'

'Mum, you're *right there*.' I raise my arm and point. 'You're closer to our bedroom door than I am.'

'Don't think I haven't noticed how you call me *Mama* when you want something, like roti.' She stops to arch an eyebrow at me again. 'But when I'm asking you to do something you don't want to do, it's *Mum*.'

'Fine,' I concede, making a point of sighing and shaking my head. 'ROSH.'

'I said *get* her, Ashana, not shout her name. I could have done that.'

It does the trick, though, because my little sister finally emerges from our bedroom wearing my old SpongeBob pyjama shorts and a Totoro T-shirt, a book between her fingers. 'You bellowed, Ash?'

'Roshaan, I've been calling you.' My mother tuts, walking to the coat hooks by the front door. She bends down for my backpack, holding it up with another tut, and I take it as she reaches for her jacket.

'Sorry, Mama.' Rosh tucks one of the dark curls that has escaped from the hastily tied pile on top of her head then points at her ear. 'I had my headphones on. I couldn't hear you.'

My mother nods towards the kitchen. 'There's a roti in there for you.'

'Thanks.'

'Daddy will be home soon. Take care of your sister.'

'I will,' we say in unison and I turn to look at Rosh with a scowl.

'Ash,' my mother says, pulling on her jacket. 'Make sure your sister takes her nose out of a book long enough to eat something. Rosh, make sure your sister doesn't set anything on fire.'

'Um,' I object with an exaggerated frown as I watch her reach up to take her handbag from the coat hook and sling it over her shoulder. 'I resent that, Mother. When have I ever set anything on fire?'

'Let's keep it that way,' she murmurs, kicking off her slippers and putting on her Crocs.

'It's comforting to know that you have such faith in me.'

She strides over to where I'm standing and curls her hand around the back of my neck then kisses me quickly on the cheek. Her fingers are cold but her breath is warm. 'Love you, Ashana. Be good, please.'

42

She does the same to my sister. 'Love you, Roshaan. Make sure your sister's good, please.'

Before I can object again, she's by the front door, kissing the tips of her fingers and pressing them to the framed print of the Sacred Heart on the wall. 'Bye, girls. See you in the morning.'

'Love you, Mama,' we call after her as she waves back at us then opens the door.

'Watch out for Dorito,' I add as she heads out into the early evening sun.

FOUR

I'd better take a shower before my father gets home from work otherwise I'll get distracted and I need to wash the smell of boat off me because I don't want my sheets to smell of it as well. Plus, showering when he isn't home is the only chance I get to actually enjoy it without him knocking on the door, telling me to get out because I'm using up all the hot water. He used to time us – three minutes per shower and not a moment more – which my mother was on board with until she came home one night after a twelve-hour shift and he wouldn't let her run a bath.

He doesn't time us any more.

I stay in the shower until the water runs cold, then immediately regret it, hoping that it heats up again before Dad gets back from work. It's worth it, though. My skin is tight and clean and my hair no longer smells like boat, rather the coconut oil shampoo I persuaded my mother to buy from ASDA last Saturday because it was on special offer. She was too busy sniffing pears to notice that the bottle was half the size of the one we usually get and I made no effort to point it out, so I'd better enjoy it because we won't be getting it again.

When I walk back into our room, Rosh is propped up against

her pillows, half-sitting, half-lying. She probably hasn't noticed as she reads whatever book she's reading with such focus you'd think she was trying to decipher the Enigma code. She doesn't even look up as I pad over to check my phone, which is charging on the bedside table between our beds. I haven't missed much since I've been in the shower, just a couple of selfies from Adara showing off her new lipstick and an alert from ASOS to let me know there's twenty per cent off everything.

I glance over my shoulder at Rosh as I head over to the wardrobe. I doubt she's even noticed that I'm back in the room, but I still open the wardrobe door and hide behind it as I put on some clean underwear and wrap the towel around me again.

'Aren't you getting backache sitting like that? What you reading anyway?' I ask, grabbing the bottle of Palmers from the chest of drawers and heading over to my bed. She just grunts, which is Rosh for *Leave me alone, I'm reading*, but I persist.

'Rosh!'

'What?' she whines.

'What are you reading?' I ask again as I sit on the edge of my bed and flip open the lid on the bottle of Palmers, squeezing some into my hand. She turns the book for me to see the cover with a pointed huff before settling back against the pillows.

'*Noughts & Crosses*. I read that last year.'

'Hm-mm.'

'I loved it. It's so clever.'

'Hm-mm.'

'Really makes you think, doesn't it?'

'Hm-mm.'

'I thought it was a GCSE text, though?' *I'm sure it is*, I think as I cream my right leg, the whole room immediately filling with the familiar smell of cocoa butter. 'How come you're reading it already?'

'Mrs Sangha recommended it.'

'I thought you had Miss Briggs for English?'

'Mrs Sangha, *the school librarian*,' Rosh says, finally bothering to look up from the book, even if it's just to roll her eyes at me. 'You know, from *the library*? That building next to the canteen with all the books in it.'

I pull a face at her as I squeeze some more cocoa butter into my palm and she pulls one back.

'I went to Rampion Wind Farm today,' I tell her, rubbing it down my left leg this time.

She chuckles and returns to her book. 'Did Mum go off about the boat?'

I stop to exhale heavily through my nose. 'Of course.'

'You know what she's like, Ash. She just worries.'

'I know,' I admit with a nod, then adjust the towel that's wrapped around my head as it tips to the side before smoothing more cocoa butter over my shoulders and down my arms. My phone is still charging on the bedside table and I glance at it. 'I wish she didn't worry so loudly, though.'

Rosh chuckles as I head back to the wardrobe. I duck behind the door and take a deep breath as I tug on a pair of leggings and my father's Guyana Amazon Warriors hoodie I stole that just fits over the towel on my head.

46

As soon as I close the wardrobe door, Rosh mutters, 'Are you going to leave that there?' without looking up. I don't even need to ask what she's referring to and bend down to pick up my school uniform, which is in a pile on the floor, then stuff it into the bag by the wardrobe to take to the launderette tomorrow.

'You're worse than Mum,' I tell her as I walk back to my bed and sit on the edge.

'Why do you keep checking your phone?' she asks as I lean over to peer at the screen again.

Rosh looks up from her book, watching as I unwind the towel from my head. 'Who is she?'

'Who's *who*?'

'Whoever you're waiting for a message from.'

'I'm not waiting for a message.'

I'm not.

Poppy doesn't even have my number.

Rosh cocks her head at me. 'So why are you so fidgety, then?'

I'm not.

Am I?

'Who is she?' Rosh asks again, closing her book this time.

'No one.' I shrug, avoiding eye contact as I rub my hair with the damp towel.

When I look up again, she's arching an eyebrow at me and she's never looked more like our mother.

We stare at each other across the room for a moment too long and I finally give in.

'Poppy,' I admit and the relief of saying her name out loud makes me light-headed.

'You've never mentioned a Poppy before.'

'I only met her today.'

'Where?'

'On the death boat to the wind farm.'

'I thought it was a school trip?'

'It was, but we weren't the only school there.'

'What school does she go to?'

'Roedean.'

Rosh's eyes light up. 'Their library is supposed to be amazing!'

'I'll be sure to ask her about it.' I chuckle gently, drying the ends of my hair.

'What's she like?'

'Nice.' I can't help but smile to myself. 'Really nice. And she's smart. You'd like her. She told me about cognitive dissonance.'

'What's that?'

I suddenly can't remember. 'I'm not sure.'

Rosh laughs. 'Wow. She must be pretty.'

'Yeah.' I can feel how warm my face is as I laugh back. 'She is.'

'So?'

'*So?*' I parrot, teasing her as I comb my fingers through my damp hair, trying not to think about how long it's going to take to dry. I keep threatening to cut it, but then I remember the ghastly bob I insisted on when I was fourteen and bottle it. I was going for Rihanna's iconic Mia Wallace cut, but my hair's far too thick so I ended up looking like Cousin It.

It was a rough six months.

'So, how did you leave it?' Rosh asks, her book forgotten as she turns to face me.

'She gave me her number.'

'Have you WhatsApped her yet?'

'I can't.' I sigh, my shoulders slumping. 'Adara says that I have to wait three days.'

'*Three days?* Why?'

'She watched this documentary about the psychology of dating or something.' I sigh again, shaking my head this time. 'Apparently, three days is the perfect time to wait, because if you message straight away, you look desperate, but if you leave it too long they lose interest.'

'That's ridiculous.' Rosh stares at me as though I've lost my mind. 'I know I'm only fourteen and I've never been attracted to anyone who isn't fictional, but even I know that's ridiculous.'

'Yeah. Well.'

'Yeah. Well. *Nothing*, Ash. What does Adara know about this sort of thing? She's been with Mark for two years and he literally lives *next door* to her. She didn't exactly have to chase him, did she?'

I try not to laugh, but Rosh is right. Adara's hardly Karamo from *Queer Eye*, is she?

'Listen,' Rosh says, crossing her legs on the bed. 'She – this Poppy – wouldn't have given you her number if she didn't want you to use it, right? She's probably waiting for you to get in touch.'

'I can't,' I whine pitifully.

'Why?'

'It's too soon. She'll think I'm a loser.'

'You are a loser. Better she know now.'

I smile sarcastically. 'Thanks, sis.'

'Just WhatsApp her.' She gestures at my phone on the bedside table between us. 'Don't listen to Adara and this stupid documentary and its "rules". Boys are different from girls, as you well know.'

'Fuck it,' I mutter, snatching the cable out of my phone and taking it off the bedside table.

Rosh claps. 'What are you going to say?'

'I don't know, but I know what I *want* to say.'

'What's that?'

'That it was really nice meeting her and we should go for a coffee.'

'Say that, then.'

'It's too needy. Wait.' I hold my finger up before Rosh can tell me that it isn't. 'I've got it. What if I WhatsApp her with the coffee cup emoji followed by a question mark?'

'Why not send the coffee cup emoji followed by the question mark emoji?'

I consider it for a moment, but when I look up from my phone and realise that Rosh is taking the piss, I scowl at her. 'I'm trying to be cool and aloof here.'

'But you're not cool and aloof, Ash. You're intense and weird.'

'*You're* intense and weird!'

'Good comeback.' She gives me a thumbs up. 'But don't waste it all on me. Save some for Poppy.'

'I hate you,' I bark as I look back down at the screen of

my phone. 'Just tell me what to say!'

'Tell her what you told me. That was nice.'

'*Nice?*' I say, appalled. 'I don't want her to think I'm *nice*. I want her to think I'm cool and sexy.'

'I thought you were going for cool and aloof?'

I have to stop myself from throwing my phone at her. 'Rosh!'

'Ash, just *be honest*. You said last time that you're sick of the games so stop playing them.'

She's right.

No more games.

I unlock my phone and open WhatsApp before I can talk myself out of it.

> Hey, it's Ash. Just wanted to let you know that now I'm back on dry land, I no longer feel the need to jump. I do feel the need for a coffee, though, if you fancy one xx

I hit send and scream when I see the single tick appear on my screen.

'Thanks, Rosh!' I hiss. 'Now I have to spend the rest of the weekend waiting for her to respond!'

I throw my phone on the bed next to me with an *UGH* and put my head in my hands.

Before Rosh can tell me not to be so dramatic, we hear the front door and she calls out, 'Dad?'

'Hey, girls,' he calls back and I immediately feel better as I hear the thud of his work boots on the doormat. A moment later he appears in our doorway and he looks exhausted. Happy exhausted. Not like when my mother gets home from work and the circles under her eyes are deeper and darker and she moves a little more slowly because her feet – her feet, her legs, her back – are so sore. No, he looks content.

Like it's been a day well spent.

He's so tall that he fills our bedroom doorway, but I can still see how much weight he's lost since he started working at the Enclosures. My mother's relieved, of course, worried about diabetes and heart disease and God knows what else, so she's happy he's keeping active. But I miss his big blanketing hugs and him, Rosh and I finishing a pack of Oreos before my mother catches us.

It's funny because most people say that they know the four of us are related because apart from the wild disparities in our height, we look exactly the same. Same dark hair and eyes. Same brown skin. Our relatives see the difference, though, insisting that I take after our father and Rosh takes after our mother, which is true I suppose. I have his nose and straight hair while Rosh has my mother's rebellious curls. It's a shade or two lighter than mine, and she's already taller than me, so by the time she's out the other side of this all-hair-and-elbows awkward adolescent phase, she's going to look more like my father. I, on the otherhand, become more like my mother with each passing day. We have the same small mole on the bridge of our noses, the same small hands and feet and the same dry sense of humour.

'I won't hug you,' my father says. He holds his hands up, which are as filthy as the rest of him, the knees of his jeans caked in mud. 'Did you have a good day? What have you been up to?'

'I went to Rampion Wind Farm,' I tell him, trying not to smile when I think of Poppy.

He raises his thick eyebrows. 'I heard.'

My mother must have called him when she was walking to work.

'Sorry, Daddy,' I wince.

'It's not your fault, darling.' He winks at me. 'I didn't read the permission slip properly. I thought it was an actual farm, you know? With cows and pigs and stuff.'

'Yeah. No. Not so much.'

'Glad you didn't fall off the boat.'

'Me too.'

He turns to Rosh. 'What have you been up to, Squirt?'

'I've nearly finished my book.'

When she holds it up, he frowns. 'Didn't you start that this morning?'

'Yeah. Can we go to the Jubilee Library tomorrow so I can get the next one in the series?'

'I'd love to, baby girl.' He stops to tug his beanie off and scratches his head with a wide yawn. 'But I'm taking your grandmother to see her friend in Bournemouth tomorrow.'

Rosh looks forlorn. 'But what about ASDA? How are we going to get all the shopping home?'

'You'll have to get the bus.'

She and I groan in unison.

'You'll be fine,' he says, waving his hand at us. 'The exercise will do you good.'

'Um, excuse you. I walked to the Marina today,' I remind him. 'That's enough exercise for the week.'

He laughs, but Rosh still looks devastated. 'But when I finish this book I have nothing else to read.'

'I'll take you to the library before we go to ASDA,' I offer. 'I need to do some research anyway.'

She turns to me with a grin. 'What about? Cognitive dissonance?'

'What's cognitive dissonance?' my father asks.

'She doesn't know. That's why she needs to do research about it.'

'Do you want me to take you to the library tomorrow, Rosh, or not?'

She turns to me then pretends to lock her mouth and throw away the key.

'How was *your* day, Dad?' I ask at last. 'Did you plant lots of pretty flowers?'

'It's mostly cutting back at this time of year, but I did sow some poppies, actually.'

I immediately flush from my scalp to my toes and when he glares at me, I think he knows why, but he nods at the damp towel in my lap. 'When were you in the shower?'

'Just now.'

'How long for?'

'Two hours and forty-seven minutes.'

He ignores me. 'I hope there's some hot water left,' he mutters as he heads to the bathroom.

Me too.

'Better sort dinner,' I realise, saying a little prayer that there's been enough time for the water to reheat when I hear my father turn on the shower.

As I'm about to stand up, though, I see the screen of my phone light up next to me and my heart throws itself against my ribs as I snatch it off the bed.

Glad you're not going to jump. I'd miss you. Let's celebrate your newfound will to live with coffee and maybe some cake too. How's Monday after school? Poppy xx

FIVE

I reply telling Poppy that Monday afternoon works and she responds immediately to ask what time. So I reply and that's how it goes for the rest of the weekend, the pair of us WhatsApping back and forth, back and forth. There's no time to think – or *overthink*, in my case – no time to agonise over what I'm going to say or question if I've said something stupid. I just *say* it and I've barely caught my breath before she's replied, asking something else, and I daren't hesitate in case she thinks I've lost interest.

Or worse, she does.

She doesn't, though, and it's just so *easy*. We talk about everything. School. What we're watching on TV. What music we're listening to. The old couple she sees on the nudist beach doing t'ai chi. The woman I pass pushing an elderly pug in a Silver Cross pram down Marine Parade. She sends me a selfie in the library at Roedean, surreptitiously pulling a face at the librarian who's just told her to put her phone away. And I send her one when I'm in the library with Rosh, posing with a book on cognitive dissonance.

I message her in the launderette, while I'm shoving my clothes in the machine. Message her in ASDA when my mother dispatches me to the bakery to get a baguette.

Message her in church on Sunday while my parents aren't looking. I fall asleep messaging her and wake up to a *Morning, babe* WhatsApp with a sun emoji.

I'm drunk on it – on Poppy – so by Sunday evening, I'm weak at the thought of seeing her the next day. I think I'm being super subtle about it, but I'm obviously not because my mother snatches my phone halfway through *Songs of Praise* and says, 'No girls until after your GCSEs.' I'm so startled that I just gape at her as she hands it back. I'm used to it – it's what she always tells Rosh and I: *No boys until after your GCSEs* – but she said it. She may have waited until my father wasn't in the room, but she did. I heard her say it and I want to grab her and hug her because I don't think I've ever loved her so much.

Girls.

Maybe she's coming around after all.

I can't sleep after that and lie in bed, looking up at the ceiling as I listen to the steady hum of the sewing machine coming from the living room and picture my mother hunched over it, working on the christening gown someone at church has asked her to make.

It's as much a part of the soundtrack to our house as the television and the dog barking next door, and it usually lulls me to sleep. But tonight it tugs me back each time I feel myself giving into the weight of my eyelids as I think about what my mother said when she caught me messaging Poppy: *No girls until after your GCSEs*. And yes, I know I'm doing it again, letting myself get carried away, but I can't help but wonder if this is it.

If Poppy is the one.

The one I tell my parents about.

The thought makes my whole body shiver and when I roll on to my side and pull the duvet to my chin, there's a faint flash of light that illuminates the dark room for just a moment. I assume it's Rosh, using the torch on her phone to read the book that my father told her to put away two hours ago, but when I look across at her, she's fast asleep, her phone in one hand and the book in the other.

That's when I realise it must be mine and reach up for it, taking it off the bedside table to find a WhatsApp from Poppy.

> 16 hours and 8 minutes xx

She's been counting down to our coffee all day and she continues to do it every hour or so until the hours become minutes. If Rosh thought I was intense, I now have proof that I'm not the only one.

I all but run out of English Lit when the bell rings. Adara follows, noticeably less excited than I am, but determined not to let me go without saying goodbye. She's forgiven me for not waiting three days like I was supposed to, but she still gives me a look when she catches up with me at the top of the stairs. I don't know what it is, if she's annoyed or wary or nervous, or some combination of the three, but she can't even bring herself to smile as she follows me down the stairs.

'Do you want me to come?' she asks as we push through the double doors, out into the sunshine.

'Why?' I frown. 'Do you really want to third wheel it?'

'In case she doesn't turn up.'

I almost trip over my feet as I stop and stare at her, everyone moving around us in their haste to get out the gates and to the corner shop or home or wherever it is they're going. I can feel the tips of my ears burning as Adara looks at me, her arms crossed, and I want to ask her why she would say such a thing, but I can't speak. It's as though I've been winded, the thrill I was feeling a few seconds ago knocked clean out of me.

When my breathing steadies and my fingers uncurl at my sides, I realise that she's isn't being cruel, she's being practical. After all, it's happened before, hasn't it? Girls not turning up and leaving me to linger outside the cinema for so long that the film we were supposed to see is over before I finally give up hope and go home. Only Adara knows about that, about all the tiny humiliations I've endured over the last year or so. But that's the trouble with best friends, isn't it? They know everything and forget nothing, no matter how much you want them to.

Sometimes I need Adara to remember these things, though. Like now, when I'm literally *running* off to meet another girl I barely know, ready to dive head first into what, I don't know, when I have absolutely no reason to believe that Poppy is any different from the others. I need Adara to remember these things so she can pull me back, to protect me even if I don't want her to. I just want to fall and see where I land.

As if on cue, I feel my phone buzz in the pocket of my leather jacket and my heart clenches like a fist as I wonder if this is it.

If this is the *Sorry, babe. Can we reschedule? xx* message. My hand is shaking so much I almost drop my phone, avoiding eye contact with Adara as I look down at the screen.

24 minutes xx

Sure enough, Poppy is exactly where she said she would be, by the café at the Old Steine, her red hair alight in the afternoon sun. I have to stop myself running to her, forcing myself to take a deep breath – then another – as I try to walk towards her at a normal pace. Before I get to her, though, she turns and when she sees me, she smiles so wide, I can see each of her teeth.

Then she's there, right in front of me, pulling me into a hug so tight I swallow a gasp before she steps back.

'Hey,' she says, her smile smaller now – just for me – and when she waits for me to meet her gaze, everything around us falls away. The seagulls flee, the traffic disappears and the buildings encircling us dissolve into dust, carried away with the breeze so it's just us and she is all I can see for miles.

Miles and miles.

This is worth it, I think, as my heart flutters and my bones ache at the thought of counting each of her eyelashes with the tip of my finger. And with that, everything else falls away as well. All those ghost girls with the careless smiles and thirsty hearts. All those hours spent waiting, waiting outside cinemas and waiting for a call that isn't coming. Just waiting to be *seen*. Poppy sees me – really *sees* me – I can feel it and when she reaches for my hand, I would do it all again for the promise of this. For the promise of whatever is going to happen next because I don't care, I just want to know. And maybe she isn't the one. Maybe we'll burn bright for a few weeks then collapse in on ourselves, but Mr Moreno says that's how galaxies are made anyway.

Poppy suggests that we grab a coffee from the café across the road, which isn't so much a café as a hole in the wall that I must have walked past dozens of times and didn't even notice was there.

'This place does the best latte,' she says, as though she's introducing me to an old friend.

'Is this a good time to mention that I don't actually drink coffee?' I admit with a nervous smile.

'Wait. What? You don't drink coffee? How do you even, you know, *do stuff*?' She looks horrified. 'I can't string a sentence together in the morning until I've had at least two.'

'I just avoid talking to people unless I really have to.'

'Words to live by.' She closes her eyes and nods sagely. 'So what do you drink, then? Tea?' she asks when she opens them again. I shake my head and she blinks at me. 'What else is there?'

'Hot chocolate?'

'Yes!' she grins, turning to the guy behind the counter.

'An oat milk latte and a hot chocolate, please.'

I take my wallet out of the front pocket of my backpack while the guy turns to make them up, but when I open it and take out a fiver, she waves my hand away.

'It's on me,' she tells me with a wink. 'You can get it next time.'

Next time.

The weather's so nice, the sun smiling down on us as we sit cross-legged on the grass outside the Pavilion. I'm not the sit-cross-legged-on-the-grass type, mainly thanks to my mother who would no doubt be pointing out how many dogs have weed on this lawn if she were here. But I try not to think about it as Poppy sips her latte, leaving behind a faint crescent of red lipstick on the rim.

When she puts the cup on the small patch of grass between us, I see that some of the foam has bubbled up through the small hole in the white plastic lid and it's all I can do not to bend down and lick it away as I wonder whether if I kissed her now, her tongue would taste of coffee.

'What are you thinking?' she asks and I look up at her, my cheeks hot, sure that she's read my mind.

'Huh?' I manage.

'You look worried. What are you thinking? Are you scared someone will see us?'

'Of course not.' Although, now I am. I can't tell her that I was thinking about kissing her, though, so I gesture at my school uniform instead. 'I was just thinking that it's a shame I didn't get time to change.'

She waves me off again. 'Don't worry about it. You look great. Exactly how I remember.'

When she smiles, I smile back, wishing I could say the same thing, but she doesn't look how I remember. She looks different. Good different, but still different.

She's in black skinny jeans and a white T-shirt that stops just above her hips and is tight enough – and thin enough – to let me know that she's wearing a black lace bra underneath. I've only ever seen her in her Roedean uniform, so I don't know what I expected. It was hard to picture her in anything else. She's even wearing it in her WhatsApp profile picture so it's almost as though I'm meeting her all over again.

The real her, anyway.

The real Poppy is cool, it seems. That effortless sort of cool people pay a lot of money to emulate but never quite achieve. Her hair is down today, a mess of thick, untidy waves that spill over her shoulders and down her back. When she takes a swig from her latte, I notice that there's a different silver ring on each of her fingers, some of them stop at her knuckle, and others are thick and weighty. A crescent moon. A cat's head. An anchor. A red heart-shaped stone with a dagger going through it on her right thumb. She's wearing a couple of silver necklaces as well, one long with what looks like a St Christopher medal layered over a shorter, chunkier one with a silver padlock.

'I only had time to change because I skipped netball,' she adds and I chuckle.

'That's where I told my parents I am.'

'How come? Wouldn't they have let you come?'

'It's a weekday, so probably not.'

'Are they really strict, then?'

'Not really.' I wrinkle my nose. 'They're *way* more laid back than my grandparents.'

'Were your grandparents born here?'

I shake my head. 'My parents were, but my grandparents are from Guyana.'

'In the West Indies?'

'Yeah.' I'm pleasantly surprised that she knows that. Most people think I mean Ghana.

'I love my parents. They're cool.' I tilt my head from side to side as I try to think of a way to explain it that doesn't make them sound like clichéd Indian parents, because they're not. 'My mum just worries. She's an A&E nurse so she's seen it all. Teen pregnancy. Stabbing. Overdoses.' I stop to take a sip of hot chocolate then raise my eyebrows. 'Yesterday I had a headache and she checked my pupils to see if I'd had an aneurysm.'

Poppy chuckles. 'Is your dad the same?'

'No. He's the complete opposite. He balances her out.'

'What does he do?'

'He used to be a psychiatric nurse, but a patient had an episode last year and he hurt his back. He's absolutely fine now, but they said that he wasn't fit to go back to work. They did the same to another nurse so he's convinced they used it as an excuse to get rid of him because their budget was slashed and they couldn't afford to keep him on.'

'That's so shit.' Poppy looks genuinely sad. 'What's he doing now?'

'He's a gardener.'

'A *gardener*? How did he go from a psychiatric nurse to a gardener?'

'No idea.' I chuckle to myself. 'But he works in the Kempton Enclosures now.'

'No way!' She points her coffee cup at me. 'My parents have access to the Kempton Enclosures!'

'Seriously?'

'Yeah. They live on Chichester Terrace.'

'Well, if you ever see a grumpy Guyanese dude in a green knitted beanie in there, that's my dad.'

'I'll look out for him the next time I'm in there.'

'If you say hello and he ignores you, don't be offended, though,' I warn as I finish my hot chocolate and put the cup on the patch of grass between us. 'It's probably because he has his headphones on. He's always listening to Radio 4, or the cricket. He *loves* the cricket.' I smile when I think of him with a shovel as he wills Guyana to score. 'It's his idea of heaven – listening to the radio all day as he digs up weeds.'

'Sounds pretty sweet apart from the digging thing. I hate worms.' She pretends to shiver.

'Same, but he doesn't mind them.'

'As long as he's happy, right?'

I nod. 'I mean, he's earning fuck all, but he's *so* much happier, which is all I care about.'

'And you have a sister, right? Rosh? How old is she?'

'Yep. She's fourteen and *amazing*. Don't tell her I said that, though.' I hold my finger up to her with a naughty smile. 'But she is. She reads a book a day and loves chemistry because it's the closest thing to magic she's ever seen.'

'She into boys yet?'

'Just Ron Weasley.'

'How about you?' I ask as she puts her empty cup down between us. 'Any annoying little sisters?'

'Nope.' She shakes her coffee cup to see if there's anything left then tips her head back, the sunlight catching on her cheekbones as she finishes it. 'Just me.'

'What's that like?'

She presses her lips together as she thinks about it and finally says, 'Lonely.'

Her honesty takes my breath away. I want to ask her more, but she won't look at me as she tugs at the grass, plucking a few blades between her fingers and bringing them up to her nose to smell them.

So I wait a beat and when she looks at me again, I ask, 'You can't be lonely at Roedean?'

'Of course not.' She makes a show of rolling her eyes and flicking her hair. 'I don't get a moment's peace at Roedean. You can't even turn your pillow over in the night without someone knowing about it.'

I wait for her to laugh, but she doesn't.

'What about your parents?' I ask, trying to change the subject. 'What do they do?'

'My mother's Margot Morgan.'

'Wait.' I frown, thinking about it. 'Where do I know that name from?'

'*Professor* Margot Morgan,' she adds, trying not to smile, but her cheeks are pink with pride.

'Yes!' I point at her. 'She did that documentary on the BBC about dark matter. Rosh made me watch that, like, three times. She's *brilliant*.'

'She is.' She lets herself smile this time. 'She won the Nobel Prize in Physics last year.'

'No way! For what?'

'I don't know.' She sighs lightly and flicks her hair again as if she doesn't care, but I can tell that she does. 'Something to do with the cosmos. She was the first woman to win it in fifty-five years, apparently.'

'Wow.'

'I love her. She's the best mum. Such an inspiration.' Poppy is practically *beaming* with pride now, deep dimples I've never seen before appearing in her cheeks. 'She grew up in Whitehawk, you know?'

'Fuck off did she.'

'She sure did. Swallow Court.'

'I live in Kingfisher!'

'The one with the sea view!'

'Sea view is pushing it somewhat,' I concede with another chuckle.

'I've never been there, but she talks about it a lot.' Poppy nods and smiles to herself. 'She was born in East County, grew up in Swallow Court, went to Whitehawk High School, like you.'

I grin. 'Like me.'

'Then she got a scholarship to Cambridge.'

'Holy shit.'

'Are you surprised?'

'No.' I shake my head as I think about it. 'Just hopeful, I guess. For Rosh, I mean. I can see her being Professor Roshaan Persaud one day.'

'It certainly has a ring to it.'

'So what did your mum study at Cambridge?'

'Maths. That's where my parents met, actually, at university. My father always says that he didn't have much choice; she was the only woman on their course.'

She laughs, but I don't.

Is that supposed to be a compliment?

'Does your dad have a Nobel Prize as well?'

'Not quite.' She laughs again, but there's an edge to it this time. The slightest hint of bitterness.

'What does he do?'

'He teaches at the Institute of Astronomy.'

'Where's that?'

'Cambridge.'

'But I thought they lived on Chichester Terrace?'

How does her father go back and forth to Cambridge every day?

'They do. They have a house in Cambridge as well. He splits his time between the two.'

Well, I guess that explains why she boards at Roedean if her parents live in Brighton.

She must know what I'm thinking, because she adds, 'Mum isn't around much, either.'

'Yeah?'

68

'She travels a lot. Since she did that documentary for the BBC she's doing more and more TV stuff. Plus, she's always giving guest lectures. She's at MIT in the US as we speak, opening a new lab, or something.'

'That must be . . .' It takes me a second to think of the word. '. . . disorienting for them.'

I'm not sure I'd like that. I need my stuff. My bed. My pillow. My towel.

I need to walk in somewhere and know that I'm at home.

'I guess, but she loves it. Dad, not so much.'

'How come?'

'Because she's more successful than he is.'

I whistle, my eyes wide at her ruthless honesty.

Poppy shrugs, the corners of her mouth dropping down then back up again. 'Don't get me wrong. He's really clever, but she's *brilliant*. The history books will remember her. His bitterness is palpable.'

She looks away as a toddler runs by, his little arms outstretched to a seagull that flies off before he can grab it. She tries to smile, but I see the change in her immediately, the warmth in her voice when she just spoke about her mother cooling now that she's talking about her father. It's as though her whole body has drooped, like a pot plant left in the sun for too long, and I decide to change the subject.

Before I can, she turns to me. 'Are you out?'

Her honesty winds me again and I blink at her, my lips parted as I try to catch my breath.

'Sorry,' she says, putting her head in her hands, her hair falling forward so I can't see her face. When she straightens, she doesn't look at me, she looks at her hands, her lips pressed together as if to stop herself from saying anything else. She stays like that for so long, I'm almost certain she won't, but then she lifts her chin to look at me from under her thick eyelashes.

'Before this goes any further, before we waste any more time, I need to know what this is.'

I don't know how, but I manage to hold her gaze. 'What do you think this is?'

'Something,' she says and I had no idea a word so small could feel so big. 'This could be something.'

'I feel the same way,' I say before I can tell myself to wait.

To think about it.

She smiles and with that, she's back – the Poppy I met on the boat – mysterious and mischievous. Her face back to the one I've stared at so many times on my phone, trying to memorise the colour of her eyes – blue, like the deep end of the swimming pool – and the stubborn sweep of her jaw.

Last night, I fell asleep counting the freckles dusted across her nose and dreamt of her laughing, the pair of us holding on to each other as we floated in a big black sea, the moon over us like a naked light bulb. Usually, when I dream about the sea, it's bad. I've been having this same dream since I was a kid, where I'm under the water and just as I break the surface, someone grabs my ankle and pulls me under. But last night, it was nothing like that. I felt free – happy – and woke up with a smile, not unlike the one she is giving me now.

'I really want to kiss you right now,' she says, and as I watch her eyes go from bright blue to black, I can feel myself shaking, this tremor that starts in the middle of my chest and ripples out – out, out – like a stone skimming the surface of a lake. 'But I already know where our first kiss will be.'

'Where's that?' I hear myself ask and I honestly don't know how because it feels like I haven't drawn a breath for a very long time.

'You'll see tomorrow,' she tells me.

And just like that, we have a tomorrow.

SIX

My instinct is to call Adara as soon as Poppy and I say goodbye at the Old Steine, but something stops me. I just want to hold on to this feeling for a moment longer – just a moment – before I tell Adara and she warns me to be careful. She'll do that thing she does whenever she's in mine and Rosh's room, touching everything and putting it back in the wrong place until everything Poppy said today is grubby and dissected to the point that it loses all meaning. The magic of it all smudged away as I lie awake wondering if it really did feel that way or if I just want it to.

No. Tonight, I want to lie awake for a different reason. I want the thought of where Poppy wants to kiss me to keep me from sleep. I wonder where it is. If she knew before she met me. If she saw it and thought, *this would be a great place to kiss someone.* Or did she think, *this would be a great place to kiss Ash?* I want to know what she was thinking when she thought of me. I wonder if she'll warn me or just reach for me, like in the movies, sweep me off my feet in the middle of the street and kiss me until it feels like my feet are no longer touching the ground.

Or maybe it's somewhere only she knows. Some secret spot that will always be ours. Somewhere we'll write our initials and revisit in ten years when we're in the supermarket and I'm tired and pissy and don't care that oat milk is on special offer. Or when we're Christmas shopping and bickering over what to buy my mother. Somewhere we can go back to that will remind us of our first kiss, when we were sixteen and our hearts felt brand new.

I know – I know – I'm getting ahead of myself again. After all, we've only been on one date. But I allow myself to wallow in it for a moment, to imagine what her mouth will feel like on mine. If she'll taste of coffee or something only I know.

Something I'll never tell anyone.

Not even Adara.

My heart doesn't just quicken at the thought, it *bangs*, each heartbeat like a bullet leaving a gun. So hard that I'm sure my ribs are going to break, that my heart's going to come straight through them and land at my feet. I press my hand to my chest and tell myself to calm down as I get on the 1A and head up to the top deck.

I usually sit at the back, but the King Seat is free – the one at the front that Rosh and I used to love sitting in when we were kids because we could pretend that we were driving the bus – and I settle by the window, putting on my headphones. I take my phone out of the pocket of my leather jacket to search for Death Cab for Cutie, the band Poppy was just telling me about. As soon as the song starts playing, it's just her and me again, even though the bus is full and there are dozens of people milling around on the street below, heading to the pub to meet friends after work or into Morrisons to grab something for dinner.

When the lead singer starts singing about following someone into the dark, I can't help but think of Poppy and the deep, deep ache her absence has left. I want to get off the bus at the next stop, run back to the Old Steine to see if she's still there. But then I think about the promise of tomorrow – and I tell myself that I can wait. I wonder if she'll taste like the cake I had on my thirteenth birthday, like the last time I remember being this happy.

My phone buzzes in my hand, making my jump.

It's Adara, of course.

'You OK, Ash? Where are you?'

'On the bus home,' I whisper so she knows I can't talk. 'But I'm good, Ad. Better than good.'

'OK. Tell me about it on the way to school tomorrow. Can't wait! Meet me outside the mini-mart, yeah?'

'See you there.'

As soon as I hang up, it buzzes again, and I think it's her, unable to wait until tomorrow, but it's a WhatsApp from Poppy.

I shouldn't have waited. I should have just kissed you.

Despite my best efforts to be cool, as soon as I meet Adara outside the mini-mart the next morning, I tell her everything. I try to slow down because I can hear myself and I sound delirious, like I have a fever or something, but I can't, all of it spilling out of me in a breathless rush that makes Adara's eyes get wider and wider. I tell her about sitting at the Pavilion,

74

about Poppy's famous mother and how she's decided where she wants to kiss me.

When I'm done, I feel like I've just run up five flights of stairs. I almost tell Adara that I need to sit down, but we're already late for school so I need to keep going, even if it's more of an effort to put one foot in front of the other than it was a few minutes ago.

Adara doesn't say anything for a long time and that scares me because, much like Poppy, she isn't the type to think before she says something, she just says it. I can't help but wonder what she's thinking, if she's trying to choose her next words carefully because she knows that she upset me yesterday when she offered to come with me in case Poppy didn't show up.

Finally she stops and turns to face me. 'This is it, isn't it, Ash?' she says, lifting her heavy eyelashes to look at me, a smile tugging at the corners of her mouth. 'She's the one, isn't she?'

All I can manage is a nod as she pulls me into a hug that lasts a beat longer than usual.

When she steps back, she's still smiling. 'I'm so happy for you, Ash. When I think about those other girls and how they mucked you around . . .' She stops to shake her head. 'I'm so relieved. I'm not gonna lie,' she admits, 'I was worried for a minute there, but maybe you'll get what everyone else gets to have.'

I smile back. 'Thanks, Ad.'

'Just be careful, yeah?' she adds with a solemn frown and I'm relieved because I was about to ask her who she was and what she'd done with my best friend.

♡

Poppy and I meet in the same place after school. I don't stop myself running towards her this time and she does the same, the pair of us meeting somewhere in the middle in a hug that nearly knocks us both off our feet. All I can think is, *Now. Please just kiss me now*, but she takes my hand and leads me into town.

I want to ask her where we're going – if she's taking me to *the place* – but at the same time I don't want to know. I just want it to happen. So I let her talk. Talk about everything. School. How nice the weather is, given it's almost October. The shoes in the shop window we pass that she'd buy if the heel was higher. The poster for a band she wants to see that are playing at The Haunt next week.

I'm listening – I am – I even manage to respond a few times, but every time she leans in to whisper something to me or our hips knock together as we're walking, I ask myself if this is it – *is she going to kiss me?* – but it isn't.

Poppy knows exactly what she's doing, of course. She's doing it on purpose, leaning in then pulling away when I blink hopefully at her, laughing in that wild, bright way that she does. I try not to take the bait each time, but it's impossible not to, because it's her and it's me and I really want to kiss her. I should be furious, I suppose, but it's hard not to laugh as well when she's laughing like that.

After half an hour of it, I give up, resigning myself to the fact that it will happen when it happens, and, in the meantime,

I might as well have some fun of my own.

'Yes, I am,' I say while we're wandering through the Lanes. She's stopped to stroke a white sheepskin rug on a table outside a shop and looks up at me with a deep frown, her hands still sweeping back and forth.

'You are what?'

'Out.'

She blinks at me. 'What?'

'You asked me yesterday if I'm out and yes, I am.'

Her hands stop. 'What? Like *out* out?'

I nod.

She blinks at me a few more times, then steps back from the rug. 'Seriously?'

I nod again.

She slips her hands into the back pockets of her jeans and turns to face me, still frowning. 'To who?'

'Adara. Rosh. My mother.'

'Your *mother*?' My efforts to convince her yesterday that not all Guyanese parents are super-strict have clearly failed because she stares at me, her red lips parted. 'Your mother knows you're, *you know*?'

'Gay? It's OK, you can say it,' I tell her with a wicked smirk.

She doesn't smile back, just continues to stare at me, hands still in the back pockets of her jeans, and I see it then, a flicker of something across her brow that passes as quickly as it appears. I don't think she's enjoying being the one made to squirm this time. Or maybe it's that she wasn't expecting me to tell her, but I did. I've opened the door to her and now, like a vampire, she's waiting for me to invite her in.

She presses her lips together for a second then asks, 'What happened?'

I just shrug. 'Nothing. My mother didn't weep and embrace me and tell me that it was OK, that she still loved me. And she didn't yell or kick me out of the flat. She didn't even suggest that I didn't accompany her to mass on Sundays like I thought she might. I thought she might tell me that I was confused, that I'd change my mind, I just hadn't met the right boy. But she didn't do any of that, she just sat there, staring at me, as I waited for her to say something. But she did cry,' I admit. 'Not in that wild, pantomime way she does when she's mad and asking God why he cursed her with such a selfish daughter because I forgot to take the rubbish out. It was quiet. Devastating.'

I try not to think about my mother's face after I said it. *How do you know?* That's all she said. *How do you know?* So I asked her how she knew that she loved my father and I saw it – the hesitation – the shiver that crossed her brow, not unlike the one that just crossed Poppy's.

'What happened after that?' she asks. 'When she stopped crying.'

'We didn't talk about it again,' I tell her, shrugging again as if it's nothing. As if it's nothing that I have no idea whether my father knows or if it's another thing we keep from him, like getting my period.

'What?' Poppy looks appalled. 'Never?'

I shake my head.

'So why did you tell her?'

I'm sure Poppy is just thinking aloud rather than asking the question, but I answer anyway.

78

'I don't know.' And I don't. I didn't have to tell her. It's not like she caught me with a girl or coming back from Pride, sticky with sweat and glitter. 'She'd been bugging me for days, saying I'd changed, that I was keeping something from her. She kept saying, *I know you, Ashana. I know something's wrong.*'

'So you told her?'

'So I told her,' I say with a sad smile, my heart stinging at the memory of it. 'I don't think it was what she was expecting me to say.' I *know* it wasn't what she was expecting me to say. 'She probably thought that I was being bullied or something. She could have coped with that.'

'And that was it?'

I nod.

'You never spoke about it again?'

I shake my head.

'Do you regret it?'

It hadn't occurred to me before now to regret it. 'It was a relief.'

And it was. I certainly feel free of it. Free of the fear that it'll fly out of my mouth one day, at church or when we're sitting at the dining table at Aunty Lalita's house, passing around a plate of dhal puri.

Poppy's frown becomes noticeably deeper. 'Was she weird with you after you told her?'

'Not weird, just careful. I mean, I know we live in Brighton and it feels like everyone is a rainbow-flag-waving liberal, but it's hard for her. It's still illegal in Guyana.'

Poppy blinks at me again, her blue eyes wide. 'What? Even now?'

I nod. 'So if you throw the whole Catholic thing into the mix, I'm asking a lot,' I concede with a small shrug. 'I'm asking her to ignore everything she's ever been told. Everything she's ever been taught.'

'Do you think she can do that?'

'It's not that she *can't*, it's that she doesn't know *how* yet.'

'But you're her daughter,' Poppy says, her eyebrows almost meeting, she's frowning so hard.

I don't know if she's angry or shocked, but her cheeks are suddenly bright red.

'I know,' I tell her with another shrug. 'But trust me, it's the best possible outcome.'

Maybe not the *best* possible outcome – I still lie, still hide that side of me – but at least things almost feel normal again. Maybe my mother's happy to keep it that way as long as I don't embarrass her. Or maybe she just doesn't want to be the first. The first in our family with a gay kid. She isn't – she can't be – but she'd be the first to say it out loud.

So while I want more than anything for her to stand up for me – stand by me – I get it. She doesn't want to be different. She doesn't want Aunty Lalita to tut and say what a shame it is. She doesn't want to be whispered about, felt sorry for. She doesn't want anything to change and why should it?

She's not gay, I am.

I wonder sometimes if she looks at me now and sees everything she's lost. The big wedding, me in a white dress walking down the aisle of the church we go to every Sunday, my aunties singing *Ave Maria* while my uncles will the service to end so they can have a drink. She can still have that, of

80

course, and the grandkids and the rowdy Christmas dinners with everyone squeezed around the table, talking at once.

The picture just won't look the way she thought it would.

'I'm sorry,' Poppy says, taking her hand out of the back pocket of her jeans to reach for mine.

When she squeezes it, I squeeze hers back. 'Thanks.'

'Do you think she'll come around?'

I feel the tiniest spark of hope as I remember what my mother said the other night when she took my phone – *No girls until after your GCSEs* – and I give into the smile tugging at the corners of my mouth.

'Of course she will. She just needs a minute. My mother's first reaction is to say no to everything. Then she thinks about it for a couple of days and comes around. I mean, if she's like that about me going to the cinema with Adara, it's gonna take more than a couple of days for her to come around to me being gay.'

I laugh and when Poppy does the same, she's back to her usual playful self.

'Are you gonna tell her about me?'

'When there's something to tell.'

Her smile sharpens into a smirk. 'I like a challenge. So are you . . .'

'A lesbian?' I finish her thought with a nod. 'Yeah. I thought I was bi for a while, but that's only because Zayn Malik had me fucked up for a minute there. Then I realised he was the only one.' I shrug again. 'You?'

Poppy nods as we turn and walk up Kensington Gardens, her hand still in mine.

'So you're out as well?'

'Yeah. I told them last year. Apparently, fifteen is the right age to tell your daughter about the birds and the bees. So I said they shouldn't bother telling me about the bees, just the birds.'

I can't help but laugh at that. 'What happened?'

'They weren't surprised.' She lifts her shoulder and lets it drop again. 'My father always assumed my best friend Charlotte and I were, you know.' She waggles her eyebrows. 'But we were just close, like you and Adara. That's why I've only come out to a few friends I trust. I go to an all-girls' boarding school, don't I?' She turns to me, eyes wide. 'I don't want everyone to think I fancy them just because I'm talking to them.'

I get that.

'I can't complain.' She flicks her hair with another shrug. 'My parents reacted exactly how they should have. They were kind and compassionate and let me know that they still loved me and I know Mum does. She has such an open mind. She knows that the earth is just a pale-blue dot on a limitless cosmic canvas. If she knows that, how can she not consider the possibility that somewhere out there, there's another species, just like us, that, when they're born, they're not told that they're male or female or heterosexual or whatever and are just allowed to work it out for themselves. Wouldn't that be nice?'

It would.

'My father, however,' she continues with a pointed sigh, 'likes to think of himself as liberal because he lives in Brighton, even though he *technically* doesn't live here full time. He's not, though. I'm pretty sure he voted Tory at the last election.' She rolls her eyes and flicks her hair again. 'So while he said all the right things, I can't help feeling that he just thinks it's a phase. Like being vegan.'

'Is it?' I hear myself ask and immediately want a hole to appear beneath my feet and snatch me up.

Did I really just say that out loud?

Luckily, when she turns to look at me, her blue eyes are bright. 'I guess we'll see.'

By the time we approach the train station, I've forgotten about *the kiss*. We've wandered through the Lanes and sat outside another café Poppy loves on Sydney Street, her eyes closed and her face tipped up to the sun as she told me that there won't be many more days like these, that we have to make the most of them. There's something about the way she said it that made me feel like I was on the boat again, that made me hope that she was referring to the slow approach of autumn, not us.

When we stop outside the station, she turns to me. 'There's something I want to show you.'

'What?' I ask as she squeezes my hand so hard, I feel the bite of her rings.

She doesn't tell me, of course, and I brace myself, sure that she's going to suggest that we get on a train to London. The way she looks at me, her eyes alight, makes me think of what she said earlier about her mother and how we're just a pale-blue dot on a limitless cosmic canvas.

Maybe that's all we are, but right now it feels like she and I are at the very centre of it and I've never felt like the centre of anything before. I've always felt off to the side, like I'm watching on. An extra in everyone else's story. But here I am and here she is and I finally get the lead role and while I don't know how this story ends, this is how it starts: outside this station, commuters bustling past in their effort to catch the 17:58, her hand in mine.

'Do you trust me?' she asks and I can feel her whole body shivering, shivering with some idea she's just had and can't wait to tell me. When she smiles at me, I realise with a joyous jolt that this could be it.

This might actually be it.

The kiss.

Maybe she wants to kiss me on Millennium Bridge, St Paul's Cathedral watching over us and the Thames beneath our feet. Or while we're strolling through Borough Market, sharing street food. Or on the London Eye. Maybe she'll wait until we're at the very top even though she's terrified of heights and can't look out, only at me. Or maybe she wants to do it in the V&A, on the blue-cheese marble steps. All those places I've daydreamed about being kissed every time the coach passes them when I'm on a school trip to somewhere infinitely less exciting.

I don't know.

All I know is that if Poppy asked me to go with her to London right now, I would.

'Come on,' she says, squeezing my hand again. But she doesn't lead me into the station, she leads me past it and down Trafalgar Street – down, down, underneath the station – past

84

the graffiti-bruised walls dotted with pigeon shit towards the creepy Toy and Model Museum.

I wonder where she's taking me when I remember that the Real Patisserie is near here and I can't stop myself from smiling as I remember the day we met on the boat and I thought I'd never see her again. That she'd be just some girl I'd think of sometimes when I looked out at the wind farm or when I ate a croissant. But here she is and here I am and when she turns to look at me over her shoulder, her eyes even brighter in the dim light as we head under the bridge, I know that I'd follow her off the edge of the fucking earth.

Finally, she stops, but before I can ask why, she looks up. I do the same to find that someone has spray-painted *JUST KISS HER* under the bridge. I look at her and there's this moment, this moment where my whole world divides into Before Poppy and After Poppy and I know then that I will spend the rest of my life comparing the two.

That's when she reaches for me and I hear myself gasp as she pulls me to her, one hand fisted in the lapel of my leather jacket, the other on my face. My eyelids stutter shut as our mouths meet in a kiss that makes me reach for her as well, fingers digging into her hips and holding on as though I may float away if I don't, the trains rolling away in the distance, almost as loud as my heart.

SEVEN

After that, it becomes a regular thing. I meet Poppy every day after school. While the weather's still warm, we find a bench or sit outside the café on Sydney Street, me in my uniform, her in her red glitter sunglasses, trying to absorb the last of the autumn sun. She keeps saying that there won't be many more days like these, that we have to make the most of them, but I know now that she's not talking about us.

Most of the time, though, we just walk around until the shops start to close and we realise it's time to go home. Poppy isn't like Adara. She doesn't want to sit in Starbucks for hours, talking about make-up or complaining about school. God, I hope that doesn't make me sound like an asshole. That's not all Adara cares about, of course. She cares about her family, Mark, me. She cares that the world is burning and no one seems to give a shit. She cares that her baby cousins will grow up having only seen polar bears and orangutans in books. She cares about school and going to university and becoming a biologist so she can do something about it.

I never thought I'd be the type of person to forget about their friends as soon as I met someone. I *hated* it when Adara did it after she got together with Mark. But Poppy is just this *force* – this tornado – that sweeps you off your feet and takes you with her when she goes.

I didn't realise how small my world was until I met her. We go to art galleries I didn't know were there and down streets I've never been on, even though I've lived here my whole life. Her restlessness is infectious. There's always something she wants to show me – a second-hand shop with taxidermy rats in top hats or that weird vegan shoe shop on Gardner Street, where she attempts to persuade me to ditch my leather DMs after reading something on the Greenpeace website about greenhouse gas emissions.

There's always a dog she wants to pet, a lost cat she has to find, a busker she wants to listen to. She looks at everything as though she's seeing it for the first or the last time and now I do the same. I wonder if she gets it from her mother, this incurable curiosity. When she's like that, I can see her as a child, making mud pies in the garden and picking through the rock pools at Ovingdean Beach and I wish I'd known her then. But I know her now and even though she's only sixteen, I already know that she's going to live a long, loud life.

There was nothing wrong with my life before I met Poppy, but now I can see a future beyond it. Beyond Brighton and our boisterous, little flat. Beyond school and homework and sneaking out to parties when my parents are asleep.

I've thought about it, about what happens next. College. University. Maybe travelling first so I get to see a bit of the world before mine narrows to lecture halls and student nights. But before I met Poppy, it was just something that was *out there*, on the horizon. This bright, brilliant future coming towards me like a train through a tunnel. A train I'd get on and it would take me away.

Next stop: adulthood.

College.

University.

An internship.

A job.

A better job.

Marriage.

A house.

A kid.

A better job.

A bigger house.

More kids.

Grandkids.

A smaller house.

A hospital bed.

The end.

Isn't that how it goes?

But when I'm with Poppy, I see so much more than that. I see our first car that we'll call Jezebel because it's a cheap little red number. Our first flat and first sofa and first armchair that we buy from that second-hand shop with the taxidermy rats in top hats and have to get home on the bus somehow. Maybe even a dog. A lazy Lab that sleeps between us every night or a boisterous Miniature Schnauzer that follows our rescue cat around, sniffing her bum.

I see it all.

I want it all.

My future.

Different from my parents'.

Different from Rosh's.

Mine.

One day, Poppy brings me flowers.

'Here,' she says and she looks like a little kid, the dimples I'd forgotten were there, reappearing in her cheeks. 'These are for you.' She thrusts an assortment of flowers at me – a lilac-coloured rose; an orange tulip; a peach carnation; a white daisy with a yellow button centre; a sunflower; a hydrangea bruised purple and blue, all at once; a lily that's beginning to open to reveal a pink freckled centre and, in the centre of them all, a single red poppy.

No one has given me flowers before.

I've daydreamed of getting them, of course. Wanted red roses on Valentine's Day. Waited for the buzzer on my birthday, hoping to open the front door to discover my latest crush standing there with a bunch of peonies.

These are certainly beautiful, but odd. I don't think to question it though, because it's Poppy and this is the sort of thing she does. I mean, I can't even imagine her going into a supermarket and picking a plastic-wrapped bunch of carnations out of a bucket. But then she shrugs and says, 'I don't know what your favourite flower is, so I got you one of each,' and I can't catch my breath for a moment or two.

When I take them home, I have to tell my mother that the florist on Manor Road gave them to me because she didn't want to throw them out, so I can't object when she puts them in a vase on the kitchen window. I'd rather they were on my bedside table so I can fall asleep and wake up to them, but they're there, which is all that matters, and I smile every time I think of Poppy in the florist, picking one of each flower.

And so it goes. Days melt into weeks, weeks into a month then another. I don't know when I stop counting, but I don't have to because Poppy is always *there*. She always answers her phone. Always replies to my messages.

I didn't know it could be like this.

That it could be this easy.

I should feel bad that I only ever see Adara at school now. I know her well enough to know that she's not happy about that, but every time I apologise, she just reminds me that she did the same thing to me when she first got together with Mark.

Eventually, I stop worrying if it's *too* easy. Stop worrying if anyone will see us. If someone will pass us kissing goodbye at the Old Steine and tell everyone at school that I'm a lezzer. Or if one my mother's friends – another Gillian – will tell her that they saw Poppy and I trying on hats in Snooper's Paradise when I was supposed to be studying homeostasis in the library.

I don't know. Maybe I want to get caught. Maybe I want to get caught so I don't have to pretend any more – hide who I am – and my mother and I can have a proper conversation about this.

Until then, though, I intend to enjoy every moment.

When it's too cold to sit outside any more, we retreat inside the café on Sydney Street – *our café* – claiming the table in the corner by the window as our own, the first thing that is ours. It's so small that our knees touch and it feels like the earth is turning a little slower.

One afternoon, Poppy turns to the condensation-clouded window and writes our initials with the tip of her finger. When she draws a heart around them, I make a show of rolling my eyes, but I have to hide my smile behind my mug because my heart is knocking against my ribs like a sparrow trapped in a bathroom.

And that's how we spend our afternoons, talking and kissing in our café, at our table by the window, like we have no place else to be. We do, though. With mocks approaching, I should be in the library or in study group, circling the vectors that translate B to A. At least, that's where I'm telling my parents I am, which they don't think to question. If anything, they're pleased I'm being so diligent. I feel bad, lying to them, but then I see Poppy again and I don't care.

I should. Adara keeps saying that we're in our 'honeymoon period' and I'm waiting for it to pass, to get bored of wandering the streets every day. For this to mellow into something normal, whatever that is. But it hasn't, because everything is an adventure to Poppy. We'll climb mountains, one day. Swim seas. Fall asleep under the stars as the moon watches over us.

We'll indulge every whim.

And I can't wait.

Before we know it, it's almost Christmas. We take a selfie under the lights on North Street that spell out LOVE and sit in our café talking about next year, about all the things we want to do, and I go home with the smell of gingerbread latte in my hair and a lightness in my heart.

Poppy helps me pick out a present for Rosh – a Studio Ghibli satchel I know that she'll love, and I help her choose some bath salts from Neal's Yard for her grandmother. But whatever we do, there's a jewellery shop on Kensington Gardens – opposite the place that sells the sheepskin rugs – that we always seem to find ourselves outside. There's a gold bumblebee necklace in the window that she wants for Christmas. She's been dropping some serious hints to her parents about it, so each time we go and it's still there she smiles with relief, then her shoulders sink as she realises it's because they haven't bought it yet. Her mood shifts after that so we go to our café and I buy her a gingerbread latte and we talk and kiss, talk and kiss, talk and kiss, until she comes back to me.

Every afternoon is a series of firsts. The first time I cry in front of her. The first time I feel her cheeks warm under my fingers. The first time her hand slips under the collar of my school shirt, her thumb pressed to my throat as though seeking out my pulse.

Sometimes she pushes it, trying to persuade me to stay another fifteen minutes or to go to the cinema with her so that we can sit in the back row and kiss through the film. I'm tempted, but this only works if I'm home by dinner. It was a hard-fought battle – not having to come straight home if I'm doing school stuff – that I won long before I met Poppy. And while I'm not actually doing 'school stuff', as long as my parents continue to think that I am, she and I can have our afternoons together.

It's not enough, though.

Poppy hasn't said anything, but I know it's annoying her, not being able to spend more than a couple of hours with each other. She keeps saying that she wants to see the Jean-Michel Basquiat exhibition at the Tate Modern so, one afternoon, I suggest we go and she's thrilled.

I leave it until the last minute to tell my mother, of course, waiting until my father is in the shower and she's heading out to work to remind her about my school trip. It's a Saturday so I'm ready if she objects, a speech prepared about how we're so busy preparing for mocks that Miss Otwell doesn't want to lose a whole day of lessons, but luckily she's so distracted by trying to find her door keys that she doesn't even notice. She just gives me a tenner when she finally finds them and tells me to have fun as she sweeps out the door.

I meet Poppy at the station and we run hand in hand to the train. We find a two-seater and sit, curled into one another like a couple of commas, all the way to London, playing songs for each other on our phones.

When we get to Blackfriars, we run down the stairs and out, out on to the Thames Path, Poppy's red hair as wild as ever in the bright December sunshine. It's so cold that the air puffs out of me in great clouds as I try to keep up with her, but I don't feel it, my cheeks hot as I watch her run away from me.

I don't like much at school, but I like art. I like Magritte's pipe that's not a pipe and Hokusai's curling waves, so I've always wanted to go to the Tate Modern. I've seen photos of it, of course, so I know it's not like the other art galleries I've been to with their polished floors and sharp white walls, but as we head down the slope to the entrance, I'm still not sure what to expect.

As we go inside and I get my first dizzying glimpse, I'm so stunned that I don't hear the security guard asking if he can check my backpack. Poppy nudges me and I apologise, swinging it off my shoulder and unzipping it so that he can see that there's nothing much in there apart from a flask that I need to refill with water at some point, an umbrella, some used tissues and my gloves, which I haven't worn yet because I'd rather suffer stiff fingers if it means I can feel Poppy's hand in mine. She does the same, unzipping her handbag and opening it up for him as I sling the strap of my backpack on to my shoulder. I hear her thank him then follow in awe as we walk down the slope into the muted grey light of the Turbine Hall.

'Here she is. Isn't she beautiful?' Poppy says proudly, like she did on our first date when she took me to that coffee shop near the Pavilion and introduced me to it as if it was an old friend.

It's so stark – nothing but hard lines – that I'm not sure 'beautiful' is the word I'd use to describe it. Still, it's enough to stun me into silence for a moment or two. It looks more like a . . . I don't know what it looks like, but it certainly doesn't look like an art gallery. It's *vast*. Smooth and grey, like the inside of a stone. And it's loud. The art galleries I've been to have all the stiffness of a library. No photos. No touching anything. No getting too close to the paintings. But here it's a cacophony of laughter as kids chase one another back and forth, their squeals skidding along the polished concrete floor and up the walls to join the cloud of commotion hovering high above our heads.

'We've got just over an hour before our slot,' Poppy tells me, checking her phone.

'Slot?' I ask, still distracted as I follow the thick black beams up to the impossibly high ceiling. There's a red heart-shaped foil balloon trapped in the right-hand corner, by the entrance, where it will no doubt remain until it withers and finally sinks to the ground. I can only imagine the horror on the kid's face as they let go out of it and watched it float up where no one can reach it, and wonder if the staff have a bet on when it will fall.

'Our slot to see the Basquiat exhibition,' she says, her voice noticeably louder than it was a moment ago. I think she's said it more than once, because when I look at her, she's frowning as if to say, *Earth to Ash*.

'We need a slot?' I frown back. 'Can't we just go in?'

She chuckles softly. 'Unfortunately not. Everyone gets a one-hour slot. Well, not *everyone*. Today's slots are already sold out. Thank goodness I had the foresight to book the tickets online the other night.'

'Tickets?' I panic. I didn't know we needed to buy tickets. 'How much were they?'

'£17. Don't worry, though.' She waves her hand at me. 'My parents are members so they were free.'

Seventeen pounds? Bloody hell. What an idiot. I should have checked that before we came. Can you imagine if her parents weren't members and I had to buy one? Given I just used what

95

was left of my birthday money to buy the train ticket, I now only have the tenner my mother gave me, which would only just cover half a ticket so we would have come all this way and not been able to see the exhibition.

Not that Poppy would have let that happen. She insists on paying for everything. She relents sometimes and lets me buy her the odd coffee but, for the most part, she pays before I can stop her. It used to make me super uncomfortable, like I was a charity case or something, but she's deeply logical about it, pointing out that I'd be using my own money, while she's using her father's and he owes her. For what, I don't know, but she always has a wicked look on her face when she taps her credit card to the card reader.

'Come on,' Poppy says with an eager smile, holding out her hand. 'I want to show you something.'

I take it and let her lead me towards the other end of the Turbine Hall, which seems to be where everyone else is heading as well. There's a crowd gathered and as we get closer, I realise that they're looking at a massive iceberg that's so high, it almost reaches the ceiling.

Poppy, tenacious as ever, manages to slip between everyone, bringing me with her, and we get to the front to find that the iceberg is sitting in a deep, round stone tub. I feel myself shiver as I look up at it, my lips parted. When I see my breath, I realise that the iceberg is real, steam coming off the sides so the peak is obscured. As I lean in closer, I can see tears of melting ice chasing one another down to settle in the tub beneath and ask, 'What is this?'

Is it a sculpture? The ones I've seen in galleries or on the street are usually of solemn-looking men with strong jaws and long coats that are carved out of smooth cool stone or bronze that has weathered to the colour of maple syrup over the years. But it's as though this is determined to be the opposite of that.

It almost feels alive.

'They always have a commission in the Turbine Hall,' Poppy tells me, which I know, but I'm happy for her to go on as I stare at the iceberg. 'They've had all sorts of wild stuff. It's usually interactive. They had a garden once with a path you could walk around and they've had swings and a massive slide. This is called *No Icebergs Ahead*.' She nods at it with another proud smile. 'I read about it on the Greenpeace website.'

I can't take my eyes off it. 'It's beautiful.'

'They reckon it's going to take about six months for it to melt and when it does, it's gone.'

'Well I guess it makes sense, seeing as it's ice.'

'Yep.' She nods again, her smile a little sadder this time. 'According to the Greenpeace website, the artist wants us to *see the reality of climate change and ignite a sense of urgency about rising sea levels.*'

'I've always thought of art as something that would outlive us,' I say.

Poppy looks thoughtful. 'Yeah, just think about the wars that paintings have survived – wars, fire, theft – moving from house to house, gallery to gallery. All those priceless pieces that were lost or relegated to dusty attics because the owners didn't know how valuable they were. You used to have to go to an art gallery like this to see them, but art is everywhere. People buy framed prints of Warhol's soup cans or Gustav

97

Klimt's *The Kiss* and hang them in their homes having never seen the real thing. Yet there they are, over their beds and in their living rooms, next to photos of their family. It's such a part of our lives now that we barely notice it, do we?' She shrugs. 'We just laugh at the photos friends WhatsApp us of Grant Wood's *American Gothic*, the faces changed to Miss Piggy and Kermit. Or buy a special edition lip balm because the lid has been "inspired by" van Gogh's *Almond Blossoms*, or something.'

Usually, I could listen to Poppy talk for hours, but knowing that this iceberg is going to melt to nothing and be gone in six months makes my chest hurt in a way it never has before.

She leans in, nodding at the people around us taking photos of it on their phones. 'There's too many people here right now, but the staff say that when it's just them, they can hear it beginning to crack.'

I listen out for it, but when I can't hear it, I turn to look at her. 'Can we come back in six months?'

I don't realise what I've said – that we'll still be together in six months – until I hear myself say it and my whole face starts burning. But hers lights up the way it does every time she sees me approaching her at the Old Steine.

'Of course. We can come back every month, if you like, take a photo each time and see how much it's changed.' She squeezes my hand. 'Come on. Let's go upstairs and take a photo of it.'

'I thought you were scared of heights?'

She just grins. 'I've since learned there are better things to be scared of.'

My heart shivers as I let her lead me through the crowd towards the stairs, following her up to the runway overlooking the iceberg. We take a selfie with it – her grinning, my eyes closed – then take photos from every angle, making sure to get one of the steam clouding around the tip.

When we're done, we wander around, hand in hand, going from room to room and eventually settle in the Rothko room. As much as I like modern art, I don't *understand* it. I enjoy how playful it is, how different it is, but I guess it doesn't move me. Or it didn't until I saw the iceberg. Maybe it's made me more open to this Rothko guy. Twenty minutes ago, I would have looked at the blocks of colour and asked how it was art. But here, in this dimly lit room, Poppy by my side, it's actually kind of soothing. So I stare at the thick, uneven lines until they blur together and become a single colour that I'd find impossible to describe if someone asked me to.

'This one reminds me of you,' she whispers, leaning into me when I turn to meet her gaze.

'Yeah?' I ask, our mouths so close now that if we were just half an inch closer, they'd be touching.

She points at the painting. 'See that hollow rectangle in the middle? See how red it is?'

I turn to look at the painting as well, then nod. 'Yeah?'

'That's what colour I imagine your heart is.'

I turn back to her as she does the same and we kiss – just for a second, more of a brush than a kiss – but it lasts just long enough to make us both tremble.

We sit there for so long, her head on my shoulder as we stare at the Rothko, that we almost miss our slot for the Basquiat exhibition and have to run around the art students sitting cross-legged on the floor with their sketchbooks. Past the tourists and the delighted children who think it's a game and try to run after us, and up the escalator, making it with about four seconds to spare.

Poppy takes my hand and leads me in. It's busy. So busy that we can barely see the paintings. She doesn't seem bothered, though, managing to squeeze us in front of each one, her cheeks pink as she tells me about them. I googled Basquiat last night, so I knew what to expect, but I'm still overwhelmed to see his work in front of me. It's wild – fierce – smears of orange and blue and yellow that make me feel breathless if I look at them for too long.

They remind me of Poppy, I realise, as we're leaving, her hand in mine. And I can't help but feel that I know her a little better now than I did before I saw them. But then she stops in front of a poster for Tate Britain with a painting of a woman in a boat that kind of looks like her, her hair long and red and her chin raised defiantly.

John William Waterhouse
The Lady of Shalott
1888

As we stand there, gazing at it, I realise that it isn't anything like the paintings we've seen today. It's much calmer, less frantic, the colours muted, almost ethereal. It's normal, I hate to say, like something you'd see in the grand drawing room of a stately home.

'This is my favourite painting at the Tate Britain,' she breathes, her cheeks pink. 'Isn't it beautiful?'

'Yeah,' I say, turning my cheek to look at her with a smile. 'So beautiful.'

By the time the train begins its slow approach to Brighton, the day is beginning to dim, the pair of us a little groggy from falling asleep on one another as we listened to a podcast about the exhibition.

'Are we home?' she asks with a long yawn.

'Yeah,' I tell her, kissing her quickly on the cheek.

'Oh no.' She sits up suddenly. 'I was meant to give you this.'

She reaches down and pulls a purple plastic bag from between her feet and hands it to me. Before we left, she'd hung around the gift shop while I was in the seemingly endless queue for the toilet and when I returned to find her holding the bag, I'd assumed she'd bought something for herself, not me.

'Well, go on,' she grins at me, her deep dimples back.

I reach into the bag and pull out a book about Basquiat.

She winks at me. 'So your mother knows that you were really at the Tate Modern today.'

'Thanks, babe,' I grin, kissing her cheek again.

'Open it. *Quickly*. We're nearly at the station,' she reminds me, looking up to see where we are.

The book falls open and there's a postcard between the pages. I don't even need to see what it is to know, my chin trembling as I reach for it to find that it's the Rothko painting she said reminds her of me.

'Pop,' I breathe, turning it over carefully so I don't smudge it with my fingers.

Mark Rothko
Red on Maroon
1959

'Do you like it?' she asks with an eager smile.

'Of course I do.' I press it to my chest and sigh. 'I love it.'

'Good,' she says, kissing me on the mouth. 'I got one for myself as well.'

She pulls another purple bag from between her feet and holds it up.

'Did you have a good day, Poppy Morgan?' I ask as the train finally pulls into the station.

'I had the best day, Ash Persaud,' she tells me, kissing me again.

I check my phone as we're getting off the train to find nothing from my parents, which is good, and that it's only three o'clock, which is even better. I told them that I'd be home by seven and

I'm about to let Poppy know that we have another four hours together when I'm aware of a commotion behind me. I turn to see what's going on just as someone shouts, 'He's got a knife!' and a guy barrels into me, knocking me clean off my feet, the shock of it enough to make me see stars as I land on the station concourse with an *Ooof.*

It hurts so much that my eyes swim out of focus for a second. Then all I can hear is Poppy screaming.

EIGHT

'I'm OK,' I hear myself say, but Poppy is hysterical. So hysterical that a man in a suit runs over.

'Are you guys OK?' he asks, staring at Poppy, who is sobbing and incoherent, then down at me.

'I'm OK,' I say as he takes me by the arm and helps me up. My knees almost buckle when he pulls me to my feet, but I don't give into it, forcing myself to stand up, saying it again, 'I'm OK.'

'Are you hurt?' he asks. 'You haven't broken anything, have you?'

'Just my arse.'

He chuckles, his nose wrinkling, as I turn to glance at Poppy. She looks distraught, her face wet with tears as she frowns at me so fiercely her eyebrows are almost touching.

'Pop, I'm OK,' I tell her, trying to smile, even though every bit of me aches.

'If you're sure?' the guy in the suit says. I nod and he nods back. 'Better call the police.'

I watch as he takes his phone out of the pocket of his suit jacket then runs back towards the ticket barriers.

That's when I see him, the guy in the foetal position on the concourse. There's a group of people gathered around him, looking at one another as a man in a neon yellow jacket paces back and forth, speaking into a walkie-talkie. Then I see the blood – bright and Rothko red – spreading out from under him, almost touching the shoes of the people around him as they gasp and step back.

I realise then why Poppy is so hysterical.

I turn back to her, taking her face in my hands and waiting for her to look at me. 'I'm OK.'

She lifts her eyelashes to look at me, her eyeliner smudged and mascara-coloured tears skidding down her cheeks as she reaches for the front of my leather jacket and fists her hands in it.

'I thought he stabbed you,' she says with a heave and a sob.

'I'm fine. See?' I pull up the front of my jumper to show her my bare stomach.

She spins me round, lifting the back of my leather jacket to check there as well, the cold air against my exposed skin making me shiver.

Content that I really am OK, she spins me round again and pulls me into a hug.

'I thought he stabbed you,' she says again, sobbing into my neck.

'It's OK, Pop,' I whisper into her hair, hugging her back. 'It's OK.'

When she steps back and finally takes a breath, I reach for her hand. 'Let's get out of here.'

105

Poppy insists on getting a cab, saying that she just wants to go home. We sit in silence in the back seat, forced to listen to a piece on LBC with Ann Widdecombe insisting that science could *produce an answer* to being gay. Or at least I'm listening to it, but when I turn to Poppy, she's looking down, playing with the ring on her thumb – the silver one with the red heart-shaped stone with a dagger going through it – as the cab rolls down Marine Parade, the sea to our right.

I can't help but think of my mother then, wondering how she'd react if she knew what just happened at the station. I haven't really thought about it until now, too concerned with reassuring Poppy that I was OK and getting her out of there. But now everything is quiet – too quiet – Poppy stiff with shock on the back seat next to me, her face paler than I've ever seen it, I allow myself to think about it.

Why him? Why did he stab that guy? Did they know each other? Did he try to snatch the guy's phone out of his hand as they were getting off the train, but the guy wouldn't let him? Something similar happened to my mother at the bus stop outside the hospital last year and my father told Rosh and I that if anything like that ever happens to us, to give them what they want and let them go. Don't cry out for help or tell them to get a job (which my mother did and the bloke was so stunned, she was on the bus before he recovered) just give them our phone or our purse or whatever they're demanding, because it isn't worth it.

Everything can be replaced.

It's stuff like that scares me. *Really* scares me. Not serial killers or axe murderers or those things that go bump in the night.

But those senselessly random things you can't avoid or prepare for or even ask yourself why because you just happened to be there, on that street at that time, and there's no explanation other than that.

Maybe that's what happened to the guy who was stabbed at the station. Maybe he wouldn't let the other guy off the train first or looked at him the wrong way and that was it. Maybe if he'd sat near us on the train and thought Poppy's laugh was too loud or if she hadn't insisted we sit in the first carriage so we were the first ones to get off, it could have been one of us.

The thought makes every muscle in my body clench as I wonder if the guy who was stabbed is OK. If he's in A&E right now and my mother will tell us about him when she gets home from work. Tell Rosh and I to be careful as my father gives us the lecture again, telling us not to do anything stupid, that everything can be replaced.

'I thought he stabbed you,' Poppy says then, still playing with her ring.

'Pop, I'm fine.' I wait for her to look up at me, then smile. 'See? All in one piece.'

'Yeah, but what if you weren't?' she asks with a furious frown. 'There we were, coming home from the most amazing day, and just like that,' she stops to click her fingers, 'you could have died and for what? Because we got that train and not the one after it? Or because you didn't tell him to watch it when he barged into you?' She finally meets my gaze, her eyes wet. 'That's the trouble, Ash, we're sixteen and we think we have time. We think we have our whole lives ahead of us, years and years, but what if we don't? Something like that could happen at any moment.'

'Poppy,' I coo, taking her face in my hands. Her skin is *burning*. 'It's OK.'

'It's not, though. It's just made me realise how much you mean to me. What if I'd lost you today?'

'I know,' I sigh tenderly, letting go of her face to curl my arm around her shoulders and pull her into me. She lets me, her head falling on to my shoulder, like in the Rothko room. 'I'm not going anywhere, I promise.'

She tips her head back to look at me from under her wide eyelashes. 'Promise?'

I lean down and press my mouth to hers, then pinch her chin between my forefinger and thumb. 'Promise.'

The cab stops then and we jerk forward so suddenly, we almost slam into the front seats.

'What the hell?' I hear Poppy mutter as I look around to see what happened.

'Is everything OK?' I ask, wondering if someone tried to cut the driver up, or something.

He turns to me, his whole face red. He's bald, so he looks like the angry face emoji. 'Get out.'

'Excuse me?' I blink at him, looking around the cab again.

Did he hit someone?

Did a cyclist pull out of a side road from nowhere?

But the driver doesn't look worried, he just looks angry. 'Get out of my cab!'

I hold my hands up. 'All right. Calm down, Peggy Mitchell,' I say, which makes him even redder.

'You're disgusting, the pair of you!'

It's Poppy's turn to blink at him. 'We're what?'

'*Disgusting!*' He spits and she recoils, her hand to her chest as he jabs a finger in our direction, looking between us. 'This is *my cab*. I get to choose who I have in it and I want you two *out!*'

'OK.' Poppy realises a moment before I do what he's getting at.

I'm still confused, though, unsure what we've done to piss him off. We're not drunk or loud or having a screaming fight. We haven't even asked him to turn off the awful Ann Widdecombe interview.

'What's going on?' I ask, looking at him, then at Poppy. 'What's happening?'

Poppy rolls her eyes, opening the car door. 'It's because we were kissing, babe.'

Really?

It's not like Poppy and I were snogging each other's faces off and feeling each other up.

It was just a peck.

'Yes!' The cab driver confirms. 'And it's *disgusting!*'

Poppy laughs and when he sneers at her, I go from zero to *I will burn this fucking cab down*.

'Don't you look at her like that, you homophobic prick!'

He turns to me now, smirking this time. 'Nice mouth.'

I make sure I don't take the bait because I know how this goes: say something so bone-breakingly offensive that it will make me angry then mock me for getting angry.

I smirk back. 'Thanks.'

'It's ungodly!'

'Ungodly?'

When I chuckle sourly he glares at me. 'That's right. Ungodly. It's an abomination!'

'An abomination? If God didn't want me to be gay, why did he make me this way?'

'He didn't *make* you that way. You *choose* to be that way. God doesn't approve of *this*.'

When he gestures between us, I lean forward. 'My relationship with God is between us. It's nothing to do with you or anyone else. Don't you have anything better to worry about?'

'Your relationship with God.' He scoffs. 'What relationship?'

'I've been going church every Sunday morning my whole life.'

He leans forward, so close that I can see the dot of spit that has settled on his bottom lip. 'Well, you should know better then, shouldn't you? The Bible – if you'd read it – clearly says, *You shall not lie with a male as with a woman; it is an abomination.* Leviticus, chapter eighteen, verse twenty-two. I suggest you look it up.'

'And I suggest you read a bit further. The *next* chapter of Leviticus – chapter nineteen, verse twenty-eight, to be precise – says, *Do not cut your bodies for the dead or put tattoo marks on yourself.*' I point at the tattoo that spells out *Casey* in calligraphy on the side of his neck. 'If you had, you'd know that, wouldn't you?'

'Get out of my cab!' he says again and he looks so mad, I'm sure his head's going to explode.

It's enough to make my anger dissolve as I laugh. 'OK, mate.'

'I'm not your *mate*,' he tells me as I reach for the door handle. 'Just get out of my cab!'

'Fine. But we're not paying you.' I tell him, one leg already out of the open car door.

'I don't want your money! It's filthy.'

That makes me laugh harder. 'You should. You're gonna need it. You're not going to get much work around here, with that attitude. It's Brighton. There's *a lot* of us here,' I remind him with a proud smile.

'And you're all going to hell!' he tells me as I climb out of the cab.

'See you there,' I tell him, before slamming it shut.

He speeds off, wheels spinning, and Poppy and I look at each other, then burst out laughing.

Luckily, we're only by Eaton Place, so we can't be that far from Poppy's house.

'Oh, Miss Persaud,' she says, hand on her chest, putting on a posh accent – or an even posher one, I should say – as we start walking towards Chichester Terrace. 'You're ungodly!'

She does it so well that I can't help but wonder how many people at her school talk like that.

I do the same, even if it isn't as convincing. 'And your money is filthy, Miss Morgan.'

'I can't believe you called him Peggy Mitchell!' She stops, reaching for my arm as she throws her head back, laughing wildly. So wildly that someone across the street turns to look at her.

'I know. He looks more like Phil,' I say, stopping as well. 'What about you, though? When he said we were disgusting.'

I press my hand to my chest and recoil with theatrical horror. 'Back rolls?'

'Back rolls!' she shrieks, so loudly a seagull flies away. 'I love Alyssa Edwards!'

'Of course you do. She's the best one.'

'Her and Sharon Needles.'

I pull a face as if to say, *Of course*.

'This is *my cab*,' Poppy says, putting on a cockney accent this time. 'And I want you two *out*!'

'No, posho, it's *aaahhhhhht*!' I correct, like it doesn't have an O or a U, just a string of As and Hs.

'Aaaaahhhhhhhht!' She tries again, succeeding this time.

I'm impressed.

'Maybe your mum was a Whitehawk girl after all.' I nudge her with my hip and she cackles.

We stand there, in the street, Poppy doubled over she's laughing so much. Her hair falls over her face so I can't see her – only hear her – and I'm glad we're finding it funny. Or maybe we're not. Maybe we're laughing because what else can we do?

As much as Brighton prides itself on how open it is to people like us, it's hardly the utopia of liberalism and rainbow flags it advertises itself as, so I knew something like this would happen eventually.

The reality of it is sobering, though.

I think of my grandparents then and I finally understand why my mother didn't say anything when I told her that I was gay. It's not because she doesn't approve, is it? It's because she's scared.

Like me, she grew up listening to the stories of how my grandparents moved to London from Guyana. About how they saw the newspaper ads from the Mother Country seeking help to rebuild the NHS and London Transport after the Second World War and thought they were wanted, but swiftly realised that wasn't the case at all. The white nurses took the best rooms in the nursing home and the best shifts and the patients would ask my grandmother for someone who spoke English because they couldn't understand her accent. And the story of how they met on the bus after my grandfather intervened when a white woman told her to get up so she could sit down. How the pubs had signs that said, *No Irish, No Blacks, No Dogs*.

My mother doesn't want me to go through what they went through, does she? To be spat on in the street or refused service in a pub. Or, I'm sure, to be kicked out of a cab for kissing my girlfriend.

'That's never happened to me before,' Poppy says, letting go of my arm as we carry on walking towards Chichester Terrace and I wonder if she knows what I'm thinking. 'Has it you?'

I shake my head.

'I didn't think people like that still existed, especially in Brighton.'

'Oh they do,' I tell her with a sad sigh, tucking my hands into the pockets of my leather jacket.

'I can't believe it.' She looks genuinely shocked, raising her hand to sweep her hair out of her face.

'You OK?' I ask with a frown.

'Yeah,' she says and I believe her. 'It's just funny, because as

113

a girl, you worry about cab drivers locking you in their cabs, not kicking you out of them.'

She stops and I realise that we must be outside her building. It's one of those wedding-cake white houses with the wide windows that look out on to the sea that were converted into flats years ago.

'You coming in?' she asks, unzipping her handbag and pulling out a set of keys.

I want to, of course. I've been desperate to see where she lives. Her room. Her clothes. The photos she has stuck around her mirror. I hope her flat is on the top floor because, while not as high as Kingfisher Court, it will finally give me a chance to see what the sea looks like when it isn't interrupted by rows and rows of rooftops. But I hesitate, wondering if her parents are home and if this is it, she's going to introduce me to them.

I'm not ready, I realise. I'm wearing jeans and a hoodie. They can't meet me looking like this. Plus, I'm only halfway through her mother's book about the Wonders of the Cosmos because Rosh nicked it when I came back from the library with it and read it first.

Poppy must know that I'm panicking, because she turns to look at me and licks her lips with a wicked smirk. 'Don't worry. My parents aren't home.'

That's even worse! I'm not ready for that, either, to be alone with her. I mean, I've been alone with her, but not *alone* alone. I was hoping it would happen eventually, but I didn't know it was going to happen today. I have special underwear that I was going to put on and I didn't shave my legs this morning because my father insisted on standing outside the

114

bathroom door, yelling at me to get out of the shower.

'Stop overthinking it, you.' She laughs, reaching for the sleeve of my leather jacket and leading me up the steps towards the front door. 'You'll give yourself a headache.'

She puts her key in the door, nudging it with her hip to get it open. She turns the light on as soon as I follow her in then spins round to face me and points at my jeans. 'Right. Get 'em off.'

I stare at her, horrified, my eyes wide and my mouth open.

'I'm kidding!' She laughs, then tosses her keys on a table under a massive mirror with an elaborate gold frame. She stops to check her reflection in it, fussing over her hair, before walking over to close the front door behind me. I watch her do it and when she comes back to stand in front of me, I finally get a look at the hallway to find that it looks like something from a BBC period drama. Black and white tile floors, a heavy crystal chandelier and a staircase that sweeps up, up, to a domed glass ceiling.

'Which one's yours?' I ask, looking at the doors for the flat numbers, but there aren't any.

She shrugs. 'All of it.'

'This is *a house*?' I turn back and blink at her. 'Like a whole house?'

She nods.

'How many storeys?'

'Four and the flat downstairs.'

'There's a flat downstairs?'

It's probably bigger than the one I live in, judging by the size of this hallway.

'It's beautiful,' I say, bending down to unlace my DMs but she gestures at me not to bother taking them off.

'It's been in my father's family since it was built in 1828. They're the only ones who have ever lived here.'

'We have a house in Guyana that my great-grandparents built. It's not as big as this one, obviously, but it has this *huge* backyard with a cashew tree and a cannonball tree which has these massive fruit-like nuts that look like rusty cannonballs.' I make a ball with my hands. 'You can't eat them, but my grandmother says that when she was a kid and she got toothache, her mother would make her chew on the leaves. The flowers are gorgeous, though. Big and pinky orange and they smell incredible.'

When I look at her, she's smiling, clearly enchanted by what I'm saying. 'Who lives there now?'

'My grandparents. They moved back there a couple of years ago because it was falling apart.'

'Same with this place. My grandmother was living here until last year, but she couldn't cope with it. It costs a fortune to maintain and when you add in all the stairs . . .' She gestures at the staircase. 'She moved into a home in Rottingdean and as soon as it passed into my father's hands, he completely gutted the place.'

'Why?'

'My grandmother couldn't take care of it so it was in a state. There were seagulls nesting in the attic rooms, apparently.' She chuckles gently, her mood softening now that she's talking about her grandmother. 'Plus, my father wanted to bring it back to what it looked like when it was built.'

'He's done an amazing job,' I tell her, looking up at the chandelier. 'It's stunning.'

'Glad you're impressed.' Her mood snaps back again. 'I think it's *obscene*. The two of them rattling around in this big house when there are people literally sleeping in the bus shelter across the street.'

'Yeah, but it's been in your family for ever—'

She claps her hands together, letting me know that she's done talking about it. 'Let me give you the tour.' She strides over to the door nearest us. 'Drawing room, which is basically a posh living room no one's allowed to sit in.' She turns on the light and I stick my head in.

It looks like a doll's house. Pale-grey painted walls with panelling beneath, parquet floors, a fireplace and, in the middle of it all, two delicate pink velvet sofas on wooden legs. There's a Christmas tree between the two wide windows and she walks over to it, bending down to turn the lights on. As soon as she does, I gasp. I smelt it as soon as I walked in, the warm smell of pine making me wish that my parents would get one, but I don't blame my father for not wanting to lug it up – and then back down – six flights of stairs every year.

It's massive – at least fourteen feet tall – but still doesn't reach the ceiling.

'There might be a present for you under here,' Poppy tells me with a sly smile.

'Pop, I told you. I—'

She holds up her hand. 'Don't. I don't care what you get me as long as you've thought about it.'

'Fine, but you know that I'm probably not going to be able

to escape over Christmas, right?'

'I know. You said. But you're still coming out on New Year's Eve, aren't you?'

'Yes!' I grin. 'I can't wait. I just need to find an excuse to get out of my Aunty Lalita's party.'

'I told you, food poisoning. Works every time.'

'I know, but as much as I want to see you, I don't think I can make myself puke. You know I hate it.'

'Fair enough.'

'Besides, I'm worried my mother will want to stay home with me.'

She points at me. 'Good point.'

'So I'm thinking period pain. According to that app you made me download, I'm due on.'

'OK. So no under the belt stuff that night.' She gives me the thumbs up. 'Got it.'

If she was close enough, I'd whack her.

She takes my hand and gives me a tour of the rest of the house. The dining room. Her mother's study. Her father's wine cellar. Up to the first floor to her father's office and the open plan living room and kitchen, which is much less formal. I mean, it still looks like something out of an interiors magazine with its tall windows and white marble fireplace. It's not the sort of room I could imagine sitting in, on the sofa under a blanket, watching *EastEnders*. But then, I don't imagine Poppy's parents watch *EastEnders*, do they?

Still, I'm not scared of disturbing anything here. It just looks like a normal living room, even if everything is oversized. The television. The bookcases on either side of the fireplace.

The sofas. The purple velvet buttoned footstool, a glossy black tray on top with some equally glossy hardback books stacked on it, a candle on top of them. I walk over to it and lift the lid, giving it a sniff to find that it smells like her.

'This is your perfume,' I say, turning to her and holding up the candle.

'Well spotted.' She seems genuinely impressed. 'My grandmother wears it.'

'So you get on, then? You and your grandmother?'

'Yeah. She's my favourite. I can't wait for you to meet her.'

We share a smile that goes on for a beat too long. She turns away first and as soon as she does, I put the candle back on the pile of books before I drop it. I walk over to one of the windows then and look out at the sea. It's dark now, the light from the moon picking out the tips of the waves so they look gilded in silver.

'This must be magnificent in daylight,' I tell her and she comes over to stand next to me.

'I guess. I'm not here much to look at it, though.'

I sneak a look at her and she suddenly looks so sad, I almost reach for her hand. But before I can she catches herself, smiling and asking if I want to see the rest of the house. I tell her that I do, so she takes me up to her parents' floor (yes, they have a whole floor) with its dressing room and shiny copper bathtub and what is quite possibly the biggest bed I have ever seen.

'Should we turn off the lights? My father would have a stroke. He's always going on about saving energy.'

She shakes her head. 'When you live in a house like this, you want people to know that you're home.' She raises her eyebrows and I do the same. 'We were broken into last year. They didn't take anything of sentimental value, just the televisions, a camera and a couple of laptops, but ever since my father has been militant about making sure that all the windows and doors are locked and the lights are on. Everything's on a timer. The windows are alarmed.' She thumbs down the stairs. 'I know the front door looks original, but it's not. You'd need a steamroller to get through that thing.'

'Comforting.'

'He's getting a whole new security system installed in the New Year, with cameras *everywhere*, so I'm trying to take full advantage of hanging out here when they're not home before that happens.'

'So where's your room, then?'

Poppy points up. 'I've been banished to the attic like Bertha Mason. Not quite the attic,' she admits, nose wrinkling. 'There's still another floor above me, but it feels like it sometimes.'

'There's *another* floor? What's that for?'

'Nothing at the moment. It still hasn't quite recovered from the seagulls, but my father's converting it next year because that's exactly what two people in a house this big need . . . *more space.*'

She sighs heavily as she stomps up the stairs and I follow.

'Bathroom.' She points at a door when we get to the top, then at another door. 'My room.'

I follow her in and when she turns on the light, it's not what I expected at all. There's lots of pink. Pink walls. Pink fluffy rug. Pink curtains on either side of the windows, dotted with gold foil stars. There's a framed black and white print over the

120

bed of a woman in a flowing dress leaning off what looks like the side of the Eiffel Tower, the whole of Paris at her feet. It's nice. Pretty. But that's just it: it's pretty. Poppy likes horror films and Basquiat and wants to get a Kurt Vonnegut quote tattooed across her ribs.

It's all a little soft for her.

A little dreamy.

I wonder if it's even her room, but she moves around it like it is, walking over to plug her phone into the charger on one of the bedside tables, before throwing herself on to the bed with a theatrical sigh. I sit on the edge, unlacing my DMs and toeing them off before lying down next to her. I'm careful to keep a polite distance, which she doesn't observe, elbowing me as she sits up and reaches for the pink chenille blanket draped across the foot of the bed. She pulls it over us and immediately curls into me, slinging her arm across my stomach with a more content sigh this time, her breath hot and slow against my neck.

'I'm so glad I finally have you in my room,' she says, hooking her leg over me.

I nod, suddenly aware of the nearness of her.

The heat.

I'm not sure what I should do next – if I should kiss her or wait for her to kiss me.

So I panic and say, 'I thought you'd have a dog.'

Nice, Ash.

That'll get her in the mood.

'Yeah?' She searches for my hand under the blanket then threads her fingers through mine.

'A big one,' I tell her, tucking my other hand behind my head on the pillow and looking up at the high white ceiling. 'A Lab or a golden retriever, or something.'

'I love golden retrievers.' She sits up, her chin on my chest. 'The family next door have one,' she tells me with a grin, her dimples back. 'He's the best. His name's Iggy. Iggy Pup.'

'Cute.'

'He is cute,' she says, her smile a little naughtier now. 'But not as cute as you.'

I laugh, my cheeks suddenly too warm. 'Nice line, Miss Morgan.'

'Did it work?' She waggles her eyebrows at me.

'Well, I'm already in your bed, aren't I?'

'You are indeed, Miss Persaud.'

She kisses me – just gently, just for a moment – then pulls back to look at me. I nod and she does it again, my heart hammering so hard she must be able to feel it as she lets go of my hand under the blanket and straddles me. Her hair falls forward as she does and I reach up to sweep it back with my hands, her tongue warm and slow in my mouth.

She pulls away suddenly and I gasp at the absence of her, watching as she sits up and takes her jumper off. She gets her head stuck, though, and I can hear her laughing as I try to rescue her, her hair rising then falling like a red Hokusai wave when she does. I'm lying down so it's harder to get mine off, which only makes us laugh more. I manage it eventually, then her hands are on the belt of her jeans and it's all a bit clumsy as I follow her lead, the pair of us kicking each other as we try to get them off, which only prompts another shiver of giggles.

She kisses me again and that's clumsy as well, our mouths not quite aligned and our noses knocking together as I reach up to undo her bra. I can't see what I'm doing, though, so I snap the strap like a horny teenage boy in my haste to get it off, which makes her giggle against my mouth. Then I succeed, and when it falls open in my hands, it isn't funny any more. I don't care what underwear I'm wearing or that I haven't shaved my legs because she's breathing my name in a way she never has before.

In a way no one has before.

Ashana.

I've always liked my name, but I don't truly love it until I hear her say it like that. And I love the way her breathing changes when I touch her, how her skin warms under my fingers and the bite of her silver rings against mine. I count each of the round bones up her back that connect like a string of pearls. When I feel her ribs fanning out like an angel's wings beneath my hands, I rise off the bed to meet her, needing to be closer to her, wanting no space between us at all, not even a thread of light.

She breathes my name again, kissing me more urgently as I trace the lines of her collarbone with my fingers then curl my hand around her throat, the pad of my thumb seeking out her pulse. I feel it beating – strong and quick – and I just want to be inside her. Inside her in the truest sense of the word. I want to crawl inside her, swim in her warm blood then climb her ribs like a ladder and lick her heart. I want to bite her. I almost have to stop myself from sinking my teeth into her neck and drinking her up.

Devouring her.

I didn't know it would be like this. Even after all this time, it feels like I'm getting to know her all over again. The colour of her skin, pale as moonlight, and her mouth, warm as sunshine. Then she touches me – really touches me – and it's enough to make something in my chest flare then collapse in on itself.

And I understand then what Mr Moreno means when he says that's how galaxies are made.

NINE

As soon as I put my key in the front door, I can hear Keith Waithe, which means that my father is cooking.

Could this evening get any better?

I walk into the flat to find him and Rosh dancing in the kitchen as he stirs something on the stove. The scene couldn't be more different from the one I just left at Poppy's. Music fills the flat and as I stand in the doorway of the kitchen, I realise how small it is. So small that my father and Rosh barely fit in there at the same time.

When I first walked into Poppy's house, I might have been embarrassed to bring her back here, given her parents have an entire floor to themselves while Rosh and I share a room. But watching my father and sister, dancing around each other as the window steams up, how could I be?

There's more life in this tiny, hot kitchen than in the whole of her house and I think she'd love it. I think she'd love Keith Waithe and helping my mother clean and cut up okra while Rosh asks her question after question about the library at Roedean.

I know then that I want to tell them about her.

I want to bring her home.

Not now, though. The kitchen is a mess. There are onion

peelings on the counter and the floor beneath and a splatter of tomato sauce up the tiles behind the stove. My mother would cuss us all out if she was home right now.

'Ashana!' my father sings when he sees me standing in the doorway. And I wonder if he knows.

If he knows what I just did.

He mustn't because he beckons me into the kitchen, still dancing.

There's no room, but I step in anyway. 'What are we having?'

'Spag bol!' he and Rosh say in unison.

I punch the air. His spaghetti bolognese is undefeated, even if he refuses to add carrots and celery and uses too much chilli and garam masala for it to be regarded as an authentic spaghetti bolognese.

'How was the Tate Modern?' Rosh asks, taking three plates out of the cupboard.

'Cool. Very cool.'

'Did you see the iceberg?'

'Yes! It was incredible. Surprisingly moving.'

'Did you take photos? Can I see?'

'After dinner, OK?' I hope my father doesn't see the face I pull at her behind his back.

She looks confused and I mouth, *I'll tell you later* as he continues dancing around the kitchen, utterly oblivious to the fact that I've broken my phone. I didn't realise until I was getting dressed at Poppy's, but it turns out my phone was in the back pocket of my jeans when that bloke knocked me on my arse at the train station so now the screen's cracked. I can still use it, but it's not even a year old.

My mother is going to kill me dead and I can't even tell her that it wasn't my fault.

Still, until then, at least there's my father's spaghetti bolognese.

I know I'm going to tell my mother about Poppy before I hear her key in the door, but the reality of it – of actually saying it out loud – is making my heart beat so hard, I'm pretty sure that I'm going to throw up.

I shift on the sofa, trying to act natural, adjusting Rosh's favourite Christmas blanket – the red fluffy one with the white snowflakes – so it just looks like I'm sitting here, reading a book.

No big deal.

I hear the front door close then she's in the hallway, hanging her handbag on the coat hook and kicking her Crocs off before unbuttoning her coat. She must see the light on in the living room, because the next thing I hear is her padding down the narrow hall towards me and I tell myself to calm down.

'Ashana,' she says, walking over to stand by the arm of the sofa. 'Where's Daddy and Rosh?'

'Bed,' I tell her with a small smile. 'How was work?'

'Fine,' she says, clearly suspicious that the TV is off. 'Why are you still up?'

'I was just reading.'

'Reading?' She looks even more suspicious. 'What are you reading?'

'About Jean-Michel Basquiat. The exhibition I went to see today.'

I hold up the book Poppy gave me and she gestures at me to hand it to her. I do, watching as she takes her glasses from the top of her head and puts them on. She squints at the cover for a couple of seconds, her brow furrowed, then drops her chin to peer at me from over her glasses as she hands the book back.

'This isn't art, Ashana. It's just lines and colours.'

'Isn't that what all art is?'

She thinks about it for a moment, then tilts her head from side to side. 'True.'

She puts her glasses back on top of her head and when she turns to leave, I panic.

'Mama, can I talk to you?' I say, my voice far too loud.

So loud that she turns back to me with another suspicious frown. I can see the look on her face – a look that says, *What are you going to tell me now?* – but then she catches herself.

'Of course,' she says sweetly, coming to sit on the edge of the coffee table.

I've been practising what I'm going to say all evening. On the bus home from Poppy's. While Rosh, Dad and me were huddled in the living room, eating spag bol and watching the Strictly final. While I was washing up and idly gazing out at my estate, wishing I had a view like Poppy's parents. But now my mother is looking at me, the words that were so carefully lined up on my tongue abandon me.

So I blurt out, 'Mama, I've met someone.'

She's quiet for a beat too long, then nods. 'I thought so.'

I blink at her. 'How?'

'The flowers.'

I nod and she leans forward, resting her wrists on her knees and starts playing with her wedding ring. I can see from the way she's blinking and nodding gently to herself that she's thinking about what she's going to say – how she's going to handle this – which isn't like my mother at all.

'What's her name?' she finally says.

'Poppy,' I say proudly, my back a little straighter. 'Poppy Morgan.'

'Does she go to your school?'

'No. She goes to Roedean.'

My mother raises her eyebrows. 'Roedean?'

'Yes, Mama. She's kind and brave and smart,' I gush, smiling and gesticulating wildly, as though I'm trying to sell her a used car. 'Her father teaches at Cambridge and her mother is Professor Margot Morgan.' I point at the television. 'She did that documentary on the BBC about dark matter that Rosh made me watch, like, three times. She's *brilliant*. She won the Nobel Prize in Physics last year.'

She nods, obviously impressed, but then says, 'Smart parents don't always equal a smart child.'

That's a dig at me, I'm sure, but I carry on anyway.

'I know, but she is, Mama. I swear. So *smart*. And funny.'

'Funny?'

OK. Funny wasn't the right way to go. Guyanese mothers don't care about funny. They only want to hear three things: doctor, lawyer or engineer. Actually, that's not fair – she's married to a gardener, after all – but I know that it's the only thing my grandparents will want to hear.

129

'And she's vegan,' I add, then immediately regret it as she sits up.

'Vegan?' she says, like I've just told her that Poppy is Vulcan or something.

Why did I say that?

Now she's worried that Poppy's going to make me vegan as well.

I try to say something to reassure her that she won't, but the only thing I come up with is, 'I love meat.'

She looks appalled.

This isn't how I thought this conversation would go at all.

Why didn't I write down what I wanted to say?

'I *mean*.' I try again. 'She has a good heart, Mama. She's a member of Greenpeace.'

That does nothing for her, clearly. 'OK.'

'And I like her.' I finally tell her the only thing that matters. '*Really* like her.'

It works, because she softens. 'I know you do. You wouldn't be telling me about her if you didn't.'

She leans towards me again and when she reaches over to cup my face with her hand, stroking my cheek with her thumb, I wonder what she's thinking. If she's asking herself what happened to her little girl, the little girl who always made her dance with her at weddings and insisted that they call her little sister 'Toast' when she was born. Or if she's thinking about how hard my life's going to be now. How that isn't what she wanted for me.

She gives my cheek one last stroke and lets her hand drop back to her knee. 'Do you love her?'

I don't hesitate. 'Yes.'

I can't believe I told my mother that before I told Poppy.

She goes quiet again and I'm shaking, ready to melt, like that iceberg at the Tate Modern as I wait for her to say whatever she's going to say next. Whether she's going to tell me that it's OK, that she loves me. Or if she's repulsed at the reality of her daughter being in love with another girl.

My hands fist in Rosh's Christmas blanket as I wait, watching her absorb everything I've just told her. For a terrible moment, I don't think that she's going to say anything at all, like when I came out to her, that she's just going to thank me for telling her, then go to bed. But then she lifts her chin to meet my gaze.

'Can she clap roti?' she asks, a smile tugging at the corners of her mouth.

The relief makes me so light-headed that it's a moment or two before I can speak.

'I doubt it.' I laugh, swatting a tear away with my fingers.

She arches an eyebrow at me. 'Not *that* smart then, is she?'

I laugh again, wiping my cheek with the back of my hand.

She leans forward to kiss me on the forehead. When she sits back she reaches out to tuck my hair behind my ears. 'Let's tell Daddy and Rosh in the New Year, OK? We'll have Poppy over for dinner.'

I'm trying so hard not to dissolve into tears that I can only nod.

'Although, what I'm going to cook a vegan, I don't know.'

TEN

I know it's New Year's Eve, but I didn't expect so many people to be on the beach tonight. When Poppy told me to meet her here, I thought she was mad. I mean, it's *freezing*. Adara refused to come, saying she'd get pneumonia, so she's gone to Donna Niven's party instead. I don't blame her. Why would she want to sit on the beach when she could be in a nice warm house, dancing with Mark and spilling beer on Donna Niven's parents' rug?

Poppy must have known something I didn't, though, because it feels like the end of world and everyone is here. There are parties happening down the length of the beach, from the Pier to the Marina. Knots of friends, from middle-aged stoners to teenagers ten minutes away from puking up the whisky they stole from their parents' sideboard. Groups of people who might never have met are laughing and drinking and dancing to whatever music is playing.

By midnight, you'll no longer be able to tell where one party ends and another begins. I've never experienced anything like this before. No one cares. It doesn't matter what you're wearing or who you're talking to. No one's trying to be cool – to fit in – because no one does and everyone does, each of us united in this shared moment of anticipation as we await the turn of the year. Everyone is friends. Everyone is in love. Nothing else matters but midnight because next year will be different. We will be different.

It's our year.

Tomorrow morning, the beach will be a mess of broken glass and lost shoes. Perhaps it will rain later and cleanse it all away, but for now, it's like the Kurt Vonnegut quote Poppy wants to get tattooed across her ribs – *everything was beautiful and nothing hurt.*

Above us, the congregation of stars makes the sky look so big that if it fell, it would smother us all. To our right, the Pier stretches out over the sea in all its neon glory, the lights from the sign pooling on the surface of the sea in puddles of pink, yellow and blue. Ahead of us, the red flashing lights from the wind farm line the horizon. It's a clear night, so you can see each one, all 116 of them, and when Poppy squeezes my hand and turns her cheek to look at me with a slow smile, I know that she's thinking about that afternoon in late September we met on the boat.

Maybe it isn't such a bad story to tell our grandkids after all.

Now, here we are, sitting on the beach, the sea at our feet. I know now that the happiness – that thirteenth-birthday-cake happiness – didn't go away. It's always been there, like when you can see that the sun is shining, but you can't feel it on your cheek. I can feel it now – I'm happy. Not just when I'm with Poppy, but on the bus to school with Adara and at night, when I'm on the edge of sleep and I can feel myself tipping. It's just there – all the time – and whatever happens next year, I hope we remember this night, that we never, *ever* forget it.

Even when we're forty and all of this feels so very far away. I hope we remember that inside, we will always be the people we are tonight.

A few minutes ago, I was freezing, the tip of my nose sore from the sharp breeze coming off the sea. Now I'm burning up, my cheeks hot and my heart flickering red, like a neon *VACANCY* sign that I'm sure Poppy can see, even through my hoodie.

Now I've told my mother about her, I know what it's like to be a normal couple, to just sit and talk without worrying who'll see. We're making lists of all the things we want to do next year. I let her go first, on and on until she runs out of breath. Then it's my turn and it tumbles out of me. I don't know whether I'm high on the promise of the New Year or the nearness of her, but I can't say it quickly enough, the words getting on top of one another in my effort to get them out. Brighton Pride. Downstairs at Twin Pines. The Photomatic booth at Snooper's Paradise. I don't hold back and when I'm done, I don't know whether I've told her all the things I want to do next year or made a list of all the places I want to kiss her.

We're spent and settle into a silence I feel no urgency to fill. I can see our breath and remember that there's talk of snow. I feel a tickle of joy at the thought of Poppy in red mittens, snowflakes melting in her hair. I know it's cheesy, but I want that. Normal stuff. Snow angels and hot chocolate and selfies in matching scarves. Stuff from movie montages when the couple are falling in love but they don't know it yet.

Except we do.

Or I do.

I just haven't told her.

As we lean into one another, I wonder if I should tell her now – but then I hear the first firework pop and see a sudden blossom of hot pink in the black sky off to our right, past the Pier. I gasp, startled, and when Poppy does the same, we look at each other and giggle.

'What time is it?' she asks, leaning into me. 'It can't be midnight yet.'

I check my phone. '11:16.'

'Must be the time difference between here and Hove,' she chuckles again, taking a sip from the can of beer we've been sharing then handing it back to me.

When I look back out at the sea, I notice some red nail polish on the toe of my right DM, just a dot, like a glossy drop of blood on the black leather. I must have done it when I was rushing to get ready earlier and I'm tempted to reach over and pick it off, but then Poppy brings my hand up to her mouth and kisses it and I feel the firework in my chest this time. She smiles at me and I didn't know that it could be like this.

That you can like someone and they can like you back and no one gets hurt.

My phone rings then and I ignore it, letting it go to voicemail.

There's a beat, then it starts again and I glance at the screen to see who is being so persistent.

It's my mother.

'Shit,' I hiss, letting go of Poppy's hand as I almost jump clean out of my skin when I see her name on the screen. I quickly make the sign of the cross and say a little prayer that she's just calling to check on me, but when I answer and there's a painful stretch of silence, I know that isn't the case at all.

If we were closer to the Pier, I'd jump off it.

Finally, she says, 'Ashana? Where are you?'

'Hey, Mama. How's Aunty Lalita's party?' I ask, trying to sound casual as I curse the group of lads who have decided that of all parts of the beach to have a wrestling match, they want to do it in front of me.

My mother waits a beat then says it again. 'Ashana? Where are you?'

Before I can answer, the lads start cheering as one of them succeeds in pushing his mate in the sea and she must have heard – she can hear the opening of a biscuit packet three rooms away – and I know I'm done for, so I don't even try to lie. 'At the beach with Poppy,' I admit with a defeated sigh.

'Come home now, please.'

'Fuck,' I spit when she hangs up on me and reconsider my plan to jump off the Pier.

Rosh was supposed to call when they were leaving Aunty Lalita's so I could get home in time.

What the hell happened?

When I check my messages, sure enough, there's one from Rosh that she sent fifty-one minutes ago.

> Phone on 1% and about to die so can't call. Dad has a headache so we're leaving the party now. GET HOME.

Followed by another one, a minute later.

Really hope you get this, Ash.

Bollocks.

I was so distracted by Poppy that I forgot to check my phone.

When I turn to look at her, she's smiling grimly. 'You got busted.'

'Yep.'

'But it's New Year's Eve,' she reminds me with a pout. 'It's our year.'

'I know.' I sigh, getting to my feet then helping her up.

We've been sitting on her coat and when I reach down and pick it up off the pebbles, she puts it on with a determined frown. 'You're already in trouble, though. You may as well stay until midnight. It's only . . .' she stops to take her phone out of the pocket of her coat, '. . . 11:21. That's, what, thirty-nine minutes?'

I'm tempted. When she says it like that it doesn't feel like that big of a deal. I know what my parents are like, though: thirty-nine minutes now and I'll pay for it for *weeks*.

She reaches for my hand and I immediately feel heavy with sadness. It's our year and we're starting it with me getting *annihilated* by my parents and no doubt grounded until the next one.

This is not how I wanted this evening to go. At all. I was going to kiss her at midnight, tell her that I love her, tell her that I told my mother about her, that she wants her to come for dinner in the New Year.

That's not going to happen now, is it?

When she squeezes my hand, I look up to find her grinning. 'Can I tell you a secret before you go?'

I grin back. 'Always.'

She leans in and presses her mouth to my ear. 'I was going to tell you that I love you at midnight.'

'I love you too.' The words are out before I can stop them, as though I can't keep them in my mouth a moment longer. 'I told my mum that I loved you before Christmas.'

Her eyes widen. They look almost neon blue in the dark. 'You did?'

'Yeah. The night we first, *you know*.' I waggle my eyebrows.

'You told your mother we had sex?'

'Of course not!' I shudder, horrified at the thought. 'I told her about *you*.'

'What did you tell her?'

'That you were kind and smart and funny.'

'And what did she say?'

'She's concerned about the vegan thing.'

'Fair enough.' Poppy nods. 'Listen. Don't worry. I know your mum is pissed that you snuck out tonight, but when she calms down, I'll come over for dinner and charm the socks off her. I'm great with parents.' She stops to tilt her head from side to side. 'Everyone else's but my own. Speaking of.' She raises her eyebrows at me. 'I almost told my mother about you as well before Christmas.'

'Yeah?' I ask, biting down on my bottom lip as it quivers.

'The last time I spoke to her she said I sounded different. *Happy*.'

'How do they notice this stuff when no one else does?'

She looks at me as if to say, *Right?* then says, 'So I almost told her why I was so happy, but she was in Boston and I didn't want to tell her about you over the phone, you know?'

I nod.

'So I'm going to tell her now.'

'What? *Now* now?'

'*Now* now. I'm going to go home now and tell her.'

My heart flutters at the thought. 'You sure?'

'Absolutely.' She nods, finding my gaze and holding it. 'Do you know grateful I am to you, Ash?'

I blink at her. 'Me?'

'Yes, *you*. I was in such a bad way when we met.' Her gaze dips and when she trails off, my heart starts to beat very, very slowly. 'I was so sad, but then I met you.' When she looks up at me with a slow smile, my heart speeds up again, twice as fast. 'And I know it isn't up to you to fix that. What is it that Amy Poehler says? Other people are not medicine? She's right, but the day I met you, it was like a light turned on and I could see everything in magnificent, magical technicolour. You didn't *fix* me, only I can do that, but you made me care about stuff again, you know?'

I nod.

I know.

'You made me want to walk down roads I've never been on just to see where they lead. Discover a café and claim it as our own.' She smiles to herself at the memory and I can't help but do the same. 'You made me plant flags all over Brighton and say, *That's ours*. And you made me want to do that all over

139

the world, in every corner, because I can *see* a future. Memories. Stories. And I want it. I want all of it. I want to do and see *everything.*'

I just stare at her because I don't know what to say.

I thought she was the one who did that for me.

It hadn't even occurred to me that I was doing the same for her.

'But it's more than that, Ash,' she says and she's breathless now, her eyes wide and her cheeks flushed. 'You speak about your family and Adara with such affection, such love, that you made me want that as well. I was so angry with my mum for not taking my side when I wanted to come home after I got kicked out of Wycombe Abbey, but I know now that she was doing what your mum does – she was trying to protect me, because if I'd come home, I would have been on my own most of the time because they're never here, which would have been no good for me, would it?' I nod. 'So while I may never get on with my father, hearing you talk about your mum made me fight for my relationship with her and I'm so grateful.' She makes sure I'm looking at her, then smiles again, loose and warm. 'You literally saved my life, Ash.'

'Pop—' I start to say and now I'm breathless.

'No. Listen.' I'm relieved when she doesn't let me finish because I honestly don't know what to say to that. 'When I say that I love you, Ash, I don't mean that I love you in the way that I love Basquiat or oat milk lattes, I mean that I love *you.* All that you are and all that you will be and I can't wait to find out who that person is.'

I don't realise that I'm crying until she swipes the tear from my cheek with her thumb then takes my face in her hands, her rings cool but her forehead warm as she presses it to mine. 'Happy New Year, Ashana Persaud.'

'Happy New Year, Poppy Morgan.'

ELEVEN

I wait ages for the bus and when it finally arrives, it's packed. The only seat left is on the top deck next to a guy who has passed out, his mouth open and his cheek to the window, his breath clouding the glass.

Great, I think, plonking down next to him and taking my phone out of the back pocket of my jeans to message my mother and tell her that I'm on the 1A. She calls immediately, obviously not believing me.

'Ashana, where are you?'

'On the 1A, Mama.'

'It's very loud.'

'It's New Year's Eve. Everyone's wasted.'

'Are you?'

'Of course not.'

Poppy and I shared *one* beer, which we didn't even finish. My mother will still check my breath, so I'd better get some chewing gum from the mini-mart before I go home.

'Call me when you get off the bus,' she tells me, without her usual gentle tone.

'Yes, Mama.'

'No *Yes, Mama*, Ashana,' she says, clearly still furious with me. 'Just make sure you do it.'

'I will, Mama. I promise.'

'If you don't, I'll think something has happened to you and I'll call the police, OK?'

'OK, Mama,' I say, glad that I didn't give in to Poppy and stay at the beach until midnight. My mother would have released the hounds.

'And send me a picture.'

When she hangs up, I take a selfie with the passed out guy sitting next to me and send it to her.

She doesn't respond.

I consider waking the drunk guy next to me as I'm getting off at my stop, but he wakes with such a jolt that I jump in my seat as he turns to me, his eyes red. 'Where am I?'

'Haybourne Road,' I tell him, hoping he hasn't missed his stop.

'Next one.' He nods then promptly passes out again.

It's the last stop, so if the driver's feeling generous, they'll wake him up before the bus turns round and heads back to Portslade. I can't help but smile as I'm heading down the stairs, picturing him going back and forth between Whitehawk and Portslade until he sleeps off whatever he's drunk. At least he'll get his money's worth.

My phone rings as soon as I step off the bus and I don't even need to check.

I don't know how she does this.

She's a witch.

'I just got off the bus, Mama,' I tell her when I answer.

'Why didn't you call me? I told you to call me, Ashana.'

'Because you called me before I could.'

She exhales heavily. 'Your father needs paracetamol for his headache.'

'I'll pop into the mini-mart. I'm almost there.'

I need chewing gum anyway. At least going to the mini-mart to get paracetamol for my father will account for the walk home from the bus stop taking two minutes longer than usual.

'Come straight home, Ashana,' she warns me.

'Of course, Mama.'

'*Of course, Mama*,' she mocks, but I can tell she's softening. 'I'm very disappointed with you.'

'I know,' I concede with a sad smile.

'I trusted you.'

'I know.'

'You could have just told me that you wanted to see . . .' she stops to lower her voice, '. . . *her* tonight?'

Is that who Poppy is now?

Her?

'I know.'

'Stop saying I know,' she snaps and she's back. Still cross, but less likely to actually murder me.

'I'm at the mini-mart,' I tell her.

'Just paracetamol then come straight home, OK?'

'I love you, Mama,' I say sweetly, because I'm evil and my mother has this thing where if you tell her that you love her, she *has* to say it back, no matter how mad at you she is.

'I love you too, Ashana,' she says with a huff, then hangs up.

144

I stride into the mini-mart to find Nish behind the counter, as always, watching something on his laptop.

'Hey, Ash,' he says, standing when he sees me walking towards him.

'You got any paracetamol, Nish?'

He grabs a pack from the shelf behind him and puts it on the counter between us. '£1.99.'

'This too, please,' I say, chucking a pack of chewing gum on the counter.

'£2.58.'

I slip my hand into the pocket of my leather jacket for my purse and hand him a tenner.

'Happy New Year,' I say when he hands me the change.

'Yeah.' He nods as though he's forgotten what night it is. 'Happy New Year, Ash.'

I take my phone out of the back pocket of my jeans as I turn to leave, checking the time.

11:58.

Two minutes isn't enough time to make it home, even if I run.

Looks like I'll be ringing in the New Year by myself.

Brilliant.

I open the chewing gum as I'm heading out the door, popping one into my open mouth. I miss, though, chucking it at my eye, and as it bounces off, I trip over the sign for the National Lottery outside. Thankfully, a girl is passing and she grabs my arm before I face plant the pavement. I turn to curse the sign.

Could you be a winner tonight? it says.

Clearly not.

'You're Ashana, right?' the girl asks when I'm a safe enough distance away from the sign.

'Yeah,' I say before I try again with the chewing gum, succeeding this time.

'Ashana Persaud?'

'Yeah.' I stop chewing the gum for a second. 'Who are you?'

At first glance, she looks about Rosh's age – thirteen, maybe fourteen. She's the same height with that same softness around her face that makes me wonder if she rereads His Dark Materials every Christmas and loves chemistry because it's the closest thing she's seen to magic. The massive black teddy-bear coat she's wearing doesn't help, swamping her, making her legs look like they might snap under the weight of it.

We stare at one another in the doorway of the mini-mart. Now I look at her – really look at her – I realise that she's older than I thought. She doesn't have the same fidgety energy Rosh has and her hair is tamer, a sharp white-blonde bob that stops just above her jaw, the colour of printer paper. She smiles and I see that her eyes are the same colour as Poppy's but again with none of the warmth, like someone's coloured them in with a blue felt-tip that's almost run out.

Cold, that's what I feel looking at her, despite her pink cheeks and smile.

She leaves me cold.

'I'm Dev.' She persists with a sweet smile that is doing nothing to convince me that she actually is sweet.

So? I almost say as I resume chewing the gum. Something

tells me that I'd rather ring in the New Year alone than with her. So I pop another chewing gum in my mouth for good measure and cross the street.

I admit, I'm not paying attention, too concerned with getting away from her to check if anyone's coming, but mercifully, I see the car that comes screaming towards me – far too fast – a second before it hits me, jumping out of the way as it swerves and slams into the railing outside the mini-mart.

It's the last thing I hear, the shrill shriek of metal hitting metal, of something hitting something it shouldn't, followed by the snap of breaking glass as the windscreen breaks into a million pieces that soar up into the air and hang there like stars. Then there's nothing, just an aching stretch of white noise that goes on and on until *BOOM*. The glass falls around me and I hear fireworks chasing one another over my head – *POP POP POP* – sending the seagulls fleeing.

I look at the car, at its back wheels spinning – spinning and spinning – the front of it folded around the railing. I'm suddenly, painfully aware of the nearness of it, the patch of road separating me from the car so slight, I could reach out and touch the back of it if I wanted to.

Broken glass crunches under my feet as I stagger back and press my hands to my face as if to check that I'm still here. I pull them away and look at them. No blood. I touch the back of my head, my chest, my stomach. Nothing. Nothing hurts. I'm here. I'm still here.

Thank God.
Thank God.
That was close.

Oh my God, that was close.

That was so close.

The relief is giddying as I mutter nonsense, over and over. I realise then that the girl who helped me when I tripped is still there. She reaches for my elbows and starts jumping up and down, clearly thrilled as she says something, something about it being midnight and something else I can't hear over the sound of fireworks and people singing.

Should auld acquaintance be forgot,

And never brought to mind?

I turn back to the car as the doors open and two blokes jump out then leg it up the street, the way I was going before they nearly hit me.

'Hey!' I shout after them. 'You could have killed me!' but they're gone.

That's when Nish rushes out of the mini-mart to see what's going on. 'Did you see that, Nish?' I point at the mangled car. 'That car almost ran me over!' but he doesn't hear as he looks down and gasps. I try to see what he's looking at, but then the girl in the teddy-bear coat is back, standing between us.

'We have to go.' She reaches for my arm, but I shrug her off as Nish rushes back into the shop.

When he returns, he has a phone pressed to his ear. 'Yes, ambulance, please. Quickly.'

'We have to get out of here, Ashana,' she tells me and I stop and stare at her.

'Who are you? How do you know my name?'

Before she can answer, I hear Nish say, 'Please. Come quick. Someone's been hit by a car.'

148

She tries to stop me, but I look around her and there, lying across the street is a body. It's dark and they're all in black so, I didn't notice them. They must have been going into the mini-mart as I was leaving.

The girl in the teddy-bear coat – Dev? Is that what she said her name was? – reaches for my arm again as I take a step towards the body, but I pull away and see the dot of nail polish on the toe of their right DM, like a glossy drop of blood on the black leather, and everything becomes white noise again.

It's me.

I open my mouth to scream, but nothing comes out, and when I turn to the girl, she's looking up at the fireworks fizzing over our heads, scattering shards of coloured light across the sky.

'I knew it.' When she looks down, she smiles at me in a way that makes me want to turn and run. Before I can, she holds out her hand to me. 'I knew it was going to be you, Ashana.'

After

ONE

I wake up with such a jolt, I half-expect to find my mother standing over my bed, telling me off for getting make-up on my pillowcase again. My head doesn't feel good. God help me, how much did I drink last night? I shared a can of beer with Poppy and we didn't even finish it so I shouldn't feel this awful.

Before my eyes can adjust, everything goes blurry again and not that nice kind of blurry, just woken up from a nap on a drizzly Sunday afternoon kind of blurry, but the bad kind. The kind that makes you feel like you're being swallowed whole.

It's then that I know that I'm having that dream again, the one where I'm under water and just as I break the surface, someone grabs my ankle and pulls me under. I tell myself not to give into it, but I'm already gone. Arms out. Palms up towards a sky I can no longer see as the water fills my nose and mouth until it's inside me. My bones washed clean and my heart bobbing like a red rubber buoy in my chest. I can taste salt, the sharp burn of it on my tongue, stinging my eyes as I sink down.

A moment later, I hear a pained sound and realise it's me, groaning at my mother that I'm awake as I force myself to peel open my eyes. Even that hurts, my eyelashes stuck together and my eyelids so heavy it takes more effort than I am capable of not to close them again.

No one's there, though.

No Mum.

No Rosh on her bed, reading a book.

It's just me.

It isn't until I kick off my duvet that I realise that it isn't my duvet at all, but a tartan wool blanket I don't recognise.

Wait.

This isn't my bed, it's a sofa I don't recognise, either.

Why am I dressed?

I press my hands to my chest and find something familiar. Leather, smooth then creased around my elbows and smooth again over my shoulders. My fingers catch on something cold. Sharp. The zip. It's my jacket. I bring my arm up and press my nose into the sleeve.

Home.

That thing I can only smell when I'm not there.

I didn't even know that my house had a smell until the first time I went away without my family. I didn't go far, just a school trip to Stratford-upon-Avon, but I opened my holdall and everything smelt like my flat. Not just washing powder, but my pillowcase. My towel. The saucepan of dhal that always seems to be on the stove, even on Christmas Day. The bottle of Estée Lauder Beautiful on my mother's dressing table that she only wears to weddings and midnight mass.

I close my eyes and inhale again and immediately feel better. Steadier. Everything feels a little more solid as I slip my hand under my jacket to find the warmth of my hoodie. That makes me feel better as well because yes, this is definitely my hoodie. This might not be my blanket, but this is my hoodie and my leather jacket. I kick the rest of the blanket away to find that I'm wearing my jeans. Definitely my jeans. Black. Slightly grey at the knees and beginning to come away at the seams between my thighs.

And these are my DMs.

But why am I wearing my DMs on someone's sofa?

Where am I?

With that, the fog clears and I'm suddenly, painfully awake.

I sit up so quickly, the sofa lets out a curmudgeonly creak. 'Ashana! You're awake,' I hear someone say and look up to find a girl sitting on what looks like a shop counter. There's a lamp next to her, the only source of light in the room, and I see then that it's the girl from outside the mini-mart.

The one in the teddy-bear coat.

She looks the same. Small. Dwarfed by her coat, her hair almost fluorescent white in the dim light. Then she smiles and that's the same as well.

All I feel is cold.

She jumps down from the counter and when she takes a step towards me, my hand fists in the blanket, pulling it to me as I raise the other to warn her not to come any closer. She takes the hint, but still smiles, 'Welcome back, Ashana.'

Back where? I almost ask, but I don't because this is another dream. It has to be. I'm dreaming and I'm going to wake up any moment.

I wait, but nothing happens. My thoughts jump in every direction as it comes screaming back to me.

The broken glass.

The fireworks.

The car, its back wheels spinning and spinning.

Then I'm dizzy again.

'Where am I?' My voice sounds weird.

Deeper.

'How are you feeling, Ashana?' she asks, the pale skin between her eyebrows creasing as she goes from being pleased to see me to concerned so swiftly that I can't help but ask myself the same thing.

How am I feeling?

Something's not right.

Am I in pain?

Should I be in pain?

Did something happen with that car outside the mini-mart?

Maybe I did get hurt.

I thought I was OK – I felt OK – but if I'm injured, why am I here and not at the hospital or at home?

Where even is *here*?

I look around and realise that I'm in a shop. It's definitely a shop. OK. I'm in a shop. I feel my thoughts scatter in every direction again and I try to grab at them before they fly away and think of the most obvious explanation.

Maybe I was in shock after what happened outside the mini-mart so she – this girl – and Nish brought me inside so I could catch my breath. But it's not the mini-mart. It's too dark. The mini-mart is bright, this unnecessarily aggressive white that makes my eyes hurt if I'm in there for too long. And it's loud. Nish is always on his phone or watching a film on his laptop behind the counter. Plus, it doesn't smell the same. The mini-mart has this smell. Orange ice-lollies and the tin of samosas on the counter that Nish's mother-in-law makes every morning and are sold out by eleven. This place doesn't smell like that. It smells like an old lady's living room. Of old paper and dust.

I look around and see books. Shelves and shelves of them. Not new ones, though, like the ones in Waterstones with their sharp, colourful spines, but old ones with battered leather jackets – oxblood and brown and what was once navy blue but now looks almost black, in this light – their gilt titles dulled from years of warm hands and lingering at the bottom of too many school bags. I look down and see that the wide, scuffed floorboards beneath my feet lead to a large window ahead of me which frames a narrow street that looks vaguely familiar, even in the dark.

Before I can work out where I am, though, two blokes stop outside the window. One is wearing a white shirt with what I hope is a red wine stain on the front and the other is swinging a bottle of champagne. They're swaying and singing 'Auld Lang Syne' and my shoulders relax again.

It's still New Year's Eve.

That's something.

Wherever I am, I can't have been here long.

When the blokes carry on down the road, I notice the shop opposite. I know it. I'm in town. I must be, because that's the weird vegan shoe shop Poppy made me go in.

'Ashana?' The girl in the teddy-bear coat is in front of me now. She's careful to keep her distance, but she's still close enough to make my hands fist so tightly in the tartan blanket the bones in my fingers ache.

'Don't be scared,' she says.

Of course I'm scared.

I don't know who she is or how I got here.

It's becoming increasingly difficult to remain calm about that.

Panic licks at my palms, my synapses firing all at once. Question after question after question until something catches light, fear burning everything away until I am left with a single, furious thought.

I have to get out of here.

That's when I see the door out to the street, but as I am calculating the number of steps between me and it, I hear a bell and it swings open.

A girl about my age sweeps in and I find myself pulling the tartan blanket closer as I wonder if I know her as well. I don't. Or at least, I don't think I do.

When she comes to stand next to the girl in the teddy-bear coat, it's like someone's been asked to draw a picture of two girls that are the exact opposite of one another. Where the girl in the teddy-bear coat is small and pale with a soft, round face and a smooth, neat bob, this girl is tall and spider-thin with a sharp nose and an even sharper smile. She's mixed with something. With what, I don't know. Her skin isn't much lighter than mine, and her eyes are the same colour. A brown that, like the navy blue books, looks almost black in this light. Like Rosh she has far too much hair, a storm of dark curls that twist halfway down her back. Except where Rosh's are loose, these are tight as springs.

She raises her eyebrows at me. 'She's awake.'

She unbuttons her black wool coat and throws herself into the armchair next to me, draping her legs over the arm. 'Have you told her yet?' she asks, peering at me from under her thick eyelashes. When I glare at her, she rubs her hands together. 'Good. I didn't miss it. I love this part.'

I lift my chin and hold her gaze for a moment longer than is comfortable, determined not to let her know how scared I am. She does the same and just as I'm about to ask her what her problem is, I see it. Not quite a smile, more of a swift twitch at the corners of her mouth, then it's gone.

I'm determined not to look away, but I'm aware of someone else, a woman who emerges from a door behind the counter and says, 'Ashana, you're awake.'

I turn as she picks up a wooden chair and walks over to where I'm sitting on the sofa. She puts it down in front of me and there's something about the way she sits, so properly – back straight, shoulders back, knees together – that makes me sit a little straighter as well.

She's older than the other two, about my mother's age, I'm guessing, but they look nothing alike. Where my mother is all soft curves with a fine halo of fluff around her hairline that always sticks up, no matter how much hairspray she uses, this woman is immaculate. Her hair is the same colour, that same poppy-seed black, but is cropped short so I can see all of her face. The light from the lamp on the counter picks out the highpoints of her face so they seem to glow. This rich, red-gold that catches on her cheekbones, the arch of her eyebrows and the tip of her nose.

She isn't all in black like the other two. She's wearing a long leopard skin skirt and a shirt, the sharp white collar making her skin look even richer, the cotton reflecting off it in a fine silver line that circles her neck.

She smiles. An effort to put me at ease, I suppose, but it doesn't quite reach her eyes. 'Hello, Ashana. My name is Deborah. Deborah Archer.' I watch as she removes her black-rimmed glasses, folding the arms down carefully and curling her fine fingers around them. 'And you're Ashana.'

'How do you know my name?'

The girl in the teddy-bear coat knew my name as well.

How do they know my name?

Deborah doesn't tell me. 'Ashana Persaud, is that right?'

She says my surname like most people do – *Per-sad* – and I correct her. 'Per-*sword*.'

I don't know why it matters.

Force of habit, I guess.

'Sorry. Ashana Per-*sword*.'

'How do you know my name?' I ask again.

She ignores me again. 'It's a pleasure to meet you, Ashana.'

'I prefer Ash.' I don't know why that matters, either.

'Ash.' She nods. 'Well, Ash, this is Isla Devlin. You met earlier.' She raises her hand and gestures at the girl in the teddy-bear coat. 'But she prefers Dev.'

Dev. That's right. She introduced herself outside the mini-mart.

'And *this*.' When Deborah pauses, I detect a hint of exasperation as she gestures at the girl with the curly hair this time. I've known her all of three minutes and I don't think to

160

question what she's done to warrant it. 'Is Esen Budak.'

Esen salutes me with two fingers and a smug smile I want to bite off her face.

'You're probably wondering why you're here, aren't you, Ashana?'

No shit.

'What do you remember about tonight?' Deborah prompts when I don't respond.

I turn my head to look at the girl in the teddy-bear coat. Dev. She smiles and my gaze immediately flicks back to Deborah. She crosses her legs and sits back, her glasses in her hand, and there's something about the way she tilts her head and looks at me with a sombre sort of concern that makes me feel like I'm in a counselling session. I wait for her to take out a notebook and start writing down everything I say.

'What's the last thing you remember, Ashana?'

I hesitate, unsure why she's asking me that instead of telling me what's going on.

I wait a beat, hoping that she'll take the hint and tell me, but she doesn't flinch and I don't know whether it's out of curiosity or politeness, but I find myself answering her. 'Being outside the mini-mart.'

She nods and I wish she wouldn't.

It feels like being patted on the head.

'I remember the car,' I say carefully. 'The fireworks.'

Me, I almost say, then stop myself because it feels like something has caught light in my chest.

I'm burning with it.

It was me. I saw my body on the road outside the mini-mart.

'What else do you remember, Ash? Dev tells me that you saw—'

'Yes,' I interrupt, crossing my arms. 'I saw. I saw it.'

I say *it* because I can't say *me* because that can't have been me in the street. I'm here.

I'm here.

'Do you understand what that means, Ash?'

Of course I don't! I want to yell, but the words get burned up in the fire in my chest.

'Do you understand that you were hit by that car outside the mini-mart tonight?'

I wasn't.

I jumped out of the way.

'Ash, I need you to tell me that you understand that you were hit by that car.'

I wasn't. I jumped out of the way.

Deborah doesn't say anything, just looks at me and waits as I buckle under the weight of what she's saying. I squeeze my eyes shut, willing myself to wake up, but when I open them again, I'm still there, on the sofa, the tartan blanket in my lap, the three of them watching me.

I feel the slow creep of dread, starting in my hands then up my arms, each hair rising – slowly, slowly – one by one at first then all at once. I'm suddenly very, very cold, yet I can feel my top lip sweating as I lift my chin to look her in the eye for the first time. I lick the sweat away, trying to swallow back the words I can feel lining up on my tongue. But they're there, I can feel them, pushing against the back of my teeth.

Don't say it.

But I do.

'What's going on?' I ask, immediately wishing I hadn't because I don't want to know.

I don't want to know.

'Ash, you're dead,' Deborah says, making no attempt to sugar-coat it. 'You died tonight.'

TWO

OK. I'll be honest, I wasn't expecting *that*.

How can I be dead? I don't feel dead. I can't be. I dig my nails into the flesh of my palm, so hard I'm sure the bones in my fingers are going to snap, and wait. It takes a moment too long, but at last, there it is. Pain, bright and fierce. The relief brings tears to my eyes. I look down at my hand, smoothing over the crescent-shaped dents with the pad of my finger as I watch them disappear.

I laugh. I can hear myself and it's one of those hysterical too-loud laughs that goes on for a beat longer than is comfortable as I wait for Deborah to join in. She doesn't, though, just watches me with a look of sombre concern as the sound dies in my throat and the whole bookshop becomes very, very still.

I look between them. First Deborah, then left to Dev and right to Esen. Why aren't they saying anything? Even Esen's smug smile has softened to something that takes me a second to recognise. Pity, I realise, the back of my neck burning. She feels sorry for me. But why? I mean, this is a joke, right?

'Listen, Ash,' Deborah says and there's a firmness to it – an impatience – that feels a little like being told off. I look frantically around the bookshop, my gaze bouncing off the shelves then down to the floor and up to the ceiling and over to the counter as I feel it again – the dread – spreading up my arms, working its way across my scalp to make the hair on my head bristle until I am aware of each one. I'm not sure what I'm looking for.

A crucifix?

A huddle of candles?

A framed print of the Sacred Heart like the one my parents have by our front door?

I look at Dev then, at her sweet face and sweet smile and sweet pink cheeks, and she has this dreamy sort of expression on her face – almost glazed – and my scalp shivers again as a thought needles at me, burrowing under my skin like a splinter.

Is this one of those conversion things? I saw a documentary about it last year, about parents who send their kids to Christian camps in America to get the gay out of them. Is that what Deborah meant when she said that I'm dead? Not dead in the literal sense, but spiritually. Did my mother do this? Did she tell someone at church that I was gay and they promised to fix me? She wouldn't, would she? When I told her about Poppy, she seemed OK with it. And why would she have been so keen for me to get home tonight if she knew I was coming here?

Maybe this is nothing to do with her. Maybe this is some sort of weird cult. Maybe Dev saw me on the beach with Poppy, followed me and brought me back here.

I turn my cheek towards Deborah again, my fingers digging into my palm so hard I don't know how I don't draw blood this time. I wait for her to say it, for her to tell me that she can help me.

Save me.

But she just meets my gaze head-on when I ask, 'What do you want?'

'I'm here to help you, Ash.'

I don't believe her.

'I'm here to help you understand what happened tonight.'

'Yeah?' I frown, feigning ignorance. 'What happened tonight, Deborah?'

'You know what you saw, Ash.'

'Do I?'

I cross my arms and sit back as I wait for it. Wait for her to tell me how being with Poppy is wrong, but Jesus still loves me. Deborah just looks at me, though, with that same infuriating, inscrutable look my mother gives me when I ask her a question she thinks I already know the answer to.

'You know what happened outside the mini-mart tonight, don't you, Ash?'

I blink at her, momentarily startled as I ask myself why she's back to this.

'You know that you were hit by that car. You know that was your body.'

'No.' It's like being punched in the chest, over and over.

That's all I can say.

No.

'You died outside the mini-mart and you're here because you were the last person to die on New Year's Eve. You're one of us now.'

I stare at her.

Where is *here*?

Who are these people?

I say the next words very carefully. 'Is this heaven?'

'It would be a bit shit if it was,' Esen responds with a sour chuckle.

Deborah ignores her. 'Not quite. The legend goes that the last person to die on New Year's Eve becomes the grim reaper for that parish.' She waits for me to look her in the eye before she says, 'This year, that person is you.'

'The grim what now?' I blink at her, but there's no hint of hesitation this time. Heat blooms in my cheeks as I feel Dev and Esen staring at me. With that, every bit of me is burning, beads of sweat bubbling up along my hairline. But Deborah just sits there, hands folded neatly in her lap.

'The grim reaper.' She licks her lips. 'You're a grim reaper.'

I wait for her to elaborate.

She doesn't.

'Wait.' I can hear myself laughing again as everything swims out of focus.

I close my eyes and press my hand to my forehead until it passes.

When I open them, Deborah is still looking at me like this is a perfectly normal conversation.

'Wait,' I say again. 'The grim reaper as in that dude with the black cloak and scythe?'

'Not quite. I suppose that's what most people imagine when they think about the grim reaper but, as always, the reality is far more mundane than the myth.'

'Huh?'

'Don't worry, Ash.' She chuckles lightly. 'You won't be required to wear a black cloak and carry a scythe.'

She's so calm. Too calm. It only makes me more untethered. I curl my fingers around the edge of the sofa cushion beneath me as though I might float up to the ceiling if I don't hold on to something.

'I don't understand.' I shake my head at her. 'You want me to decide who dies?'

'Of course not.' Deborah looks so appalled that I have to stop myself from laughing again because that's a completely unreasonable thing to assume, apparently. 'The decision has been made before you get there.'

'Who makes that decision, then?'

She carries on as if I haven't said anything. 'Grim reapers are responsible for the people in their parish who die the same way they did. So, in your case, you will be responsible for adolescent sudden deaths. We refer to you as grim reapers, but you're actually more like collectors. All you have to do is escort them down to the beach where someone will be waiting to take them to the otherside.'

'The other side of *what*?'

'Hove,' Esen says.

Deborah pinches the bridge of her nose and lets out a weary sigh. 'How is that helping?'

'I'm not trying to help.' Esen puts her hands behind her head and eases into the chair.

Deborah ignores her. 'Listen, Ash. I know this is a lot to absorb all at once.'

'Not at all.' I wave my hand at her. 'This is all absolutely, perfectly normal.'

'I understand.'

'Do you?'

I don't think she does.

'I do.' Deborah looks me in the eye and says it again. 'I *do*. But you're not alone.'

Something dawns on me then. 'Wait. Are you all grim reapers?'

'Dev and Esen are.'

'What are you, then?'

'You could describe me more as a mentor.'

'What? Like that guy from Buffy?'

'Yes.' Esen points at me. It's the most animated I've seen her since she walked in and it makes me unreasonably uncomfortable. 'Except you have to do everything she says or you'll be banished for eternity.'

I look back at Deborah. 'Excuse me?'

'Again, not helping, Esen,' she says without looking at her.

'Again, not *trying* to help, Deborah.'

'Can you stop? This is hard enough for Ash as it is,' Dev tells Esen, shooting her a look so fierce it makes Esen hold her hands up and pretend to lock her lips and throw away the key.

'That's why I was at the mini-mart this evening, Ash.' Dev's face softens as she turns and peers at me from under her neat fringe. 'To reap you.'

'You,' I point at Dev then back at myself, 'reaped me and now I'm a grim reaper as well?'

'Because you were the last person to die this year.'

'Is that what you meant when you said that you knew I was the one?'

She grins. 'Yes! I didn't know for sure, but I was hoping.'

169

'OK.' I finally summon the strength to stand up. The muscles in my legs protest at the effort, but I manage to remain upright out of sheer stubbornness, if nothing else. 'I have no idea what's happening here or what you're getting out of this, but I'm not dead.' I hold my arms out and raise my eyebrows at Deborah. 'So, as much fun as this has been, I'm going to go, because *clearly*, you're all out of your minds.'

Dev gapes at me as I step over the blanket which has pooled around my feet. 'Where are you going?'

'Home,' I tell her over my shoulder as I head for the door.

THREE

As soon as I get out into the street, I check my pockets.

They're empty.

No phone.

No keys.

No wallet.

Brilliant.

I look at the bookshop, ready to go in and demand them back, but all I have in my wallet is whatever change Nish gave me in the mini-mart. If Deborah wants to keep that and my shitty phone with the smashed screen, she's welcome to it.

Something tells me I'm getting off lightly.

I don't linger, another tingle of dread tripping down my spine as I check that she hasn't followed me before heading towards North Street. I want to run, but I'm suddenly horribly woozy, like when you sit up too quickly and have to sit down again. But I can't sit down, I have to go, and I don't know whether it's the shock of what just happened or my desperation to put as much distance between myself and the bookshop as possible, but my legs are shivering so much it's all I can do to put one foot in front of the other.

The fact that it's so quiet doesn't help. Admittedly, I've never been in this part of town so late, but usually it's littered with people and there's no one here now – not a soul – which freaks me out almost as much as what just happened in the bookshop.

Someone has left a trail of hot-pink feathers like breadcrumbs that lead to a boa that is curled up in the middle of the road. Whoever dropped it was probably too drunk to notice that it had fallen off and is now long gone. So it's just me and the feather boa and something about it makes me shiver, like I'm a character in a zombie movie, or something.

Like I'm the only person left on earth.

When I get to the corner I stop and look up. The sky is gunpowder black, the moon a perfect circle of white, as though someone's taken a knife and cut a hole clean out of the sky. I stand there and stare at it, trying to work out why it doesn't look right. Then I realise what's wrong – what's *missing* – I can't hear the seagulls. Usually they'd be squealing and diving down to pick through the bins or waddling about on the pavement looking for scraps.

They're part of the soundtrack of Brighton, like the push and pull of the sea. But tonight, I can't hear them. They're gone and everything is unnervingly quiet. So quiet that I can hear the steady squeak of my DMs as I tell myself to walk faster.

At last, there, ahead of me, is the light of North Street and my hands unclench in my pockets. A bus rolls past, the top deck empty, and when I turn left, every part of me pulses like a fresh bruise when I see the Old Steine. If I could trust my legs, I'd run. So I walk and keep walking, putting one foot in front of the other again and again and again as I tell myself that I'll be home soon and everything will be OK.

I'm crossing the road when I finally hear it, what can only be described as a *shriek* that is enough to make me miss a step. It takes a moment for the shock to pass and when it does, I realise what it is – a seagull. I never thought I'd be so pleased to see one, but I catch myself sighing with relief as something in me realigns and everything around me finally feels a little more solid.

The lawn is dotted with them, their white wings tucked in as they pad back and forth, picking at the grass. There are people too. Not many, but enough of them to make me feel safer as I head across the road. Most of them are at the bus stop, shifting from one foot to the next, breath puffing out of them in great clouds as they wait for the night bus. There are four girls on the corner and as I pass, one of them releases a torrent of vomit so violent her friend screams. I scream as well, covering my mouth with my hand and jumping out of the way to avoid the spray as I conclude, with a sob, that this evening hasn't ended the way I hoped it would.

I don't realise that I'm heading to the Pier instead of up St James's Street until I'm there, under the clock. I don't know if it's working, but it says that it's almost 3 a.m. as I head up Marine Parade.

It isn't until I'm approaching The Lanes Hotel that I notice that I'm walking more quickly and when I find myself at the top of the stairs down to the beach, I know why.

Then I'm running, my legs obeying me at last as I charge down the stairs and on to the beach, the pebbles splashing beneath the soles of my DMs as I try to remember where I was sitting with Poppy a few hours ago.

We were sitting here, weren't we? The Pier to our right, the wind farm ahead of us. I know I can't, but I'm sure that I can see the impression we made in the pebbles and oh God—

Why did I leave?

I should have stayed.

Poppy was right – it was only thirty-nine minutes. It wasn't even worth it in the end, was it? It's not like I made it home on time. If I'd stayed I could have rung in the New Year with her and none of this would have happened.

I suddenly miss her so much it's all I can do not to sink to my knees and cry. It dawns on me then that without my phone, I don't have her number. My parents made me and Rosh memorise our landline and their mobile numbers in case something happened. I had the chance to do the same with Poppy's, didn't I? When I was on the bus from town that afternoon, I stared at it until the numbers blurred together.

Furious with myself, I walk the length of the beach, right up to Dukes Mound, but there's no sign of her.

She's gone.

I give up, following the road up to Marine Parade. At least I know where she lives, I think, slowing as I look up at her big white house. I look up at her bedroom window and see that the light is on and I want to call up to her, tell her everything that happened tonight.

But that can wait.

I need to get home.

It's the police car that finally makes me slow down. It's parked in the middle of the street, doors open. People on my estate don't call the police, they prefer to handle things themselves, so if the police are here uninvited, it can't be good.

There's a huddle of people by the car, chatting furiously. Most of them are in their pyjamas, coats thrown over the top, their bare feet stuffed into shoes and trainers in their haste to get out and see what's going on. I can't help it, curiosity getting the better of me as well, and I walk over to see what they're looking at.

When I do, I realise that they're standing there because they can't go any further, a line of blue and white tape that says, POLICE LINE DO NOT CROSS stretched out in front of them. I look beyond it to find that I'm outside the mini-mart and a shiver scuttles across the back of my neck like spider.

I feel something tug at me then, telling me to go – to run – but I find myself inching closer, curiosity clawing at me, propelling me forward. I know what's there before the heads part and I see it and when I do, something in me tips too far one way. Then I'm falling and reach for the person nearest me to stop myself. It's a woman. She's wearing a pink dressing gown not unlike the one my mother has and, please, I just want to be at home.

But I'm not.

I'm here and it's there.

The car that almost hit me.

Its wheels aren't spinning any more, but the front of it is still wrapped around the railing as though it's trying to bite a chunk out of it and then I'm tipping again, hand fisting in the woman's sleeve. When she turns to look at me, I see the tears in her eyes and it's a moment before I can speak.

I feel the tug again – *Go, Ash. Run. Run.* – and I know I should, but I can't.

'What happened?' I ask and it's barely a whisper.

'Hit and run,' the woman in the pink dressing gown says with a sniff.

'Was anyone hurt?'

'A young girl.' She shakes her head. 'She died. Her poor family.'

I give into the tug then, letting it pull me back, and turn to find someone behind me.

Dev.

'Sorry. Did I scare you?' she says, but she looks scared as well, her pale skin almost see-through in the blue lights stuttering around us. She reaches for the sleeve of my leather jacket and pulls me away from the people lingering outside the mini-mart. 'We have to get out of here before someone else sees you. You're still transitioning. It's a good job that woman in the dressing gown doesn't know who you are.'

I have no idea what she's on about and I don't care.

All I care about is getting home.

Everything will be OK if I can just get home.

I see the light of Kingfisher Court ahead of me and I don't dare look away, terrified that if I do, it will disappear in a puff of smoke and I'll be back on that sofa in the bookshop with Deborah, Dev and Esen staring at me. One, two, three more strides and I'm there. I reach for the door handle, the stainless steel cool and smooth against my fingers as I curl them around it and hold on in case I give into the pull in my stomach, like a fish hook tugging me up, up.

Mercifully, I don't need my keys to open the door, my other hand shaking as I plug in the security code.

Before I can stop her, Dev follows me in through the doors and I spin round to face her, my hands balled into fists at my sides. 'Leave me alone,' I warn, my voice far calmer than I feel.

If she's intimidated, she shows no sign of it, but at least she knows better than to reach for my sleeve again.

'Please, Ash,' she says, as though she's pleading with a surly toddler. 'Just come back to the bookshop with me. You'll be safe there.'

I'm safe here.

I'm home.

I turn away, heading for the stairwell. I realise that she's followed when I hear her footsteps behind me as I run up the stairs, two at a time. My legs are shaking so much that I don't know how I make it up them without falling, but I do. One flight. Then another and another until I'm on the sixth floor.

Usually, I'd be out of breath by now, my heart throbbing in my ears, but I don't feel a thing as I turn on to the gangway. It's partially open here, the doors to each flat in a neat row on one side and a chest-high wall looking out across the estate on the other. It's so cold that I don't expect to see Dorito, but there he is, sitting on Miss Larson's doormat, his thick tail swishing back and forth. He yowls at me as I pass and lifts his little chin, no doubt waiting for a scratch between the ears, but I can't stop. I need to get home and away from Dev, who is still behind me.

I stop so suddenly, she almost goes into the back of me.

She takes a step back when I spin round to face her. 'Will you stop following me.'

I'm nearly at my front door and she needs to go. *Now*. What am I going to say to my parents? They're going to be pissed off enough about the fact that I've been missing for the last three – actually, probably nearer four – hours, but how am I going to explain Dev?

My mother is going to have a fucking stroke.

'Ash, listen—'

I don't let her finish. 'Just go.'

'Ash, *please*. Will you just listen to me for a second—'

'Will *you* listen to *me*?' I point up the gangway to my front door. 'I know you and Deborah have got it into your head that I'm dead, but I'm not. I'm about to be, though, because as soon as my mum opens that door she is going to kill me. She's actually going to kill me dead and she'll kill you as well if you don't leave.'

Dev doesn't budge, though, just stares at me.

I turn away with a sigh, but as I'm about to carry on to my flat, something occurs to me and I turn back to her. 'Do you have my keys?'

She looks confused.

'My door key. I don't have it. Or my wallet or my phone. One of you must have taken them.'

Dev shakes her head. 'Ash, you don't understand—'

'Look.' I press my palms together and hold them up. 'I don't care about my wallet. Keep the money. I don't even care about my door key, I just need my phone back. Please.'

She takes a step toward me and lowers her voice.

'They're . . .' She stops, looks over her shoulder and takes another step toward me, so close that the toes of our boots are almost touching. 'They're with your body, wherever that is. The hospital, I assume.'

I roll my eyes. 'Not this again.'

'Yes, *this again*.'

I turn away from her and stride towards my front door. She follows, but I don't care any more. My parents can add *Followed home by a weird girl* to the list of this evening's misdemeanours. There's no way Dev is going to get past my mother, anyway, as she's about to find out.

The narrow bathroom window is dark, but the kitchen light is on, so they're definitely home and I make the sign of the cross. 'Father God, pardon me for the evil I have done this day. If I have done any good, may my mother deign to remember it. Watch over me as I enter this house and protect me from any danger that may befall me from slippers or other inanimate objects. Amen.'

I make the sign of the cross again and ring the bell.

Nothing.

I wait then try again – twice this time – but again, there's no response. I can hear the bell ringing through the door so I know it's working. I try knocking instead and when there's no response, I press my ear to the door.

'They're not home,' I hear Dev say.

'Where else would they be? It's nearly four a.m.'

'At the hospital, probably. Or with the police.'

I ignore her, panic pinching at me as I step back and open

the letterbox. 'Mum? Dad? Rosh?'

'Ash, stop.' Dev hisses. 'You can't let anyone hear you. It's dangerous.'

Dangerous?

And my mother says that *I'm* melodramatic?

'They must be asleep,' I say, more to myself than to Dev.

Charming, I think, banging my fist against the door, this time. I know I have no right to be put out, but I'm glad to see that they're so concerned about me that they've fallen a-bloody-sleep.

Nothing.

The panic distils into something sharper. I feel the prickle of it across my scalp again as I realise that there's no way my parents would go to bed and leave the kitchen light on. My father always does a circuit of the flat before he does, checking that all the windows and doors are locked and the lights are off. He's always been militant about it, but after Grenfell, he's even worse, the microwave permanently flashing 00:00 from where he turns it off every night.

The kitchen window is close enough that I only need to take a step to the right to look through it and yes, the light is definitely on and there are three mugs lined up by the kettle, a tea bag in each.

Maybe they've gone looking for me. My mother knows that I was on the bus so unless I was lying – which I wasn't – I got off at Haybourne Road. Maybe they're retracing my steps. Is Rosh with them, her coat buttoned-up over her Totoro pyjamas? I turn and look out across the estate and when I see the haze of blue lights in the distance, I remember that my mother asked me to get paracetamol so she knows that I went to the mini-mart. But if she knows that I went to the mini-mart and they go there to check, they'll see the car and if they see the car . . .

Then I'm running. I hear Dev call after me, but I'm gone, along the gangway and back towards the stairs, one hand on the railing and the other palming the wall so I don't fall. All I can think about is how scared they must be and I have to find them.

I have to let them know that I'm OK.

When I get to the ground floor, I fly out of the stairwell door and out, out, past the lifts to the door. I punch the green button with my fist and push, but as soon as the door opens and I'm out, I run straight into someone. I jump back, holding up my hands, ready to apologise, when I see who it is and stop.

'Going somewhere?' Esen asks with a slow smile.

FOUR

'Oh, Ess. Thank God,' I hear Dev say and look back as she runs out the door.

When I turn back to Esen, I can tell that she's trying not to laugh. 'How's it going, Dev?'

'I was just mauled by a cat.' She points down at her ripped tights.

Then it's my turn to try not to laugh.

Good old Dorito.

'And she . . .' Dev stops and stands next to me. I arch an eyebrow as if to say, *She what?* and she presses her lips together, not finishing the thought. 'Well,' she says instead, adjusting her teddy-bear coat. 'Let's just say that it hasn't been as easy to persuade her to come back to the bookshop as I thought it would be.'

Esen raises her eyebrows at her. 'Shocking.'

Dev peers at her from under her fringe, clearly unamused.

'OK,' Esen says. 'You go do my reap at the station and I'll handle this.'

'Fine.' Dev huffs, smoothing down her bob with her hands. 'I'll see you back at the bookshop.'

She stomps off towards the mini-mart and I should be doing the same, but I just watch until she disappears and the road is empty again. When I turn back, Esen is still there, her hands in the pockets of her heavy black coat.

'So,' she says, rocking back and forth on her heels. 'This home, then?'

I wait for it, the sudden flare of fury – fury and fear and confusion – that I've been feeling since I woke up on the sofa in the bookshop, but there's nothing. It's as though it's burned out. If you cut me open, there would be nothing left – no fire, just smoke – and I'm really trying not to cry.

'I just want to let them know I'm OK.' I cross my arms. 'The lights are on, but no one's answering.'

She thinks about that for a moment then nods. 'OK.'

She starts walking towards the door to Kingfisher Court. When she realises that I haven't followed, she stops and turns back to me. 'Well, come on, then.'

I hesitate, suspicious of why she's being so accommodating when all Dev wanted me to do was go back to the bookshop, but curiosity gets the better of me.

When we get to the door, she gestures to the security pad and I put in the code, my hand shaking even more this time. There's a dull buzz and she opens it, heading for the lifts and pressing the Up button.

'They're not working,' I tell her, thumbing at the door to the stairwell.

'And you live on the first floor, right?' she asks, hopefully.

'The sixth.'

'Of course you do.'

Esen follows me this time, not that she's in any rush to. To be fair, I'm not feeling the same urgency I did when I first got here, either, as I hold on to the handrail and haul myself up the stairs.

'This is nice,' I hear her say as she follows me up, but I don't need to look at her to know she's being sarcastic. 'It smells like this squat I used to live in near the station.'

My jaw clenches, ready to tell her to fuck off because while OK, yes, *technically*, this stairwell does smell of piss and weed, this is my home so I can say that, but she can't. But I don't take the bait, too tired to get into it with her. She's being an asshole and she knows full well that she's being an asshole.

She seems to think it counts as personality.

When I glance over my shoulder to give her a withering stare instead, she's looking at the walls. 'This Sicko guy is certainly very proud of himself, isn't he?'

'It's not *Sicko*, it's *Syko*, like psychopath.'

'Sorry.' She rolls her eyes and holds her hands up. 'Did I offend your friend Syko?'

I stomp up the rest of the stairs until we reach the sixth floor. When I turn on to the gangway, Dorito isn't there any more, which is a shame, because he'd hate Esen.

As I told my mother, cats sense evil, don't they?

I stop outside my front door. It's exactly as I left it; the light in the bathroom is off, but the one in the kitchen is on so I can see that the three mugs on the counter by the kettle haven't moved, a tea bag still in each one. I ring the bell again and, again, there's no response, so when I look up the gangway to see Esen swaggering towards me, her dark curls bouncing with each step, I wonder why she wanted to come back here.

It's pointless.

She takes something out of her pocket and nods at me to get out of her way.

'Don't tell Deborah or Dev about this,' she tells me, raising her eyebrows.

I look around nervously as I realise that she's picking the lock, but before I can protest the door swings open and I have to swallow back a sob as I smell it.

Home.

She steps aside so I can go in first, closing the door behind her as I bend down to unlace my DMs. My fingers are fidgeting so much that it takes me a moment longer than usual and, as I toe them off, I gesture at her to do the same. She complies with a huff, unlacing her boots and kicking them off, leaving them on the doormat next to mine as I turn to look at the bathroom. The door is ajar, the light off, but I'm sure I can still smell pomegranate from the shower I took before I left to meet Poppy and every bit of me aches.

How was that only a few hours ago?

The kitchen is opposite the bathroom. It's the only room in the flat without a door, so I walk straight in and there they are – the three mugs by the kettle, a tea bag in each. Other than that, everything looks the same. The saucepan of dhal on the stove. The turmeric-stained wooden spoons in the pot next to it. The bananas browning in the bowl on top of the microwave that is flashing *00:00*.

Esen stands by the front door, watching as I head back out and down the hall to the living room. I glance into my parents' bedroom and stop in the doorway. My mother's side of the bed is made, as always, but my father's side isn't. I've never seen my parents' bed unmade – ever – and the lamp is on.

Why didn't he turn it off?

He always turns it off.

I guess he was sleeping, a glass of water on the bedside table, ready for the paracetamol that I was supposed to bring home.

My legs feel less steady as I turn and carry on down the hall to the living room, fingers reaching out to the walls on either side to steady myself. I can feel the wallpaper beneath them, the one my mother loves so much – royal red with gold elephants – that was so fiddly it took my father a whole weekend to hang.

The door to the living room is open as well so I can see that the lights are on, the television flickering steadily. I walk over and turn it off, then stand in the middle of the room. Aside from the lights and the television being on, everything is in its place. My mother's sewing machine. The framed photo of us at my cousin's wedding hanging over the sofa, me in that yellow sari that my mother loves so much because it isn't black. The Christmas tree in the corner by the television, lights slowly fading then getting brighter, fading then getting brighter.

There are some presents under it that weren't there when I left. Two – one for me and one for Rosh, I assume – which are probably from a relative who was at Aunty Lalita's party. Rosh hasn't opened hers yet, no doubt waiting for me to get home so we can open them together and I feel rotten. Then I see her favourite Christmas blanket on the floor – the fluffy red one with the white snowflakes – and I suddenly miss her so much that I want to pick it up, press my face into it and weep, but I'm aware of Esen in the doorway, watching me.

She steps back to let me pass as I head into the hall and stop at the door to mine and Rosh's room. It's directly opposite our parents, which meant that we couldn't get away with much as kids so I was constantly bribing her with sweets so she wouldn't cry and alert them to something I'd done. But I kind of like it now, that my parents are right there. Always there. They aren't the type to go to the pub or the cinema or out to dinner. I wish they would sometimes, because it might help them understand why I want to do these things with my friends, but aside from family functions, all they do is go to work, come home, eat dinner and go to bed. Saturdays are for chores – cleaning the flat, then the launderette, then ASDA – and Sundays are for church and homework.

I always know where they are and now I don't, just that something is wrong.

Something is terribly, horribly wrong.

I wait a beat before pushing open the door to my room. I know I shouldn't be surprised to find it empty as well, but every bit of me sags as I look at Rosh's bed. There's an open book on the floor, like a broken bird that has landed there and can't move. I pick it up, blowing away the biscuit crumbs that have gathered in the spine. I consider folding over the top corner of the page so she doesn't lose where she is, but I know Rosh hates that, so I close it carefully and graze my thumb across the cover.

'*The Amber Spyglass*.' I hold the book up to Esen, who is watching from the doorway like a vampire waiting to be invited in. She takes a step towards me and when I don't object, she keeps going, standing in the middle of the room with her hands tucked into the pockets of her coat.

She tilts her head to look at the cover, then says, 'I've not read them.'

'Me either, but my little sister rereads them every Christmas,' I tell her with a tender smile.

The Amber Spyglass is the last in the trilogy, I think, so Rosh was on course to finish by the end of the year.

Maybe she would have if I hadn't fucked everything up tonight.

'Rosh is the clever one.'

'What's your thing, then?'

'Disappointing my parents, mainly.'

That makes Esen laugh – really laugh – her whole face changing. 'I get that.'

I raise my chin to look at her, but she won't meet my gaze, and it makes me feel better for some reason, like she finally sees that I'm a person, not some stray Dev brought back to the bookshop. A person with a little sister who loves Will Parry and will have to fall asleep staring at my empty bed every night.

I turn away and put the book back on the pile on the bedside table, pressing my palm to it for a moment before turning away again. It only takes one step to walk to my side of the room. I suppose I should be embarrassed by the state of it, but I'm not. Perhaps if Esen was Poppy, I'd apologise for the pile of clothes I abandoned on the bed after trying everything on and before settling for the black jeans and hoodie I'm wearing, but I don't care what Esen thinks.

God. Rosh is right, though. I am messy, aren't I? I can't

help but smile as I think about the time she got a piece of masking tape and stuck it down the middle of the floor, warning me that anything that strayed on to her side of the room would end up in the bin. Not just our bin, but the big bins outside that smell foul and are too high to get stuff out of once they've gone in. I didn't believe her and that's how I lost my favourite Thrasher T-shirt.

That's when I see the nail polish that I hastily applied before I left and look down at my feet to find the red dot on the toe of my DM and I ache again as I think about Poppy, her head on my shoulder as we looked out at the sea, the New Year rolling out from our feet like a red carpet.

When I look up again, I glance at the mirror over my chest of drawers and gasp.

'What the fuck?'

'What?' Esen asks, then she's next to me. My whole arm shakes as I bring it up to point at my reflection. 'Oh.' She nods, lifting her chin to meet my gaze in the mirror. 'I guess you've transitioned.'

'*Transitioned?*'

It looks like me, kind of. I'm the same weight and height with the same dark eyes and the same smooth black hair tied back into the high ponytail I favour every day, the only evidence that remains of my Ariana Grande phase. My skin is the same colour, that same rich brown I used to scrub at in the shower until I was red raw because my Aunty Lalita would constantly tell me what a shame it is that I've inherited my father's skin tone and I'm not as light as Rosh, as though she'd won the genetic lottery. My mother would tell me not to listen to her, that she loved the colour of my father's skin and she loved mine, too.

It was years before I believed her, but now I do and when the sun hits it and my skin is as bright as a brand new two-pence piece, it doesn't feel like losing at all. But when I look in the mirror, it's kind of like looking at myself in a CCTV monitor. It's me, but it's not me, everything unique – my nose ring, the mole on the bridge of my nose, my fierce red lipstick and black eyeliner – smudged away.

I see Esen's reflection and swallow back another gasp as I look between the mirror and her. She doesn't look the same, either. Again, she's the same weight and height with the same dark eyes, but in the mirror her warm brown skin is dull and her tight, glossy curls are greasy and limp.

Esen nods at our reflections in the mirror. 'That's how we can walk around without being noticed.'

We.

I don't like that.

When I don't respond, I hope she takes the hint, but doesn't. 'The thing is, we can't look like we used to because everyone can see grim reapers, because everyone is going to die eventually. But they don't see us – like, really see us, what we used to look like before we died – until it's their time.'

I lean forward and lift my chin to find that there's nothing there. The scar I acquired when I fell off the slide in the playground when I was six is gone, but when I graze the spot with my knuckle, I can feel it.

It's still there.

'Which is why you shouldn't be here,' Esen says when I turn

back to her, my arms crossed.

'Why?' I ask, avoiding her gaze.

'Because you don't want anyone from your family to see you.'

'But they can't. I thought we were invisible, or something?'

'Not quite.' When I'm brave enough to lift my chin to look at her, I see that she's leaning against the chest of drawers with her arms crossed as well. 'It's kind of like when you're on the bus and there's someone sitting three rows behind you. If someone stopped you when you got off and asked you to describe them, you wouldn't be able to, would you? Not in any detail, anyway. Maybe the colour of their hair or what coat they were wearing, but nothing specific because you weren't paying attention to them, were you? It's the same with us – as long as we don't do anything to draw attention to ourselves, no one notices us.'

'And that's a good thing?'

'Of course.' She chuckles. 'They don't want to see us.'

'Will they die if they do?'

Esen turns her cheek towards me and when our gaze catches, she turns away again. 'A couple of years ago, I was doing a reap on the Pier when I heard someone say my name.' She goes over to sit on Rosh's bed, then leans forward and rests her forearms on her knees, looking down at her hands. 'It took me a minute because I hadn't seen him for years, but I realised it was my cousin's mate.'

'And he knew it was you? As in *you*, Esen.'

She nods.

'What did you say?'

'I panicked and tried to style it out. Put on this ridiculous, and no doubt *horribly offensive*, Spanish accent and made out that I didn't know what he was on about.'

'Did he believe you?'

'He had to, didn't he? I'm dead. How could it be me?' She stops and I wait because I know there's something she's not telling me.

Then she says it.

'He died in a car crash a couple days later.'

Jesus.

I can't process this.

It's too much.

I walk over to my bed and sit down with a tender sigh.

There's an explanation for all of this, for why I woke up in the bookshop earlier. For Deborah and Dev and Esen. For why I don't look the same. And it's not that I'm dead and it's not that I'm a grim reaper, or whatever the hell else I'm supposed to be. It's something else. Tomorrow, I'll go and tell Poppy I had this mad dream and we'll laugh and draw scythes in the steamed-up window in our café.

I look down at my hand, remembering how I dug my nails into my palm until it hurt. I'm desperate to do it again, but I'm terrified that if I do, nothing will happen.

When I look up at Esen again, she's watching me like she knows.

Like she knows this is it.

I know.

I know that I was hit by that car outside the mini-mart.

She nods and when the corners of her mouth curl up into a sad smile, it feels like I'm falling – falling and falling – even though I'm sitting perfectly still. I put my head in my hands, as though I am unable to support the weight of it any longer, and sit there until it passes.

When it does, I lift my head and Esen's still watching me, still smiling sadly.

'I'm dead, aren't I?' I say at last, but it isn't a question.

When she nods again, I feel like I should be crying, but nothing is coming out.

'It's not all bad, though.' She smirks. 'You get to spend eternity with me.'

FIVE

I go back to the bookshop with Esen because I honestly don't know where else to go.

'The wanderer returns,' she announces as we walk through the door.

Dev presses her hands to her chest. 'Thank God. I was so worried.'

Esen strolls over to the counter where Deborah is writing something in a notebook. 'I want it noted for the record that it was *me* that got her back.' She taps the notebook with her finger. 'Not Dev. Me.'

Deborah doesn't look up. 'Would you like a cookie, Miss Budak?'

'Yes, please.' She turns away with a flourish, curls swinging as she unbuttons her coat and throws herself on to the sofa I woke up on earlier. 'A big one. Preferably, chocolate chip.'

Dev walks over to where I'm standing, her forehead crinkled with concern. I can tell that she wants to touch me – perhaps put her hand on my shoulder – but thinks better of it. 'How are you feeling, Ash?'

I shrug, hands in the pockets of my leather jacket. 'Fine.'

'Are you sure?'

'She's fine.' Esen waves her hand, then tilts her head from

side to side. 'I mean, she's not *fine* fine, but she's doing way better than you did.' She chuckles, looking over her shoulder at Deborah. 'Remember?'

She continues writing in the notebook, clearly trying not to reciprocate. 'I do, Miss Budak.'

Esen looks back at me. 'Dev was hysterical,' she explains. 'We had to lock her upstairs for a week.'

'It wasn't a week,' Dev insists, all but stamping her foot. 'It was more like three days!'

Esen scoffs at her, looking back at the counter.

'Ladies, please.' Deborah takes her glasses off and pinches the bridge of her nose. When she puts them back on, she looks between Dev and Esen. 'If I could still get headaches, you two would be giving me one right now.'

Dev crosses her arms with a huff. 'I'm *just saying*, it wasn't a week. Esen is exaggerating, isn't she?'

'Fine.' Deborah looks back down at the notebook. 'It was five days.'

Dev squeaks and Esen holds her arms out as if to say, *I told you so*. 'A working week, then.'

'OK. OK. That's enough,' Deborah tells them with a weary sigh then holds up a neon pink Post-it note. 'We've got another stabbing at the station. Which one of you wants it?'

Esen sticks her arm up. 'Me! I haven't done one for a while.' She clambers off the sofa, coat swinging at her sides as she walks over to the counter and takes the Post-it before turning to me. 'You ready for one?'

'Not yet,' Deborah warns, peering over her glasses at her then at me. 'Ash needs to get some rest.'

'OK,' Esen says with a swift shrug, buttoning her coat and striding to the door. 'Laters, losers.'

The bell rings and she's gone, the bookshop suddenly much quieter.

'An eternity with *that*?'

I don't realise that I've said it out loud until I hear Dev let out a sigh. 'Now you know why they had to lock me upstairs for a week.'

Not that she needs to, but Deborah reminds me that it's been a long night and suggests I go upstairs and get some rest. I don't hesitate, for once. Dev offers to show me the way and I get the impression that she does this a lot – volunteering to help Deborah – like that girl in class who jumps up to distribute the handouts before the teacher has even asked. It's nice, I suppose – thoughtful – but I'm more of a sit-at-the-back-of-the-classroom-and-hope-no-one-notices-me kind of girl so I fear that we're not going to get on, Dev and I.

I follow her upstairs into a bedroom. It's about the same size as my parents' room and just as neat, with the same wide floorboards as the shop downstairs and a window that, even with net curtains, I can see looks out on to the Lanes. There's a double bed with bedside tables either side, a wardrobe, a chest of drawers. Normal things, but I still feel uneasy. Nothing goes together, as though someone's gone into a charity shop and said, 'I'll have that, that and that.' Even the duvet and pillowcases don't match, the cover cream with huge red flowers while the pillowcases have red, white and blue stripes. They're creased, but must be clean, at least, given that the colours are

196

dull from being washed too many times. Still, as exhausted as I am, I'm not in any rush to get in.

'Whose room is this?' I ask, because I can't tell by looking at it. I mean, my little sister is tidy, but between all her books and the posters on the wall over her bed, at least you know which side of the room is hers. There's nothing to suggest that this room is even being used. Aside from the furniture, it's pretty much empty. There's no rug, no curtains, no lamps on the bedside tables, the walls bare except for a water stain in the top right-hand corner and a cobweb softening the one opposite it. It doesn't even have a smell. Actually, it does, but it isn't a nice one, like my room, which is always sweet with the smell of hairspray and that perfume from Lush I got for my birthday. It smells like the bookshop, of old paper and dust.

'No one's,' Dev confirms with a shrug.

'Where do you sleep, then? On the sofa downstairs?'

Her forehead creases for a second then smooths. 'Oh.' She smiles sweetly. 'We don't sleep.'

I have to lean against the door frame as I realise what she's saying.

We don't sleep because we're dead.

Dev shrugs. 'You're still transitioning, though, so you might sleep.'

'You two keep saying that. What do you mean, *transitioning*?'

'From who you were to who you are now. It happens in phases,' she explains, walking over to the chest of drawers, pulling out a pair of jeans. 'Appearance first, which should only take a few hours, and then you won't, well . . .' She stops, thinking about it for a second. 'Well, you won't look like you did before.'

I'm painfully aware of that, I think as I remember seeing myself for the first time in the mirror in my bedroom.

'All the other stuff happens later,' Dev adds with a careful smile.

I'm too scared to ask what the other stuff is so I gesture at the pair of black jeans she's holding instead.

'Are they yours?'

She nods.

'From . . .' I trail off, not wanting to say *before*.

She shakes her head. 'If we need stuff, like clothes, Deborah gives us the money. Not that we need much. It's not like we're paying rent or bills and buying food and stuff.'

So we don't eat or drink, either, then.

What about everything else?

'No more periods, either,' she says with a grin, reading my mind.

This grim reaper thing does have some benefits, then.

'So is it part of the dress code?' I nod at the jeans again. 'Black.'

'Nah. It's just easier to blend in, you know?'

I want to ask her more, but she turns away from me.

'I'll leave you to it.' When she gets to the door, she turns back. 'Open or closed?'

'Halfway.'

'Shout if you need anything.'

Then she's gone.

I'm so tired, I'm weak with it – the few paces to the door to turn off the light suddenly so far that I consider leaving it on. I probably should – I certainly don't feel safe enough here to be alone in the dark – but it's too bright and my head is *fizzing*. Question after question after question until it's nothing but white noise.

Maybe being still for a while will help.

The bed is more comfortable than it looks so I take off my leather jacket and DMs and lie on top of the duvet, waiting for sleep to pull me under. I feel the tug of it – starting at my toes – threatening to swallow me up, and for a moment I let myself believe that if I give into it, when I wake up I'll be back in my own bed, swaddled in my duvet with my back against the radiator and all of this will have been a ghastly fever dream.

But I don't sleep, I lie there, aware of Deborah and Dev's gentle chatter somewhere beneath me. Eventually, the bell over the door rings and I close my eyes, hoping it's Poppy coming to find me. But it can't be because no one knows that I'm still here, do they?

Not even her.

I picture her in her pretty pink room on the third floor of her parents' big house, waiting for my WhatsApp. She'll know. She'll know something is wrong because I *always* message her when I get in. Maybe she'll tell herself that my battery died, as she lies there, looking up at the high white ceiling. Or that my mother took my phone as punishment for sneaking out. But she'll know. I wonder how she'll find out. I'm the only one who has her number so Adara will have to tell her. Send her a message on Facebook, asking Poppy to call her.

Just imagine. They've never met and that's the first conversation they'll have.

How fucked up is that?

SIX

I don't know how long I lie there, the room getting darker and darker until I can no longer see the crack across the ceiling. I'm aware of the door opening every so often then closing when I don't stir, grateful that whoever it is – Dev, probably – takes the hint and leaves me alone. I guess she's had enough of me ignoring her, because the door finally swings open and the light comes on.

'You OK?' she asks, hovering in the doorway with a mug.

'Not really,' I mutter, forcing myself to sit cross-legged on the bed.

She walks over and gestures at the edge. I nod, grateful that she asked first.

She puts the mug on the bedside table and sits in front of me. 'Did you manage to get any sleep?'

I shake my head.

'I didn't think you would,' she says with a sad smile. 'Do you at least feel a little calmer?'

'I guess.'

I don't know if calm is the right word for what I'm feeling right now.

Defeated, maybe.

She nods at the mug. 'I brought you a cup of tea.'

'Thanks,' I say, wincing slightly. 'I don't drink tea, though.'

'It's more of an experiment. If you'll humour me. What can you feel?' she asks as she hands it to me.

I'm aware of the weight of it, the heat of it against my knuckles.

'It feels like a cup of tea.'

'Would you mind tasting it?'

I pull a face because I don't really want to – I hate tea – but I'm curious.

I bring the mug to my mouth and take a sip. I can feel that it's hot, can feel the burn of it on my tongue and in my throat, but as I wait for my stomach to turn at the taste of it, nothing happens.

'It doesn't taste like tea.' I frown, looking down at the mug to check that it is. It looks like tea.

'What does it taste like?' Dev asks eagerly, as though I'm about to discover the cure for cancer.

I take another sip.

Nothing.

'It tastes like hot water.'

She looks thrilled. 'Wow!'

'What?'

'This is the fastest transition I've ever seen.'

'What do you mean?' I ask, turning to put the mug back on the bedside table.

'It usually takes a few days,' she explains. 'But you're already there, Ash.'

'Already where?'

'On our side.'

I dislike that word – *our* – as much as *we*.

'The physical stuff happens first,' she goes on. 'Your heart stops and your body no longer needs to function the way it used to for you to, you know, *be here*. Then your senses start to go. So taste.' She tilts her head towards the mug of tea. 'And smell. You can't smell anything, right?'

It hadn't occurred to me to check. I inhale deeply and sure enough the room doesn't smell like the bookshop downstairs, of old paper and dust. I raise my arm, bringing the sleeve of my hoodie to my nose and wait as I inhale again. But there's nothing. It doesn't smell of anything at all.

'What about my other senses?' I ask when I look up at Dev again.

'We need some of them – sight, hearing, touch – to be able to do what we do.' She lifts her shoulder then lets it drop again. 'But we don't need to smell or taste anything, do we?'

I suppose not.

'I can still breathe, though. How can I still breathe if I'm dead?'

I can feel it, can still feel the rise and fall of my chest and the air in my nose as I take in a deep breath and let it out, as if to prove the point. But there's no relief when I do it. There's nothing there.

'We don't need to breathe to function, but we need to breathe so we can talk.'

'OK.' I consider it for a moment. 'But how come with the tea, when I picked up the mug, I could feel that it was hot against my knuckles and when I drank it, it burned, but it didn't hurt?'

'Because pain is a *physical* response and touch is a *sensory* one. We still need to be able to feel stuff.' She stops and I can tell that she's trying to think of the best analogy. 'Like, say I'm doing a reap and it's in a house that's on fire so it's too smoky to see where they are. I need to be able to feel them so I can find them.'

I get it, I think.

'Anyway, that's enough rest,' she says, jumping to her feet. 'There's something I want you to see.'

I hold my hands up. 'I'm not doing a reap. I'm not ready.'

'Oh no. It's nothing like that.' She shakes her head. 'Come on.'

SEVEN

Dev takes me to a party on the beach, which I wasn't expecting. I don't know what it's in aid of – the first day of the year? Is that a thing? – but it's too loud to ask. It's a mess, people everywhere – almost as many as last night, when I was with Poppy – a bonfire in the centre of them, its hot yellow flames curling up to a peak like the petals of a tulip. Except this party is at the other end of the beach, at Duke's Mound, the Pier a finger of coloured light in the distance.

I tug the sleeve of Dev's coat to get her attention. 'What is this?'

She shakes her head and cups her hand to her ear.

'What is this?' I have to shout over the music and when I do, I realise it's that song by Honeyblood that I was obsessed with last year. It's called 'Babes Never Die', ironically, and I listened to it on repeat for, like, a month and drove Rosh *insane*. The memory of it should make me feel better, but it doesn't. After lying in a dark room at the bookshop for the best part of a day, the assault of, well, *everything* – people, sound, colour – leaves me dizzy.

Someone steps on my toes but I apologise, then apologise again as I'm elbowed so suddenly in the ribs it almost knocks me off my feet. I lose sight of Dev for a moment.

Mercifully, I find her on a quieter patch of the beach, the music dampening to more of a sluggish *BOOM BOOM BOOM*. I close my eyes and try to snatch at a breath, because being here feels like that time I fell into the deep end of the swimming pool when I was a kid and my father had to fish me out. When I open my eyes again, I see that it's snowing, falling in fat white clumps that catch in my eyelashes as it falls around us. My first thought should be Rosh and how happy she must be to see it. Or of Poppy in red mittens, snowflakes melting in her hair. But my first thought is of reading *To Kill a Mockingbird* at school and laughing when Scout saw snow for the first time and told Atticus that the world was ending.

I turn to look at the tangle of people. Some have their arms in the air, others their heads tipped back, laughing up at the dark sky, but something isn't right. It's like the furniture in the bedroom back at the bookshop – nothing goes together. It's a bit like last night, when wildly disparate groups of friends were thrown together. But they didn't mix, did they? They kept in their groups – played their own music and drank their own beer – until midnight and the space between them disappeared as they rang in the New Year together.

Or at least, I assume that's what happened.

I wasn't there to see it, was I?

Here everyone's blended together. A woman with a waist-length silver plait is having an earnest conversation with a guy my age while a girl with neat braids laughs and claps at a man, utterly enchanted by his dad dancing.

None of it makes sense.

And no one is touching. There are no couples kissing

or friends hugging when they're reunited after being lost in the chaos. No one is drinking, either. A couple of people are, the light from the bonfire sparking off the beer cans in their hands, but most aren't. They're just wandering around, talking and dancing.

'You all right, Dev?' I hear someone say and look back as a guy dressed in black approaches.

When she smiles and nods, he salutes her with two fingers then keeps going.

'Do you know all these people, Dev?'

She shrugs. 'Not all of them.'

'Who are they?'

'Reapers.'

'What?' I turn to look at the crowd again. 'All of them?'

'Most of them, yeah.'

I turn back to her with a frown. 'Brighton has *all* of these reapers?'

'They're not just from Brighton, they're from all over. Worthing. Eastbourne. Hastings.'

'How come I've not seen any of them at the bookshop?'

'They all have their own bookshop or café or whatever, depending on what area they cover.'

'So there's more than one Deborah?'

She chuckles, her eyes wide. 'There's only *one* Deborah.'

'So why are they here?'

'To celebrate the new reapers. We do it every year. It's kind of like a *Welcome to the Family* thing.'

'I thought you said that you aren't allowed to draw attention to yourselves?' I ask, wondering how a hundred reapers blasting music and dancing around a bonfire on the beach – a bonfire they're not allowed to be having, by the way – isn't drawing attention to themselves.

'It's Brighton.' Dev waves her hand at me. 'No one cares.'

I guess not. It certainly explains why some people are drinking. But that's Brighton. People see a party and they want to join in, even if it's snowing. They wouldn't be so keen if they knew who they were dancing with.

'Dev!' I hear someone say and look back to find a girl walking towards us.

I say girl, but she's older than us – eighteen, maybe nineteen. She grins at Dev and I'm taken aback for a moment. She looks so much like Adara. They have the same heart-shaped face, the same full, wide mouth and milky-tea-coloured skin. I've never seen Adara without her hijab. It's so much a part of her that it hasn't occurred to me to ask myself what her hair's like beneath it. This girl's hair is a bit longer than Dev's but as dark as mine with the same thick, unruly waves. I'm a bit envious because it's what I was going for when I was fourteen and cut all my hair off, except for the smooth, blunt fringe that stops halfway down her forehead, which shouldn't suit her but does.

She jumps on Dev, throwing her arms around her with such enthusiasm, they almost fall over.

'Is this Ash?' the girl asks when she lets go and steps back.

Dev thumbs at me. 'This is her.'

'Hey!' She grins at me this time. 'Danica Daniels. Kiddie cancer.'

There's something about the way she says it, like she's telling me what school she goes to, that makes me hesitate when she holds out her hand.

I look down at it, then reach out and shake it carefully. 'Kiddie cancer?'

'Danica reaps children who have cancer,' Dev explains with a solemn nod.

'I thought you reaped the people who died in the way you did?'

'We do. At first, anyway,' Dev says. 'But we can't have four-year-old reapers running around, can we?'

I guess not.

I didn't think about that.

'I got promoted,' Danica says with less enthusiasm this time.

'To children with cancer? *That's* a promotion?'

Danica shrugs, smiling sadly. 'Well, someone's got to do it.'

'I guess.'

'Hey,' she says, tipping her chin to me. 'You Indian as well?'

It's quite the segueway.

I've barely had time to recover from the kiddie cancer thing.

'Yeah.' I nod. 'Indo-Guyanese.'

'Yes!' When she smiles this time, it's so wide now that I can see the white of her teeth as she raises her hand for a fist bump. When I reluctantly comply, she winks and says, 'We need more desi reapers.'

Glad I could add to the numbers, I guess.

Dev is distracted by someone else she knows, which gives me an opportunity to slip off and find somewhere quiet to sit. As I look out at the horizon, I see the red flashing lights from the wind farm – all 116 of them – and I can't help but think of last night with Poppy, the sea at our feet. I'm suddenly exhausted and squeeze my eyes shut, sure that I can feel the heat of her next to me, but when I open them again, it's not Poppy, it's Dev, and I jump.

'Found you,' she grins.

I don't. 'Yay.'

'Oh, come on, Ash,' she coos, sitting down next to me on the pebbles. 'I thought you'd like this.'

I'm a bit startled by that. 'Why?'

'So that you can see that you're not alone. You're part of a family now.'

Dev can keep saying that we're a family as many times as she likes, but we will never be family.

I have a family.

'Well, this might cheer you up, then,' she persists, reaching into the pocket of her coat. I watch her warily as she pulls out a small black velvet bag. 'Deborah told me to give you this.'

I stare at the bag. 'What is it?'

'I got it from that jewellery shop, Cronus, in the Lanes.'

I know it. It's the one with Poppy's bumblebee necklace.

'Open it!' Dev tells me with all the excitement of a child bringing their first macaroni art home from school.

I do as I'm told, Dev watching as I untie the velvet pouch. I reach inside and pull out a fine silver chain. I hold it up and when the moonlight catches on the small scythe pendant, I almost drop it.

'We all have one,' she explains, her voice suddenly tiny

as she reaches under the collar of her teddy-bear coat and hooks hers out with her finger. 'It's kind of our thing. Esen has one as well.'

I make myself look at it and it's beautiful, actually. There's a delicate pattern on the handle and, when I turn it over, I see that my name is engraved on the curve of the blade.

'Thanks.' I try to smile as I glance towards the crowd and see Esen, standing back from the chaos, her arms crossed and the wind disturbing her curls as she chats to someone who looks as bored as she does.

'Aren't you going to put it on?' Dev asks eagerly.

She's not going to let this go, is she?

So I put it on and as soon as I do, she reaches over and presses her finger to the pendant.

'There,' she says with a proud smile. 'You're one of us now.'

I can't look at her so turn to Esen again, but she's laughing now and her whole face looks different.

'Don't worry about Ess,' Dev tells me as she picks up a pebble and lobs it toward the sea. 'She's tough,' she warns as we watch the pebble land with a heavy *plop*. 'It's going to take a while to win her over, but when you do, and I know you will, she'll do anything for you.'

I don't care if I win her over or not.

'Everyone handles this differently,' Dev admits, still looking out at the sea.

'Handles what differently?'

'*This.*' She nods at the crowd. 'Being a reaper.'

'So there's more to it than ferrying dead teenagers back and forth to the beach for eternity?'

She chuckles to herself, then continues what she was trying to say. 'Some people, like Esen, put everything they were, all their memories and the lists of things they didn't get time to do, into a box. Then they lock it and hide it somewhere at the back of their mind. It makes it easier to bury that person and become someone else entirely. Some reapers even change their names because they don't think of themselves as that person any more.'

'Is that why you ask people to call you Dev, not Isla?'

'I've always been Dev, actually. There were two Islas in my year so she became Isla McDermid and I became Isla Devlin. But then people started dropping the Isla so I was just known as Devlin, then Dev.'

It's weird. I forgot that she had a life, like I did, before she ended up in the bookshop.

'What school did you go to?'

'Queen's Park then Stringer. You?'

'I went to Whitehawk all the way through.'

'I thought so.'

I'm about to ask her why when I realise that it's a safe assumption to make, given where I died.

'What about you?' I ask instead. 'What's your way of dealing with this, then?'

She's quiet for so long that I don't think that she's going to tell me, but then she tilts her cheek towards me and looks at me from under her false eyelashes. 'I tried it Esen's way for a while, but it didn't work for me. I can't disassociate like that, you know? I may as well be dead.'

'I thought we didn't have a choice? I mean we have to

disassociate. We *are* dead.'

'Listen, Ash,' she says, but she doesn't say it like Deborah did, like she's losing her patience. She says it like she's doing the opposite, like she's waiting for me to catch up. 'I know you think you have no choice because you've won the worst lottery *ever*.' She laughs and I let myself do the same. 'But choosing not to live is still a choice.'

'What do you mean?'

'I mean, you can do what Esen does and lock it all away and pretend it's not there or . . .' She hesitates and I tell myself to be patient as I wonder if she's ever said this to anyone before.

If she's ever had to put this into words.

'It's like . . .' She tries again. 'We're all the same, right? More or less. If you cut us open, we all have a heart, lungs, ribs. But there's other stuff, isn't there? Deeper stuff. That's unique to us.'

I bring my hand up to my chin, stroking the scar with my knuckle.

'The physical stuff.' Dev reaches down to pick up a pebble, sweeping her thumb over it. 'The stuff that we all do, like sleeping and eating, is easy to let go of because we have no control over it, right?'

I nod.

'You die. Your heart stops. That's it. If it started again, you wouldn't be dead.'

'True.'

'But the other stuff . . .' She shrugs. 'The stuff deep, deep down that only we know about, is still there.'

'You mean, like, memories?'

She points the pebble at me. '*That* stuff doesn't go away, unless you lock it away like Esen does.'

I think of Poppy then, of last night and the look on her face when I told her that I loved her too.

I never want to forget that.

Ever.

'Why would you want to let go of that stuff, though?'

'Because it's easier.' Dev looks down at the pebble in her hand. 'It's easier not to feel anything, to give into it. Let go of it all and just see this as a job. All you have to do is take them to the beach. That's it. It's not your problem after that, is it? It doesn't matter what happens to them, who they're leaving behind or where they're going, because you'll never know and I get that.' She nods to herself, still looking down at the pebble. 'I get why that's easier, but eternity is a *long* time if all you're doing is sitting around the bookshop, waiting for someone to die.'

She throws it and I watch as it arcs up and then down, waiting to hear the *plop*.

'What else is there, though?'

'There's this.' Dev's gaze drifts back to the party. 'You won't feel things like you used to. Like, your palms won't sweat and your heart won't race when you see someone you used to love, but you'll *remember* how it feels.' She fusses over her fringe with her fingers. 'You'll still feel that same attachment to them, that need to be near them, to protect them, you know? That need to say something stupid to make them laugh.'

I think of Poppy and wait for the ache, but it doesn't come.

'Don't get me wrong,' Dev adds. 'Being dead is great.

I'm not scared of anything any more. What's the worst that can happen? I'm already dead. So all that stuff I used to be scared of – all the petty stuff I was self-conscious of, like whether I'm pretty enough or clever enough or funny enough – I don't care about that any more. I care about now. About this moment. Because if I don't . . .' She stops to lick her lips, her smile noticeably duller, like the underside of a leaf. 'Just be careful, OK?' she warns, picking up another pebble and curling her fingers around it, her knuckles even paler as she squeezes it. 'I know you're mad that it was you this year and you're right to be. It's not fair. But if you let it, that feeling – that bitterness – will just grow and grow until there's no room for anything else and you don't want that. Then you really will be dead.'

Before I can ask her what she means, she gasps and points up at the sky. 'Look!'

I look up as a shooting star streaks across the sky over our heads. A sharp thread of white against the black, black sky tipped with a pearl of light.

'Make a wish, Ash!'

When I see that the trail is already disappearing, panic distils everything to a single thought.

Poppy.

I want to see Poppy again.

EIGHT

When we get back to the bookshop, Esen isn't there. So we sit on the armchairs, telling Deborah about the party. Or at least, Dev does. I sit there, thinking about what she said on the beach, about how choosing not to live is still a choice.

I stroke the tiny mole on the bridge of my nose with my finger as I consider what would be better. Doing what Esen does and locking it all away and keeping it safe somewhere in the back of my mind? Or doing what Dev says and holding on to it even if it makes all of this so much harder?

The answer is obviously the latter, but if I don't lock it all away – keep it somewhere safe – will I be able to remember the feel of my father's big, blanketing hugs in fifty years? Or how Poppy's laugh sounds like the noise my grandmother's gold bangles make when she claps roti?

What if I lose it all?

What if I lose it all and I can never get it back?

An hour later, I'm still sitting in the armchair, head tipped back, staring up at the ceiling. It makes me think of the high white ceilings in Poppy's house and before I can tell myself that it's a terrible idea, I lower my chin and ask Deborah, 'Do you know Margot Morgan?'

She looks up from where she's standing behind the counter. 'Margot Morgan? The physicist?'

I nod.

'Of course.'

'Do we have any of her books? Didn't she write something called *Wonders of the Cosmos*, or something?'

If she's surprised that I'm suddenly acknowledging that this is a bookshop after doing little else but sulking on the sofa since I got here, she recovers quickly. 'I doubt it. We only deal in rare and antiquarian books here.' She takes off her glasses and gestures at the neatly arranged shelves. 'First editions, ideally, but for the most part they're either collectables or signed copies of special or out-of-print editions.'

'OK,' I say with a small shrug.

I assume that's it, but then she asks, 'Why the sudden interest in Margot Morgan?'

'No reason,' I say with a shrug, trying to sound nonchalant.

'She's a brilliant woman,' Deborah says, adjusting the collar of her shirt. 'She lives near here, actually.'

'Does she?' I say, my voice too high as I think about Poppy's big white house and her big pink bedroom and the loss is palpable.

It fills the bookshop until it feels like I'm suffocating.

Mercifully, before Deborah can say anything else, Esen barrels in.

'What a knob!' She doesn't wait for anyone to ask who she's referring to, just unbuttons her coat and collapses on the sofa.

'Can you believe that the bloke I just reaped tried to punch me?'

'Do you really want us to answer that?' Deborah asks as she goes back to her pile of books.

Esen ignores her, tipping her head back against the cushion with a growl. 'Then he did a runner. I had to chase him down Queens Road. This old dear was coming out of Sainsbury's. Almost sent her flying.'

'Let's be careful around the elderly, Miss Budak.' Deborah opens a book that's by the till and begins leafing through it. 'They'll be seeing one of us soon enough.'

Esen laughs at that, the skin around her dark eyes crinkling. 'Too true.'

'Did you catch him?' Dev asks, leaning against the counter.

'Of course. Had to drag him down to the beach by the collar of his coat, though.'

'Right,' Deborah interrupts, holding up a hot-pink Post-it note. 'Here you go.'

Dev takes it from her and looks at it. 'What've we got?'

'Overdose at the New Steine. You can take Miss Persaud, show her the ropes.'

I look up and Dev is blinking at me, looking as unconvinced as I feel. 'What? *Already?*'

Esen sits up then. 'Can I go, too?' She turns to me and grins. '*This* I need to see.'

'Absolutely not.' Deborah returns to her book with a wave of her hand.

'Why not? Don't you trust me?'

Deborah doesn't look up. 'Not even a little bit.'

I don't get a chance to protest as Dev hustles me out of the bookshop and out on to the street. It's still dark and will be for a while, I know, as the seagulls squeal furiously as though they're trying to warn me about something. While Dev is zipping up her coat, I turn to look through the window of the bookshop. Deborah is behind the counter, flicking through a book, while Esen lies on the sofa, her boots resting on one arm and her head on the other, her cola-coloured curls spilling over the edge, the ends almost touching the floor.

'You coming, Ash?'

I'm aware of Dev next to me then and slowly turn to face her.

'We don't have long,' she tells me, thumbing down the street, her white bob shivering.

I guess if this really is my life now – if you can even call it that – I can't avoid doing this for ever. So I follow, allowing myself to fall into step with her as we head towards North Street.

'Don't worry,' Dev says as we turn left at the Wetherspoons. 'You won't have to do anything.'

I nod.

'It's an overdose. So she's probably already gone.'

Dev shows me the Post-it note.

Kitty Lawrence
Overdose
New Steine

'How will we know it's her?'

Dev doesn't look at me. 'We'll know.'

When we get there, I brace myself, but the garden is empty. It would be impossible to miss her. The New Steine is much smaller than the Old Steine with its neatly kept lawn, fountain and the War Memorial which Rosh had to write an essay about for school last year. Here the garden is more modest, just a long strip of grass with the sea at one end and a weird sculpture at the other. Some of the lights in the B&Bs on either side are on, the guests either just getting in or just getting up to catch an early flight, too concerned with making sure they've packed everything and have their passport to notice what Dev and I are here to do.

I look around for her – Kitty Lawrence – but the garden is empty except for a small dark-blue tent that is pitched in the top right-hand corner of the lawn, by the sculpture. It takes me a moment longer than it should to realise that's where she is, but by the time I do, Dev is already walking towards it.

'Stay here,' she warns when I follow. Not that she needs to. I have no idea what's happening in that tent and I have no intention of finding out as I watch Dev crouch down and unzip the front of it. She peels it open and when nothing happens, when no one screams or cries or comes flying out with a needle hanging out of their arm, I can't help but lean down to peer inside.

There she is – Kitty Lawrence, I assume – sitting cross-legged, clutching a white fleece blanket. Her fingernails are dirty, but the rest of her is in pretty good shape. Her long dark hair looks clean enough and is parted in the middle, falling on either side of a small face that is almost the same colour as the blanket she's holding and I look away as I wonder how she ended up here, in this tent, all by herself.

That's when I see it, the body lying next to her, curled up in the foetal position, and for a moment I think that it's someone else, until Kitty points to it and says, 'That's me.'

Dev nods.

'How is that me?'

'Come with me, Kitty.' Dev holds out her hand to her.

When Kitty gets out into the cold, she sways a little and when she steadies herself, she looks up at the sky. It's pure black and there's something about the way she just stands there, looking up, that makes me wonder if she knows.

If she knows that she's dead.

I turn to look back at the tent. The front of it is down now, but Dev didn't zip it back up so it flaps open in the breeze and I can't help but think about Kitty's body inside, wondering how long it will be there before anyone notices.

When I look back at Kitty, she's smiling at me. This silly, dopey smile, her pale-green eyes on me, but not, like she's just woken up from a nap. 'Who's this?' she asks.

'This is Ash,' Dev explains. 'She's here to help as well.'

'Hello, Ash,' Kitty says and she's swaying again, not enough to make me reach for her, but enough to make me wonder if I was like this as well. I don't think I was. I can remember it all so clearly. The sharp *POP* of the fireworks, the seagulls fleeing, the wheels of the car spinning and spinning, the crunch of the broken glass beneath my feet, 'Auld Lang Syne'. I remember every detail. But then after that there's nothing. I don't remember getting from the mini-mart to the bookshop, just being there, on the sofa, and everything spinning again.

'We're not going far,' Dev says, nodding towards the beach.

'Where are we going?' Kitty asks but follows anyway, out of the New Steine and across the road.

The sea is almost as black as the sky and uncharacteristically calm for January. As I look out at it, I remember then what Dev said earlier about not having to hold on to the stuff you don't want to hold on to. So I let go of it then – my fear of the sea – hoping it will make room for something else.

Something that scares me in a better way.

'I couldn't sleep,' Kitty tells us as we walk towards it. 'I was so cold.'

There's something about the way she says it that makes me turn my face away as I look out across the beach. I know it's almost four in the morning, but I've never seen it empty like this. Apart from the seagulls, we're the only ones here. The stones crunch beneath our feet as I look at the Pier stretching out over the sea, the only trace of colour for miles and miles. It's not open yet, the long arm of the Booster still, like a broken clock stuck at two forty, but in a few hours, it will be alive with noise. The rise and fall of the carousel. The roll and splash of coins in the slot machines. The hiss and spit of the fryers as people wait for paper bags of hot sugared donuts and churros.

For now at least, everything is still.

Even the sea.

Then I hear Kitty ask, 'Who's that?'

I turn back to see the shadow of a man standing on the shoreline ahead of us. He's tall and thin and dressed completely in black, just a smudge against the sky. He wasn't there a moment ago and I'm about to turn and ask Dev who it is when I see the wooden boat next to him, bobbing gently on the sea.

Dev stops so I do as well, glad to be keeping my distance from whoever it is.

Kitty does the same, standing between us, looking confused for the first time. 'Aren't you coming?'

Dev shakes her head. 'That's Charon. He's going to take you where you're going.'

'Where am I going?'

'Where do you want to go, Kitty?'

She thinks about it for a moment then says, 'Home.'

'Well, then you're going home.'

She turns to me, then. 'Can you tell my mum something, Ash? Can you tell her that I'm sorry,' she says with a deep frown, her eyes suddenly wet. 'I wanted to come home before now, but I couldn't.'

I don't know what to say, so I just nod as I watch her walk towards Charon. For a moment I don't think that she's going to look back, but then she stops and turns back to face us with a smile.

'I'm not cold any more.'

NINE

I spend the next week with Dev, watching as she does her reaps, making sure I keep a comfortable distance, like a junior doctor learning how to attach an IV. The first thing I learn is that not many teenagers die every day in Brighton. That's no bad thing, don't get me wrong, but it means that between Dev, Esen and I, we only have to do one – maybe two – reaps a day. Dev says it's busier at Christmas and over the summer – when people are taking exams or getting their results – so, for now, it's quiet.

Not that I'm complaining, it just leaves yawning stretches of time with nothing to do. So the three of us spend most of our days skulking around the bookshop, sprawled on the sofa, bickering with each other like curmudgeonly cats.

My second reap – after Kitty Lawrence – is Jennifer Craig from Preston Park who kills herself but doesn't leave a note, which bothers me more than it should. Then there's Imran Mahmood who was jumped on his way back from a gig at The Haunt but won't tell us why. Then, this afternoon, there was Charlie Graham, who died at Jubilee Library, of all places. It took us ages to find him because he was at a desk on the second floor, slumped over his books, so we thought he was taking a nap. Or at least his body was there, Charlie was actually sitting on the floor, his back to the wall, which is why we didn't see him.

It turns out he hit his head playing rugby the day before and didn't know it was that bad until his brain short-circuited halfway through his essay on the *Domesday Book*.

As Dev and I are walking back to the bookshop after handing Charlie over to Charon, I can't help but ask myself what he would have been doing if he'd known today was, you know, *the day*.

Dev must be thinking the same thing because she asks, 'Where would you have been? If you'd known that you were going to die on New Year's Eve?'

'You mean if I wasn't outside the mini-mart?' She nods. 'I don't know.' I don't. I haven't even thought about it. 'I sure as shit wouldn't have been in the library writing an essay about the *Domesday Book*.'

She giggles, her nose wrinkling. 'What a way to go.'

I'm glad she doesn't push, even though I know where I would have been if I'd known.

Under the bridge at the station, kissing Poppy until there was no breath left in me.

A few days after Charlie Graham, Dev and I head into town because I can't keep wearing the same black jeans and hoodie for eternity.

'Isn't it weird?' I say to Dev as we're in Primark looking at jeans. 'It's been, what? Almost two weeks and I haven't seen anyone I know. Like now. It's five o'clock on a Saturday afternoon. You'd think I'd see *someone* in town. Even if it's just someone I went to school with or one of my neighbours.'

'Uh-huh,' she mutters, distracted by a pink sequinned dress on the other side of the shop.

'Have you?' I ask, trailing after her as she walks over to it.

'Have I?'

'Seen anyone from, you know, before?'

'I saw my old history teacher once.' She takes the dress off the rail then wanders over to the mirror. 'He was coming out of the station.'

I follow, standing behind her as she holds the dress to her and tilts her head at her reflection. 'Did he see you?'

She shakes her head.

'What would have happened if he had?'

She laughs. 'What do you think?'

'I honestly don't know. All you said when I went home on New Year's Eve is that it was dangerous.'

Actually, that's not true. Esen told me the story about her cousin's mate seeing her on the Pier, didn't she?

I guess I just want to know if that was a coincidence. Not that I'm hoping I'll see anyone. Or maybe I am.

Maybe I'm thinking that if I hang around near Roedean, I might see Poppy.

Just once.

Just for a second.

'It's dangerous because people only see us how we looked before, when it's their time.' Dev waits for me to meet her gaze in the mirror then goes on. 'So if my old history teacher had recognised me at the station that day, he would have known something was wrong.'

'Wrong?' I ask, stomping after her as she walks to the rail and puts the dress back.

I wish she'd stay still.

'Yeah.' She turns to look at me with a curious frown, no doubt trying to suss out if I'm joking. When she realises that I'm not she nods at me, her eyes wide. 'Why do you think it would be a bad thing if he recognised me?'

It takes me a moment and when I finally realise what she's getting at, I shake my head and curse myself for being so dense. 'Because if he recognised you that would have meant that it was his time.'

She holds her finger up and gives me a look as if to say, *There it is.*

'But what does it matter?' I shrug. 'He was going to die anyway.'

'*Because*,' Dev says, making the word sound about a minute long as she takes another dress off the rail and looks at it before pulling a face and putting it back. 'It messes with the natural order of things. Like.' She turns on her heels to face me. 'What if he had recognised me that day and keeled over at the shock of seeing the girl in his history class who's been dead for eleven years?'

'Maybe that's how he was going to die, though?'

'Maybe, but what if he was supposed to be hit by a bus two hours later, saw me, and died of a heart attack instead?' She raises her right shoulder and lets it drop again. 'Seeing me disrupted the chain of events.'

'Like the butterfly effect,' I say, remembering what Mr Moreno told us when we were discussing climate change after our visit to the wind farm. Apparently, some scientists believe that the ripple effect of just one butterfly dying could be far-reaching enough to alter the course of history forever.

'Exactly. There's an order to this.' Dev gestures at the neat row of dresses on the rail in front of her. 'If we intervene,' she sticks her hand between two of them, making the space between the hangers wider, 'even if we don't mean to, and someone dies before they're meant to, or in a way they weren't supposed to, it doesn't just mess up that person's timeline, but everyone else's. My old history teacher, for example.' She pulls out one of the pink sequinned dresses that she was just admiring and holds it up to me. 'If he'd died of a heart attack when he saw me, that means that he didn't get hit by a bus two hours later, like he was supposed to, and *maybe*.' She puts the pink sequinned dress back on the rail between two black ones. 'That bus hits someone else. Someone who wasn't meant to die that day.'

I stare at Dev as the horror of it finally begins to register, and it's like putting a two-pence coin in one of the arcade games at the Pier and hearing the slow roll then waiting for the splash.

'So *that's* why it's so dangerous? In case someone else dies when *they* were supposed to.'

'I don't know.' She stops to shrug again then reaches for a lime green fake-fur bag on the shelf over the clothes rail. 'Not for sure, anyway. No one does. Only Deborah. But there must be a reason she doesn't send us near where we used to live. I'm sure she does it on purpose to avoid us bumping into anyone we used to know.'

So that's why our reaps have been on the other side of town – Seven Dials, Preston Park, the Level. Well, that explains why, despite my best efforts, I've been unable to engineer it so we pass either my estate or school on the way back from one of our reaps so I can check on my family and Adara. I just want to see them once – just once – to make sure they're okay. Maybe, one day, when Deborah trusts me to do a reap my myself, I'll be able to. But, until then, I'm stuck with Dev who is obviously under strict instructions not to go anywhere near Whitehawk.

'But what if we do bump into someone we know? By accident, I mean?'

Dev doesn't seem worried about that. 'As long as they don't recognise us, it doesn't matter.'

I suppose.

'Besides, after a while, you stop looking, I guess,' she adds, putting the bag back on the shelf.

'Feels like it's going to snow again,' Dev says, looking up at the sky as we walk back to the bookshop. But I'm not thinking about that, all I'm thinking about is what she just said and how much it scares me. Scares me more than dying. More than being a grim reaper. More than being stuck here and not being able to see my family or Poppy again. The thought that, one day, I'll stop looking for them. I won't check if it's Rosh when someone passes me in the street with a Studio Ghibli satchel or I won't have to fight the urge to run when I see a girl ahead of me with red hair.

If all of this – the reaps, hanging out with Dev and Esen in the bookshop – has begun to feel normal without me noticing, what if I don't notice that, either? What if, one day, I realise that who I was is just a memory, like that framed photo of me in the yellow sari hanging over the sofa in my living room.

A bug trapped in amber.

TEN

As we're heading back to the bookshop, I see someone coming out of Boots and if my heart hadn't already stopped on New Years Eve, it would right then. Adara. Adara and Mark, actually, laughing and nudging one another as she peers into the small paper bag she's holding. When she tells him to shut up, I wonder if he's teasing her for buying another rose gold eyeshadow palette that looks exactly the same as the four others she has. 'Who's that?' I hear Dev ask, but I don't look at her, only at Adara. She's wearing a pale pink hijab that matches her pale pink padded jacket, her eyeliner as sharp as ever, and as she turns to face me, I'm sure she's wearing the lipstick she bought the day I met Poppy at the wind farm. I smile and wait, but she doesn't even glance at me as she and Mark pass. The shock of it makes me turn on my heels and watch as she walks away.

She didn't even see me. Adara, who I've known since the first day of school when she complimented my Elmo lunchbox and said it matched her Cookie Monster one. Adara, who was the first person I told when I got my period and was the first person to tell me that I didn't just think Rachel Boyd was pretty, I had a crush on her. Adara who has always been there – always – and isn't any more. Actually, she is still there, isn't she? It's me that's gone, I realise, as I stand there, on the pavement outside Boots, watching her and Mark until I lose sight of them. I suddenly feel very, very alone, but then Dev is there and when I tell her who Adara is – who she was, I guess, to me, anyway – she insists that we sit on the beach and wait for the snow. It's almost eight thirty by the time we get back to the bookshop, but if Deborah's wondering where we've been, she doesn't say, just welcomes us with a nod while Esen lies on the sofa with her arms crossed and her eyes closed. If she hears the bell over the door announcing our arrival, she doesn't stir and I'm tempted to click my fingers at her.

'How did it go?' Deborah asks from behind the counter, without looking up from whatever she's writing.

She's changed since the last time I saw her, into a neat black-linen shirt-dress, her cropped hair covered with an intricately twisted leopard-skin headwrap that sits in a generous knot on the top of her head.

I didn't realise that leopard skin was part of the dress code, but then I don't think she's ever left the shop.

'Good,' Dev tells her with a nod. 'We went shopping.'

That makes her look up. 'Not *more* make-up? That money I gave you was for *clothes*, Miss Devlin.'

'No make-up.' Dev smiles brightly. 'Just something for Ash to wear that isn't *those* jeans and *that* hoodie.'

'Very wise,' Deborah mutters, looking back down at her notebook. 'Make sure you wash them first.'

I almost laugh because that's *exactly* what my mother would have said. I've never understood it, but she has a thing about washing clothes before you wear them, even if they're brand new.

We do as we're told, heading upstairs into the kitchen. I've never been in here, I realise, as Dev starts taking everything we've just bought in town out of the bags. It's a bit bigger than my kitchen and just as clean, but a stark, hospital clean that, like with the bedroom, makes me wonder if anyone ever comes in here.

We're taking the tags off and putting it all in the washing machine when we hear Deborah's voice again.

'Dev?' she calls up the stairs.

She sticks her head out of the kitchen door. 'Yeah?'

'Can you come here please?'

I immediately panic, wondering what she's done wrong, but Dev doesn't seem concerned as she shuts the door of the washing machine with her knee and turns it on. I make sure she goes first, following her down the stairs. As we stroll back into the bookshop, Esen is leaning against the counter, looking bored, as always.

'There you are,' Deborah says, peering at us over her glasses as we walk around the counter to stand by Esen.

'What's up?' Dev asks with an eager smile.

'I need you to go to the Pier.' She pulls a Post-it note from the top of the pad and hands it to her. 'Drowning.'

'Another one?' Esen doesn't look amused. 'What's going on today? We've had, like, three reaps already?'

Deborah shakes her head. 'Must be something in the water.'

'Literally,' Dev chuckles, holding up the Post-it note, then turns to me. 'Let's go, Ash.'

'No,' Deborah says, holding up her hand. I look at her with a frown. 'You can't swim, can you, Ash?'

How did she know that?

'Besides, we have three at once.'

She pulls another Post-it note from the pad and hands it to Esen, and another to me.

Esen looks at me, then at Deborah. 'She's not ready.'

'It's been almost two weeks. You did your first reap by yourself within twelve hours,' Deborah reminds her.

'Yes, but you forget, I was already dead inside. Dying just made it official.'

Deborah chuckles, looking at Dev, who is standing next to me in the middle of the shop, her lips parted. 'Dev, you said that Ash has been doing well, right? That you haven't had any issues.'

Dev looks at me, but when I raise my eyelashes to meet her gaze, she looks away.

She nods at Deborah and Esen stares at her, her eyes wide, as though she's just been slapped across the face. When Esen recovers she turns back to Deborah, her hands pressed to the counter.

'She's not ready,' she says again, her voice lower. Firmer.

'Well, we have three at once in three different parts of Brighton, so now is as good a time as any,' Deborah tells her, handing her one of the Post-it notes. She holds up the other one to me. 'Well, come on, then.'

I walk over to the counter, aware of Dev and Esen staring at me as Deborah hands the Post-it note to me.

'Saltdean? That isn't our patch,' Esen says, reading it

before I do.

Deborah looks down at her notebook. 'Katrina's busy with another reap so asked if we could help.'

'Get someone else to do it. Ask Danica. I'm sure she'd do it.'

'Ash is ready.' Deborah looks up at me with a firm smile. 'Aren't you, Ash?'

I don't respond, looking down at the neon green Post-it note between my fingers.

Alice Anderson
Fall
Longridge Avenue, Saltdean
21:12

ELEVEN

Alice Anderson is exactly where Deborah said she would be, on the cliff in Saltdean looking out at the sea. Not that I could have missed her in that hot-pink fur coat she's wearing. It's the sort of thing I'd make a beeline for in a shop, but never be brave enough to buy. I'd try it on, take a selfie, then put it back in favour of something more sensible. Something black that I could wear to school without getting detention.

That's one of the hardest things about this, how hopelessly normal they are. Alice could be from my year or the girl behind me in the queue at Primark, waiting for the changing rooms. Someone I could have passed in the street and never noticed until tonight.

It's hard to tell in the dark, but from here she looks my age – sixteen, maybe seventeen – with a froth of blonde curls that the wind lifts up and away from her face so I can see her profile. I can't see the colour of her eyes, but I can make out the sweep of her jaw and her neat button nose, her lipstick the same colour as her coat. Judging by her knee-length dress and heels, she's been out tonight.

It's far too cold for bare legs, but maybe she thought she'd be OK because she was getting a cab home, then lost her purse and had to walk instead. Or maybe she had a row with her boyfriend and told him to stop the car here, insisting that she'd make her own way home.

I don't know why I do this, why I make up stories about them. That will pass, I suppose. Maybe in a few months when I've done this enough times that I won't even remember their names any more.

Until then, I can't help but ask myself why they're there.

Why them.

The sea is rough tonight, the waves a rolling boil that will snatch you clean off your feet and drag you in if you get too close. Not that I ever do. I've always been scared of open water and nights like this remind me why. The waves are so loud that Alice doesn't hear me approach, but I keep my distance because I can see that she's shaking.

There's something about that moment, when you're stuck in that woozy midpoint between being here and not, when you feel everything at once – fear, joy, hope. It's not so much a rush as a flood and it's like you're drowning, like someone is holding your head under water and if you can just find your way back to the surface, you'll be OK.

That's what's so cruel about it. There's a split second when you're sure that you got away with it and the relief is dizzying. It's kind of like that moment right after you kiss someone for the first time and you feel untethered, like you could float up and touch the sky. That's where I come in, to make sure you don't.

I give Alice a minute to steady herself, watch as she closes her eyes and sucks in a breath. Her whole body shudders and I wonder if it's then that she knows that there's nothing there.

Finally, Alice turns, her blonde curls swirling in the wind, and when she sees me, she takes a step back.

I wait a beat, then another.

'Alice Anderson?'

The crease between her fair eyebrows deepens. 'How do you know my name?'

'I'm Ash.'

She stares at me so I nod at her. It takes her a moment, but when she realises that I'm gesturing at her to look over the cliff, she does, then lets out a wail that sends the seagulls scattering in every direction. She staggers back from the edge and covers her mouth with both hands. When she spins round to face me again, I have to fight the urge to turn and run because what if she wants me to say something?

This is what she'll want me to say: everything is going to be OK.

This is what I can't say: everything is going to be OK.

She doesn't say anything, though, and I'm glad, that she doesn't ask me how or why or any of those impossible questions I can't answer. Maybe she'll want to know when. I can tell her that. If there's one thing I've learnt doing this, it's that in that moment, when all the years you thought you had ahead of you dissolve into a few seconds, why doesn't matter. What matters is who you'll leave behind and I get that more than anyone, believe me.

Like I said, there's something about that moment. Everything – all those things you did and didn't do and said and didn't say – falls away and you see everything with absolute, startling clarity. People go their whole lives waiting for that moment.

They climb mountains and swim seas and read books hoping to find it. A lucky few do, but most of us – people like me and Alice Anderson and all the ones who went before us and all the ones that will follow – don't until it's too late and, God, it's cruel, isn't it? How, when there's no time left, you suddenly know exactly what you should have done with it.

When Alice lifts her chin to look me in the eye for the first time since she found me standing here, I wait and wonder if this is it. She knows and it will all come out in a rush. All the things she should have done. The lies she told and secrets she kept. She can't take it with her, so she'll leave it with me. Everything she wished for when she blew out her birthday candles. I'm there and this is it, her last chance to say *I'm sorry* or *I love you* or *Forgive me*.

All the times she should have jumped and didn't. All the people she should have kissed and didn't. All that time she wasted being too careful or too polite or too scared when, in the end, nothing is as scary as watching your whole life narrow to a single moment that's about to pass, whether you're ready for it to or not.

Maybe I'll see it then – the regret – burning off her, right through her clothes, and she'll never look so alive. She'll laugh and cry and scream, exhaust every emotion until there's nothing left and it will be like watching a light bulb flare then burn out.

But Alice doesn't do any of that though. She doesn't tell me her secrets, doesn't tell me about her dog, Chester, who sleeps at the bottom of her bed at night. Or about the lipstick she stole from Boots last year, the red one that wouldn't come off, even when she scrubbed it so hard her mouth felt bruised for days.

I should be OK with that because it means that I don't need to explain, we can just go. But I want to. I want Alice to ask me who I am. If she did, I'd tell her that I'm Ashana Persaud and that I'm sixteen. I'd tell her that my favourite song is 'Rock Steady' because it always gets my parents on the dance floor at weddings and my favourite film is *Dilwale Dulhania Le Jayenge*, even though I tell everyone it's *The Shining* because it's easier. I'd show her the scar on my chin that I got falling off a slide when I was six and tell her about the tattoo I was going to get on my eighteenth birthday. I'd tell her that I'm scared of open water and clowns and being puked on and that from here, you can see where I had my last kiss, a couple of weeks ago, right there on the beach. And most of all, I'd tell her that it's not fair.

It's not fair that she gets to go, when I have to stay and do this.

She doesn't ask, though, so we just stand there, on the edge of the cliff, the moon watching over us and the sea beckoning beneath until finally she says, 'The moon looked so pretty. I just wanted to take a photo of it. I didn't realise I was so close to the edge and then it just . . .' she stops to look up at the moon, '. . . wasn't there any more.'

When I see her smudged eyeliner, a mascara-coloured tear skidding down her cheek, I realise that her eyes are brown, like mine, but the light behind them has gone and I wonder what they were like before. Before I got here. I wonder who's waiting for her at home. If her parents are up, pretending to be engrossed in *Newsnight* so it doesn't look like they've been waiting up for her. Her mother swaddled in a thick dressing gown, phone in hand, while her father listens out for the curmudgeonly creak of the gate, followed by Alice's careful footsteps as she navigates the gravel path in her heels.

But she isn't going home, is she? The thought makes me want to turn and run into the sea, let it pull me under, carry me to wherever it is that I'm supposed to be. But I can't. I can't leave her. So I walk over to where she's standing and peer over the edge. It's dark, but I can see her – Alice Anderson – on the path, her limbs at unnaturally odd angles on the concrete, a halo of fresh blood beneath her head.

We stand there for a while, my hands in the pockets of my jacket and Alice's in the pockets of her hot-pink coat. Eventually, she tilts her cheek towards me. 'Are you an angel?' I try not to laugh. 'If you're not an angel, what are you, then?' She looks me up and down and I let her. Let her take in that I'm in black, from my DMs and jeans to my hoodie and leather jacket. Her gaze narrows when she sees my silver scythe necklace.

With that, her pale skin becomes almost see-through against the dark sky, her edges blurred, like she's already disappearing. A whisper of moths gathers, settling in her curls as she watches me look over the cliff again then does the same. When she sees the sharp shadow of Charon on the beach below, the moonlight picking out his wooden boat as it bobs gently on the suddenly still sea, she turns to me with a curious frown.

'Is he here for me?'

I nod.

'Where am I going?'

I hold out my hand. 'You'll see.'

TWELVE

When I call Dev to let her know that the reap went OK, she insists I meet her and Esen on Ovingdean beach. When I get there, it's still snowing and we sit on the wall, the three of us uncharacteristically quiet as we watch it fall and settle silently on the pebbles below. There's no bickering. No swapping stories about the reaps we've done that day. We just sit there, waiting for Deborah to dispatch us somewhere else.

She doesn't, though, so I do what Dev told me to and remember it – this moment – terrified that if I don't, my life will narrow to a pinhole that allows for nothing more than being a taxi driver for the undead, everything in between just yawning gaps of time to be whiled away in the goldfish bowl of the bookshop, looking out the window as the world floats by.

Dev's right, the physical stuff is easier to let go of – not feeling cold or hungry or tired – but while I no longer feel my heart beating, I still feel the weight of it every time I think about my parents dancing to 'Rock Steady' at a wedding or the first time I heard Poppy laugh – how it was a brand new sound that I wanted to hear again and again.

I remember it all and I promise never to forget.

In the meantime there's this:

Dev's hair is the same colour as the snow beneath our feet.

She hasn't left my side since I woke up on the sofa in the bookshop and I know she never will.

Esen's hair is as black as the sky stretching over us.

It would be easy to dismiss her as a shadow that sucks away the light, but standing beside her is like standing in the shade of a great oak tree on a summer's day. Cool and steady and every now and then, there's a thread of light.

And then there's me, sitting between them as we look out at the wide, wild sea.

No, this isn't how I thought my life would end, but if this is how it starts again, at least I have them.

As we walk back to the bookshop, I hear something when we're passing the Dome and stop.

It's her.

Her laugh.

The fake one she puts on when she's talking to her father on the phone.

I swear I feel my heart for the first time in weeks, or at least some echo of it, like a song playing in another room. I tell myself that I'm imagining it, that it can't be, that I've conjured the sound because I'm here, surrounded by people when she's the only one I want to see. But then I see a flash of red ahead of me and before I can stop myself, I'm running.

I hear Esen and Dev shouting my name, but I don't look back. I get caught up in the mess of people leaving the Dome. Whatever was on must have just kicked out because there are people everywhere, going in every different direction, back towards the Old Steine and up towards the station. They're all talking at once, stopping to pull on coats and gloves as I try to move around them. A bloke hits me in the face with his scarf, but doesn't notice as he steers his mate to the pub across the road. 'Excuse me,' I say, but he doesn't hear, too concerned with getting one last drink before closing.

This is taking too long.

I'm going to miss her.

I'm going to miss her.

I don't think, just step into the road. There's a cab coming so I jump back on to the pavement and wait for it to pass before running after it.

When I get to the corner, there she is, outside the Mash Tun, the light spilling out of the open door picking her out like a spotlight and oh God, it's her. She's there. She's really there. I want to run to her, fist my hands in her coat and pull her to me, press my face into her neck and inhale her.

Poppy.

Her name is out of my mouth before I can stop myself, like a dog slipping its leash and running towards her. She turns her cheek towards me and this is it, the moment I've been waiting for. I know I don't look like the same, but she'll know it's me, because it's her and it's me and she'll know. So I wait. Wait for the shiver of recognition to cross her face, for her to cry and run to me, hold me so tight my feet leave the ground, but she just smiles and tips her chin at me.

When she turns away I feel a knock, like I've walked into the corner of a table, followed by a wobble. It's as if there was a glass vase balancing on one of my ribs and now it's falling, down, down.

It's funny because I always thought she was the one who was left behind, but it was me, wasn't it? She gets to move on, to laugh and go out with her friends. Drift on and on, unfazed, unaltered, unaware that I'm still here.

Then she's gone and as I watch her go, hips swinging and hair ablaze, it feels like dying all over again.

THIRTEEN

When I look up, Esen is there and I stiffen because she isn't like Dev. She isn't going to hug me and tell me that it's OK. Sure enough, she looks at me carefully, her hands in the pockets of her heavy wool coat. Her hair is wild now, the wind lifting her curls up and away from her face so that I can see the sharp sweep of her jaw.

I brace myself, sure that she's going to rip me a new one, but she looks at me and I realise it's the way I looked at my little sister that time she got lost in Churchill Square. A look that's equal parts relief and *DON'T YOU DARE DO THAT AGAIN* and something else. Something I realised when I was looking for Rosh in Churchill Square and turned the corner to find her by the cookie stand and I knew I'd go to the ends of the earth to find her.

The urge to hug Esen then is so fierce it startles me, but I resist as I watch her take her phone out of the pocket of her coat and call someone. 'I've got her,' she says, then hangs up.

'Is that Deborah?'

Esen shakes her head then slips her phone back in her pocket. 'Dev. She went back to the bookshop to distract Deborah while I followed you.' The skin between her dark eyebrows pinches, the light spilling through the open door of the Mash Tun making her eyes look alight. 'What was that about? Why did you run off like that?'

I don't know what to say, so I say sorry.

'Don't be sorry. It's my fault.' She shakes her head. 'I told Deborah you weren't ready.'

It takes a moment to realise what she's getting at. 'Alice Anderson? Oh she's fine. She didn't give me any trouble.' Esen doesn't look convinced and I hold up my hands. 'Honestly. I just took her to Charon.'

'So what just happened?'

I consider not telling her, but I can feel myself tipping. Into what, I don't know, but I need her to pull me back.

'I just saw my girlfriend, coming out of the Dome. That's why I ran, to catch up with her.'

'What?' she snaps, bringing her hand up as the wind blows her hair forward, into her face.

'She didn't recognise me.'

Esen visibily relaxes at that, but still arches an eyebrow at me. 'You sound disappointed.'

'I'm not.' I can't look at her. 'I just thought she might.'

'Thought or hoped?'

There's a pause and the seagulls fill it.

First Adara, now Poppy? I know it's good that they didn't see me, but that doesn't make it any easier.

'This doesn't feel real,' I say, more to myself than to her. 'It's like I'm waiting to wake up and be back, you know? Like nothing happened. Like all of this is a bad dream, or something.'

My gaze catches on Esen's scythe necklace and I can't help

but reach for mine. I press the sharp silver pendant between my finger and thumb and think of Alice Anderson's parents waiting for her to come home. 'Does this get any easier?'

I don't realise that I've said it out loud until I hear Esen say, 'I don't think it's supposed to be easy.'

FOURTEEN

It's stopped snowing, the little that did settle melting away as Esen and I walk back to the bookshop. I'm so distracted by what just happened with Poppy, that it's a moment or two before I notice we're turning on to a road I don't recognise. I ask her where we're going. But she doesn't respond as she takes her phone out and frowns at the screen before putting it back in her pocket.

'Where are we going?' I ask again. Not that I mind the detour, happy to delay the bollocking I'm no doubt going to get from Deborah as soon as I get back.

Esen nods down the road. 'There's something I want to show you. Something that will help.'

'Help with what?'

'Help to make all of this feel more real. It's just down here.'

There doesn't seem to be anything *here*, though, just a row of houses to our left and a high brick wall to our right, but she's walking with such purpose I practically have to run to keep up with her. A cab rolls past, its light on, and as I look over my shoulder to watch it go, back towards the seafront, I don't see the orange cones blocking our path and almost walk straight into them. Luckily, Esen stops me, sticking her arm out.

'Here,' she says, looking down at them.

I do the same, then glance up at the wall to find there's a huge hole in it, broken bricks tumbling out on to the pavement, the cones there to stop idiots like me from tripping over them.

'Come on.'

Instead of walking around, she steps over them, through the hole in the wall.

'Where are you going?'

Esen doesn't respond, disappearing into the darkness. I check over my shoulder then do the same, stepping over the pile of bricks and through the break in the wall into a dense copse of trees. A branch snaps under my foot as I do, making me lose my footing, Esen is there, reaching for the sleeve of my leather jacket. She gives me a second to regain my balance, then lets go, telling me to follow her.

I do, but as we move further away from the street light spilling in through the hole in the wall and the ceiling of leaves above our heads gets thicker, it becomes harder to see where I'm going. It doesn't help that Esen is all in black, just a shadow ahead of me that I try not to lose sight of as I pick my way through the uneven carpet of broken branches. My toe gets caught in a tangle of weeds and I stumble forward, heading face-first into a spider's web. I gasp, arms flailing, as the fine threads melt into my cheeks, but Esen catches me again, telling me to be careful as she takes me by the arm and leads me out on to a large lawn.

Now that we're away from the embrace of the trees, I can see the moon, high and bright in the sky, casting enough light to illuminate where we're standing. But before I can see where we are, a small bird swoops over our heads and I gasp again, ducking and covering the top of my head with my hands.

'Will you calm down?' Esen hisses. 'It's just a bat.'

'A bat?'

That's even worse.

She doesn't seem fazed, though, pointing to the left. 'That's the entrance, so it must be this way.'

'What is?' I ask, but she's already walking away. I have to trot to catch up and when I do, I stop, turning in a circle, my eyes wide as I realise that we're surrounded by gravestones.

'Is this a cemetery?' I frown. 'You're taking your goth aesthetic way too far, Esen.'

'Don't worry. I haven't brought any cider.'

She laughs, but I don't.

We pass under the shadow of a huge tree, its branches twisting up as if trying to touch the sky. As we do, the gravestones begin to straighten, becoming more evenly spaced, the flowers on them fresher, as old stone gives way to smooth, sharp granite. These headstones are easier to read, the gold lettering seeming to glow in the moonlight, but I don't dare look at them, focusing on Esen, who is a few steps ahead. Her pace finally eases and as it does, I notice that these graves don't have headstones at all and are covered with wreaths and flowers spelling out *NAN* and *DAD*, each one seeming to compete with the next. Some have those brightly coloured pinwheels, the ones you get at the beach, and others are flanked by fat church candles, long blown out by the wind or melted into waxy puddles on the grass. One even has a blue and white Brighton & Hove Albion scarf draped over the top and I can't help but think about who put it there. How careful they were not to disturb the mound of wreaths beneath.

I've never been to a cemetery before. The only person I know who has died is my father's father, but I was two and I don't remember his funeral, just the story of how I cried for the entire flight to Guyana and didn't stop until one of the cabin crew took me into the cockpit and let me sit on the captain's lap. I don't know where my grandfather is buried – or if he is even buried, maybe he was cremated, I never thought to ask – but I wonder if it's somewhere like this. Somewhere big and quiet with the moon watching over him.

The procession of flowers stops abruptly and when I see why, I have to look away as I pass a plot that is completely bare. As I do, I see that Esen has slowed as well, stopping to read the cards on each grave – checking each side of the path – and in an effort to avoid walking into the back of her, I find myself doing the same. I linger by the one that has the most flowers, a virtual mountain dotted with teddy bears, a foil monkey balloon rising from the centre, bobbing gently. I lean down to read one of the cards. It's limp from the snow and beginning to curl in on itself, the ink dotted away, but there's enough left to see what it says.

Sleep tight, sweet monkey.
You're not alone.
You took our hearts with you.
Mum and Dad xx

I step back as though I've been punched, turning away from it and striding up the path towards Esen, who has stopped by one of the plots and is standing in front of it, her head bowed and her hands in the pockets of her coat. She looks up as I stop next to her then nods down at the blanket of flowers at our feet.

'What?' I ask, but she doesn't look at me, just keeps her gaze fixed on the grave. So I glance down to see who it belongs to. It's the same as the others – the same spent candles surrounding the same mound of wreaths and teardrop bouquets of lilies. All white, of course, except for a bunch of more colourful ones on top. I'm wondering why Esen has brought me here, when I see the A made of white chrysanthemums, and step back.

'What is this?' I ask, but I know.

'Don't tell Deborah and Dev,' Esen says, but she doesn't say it in the cocky way she did the night she picked the lock to my flat. 'Deborah will kill me again if she finds out that I brought you here. We had a massive row about it last week.'

'About what?'

'I thought it would help, you know? Seeing your grave. Help with coming to terms with what's happened. It helped Dev,' she explains as I shake my head at her, utterly appalled. 'When we finally lured her out of the bedroom, we took her to her funeral and she said it made her realise that it was real. That she was dead. I wanted to do the same with you, but Deborah wouldn't let me. She said you weren't ready.'

'What makes you think I am now?'

'I don't.' She lifts her shoulder and lets it drop again. 'But after seeing your girlfriend tonight, I thought it might help. I just don't want you getting your hopes up, Ash.'

'You don't want me to get my hopes up?' I stare at her, stunned. 'Poppy looked *right at me* and she didn't recognise me.

How would that get my hopes up? If anything, it brought it home that I really am dead, so this . . .' I gesture at the grave and almost say, *Is the final nail in the coffin* but think better of it.

Jesus, it would be funny if it wasn't so tragic.

When I don't finish the thought, she puts her hand in her hair and fists it. 'I'm sorry, Ash. I'm not trying to make you feel worse. I just thought it would make it more real, you know? Give you closure.'

Closure.

I turn away from her and look down. 'There's no headstone,' I realise with a frown.

She stands next to me, so close her sleeve brushes mine. 'There won't be. Not yet. It takes a couple of weeks for them to put one up.'

I didn't know that.

We stand in silence for a while, looking down at the grave.

My grave.

I realise then that I'm not angry. Not bitter or sour or burned-up by the injustice of it all.

I'm just sad.

Desperately, unreachably sad because it's not fair.

It's not fair.

'Where do they go?' I ask, at last.

The one question I haven't dared ask Dev.

Esen doesn't look at me. 'Who?'

'When they get on the boat, where do they go?'

'I don't know,' she says and I believe her. 'No one I know has got on the boat and come back.'

'Dev says it's wherever you want to go.'

'Dev says a lot of shit.'

I chuckle and it's nice, this warm tickle in my chest.

'You're Catholic, right?' she asks, nodding at the wreath in the shape of a crucifix.

I hadn't even noticed it.

'Technically.' I shrug. 'But it's complicated.'

'Because of the gay thing?'

OK. Maybe it isn't that complicated.

'I don't know for sure, *obviously*,' Esen goes on, 'but I don't think it's the same place for everyone. I mean, we're all different, right? Some people believe in heaven or Jannah or She'ol. I think they end up wherever they *believe* is beyond the sea.'

'What do you believe in?' I ask, looking down at the crucifix of white carnations at our feet.

'You mean other than the power of a well-tailored coat?'

She turns up her collar and arches an eyebrow at me and I roll my eyes.

'I don't believe in anything,' she admits with a shrug. 'It's hard to, after everything.'

For a moment, I think she's talking about this – being a reaper – but then I realise that somewhere, out there, there is a grave, much like this one, with her name on it. She had a funeral, left people behind. A mother. A father. Brothers. Sisters. Maybe even someone like Poppy. And with that, Esen goes from a pain in the ass to a person. A person who had this whole other life before she got stuck in the bookshop, like I did.

What a thing to have in common.

'We should go,' she says, but when she takes a step back,

I turn to face her.

'Where would you have gone?' I ask, tucking my hands into the pockets of my leather jacket. 'I mean if you had got on the boat with Charon instead of becoming a reaper. Where would you have gone if you don't believe in anything?'

She thinks about it for a second, then says, 'Nowhere, I guess. I would have just kept going.'

I don't know if that sounds soothing or terrifying.

'I think that might actually be worse than this,' I say with a tender sigh.

'It's not so bad. It's not,' she adds when I scoff. 'It's shit and I hate it sometimes, but at least I'm still here.'

'Are you, though?'

'It feels like I am, when I look out at the sea. Or when the sun's coming up and it's just me and the people doing the walk of shame home. Or when some old dear swears at me for almost knocking her over as she's coming out of Sainsbury's.' She stops and finally meets my gaze. 'It's not the same, but it's enough, you know?'

I don't, but I nod anyway.

'Plus, I get to have a laugh with my family.'

'You're not even allowed to see your family.'

'Not *them*,' she sneers, 'I don't care about them. I don't even know who my dad is. Not that my mum is around to tell me.'

'I'm so sorry. Did she die as well?'

'No, she put me in care when I was eight. I haven't seen her since.'

'I'm sorry. I—'

'I mean *this family*. My new family. Dev and Deborah.' She

kicks at a tuft of weeds on the path between us. 'And you.'

Me?

'Oh,' I say, lifting my chin to look at her. She won't look at me, though, and I have an overwhelming urge to reach for her hand, but before I can, I hear someone say my name.

They say it again. 'Ash, is that you?'

I turn to see who it is and there she is, red hair ablaze in the moonlight as she stares at me.

Poppy.

FIFTEEN

I wait for her to disappear, but there's no puff of smoke. No cruel cackle as my mind, satisfied to have played its trick, goes back to plotting the next one. Her cheeks are so red that it's all I can do not to reach out and cup her face with my hand, feel the burn of her skin against my palm, but I can't move and it's like the day we met on the boat, like she and I are encased in a soap bubble that will pop if I'm foolish enough to do anything to disturb it.

She speaks first, her voice low – careful – in a way I've never heard it before. 'Ash?'

I just stare at her. 'Oh my God, Poppy.'

It's her.

It's actually her.

But it can't be.

I feel it then – hope – my wicked brain tricking me into thinking that it's some sort of miracle before the reality of it comes barrelling towards me like that car outside the mini-mart on New Year's Eve.

'Go, Poppy! Run!' I tell her as if that will stop it.

As if her running away will halt the chain of events that were set in motion as soon as she recognised me.

She steps back, her eyes wide, tears streaming from them.

She looks at me one last time then she's gone, doing as I say and running away down the path, her hair *everywhere*, the only thing I can see in the dark. And I should let her go, but before I can stop myself, I'm running too, calling out her name. She turns to look back at me, her face pale now and her mouth open as she lets out a scream that sends the seagulls fleeing, wings batting wildly, echoing her cry.

'Get away from me!' she yells, hair whipping around so that it covers her face as she turns away again. And with that she stumbles, falling forward and holding her hands out to stop herself as she spills on to the path with such force the pebbles fly away, much like the seagulls just did. And it's the most terrible sound, this heavy *HISS* as the air leaves her lungs, punctured by a sharp yelp as she lands on the path and her hands leave two grooves in the pebbles.

By the time I get to her, she's turning on to her back. 'Get away from me!' she warns again, crawling backwards, away from me, up the path. I see the blood on the heel of her palm as she stops and holds her hand up – wet and bright, bright red – and when I see the harsh scrape on her chin, something kicks in, some need to bend down and scoop her up, hold her to me until she stops shaking. She's looking at me, utterly wild, and when a single tear skids down her cheek, I know what it means that she can see me, but I can't leave her because what have I done?

What have I done?

'Poppy, I'm so sorry,' I gasp, reaching for her. 'Are you OK?'

'Who are you?' she asks with such contempt that I pull my hand away and take a step back from the path, on to a wreath that is propped against the pile of flowers on the grave we've stopped by. When I regain my balance, I look down to find that it has toppled over, a patch of it balding from where I stepped on it. The grass beneath my feet is dotted with white chrysanthemum petals and I'm so ashamed that I've disturbed it – destroyed it, actually, this wreath some poor soul laid for someone they loved and lost – that I want to bend down and stand it up again, but I can't move as I look back at Poppy and she says it again.

'Who are you?'

It takes me a second, but she isn't speaking to me, she's speaking to Esen.

I'd forgotten she was there.

'I'm Esen,' she says, crouching down next to her. 'Can I help you up?'

'I'm fine.' Poppy winces as she puts her hands down on the path to heave herself up. As soon as she does, she pulls away so suddenly that she almost loses her balance again and I realise that it's because I've reached my arm out to help her. 'Don't touch me!' she spits this time, taking a step back.

'Why don't you sit?' Esen nods at the bench under the tree.

She looks down at the blood in her hands, then up at me. 'What the fuck is going on?'

I don't know.

This isn't it.

This isn't how it's supposed to go.

This isn't the moment I've been waiting for since I left her on the beach on New Year's Eve. I've imagined it so many times. It's the only thing that's kept me going while I was languishing on the sofa in the bookshop, listening to Deborah and Esen go back and forth. Or each time I walked back from the beach with Dev to distract myself from thinking about whoever we'd just reaped. I'd tell myself that when I turned the corner, Poppy would be there and she'd see me – really *see* me – throw her arms around me and hold me the way I want to hold her now.

Like I'm not going to let go this time.

But then I did see her, didn't I? A couple of hours ago, outside the Dome. She looked right at me, but she didn't see me and it felt like dying all over again. Now she can and she's bleeding, bleeding and looking at me like I did this to her and this isn't how it was supposed to go.

'I thought you were dead, Ash!' she roars – actually *roars* – so loud that the birds in the branches over our heads scatter. I didn't even realise they were there and now they're gone, a flutter of black lines against the moon.

'I went to your funeral, Ash!' She stops to swat away a tear with the back of her hand. 'I put *those* on your grave!' She points back to where we were just standing, at the mismatched flowers on top of the heap of wreaths and bouquets.

My gaze darts to them and I feel rotten.

I was so freaked out by seeing my grave that I didn't even notice them.

With that, whatever tiny thread is holding me there – rooting me to the spot – snaps and it's like I'm floating, like I'm sitting on one of the branches over our heads, looking down, watching everything unfold.

'How could you do that to me?' I hear Poppy say. 'How could you let me think that you were dead?'

When I don't respond, she says my name and I'm back in front of her, watching as she shakes her head furiously, so furiously that it sends another tear skidding down her cheek. 'I've been here every night this week because I can't sleep for thinking about you! Thinking about you, lying here, all alone, and you're not even dead!' She stares at me, waiting for me to say something, and when I don't, she shoves me, so hard that I stagger back. 'Ash, you broke my fucking heart!'

Esen reaches for me, but I wish she hadn't. I wish she'd let me fall, because it's too much. The pain – the unbearable, uncontainable pain – in Poppy's voice. I wish she'd let me fall so the earth can swallow me up.

Keep me there.

Where I belong.

'If I can interject for just a second,' Esen says then, but Poppy doesn't look at her, just at me.

'Who the fuck is she?'

'I told you, I'm Esen.'

Poppy ignores her, holding up her hand as if by blocking Esen's face she isn't there.

'Seriously, Ash. Is she your new girlfriend or something?'

If I could laugh, I would.

'If you weren't interested, Ash, you could have just ghosted me. You didn't have to fake your own death.'

'Technically,' Esen says with a smirk, 'Ash did ghost you. Literally.'

She laughs and I turn to glare at her as if to say, *Really, Esen? Now?*

'Fine.' Esen rolls her eyes and I have no idea how she can be so calm.

It feels like someone has left a tap on in my head and it's about to overflow.

Esen gestures at the bench for Poppy to sit down again, but Poppy crosses her arms.

I need to, though, my legs about to give way as I turn and sit on the bench, my head in my hands.

When I look up again, they're both standing over me, staring.

Poppy with her arms crossed.

Esen with her hands on her hips.

'What is happening?' I say, looking between them. 'I don't know what's happening.'

'You don't know what's happening?' Poppy scoffs. 'I just found my dead girlfriend in a graveyard!'

'OK.' Esen holds her hands up. 'OK. Everyone just calm down.'

Calm down? I want to scream. *My girlfriend's going to die!*

When she takes her phone out of the pocket of her coat, I panic. 'Who are you calling?'

I hope it's not Deborah.

'Dev,' she says, holding it to her ear. 'I'm no good with shit like this. She'll know what to do.'

'Who the fuck is Dev?' Poppy asks and I let my head fall back into my hands.

'A cemetery? Really, Ess?' Dev tuts as she stumbles into the clearing. 'You're taking this goth thing too far now.'

Esen ignores her. 'Dev, this is Poppy.'

When Dev says hello and gives Poppy a small wave, Esen looks between them with a deep frown, clearly waiting for a reaction. When she doesn't get one, she turns to me. I raise my eyebrows at her and Esen blinks at me as she realises that I haven't told Dev about Poppy yet. Only her.

'Poppy is Ash's girlfriend,' Esen tells Dev, gesturing at her.

'Oh.' Now Dev looks confused and I know what she's thinking – *I haven't left her side since New Year's Eve so how could she have met someone?*

'Ash's girlfriend from *before*,' Esen clarifies, waiting for the penny to drop.

When it does, Dev's eyes widen. '*Before* before?'

Esen nods.

'Shit,' she mutters under her breath. 'Wait. Hang on. *You*,' Dev points at Poppy then at me, 'are *her* girlfriend?'

'I *was*,' Poppy says pointedly. 'Until she faked her own death.'

'Faked?' It takes Dev a moment, then she turns to Esen. 'You haven't told her yet?'

'Told me what?' Poppy asks, gaze flitting between the three of us.

'And *she*,' Dev looks at Poppy and points at me again, 'looks the way she always has?'

'Of course.' Poppy shrugs, foot tapping. 'Who else would she look like?'

'Oh.'

That's all Dev says: *Oh*.

Not quite the explanation I was hoping for and I can tell by the look on her face that it isn't good.

'Oh,' she says again, then turns to Esen, her frown even deeper now. 'Oh no.'

Esen nods, exhaling heavily through her nose as the two of them turn to look at me.

'Oh God, Ash. I'm so sorry,' Dev says with a sad sigh.

'It's OK,' I say with a shrug and I don't even know why I say that because it isn't OK.

It's the farthest thing from OK.

'So?' Poppy says then, looking between us. 'Can one of you tell me what the hell is going on?'

SIXTEEN

I tell Poppy everything. Everything I know, anyway. Everything Deborah told me that night I woke up on the sofa in the bookshop. About me being hit by the car outside the mini-mart. About how I was the last person to die on New Year's Eve. About the legend. About being a grim reaper.

Saying it out loud sounds even more ridiculous, as though we're sitting around a campfire, telling Poppy about the patient that escaped from the insane asylum who now lives in this cemetery. She doesn't laugh, though. She doesn't laugh or cry or tell me that I'm mad. She listens, her eyes getting wider and wider as she turns the ring on her thumb – the silver one with the red heart-shaped stone with a dagger going through it – around and around and around until I've run out of ways to tell her – to explain – and I have to wait and see if she believes me. If she's going to ask the question we're all asking ourselves, but none of us wants to be the first to say it.

But Poppy doesn't say anything, her gaze drifting to my neck. It takes me a second, but I realise that she's staring at my necklace and I instinctively reach for it, pressing the scythe pendant between my forefinger and thumb. She copies me, pressing her St Christopher pendant between her forefinger and thumb as she lifts her chin to look at me. Our eyes meet and it's the first time I've really let myself look at her, avoiding it until now in case I saw how angry she is and everything would change and I'd no longer be the person she met on that boat.

Or maybe it's not what I'd see, it's what I wouldn't see.

That she wouldn't look at me the way she used to – like I'm the only thing she can see for miles and miles.

Sometimes, when I'm lying on the sofa in the bookshop, looking up at the ceiling, I wonder if I've conjured her out of some heady mix of loneliness and nostalgia. If time has softened her, made her eyes bluer and her hair redder, blurred it all away until she becomes this fanciful, too-perfect thing, like a fairytale princess trapped in a castle, waiting for me to rescue her. But, looking at her now, I know I didn't. Even with an angry scrape on her chin and mascara lines down her face, as though someone has been drawing on it with pencil, she's beautiful. Her cheeks pink and her eyes as blue as I remember, the mascara cried away so that the moonlight catches on the curve of her eyelashes. And even though I'm scared because I know what it means – why she can see me, what's going to happen to her – I can't help but feel unspeakably lucky.

Lucky that she's right there.

Lucky that I get to see her face one more time.

And she gets to see mine.

'I knew it was you outside the Dome earlier,' she says, at last. 'It didn't look like you, but, I don't know.' She stops, looking at my scythe necklace again. 'That's why I came here. Because I was thinking about you.'

I knew it.

I knew that when she saw me, she'd know it was me.

I feel a sharp shiver of hope as I remember that it's her and it's me and it's *us* and maybe it really is that simple. Maybe she wanted to see me so much and I wanted to see her so much that the sheer force of it was enough to shift her world closer to mine, or mine closer to hers, and now we're both here, at the same time.

But then I think about all the graves we're sitting among and the people who visit them each day, who polish the granite and clear the weeds and leave fresh flowers for their husbands and wives and friends. The people they love and miss as much as I love and miss Poppy and would give anything for one more day with them.

As much as I'd like to think we are, we're not special, are we? It may feel that way sometimes, when I think about those afternoons we spent in our café, knees touching under the tiny table, when it felt like the earth was spinning a little slower. When we talked and talked, every conversation like our first, and last, all at once. Opening each of the doors inside us that, until then, we'd been so careful to keep locked, only to find that it wasn't as scary – that *we* weren't as scary – as we thought.

That we weren't so wild and difficult to love.

After being so sure that I wasn't made for anyone, just those girls who were fond of playing with matches around my paper heart, I found her. And maybe we're not special – cure cancer and change the world kind of special, special enough to deserve to be reunited when no one else does – yet here we are. We've found each other again. Of all the people, her. Not my mother

268

or my father or Rosh or Adara, who I love and miss just as much as I love and miss her.

And that has to mean something.

It has to.

With that, I feel the surge of something I haven't felt since New Year's Eve.

It takes me a moment to realise what it is and when I do, the relief is dizzying.

Purpose.

'Right,' I say, zipping up my leather jacket. 'Let's go to the bookshop.'

Esen watches me, clearly confused. 'Why?'

'So I can ask Deborah what the fuck is going on.'

SEVENTEEN

Esen just laughs, but when she realises that I'm serious, her face hardens. 'Are you out of your mind?'

'Absolutely not,' I tell her, shaking my head.

The opposite, in fact.

For the first time in weeks I know *exactly* what I'm doing.

Esen turns to Dev, who looks equally horrified, then back at me. 'You can't tell Deborah about this.'

'Why not?'

'What do you mean, *Why not?*' She looks at Dev as if to say, *Are you listening to this?* When Dev shakes her head, Esen turns to face me again. 'You know why not, Ash. I know it seems like all Deborah does is hang around the shop all day, handing out Post-it notes and dusting books, but do you even realise how powerful she is?'

'No, I don't and neither do you,' I remind her. 'None of us do, Esen. Not for sure.'

'That's true,' she concedes. 'But how do you think she knows who's going to die? She must have a direct line to *someone* and if she tells them about this, what do you think is going to happen to you? To Poppy?'

I don't even want to contemplate it.

'I'm not going to tell her,' I say through my teeth. 'I'm just going to *subtly* ask her what's going on.'

Esen scoffs at that then throws her hands up and turns to Dev. 'I give up.'

'Ash, listen. You can't.' Dev tries this time, her forehead creased with concern. 'You can't risk it.'

'She's the only one who can tell me, Dev. Who else can I ask?'

'What do you even want to ask Deborah?' Esen says, unable to help herself, as always. 'You *know* what's going on.'

'Yeah, but maybe—'

'Yeah, but maybe *nothing*.' Esen points her finger at me. She takes a step towards me, and looks me right in the eye. 'You want to ask Deborah if there's a way around this, don't you? If you can stop it.'

She's right, but I ignore her, uncrossing my arms and turning to look down at Poppy who is still sitting on the bench looking up at us. 'Let's go, babe.'

I half expect her to refuse, but to my surprise, when I hold out my hand to her, Poppy takes it. I feel her tremble as our palms touch and with that, we're both completely calm as she stands up to face me.

'Ash, please.' Dev tries again. '*Please* think about this.'

I don't want to think about it.

I want to know what this means.

So Poppy and I walk and keep walking, out of the graveyard and back to the bookshop, while Esen and Dev follow, trying to talk me out of it. We're approaching the Komedia when Esen finally reaches for my arm to stop me.

'For fuck's sake, Ash,' she spits, when I shrug her off. 'Do you know what's going to happen if Deborah finds out that your girlfriend can suddenly see you again?' She tips her chin towards the light of the bookshop ahead of us. 'That Poppy knows you're a reaper?' She looks back at Dev then at me again. 'That we're *all* reapers.'

I stare at her, Poppy's hand in mine, warm and familiar. 'I don't care.'

'You should care,' Esen barks. 'No good can come of this. You know that, right? I appreciate that you're in shock, but you *must* know that.' When I don't respond, just squeeze Poppy's hand, she waits for me to meet her gaze then shakes her head. 'You've been doing this long enough to know that there are no happy endings here, Ash.'

Actually, *that* feels like dying all over again.

I ignore her and turn to Poppy with a patient smile. 'Stay here, OK?' I know Esen and Dev think I've lost it, but as much as I don't want to leave Poppy out here by herself, even in the self-destructive mood that I'm in, I'm not foolish enough to take her into the bookshop with me. 'Don't move, OK? I'll be right back.'

I prepare for Poppy to put up a fight, but she just smiles at me then nods before I stride off.

I'm almost at the door to the bookshop when I feel someone reach for my arm. It's Esen, but she doesn't let go this time.

'It's Poppy's time, Ash. You know it is,' she says when I whip my head round to hiss at her. I try to shrug her off, but she holds on tighter, pulling me to her. 'Do you really want to go *in there?*' She nods at the door then lowers her voice. 'And risk Deborah finding out? You'll make whatever time Poppy has left even shorter.'

That makes me falter for the first time since we left the cemetery.

'What do you think Deborah is going to do when she finds out, Ash?' Esen shakes me so hard I swear I feel something in me come loose. 'Do you think she's just going to let you two skip off into the sunset?' She shakes me again. 'She's going to send Poppy straight to Charon and you to, *God knows* where. We'll never see you again.'

When Esen finally lets go, I stagger back as Dev runs over.

'What am I supposed to do?' I ask and it comes out as a howl.

'Just *wait*,' Dev says softly, her palms pressed together. 'I know you're scared, Ash, but we'll work it out.' She looks at Esen who exhales through her nose then nods. 'Between the three of us, we'll work it out. I promise.'

I look between them, then back at Poppy who is standing outside the Komedia, watching us, and sigh.

'Fine,' I say, adjusting the sleeve of my leather jacket.

'Thank God.' Dev looks so relieved that if I didn't know better, I'd think she was going to faint. 'Everything's going to be OK.'

Will it? I think as I follow them into the bookshop.

If Deborah was concerned about me going AWOL earlier, she doesn't show it as she emerges from the door behind the counter when the bell rings. She's carrying a pile of books, which she puts down next to the till. It never ceases to amaze me how busy she keeps herself. She's always fussing over them, arranging and rearranging them and running a feather duster over the shelves, even though I've never seen a single customer come in here.

Not once.

'Perfect timing, ladies,' she says, reaching across the counter to pluck a neon orange Post-it note from the stack. 'Dev, do you want to do this suicide by Queen's Park?'

'Sure,' she says, walking over to her and taking the Post-it note.

'Esen, you can do this one,' Deborah says, plucking off another one.

'Two?' Esen frowns. 'I know it's Saturday, but it's busy tonight.'

'I know. This one isn't far, though.'

'Where?' we ask in unison.

'Across the road.'

'Where across the road?' I ask, glancing over my shoulder at the door to see if I can see Poppy.

I can't.

'The Komedia,' Deborah says and the floor immediately turns to water beneath my feet.

'Who?' I ask, my voice noticeably less steady.

Deborah looks up, her gaze narrowing suspiciously before she peers at the Post-it note.

Don't say Poppy Morgan.
Don't say Poppy Morgan.
Don't say Poppy Morgan.

'Toby Powell,' she says.

'Toby Powell,' I repeat, so relieved that I have to swallow a laugh.

'Homeless kid,' Deborah adds solemnly. 'Froze to death.'

My relief swiftly hardens to guilt as I look at Dev and Esen and wonder if they're thinking the same thing.

We didn't even see him.

We must have walked straight past him.

'Are you OK?' I hear Deborah ask.

I look across the shop at the counter and shrug when I realise that she's talking to me. 'Fine.'

'You're behaving very strangely.'

'Am I?'

I feel fourteen again, like I've returned home after my first proper kiss (Danielle Lawson, at the bus stop outside Morrisons – she ignored me the next day at school) to find my parents on the sofa in the living room watching *Chupke Chupke* and I have to act like everything is normal when it feels anything but.

I shrug again, hoping it comes off as nonchalant rather than surly, but she frowns.

'What's going on? Did something happen with Alice Anderson?'

I'd forgotten about Alice Anderson.

Was that really tonight?

It feels like two weeks ago.

'No.' I shake my head. 'I just took her down to the beach to Charon.'

'I know, but did something happen *after* that?'

How does she know? I think, sneaking a look at Dev and Esen.

'She's fine,' Esen tells Deborah, plucking a piece of fluff off her coat then walking to the counter and taking the Post-it note. 'Come on, Ash. Let's find Toby Powell before he wanders off.'

'Why don't you go?' Deborah looks past her at me. 'I want to talk to Ash.'

She knows, I think, looking desperately at Esen.

She knows about Poppy.

She knows.

She knows.

She knows.

'We won't be long—' Esen starts to say, but Deborah interrupts with a sharp smile.

'I'm sure you're more than capable of handling this one by yourself, aren't you, Miss Budak?'

It isn't a question and we both know it.

Esen raises her eyebrows as if to say, *Good luck* then she and Dev head for the door.

The bell rings and they're gone, leaving me alone with Deborah, who is watching me over her glasses.

'Is there something you want to tell me, Ash?'

Don't tell her.

Don't tell her.

'Did something happen tonight?'

Don't tell her.

'Nothing.' I press my lips together in case I say anything else.

'Are you sure?'

Don't tell her.

I think about Poppy, outside the Komedia, and I can feel the words lining up on my tongue.

'I saw someone I know tonight.'

It's out of my mouth before I can stop it, the words flying around the bookshop like startled moths.

She takes off her glasses and looks at me. 'Who?'

'Just someone I went to school with.'

'You didn't approach them, did you?'

'Of course not.'

She nods, returning to the pile of books. 'Good.'

That's all she says – *Good* – and that's the end of the conversation, as she puts her glasses back on and picks the first book from the pile, grimacing at the cover.

I should be pleased, I know, pleased that I got away with it and she doesn't want to know more, but I can't stop myself from pushing even though I know what she's going to say.

'It just freaked me out,' I go on, tucking my hands into the pockets of my leather jacket and looking down at my feet with a small shrug. 'That they didn't recognise me when I was right there.'

'Why would they recognise you?' I look up to find Deborah watching me, clearly concerned with where I'm going with this. 'Why the sudden curiosity, Miss Persaud? You know they can't see you as you were before.'

'Really? *Never?*'

'Never,' she says tightly, going back to the books, shuffling through them and picking one out from the middle of the pile. 'No one sees a grim reaper, really *sees* one, until it's their time. But you know this.' She opens the book then immediately closes it again and puts it down on the counter. 'So why are you asking?'

'I'm just curious,' I say carefully, like I'm stroking a stray cat that may turn on me at any moment.

'About what?'

'About what would have happened tonight if my friend had recognised me.'

She takes her glasses off and exhales heavily. 'Well, it's a good thing they didn't.'

'Why?' I stop and press my lips together as I try to swallow the words back, but I can't contain them any longer, they're too big – too heavy – to hold in. 'Because that means they're going to die?'

'Yes.' She makes no effort to soften the blow. The word drops, hard as a stone, to the floor at my feet. So hard I'm sure I see dust puff up from between the floorboards. 'How else are they able to see you if they're not going to die, Miss Persaud?'

I knew that, so I don't know why I let myself hope that Poppy and I were special.

That we'd discovered some secret door between her world and mine.

I finally let myself say it then, if only to myself: Poppy's going to die.

The shock of it is enough to send me flying out of the bookshop and it's all I can do not to give in to it, not to run out and take Poppy's hand, tell her to come with me and run, as fast and as far away as possible.

'Anything else, Miss Persaud?' Deborah asks, and when I look at her again, her eyebrows are raised.

'Do you only see grim reapers right before you die?'

'No.' She puts her glasses back on, clearly hoping that's the end of the conversation, but when she raises her chin to find me looking at her hopefully, she shakes her head.

If it was anyone other than Deborah, I'd think that I'd worn her down.

'When someone is going to die, Ash, there is a window of time between when the decision is made and when we're told to reap them.' She raises her finger, no doubt anticipating that I'm about to ask her who makes that decision and obviously has no intention of telling me. 'We only know when that window is *closing*.'

'How long is it open for?'

I think of Esen's cousin's friend then, how he saw her on the Pier.

She said that he died a couple of days later.

Is that all Poppy has?

A couple of days?

The walls inch closer as I wait for Deborah to respond, the books so close that I'm scared to move in case I elbow them off the shelves, and the ceiling so low I'm sure it's touching the top of my head.

Deborah just shrugs, though. 'We don't know. It could be days. It could be a few hours.'

Hours?

I open my mouth, but nothing comes out. I don't scream or cry or tell her that it isn't fair.

I just stare at her as somewhere a clock starts ticking.

Tick-tock.

Tick-tock.

I need to get back to Poppy.

'As I said,' Deborah goes on, blissfully unaware. 'We only know when that window is closing. Anything that happens before that is not our concern. That's why it's vital that you don't see anyone you used to know, Ash, because if they were to see you while that window is open.' She holds out her palms and shrugs. 'Well.'

'Well what?'

'Well.' She stops and I don't know if she's trying to decide how to put it or whether to tell me at all, but it's enough to make my hands ball into fists in the pockets of my jacket. 'People seeing grim reapers isn't a big deal as they're unlikely to notice you. So if Alice Anderson walked in here yesterday, while the window was open, she may well have seen you as you look to me now, but she would have no reason to be concerned because you're just a stranger in a bookshop, right?'

OK.

That makes sense.

'But if it was your mother, for example.' She holds up her hands, as if expecting me to recoil in horror. 'Not that I'm saying that anything is going to happen to your mother. But *for example*, if your mother walked in here, while the window was open, she may well see you, Ash, her daughter, and that would be it.' She claps her hands. 'The whole thing falls apart. She'd want to know why you're not dead and you'd have to tell her that she's going to die.'

'Would that be such a bad thing, though?' My voice sounds tiny, like it's coming from across the street.

'Of course it would,' she says, as if it's obvious. 'There are things we shouldn't know, Miss Persaud. When we're going to die is one of them.'

'Why?'

'Why?' She waits for me to meet her gaze, then frowns at me. 'Because what if they tried to change it? To avoid it? *This.*' She turns her hands in circles over the counter, like a magician at a kid's birthday party before he pulls a rabbit out of a top hat. 'What we do, only works because we don't interfere with the process, we merely facilitate it. We know more than most, more than we should, some would say, but we don't know *everything.* And rightly so. It's a delicate balance that is easily disturbed, and when it is, the universe is out of kilter and the knock-on effect could go on for years. *Generations,* in fact. That's why we must be careful.'

'And if we're not?'

'You have to be, Ash,' she says, returning to the pile of books.

I think about what Dev said in Primark then, about the black dress between the two pink ones.

'Because someone else might die when they were supposed to? Someone who wasn't going to die.'

I hear my voice quiver as I say it.

If Deborah notices, she doesn't acknowledge it, just lifts her shoulder and lets it fall again. 'They might,' she says, as if it's nothing. As if we're talking about the weather and she's told me that it might snow again tomorrow.

'What would happen to me?' I ask before I can tell myself that I don't want to know.

'You, Miss Persaud?'

'Yeah, if someone that knows me recognised me while the window is open?'

'Nothing.' Deborah shakes her head. 'It's not your fault if you bump into someone you used to know.'

'So I wouldn't be punished?'

'Of course not.'

I should be relieved because it wasn't my fault. I didn't know Poppy was going to be at the graveyard, did I? It's not like I was hanging around near Roedean, hoping to see her, like I've considered doing so many times.

I was there.

Then Poppy was there.

And now . . . what?

'I'd only be punished if I intervened, right? If I tried to stop them from dying.'

That gets her attention.

She takes her glasses off again and looks up from the book in her hand. 'Why would you intervene?'

'I don't know,' I say, trying to sound unperturbed by the look she's giving me. 'But say I did.'

I want to hear it from her.

Not Esen or Dev.

I want to her to tell me.

'Well, if you intervened.' She arches an eyebrow and shakes her head. 'That would be a very different story.'

'What would happen to me?'

'That isn't for me to decide, Miss Persaud.'

'But it would be bad, right?'

She doesn't look at me as she puts her glasses back on. 'Just makes sure you never do.'

I know then that I have two choices: tell Deborah about Poppy or not tell her about Poppy.

It really is as simple as that.

If I tell Deborah now, she'll be pissed, but not as pissed as she'll be if she finds out . . . after.

But Esen's right, she's not going to let Poppy and I skip off into the sunset. As soon as I tell her, she's going to send Poppy straight to Charon and that will be it.

I won't be able to stop it.

That's what this is about, isn't it?

Why I'm here.

Esen's right about that as well.

I'm going to stop it.

'So that's it?' I check. 'It's never happened that someone has seen a grim reaper and they haven't died?' I make sure that I say each word precisely, as though I'm reciting a spell and if I don't say it exactly right, it won't work.

'Never,' she says, opening one of the books and flicking through it.

'Why?'

'Because, Miss Persaud.' She finally looks up at me, slamming the book shut with great flourish. 'That would be a miracle and we're not in the business of miracles. Quite the opposite, in fact.'

EIGHTEEN

As soon as I get outside again, all I can see is Poppy. She's sitting on top of one of the picnic benches outside the Komedia with her chin in her hands. When she looks up to find me standing in the doorway of the bookshop, she sits up and she looks so relieved that I almost look away, because what am I going to do?

How am I going tell her?

I have no idea, so I just stand there, taking her in, like I should have before I left her on New Year's Eve. She really is beautiful. Not oil-painting beautiful or billboard beautiful – the sort of beautiful that makes blokes honk their horns as they drive past – but the sort of beautiful people sing songs about and write books about. The sort of beautiful that keeps you up at night, scared that you're going to fuck it up because you're not ready.

I smile and when she smiles back, this loose, clumsy smile, the way you smile for school photos when you're a kid, she suddenly looks so young that it's all I can do not to give into it. Fold down on to the pavement and press my cheek to the paving slab and stay there because it's not fair. How can we be so unlucky? The pair of us dying within weeks of each other. Most people get to live whole lives. Have children and grandchildren. Get to make mistakes and learn from them. Burn bridges and build new ones. Get to live and love until they've worn their hearts out then hold the hand of the person they love and think, *We made it*, before they die in their sleep at ninety.

Why can't she have that?

Even if it isn't with me.

I think about what Mr Moreno told us last year, about that guy, the astronomer called Carl Sagan, who said that we're all made of star stuff. The nitrogen in our DNA. The calcium in our teeth. The iron in our blood. All of it was made billions of years ago in the interiors of collapsing stars.

Mr Moreno says it's funny because humans have spent years and years studying the universe. We've built rockets and pointed them towards the moon. Peered through telescopes, trying to see what fills the space between the stars. But the universe doesn't have to do that because, according to Carl Sagan, anyway, we – our very existence – is a way for the universe to know itself.

Some part of us knows that, apparently. Knows that is where we came from and we long to return. I used to think that within Poppy there was a series of locked doors that, if she let me, I'd spend the rest of my life trying to open. But now that I look at her, I know Carl Sagan is right. She has the cosmos within her. I can see it, trying to free itself from the confines of her ribs and out, out through her skin. I can see the stars at the ends of her hair, tugging her towards the sky.

Back to where she belongs.

It's already happening. She's already going, being called back to settle in some corner of the sky where she can she can shine as brightly as she wants without worrying that she'll burn out too soon, like she has now.

'Did you find out what's going on?' she asks eagerly when I get to where she is on top of the picnic bench.

I should tell her, I know. But I don't want to tell her here, in the street, in the same place someone just died.

I have to eventually but, for now, I just want to stand in her light for a moment.

'How come you were in there for so long, then?' she asks, with a frown this time.

'She gave me a bollocking for going AWOL.'

'Yeah?' Esen says with a keen smile, suddenly at my side.

I roll my eyes with a theatrical sigh. 'Thought you had a reap?'

She nods at Poppy. 'Couldn't leave her, could I? I asked Danica to do Toby Powell.'

'Thanks,' I say, softening as I realise that it didn't occur to me that she'd stay with Poppy.

'So Deborah give you a bollocking, then?' She smirks, obviously hoping that she did.

'Of course. I told you she would.'

But when I look at Poppy again, she suddenly looks furious. 'Why are you doing this, Ash?'

I blink at her. 'Doing what?'

'Acting like you have no idea what's going on.'

'I don't,' I tell her with an exaggerated frown as I take a step back and fuss over the collar of my jacket.

'You do!' She looks between Esen and I, even more

angry now. 'You both do! You're *grim reapers*!'

I shake my head at her.

'You *know* that the only reason I can see you, Ash, is because I'm going to die.'

No.

That's all I can think.

No.

No, this isn't happening.

No, I can't do this.

No, I can't tell her.

I wait for Esen to say something, to make a cutting remark, some stupid joke that I can roll my eyes at so I don't have to look at Poppy who is gazing up at us from the picnic bench, waiting. But Esen doesn't say anything, just looks at me, then down at her feet, and it's up to me.

Which is only right; it should come from me.

But I can't.

'Come on,' Poppy says when neither of us answer. 'You must have been thinking the same thing?'

I shrug, stuffing my hands into the pockets of my jacket, suddenly unsure what to do with them.

'I mean, why else can I see you guys?'

'I . . .' I start to say, but I trail off as the words abandon me, hiding under my tongue.

God, I'm pathetic.

A flash of lightning could strike her now – snuff her right

out – and she deserves to know.

I feel wretched as the seagulls wail above us, shrieking like a racket of banshees.

'You're right. You can see us because you're going to die,' Esen says and it makes me feel even worse.

That it was her who had to say it because I couldn't.

When I look at Esen, she's frowning fiercely as if to say, *Just tell her*.

So I do.

I tell her everything Deborah just told me. About the window. About how when it's open you can see all grim reapers, not just the one who is assigned to reap you. About the butterfly effect and why it's so important that we don't see the people we used to know in case it fucks everything up.

Poppy listens, her mouth a straight line, mirroring her brow as she waits for me to finish. When I do, she doesn't say anything for a long time, her gaze drifting past me to the light of the bookshop.

'So that's it?' she says, finally. 'I'm definitely going to die?'

I look down and nod, kicking at a spent cigarette butt at my feet.

'When?'

When Esen and I don't respond, just look at each other then in opposite directions, like a couple still smarting from a fight, she laughs and shakes her head, but it isn't her usual wild, bright laugh.

It's dull.

Sour.

'Really?' She shakes her head. 'You have *no* idea?'

288

I shake my head back. 'Just that it will be soon.'

'How soon?'

'I don't know.'

'Yes, you do,' she says when I won't look at her. 'I know that's why you were in the bookshop so long, Ash. Deborah wasn't giving you a bollocking, was she? You were talking about me.'

Esen turns to look at me again, her eyebrows raised.

'I didn't tell her anything, I swear.' I take my hands out of the pockets of my jacket and hold them up. 'I just asked her generally, what would happen if someone I used to know recognised me.'

'So what did she say?' Poppy pushes, the crease between her eyebrows deepening.

'Not much.' She obviously doesn't believe me, so I hold my hands up again. 'It's Deborah. She knows everything and tells us nothing.'

Esen chuckles tartly, backing me up.

'All she said was not to let it happen.'

'Not what would happen if it did?'

I shake my head because I can't tell her that as well.

Not now.

It's too much.

'So where does that leave me, Ash?'

'I don't know, Pops. I'm so sorry.'

'So what? I just sit around waiting for Deborah to give you a Post-it note with my name on it?' she asks, fiddling with the cat-head ring on her forefinger. When I don't respond, just exchange another glance at Esen, Poppy is quiet for a moment, then looks at me again. 'I'm guessing this window isn't open for long.'

I consider lying. Consider giving her a tiny bit of hope, but that's not fair, is it?

Not that any of this is fair, of course.

I shake my head. 'A couple of days, maybe.'

The word – days – hangs there, filling the space between us as she sits up and crosses her arms.

'So I could die any minute, Ash? I could die right now, on this bench?'

She doesn't wait for me to respond.

'I don't want to die on this bench,' she says.

But all I hear is, *I don't want to die.*

Before I can say anything to comfort her, though, she jumps off the picnic bench and starts walking away.

'Poppy, where are you going?' I call after her, but she doesn't look back.

'I told you! I'm not dying on this fucking bench!'

NINETEEN

I don't think Poppy knows where she's going, she just wants to go. So Esen and I give her a minute, trailing behind her as she strides away from town towards the Marina. She finally slows as she passes the elevator down to Madeira Terrace and I wonder if she's tired, but she glances over the railing at the café and empty playground on the beach then starts walking with more purpose, her hair burning bright red in the moonlight.

My instinct is to walk more quickly as well, but Esen won't let me, tugging on the sleeve of my leather jacket until I slow down. She tells me again to give her a minute, but what if Poppy doesn't have a minute? What if the driver of the approaching lorry falls asleep, mounts the kerb and mows her down?

It could happen.

Anything could.

Look at that guy Dev and I reaped in the library – Charlie Graham. He was just doing research for his essay on the *Domesday Book* and *BOOM*. He was gone. The same thing could happen to Poppy. The shock of all this could trigger some secret heart defect she doesn't know about. The sky could fall or the sea could rise up over the railing and snatch her away and how am I going to stop it?

How am I going to save her?

Poppy waits for the lorry to pass then darts across the road. I try to do the same, but the lorry is there and I feel Esen's hand on my arm again as I wait for what feels like forever for it to pass. When it does, Poppy is on the other side of the road and I run towards her as she heads for Chichester Terrace. I follow, knowing now where she's going – home – just like I did the night I woke up on the sofa in the bookshop. But before I reach her, a woman walking a small, fluffy black and white dog approaches and I stop before I trip over its lead.

The woman apologises, then apologises again when the dog starts barking fiercely. 'They sense evil.' Esen nods at the dog as it struts away, taking the owner with it, but I ignore her, looking for Poppy who is almost home now. I start running, reaching her as she's putting her key in the front door. I don't hesitate and follow her up the steps, stopping as she nudges it open with her hip. She leaves it open and I take it as an invitation to come in as she turns on the light and tosses the keys on the table under the mirror.

'Is this where you live?' Esen asks when she wanders in.

Poppy doesn't look at her. 'Where my parents live.'

'Holy shit,' Esen mutters. This is a house? A *whole* house?'

She just shrugs.

Esen raises her eyebrows and whistles. 'Oh, so you're *rich*, rich.'

'My parents are.'

'Are they home?' I ask, wondering how we're going to explain all of this to them.

'How would she even know?' Esen laughs. 'This must be at least three storeys.'

'Four, actually. And the flat downstairs.'

'Fuck-*ing* hell.'

'I'm glad you're impressed. It's a waste. They're never here. Like now, they're in Paris for my father's fiftieth.'

'When do they get back?' I ask and wonder if she's thinking the same thing.

If they'll be back in time.

'Tomorrow. Their Eurostar gets in around lunchtime, I think. So by the time they get the train from St Pancras, it'll be, like, early afternoon. *Right*,' she says, before I can ask anything else. 'I need a shower. I need to wash today off me.' She gestures at us to follow as she heads up the stairs. 'You're welcome to hang out.'

When we get to the top of the stairs, she throws her hand out towards the living room then stops with a sad smile, no doubt remembering that I've been here. She heads up to her room and as soon as she's gone, Esen marches into the kitchen. I want to tell her not to touch anything, but before I can, she yells, 'There's a wine fridge!'

'Careful,' I tell her as I walk in to find her opening the glass door.

'Dom Perignon,' she says, pulling out a champagne bottle and smiling wistfully at the label. 'Man, I wish I could still taste this. The closest I ever got was a bottle of prosecco from Lidl.'

'Same,' I chuckle. 'Except mine was from the Co-op, which Adara and I drank in Preston Park.'

'Classy,' she says, sliding the bottle back on to the shelf as I walk back into the hall to see if I can hear Poppy.

I look up the stairs, considering going up to check on her,

when I hear Esen call out to me from the kitchen.

'Leave her alone, Ash.'

'I just want to make sure she's OK,' I tell Esen, coming to stand in the doorway.

'I know.' She shrugs. 'But if it happens in the shower, it happens in the shower. What can you do?'

It's Esen, so I know I shouldn't be surprised that she's being so bloody blasé, but I still want to smack her.

'So?' she asks when I walk back into the kitchen, standing behind the island with her arms crossed.

'So?'

'What did Deborah say?'

'Exactly what I told Poppy, that she doesn't know how long it will be *before* . . .'

I can't say it.

'Deborah does know,' Esen huffs. 'You just can't ask her.'

'I almost did.'

Esen shakes her head at me. 'I'm glad you didn't.'

'Isn't it better to know, though? So we know how much time Poppy has left?'

'She wouldn't have *any* time left. Deborah would send her straight to Charon. You know she would.'

Of course she would.

'I don't know.' I shrug. 'I thought maybe she'd let it run its course. Let her go when she's supposed to go.'

'Maybe, but at what cost?'

'Cost?' I try not to raise my voice in case Poppy hears. 'She's already dying. What else is there to lose?'

'I mean, cost to *you*, Ash. If you told Deborah, you'd have to tell her that Poppy knows who, *what*, you are and she'd never let that go unpunished.'

'I don't care about that.'

'Don't.' She uncrosses her arms, raising a finger to me. 'Don't even think about it.'

'About what?'

'You know exactly *what*.' She waits for me to look at her and says, 'You can't.'

I lift my chin, meeting her gaze. 'Can't what, Esen?'

'You can't intervene, Ash.'

I press my lips together, thinking about all the ways it could happen. Poppy's healthy – as far as we know, anyway – so it's got to be something that's going to happen *to* her. A drunk driver. Someone with a knife who doesn't like the way she looks at him. Maybe, right now, somewhere in this huge, old house, a frayed wire is getting hotter and hotter, or a fuse is about to blow and the whole house will go up in flames. I can't imagine just letting it happen.

Not trying to get her out.

Not reaching for her if she falls.

'I honestly don't think I'll be able to stop myself,' I admit.

When I look at Esen again, she's nodding. 'I know, but you're gonna have to. If you don't think you can, you have to stop seeing her, Ash.'

'I don't think I can stop that, either.'

'Listen. I know you think I don't get it, but I do.' She presses her hand to her chest. 'It's not fair.'

I nod because she's right, it's not fair.

'You and Poppy didn't get to say goodbye to each other,

295

did you? You didn't get an ending, but now you do and, yeah. OK. Maybe it isn't the one you wanted, but it's better than the one you had, right?'

When I don't agree, just turn to look at the pristine stove that has probably never been used, I hope that she's going to leave it at that, but then she says, 'You can't change fate, Ash. Poppy will die when she dies. You can't stop it. And yeah, that's shit and not fair and everything else you're feeling right now, but look at it this way – you'll never disappoint her, will you? She'll never get bored of you or cheat on you, break your heart so bad that you can't bear to hear her name again. It will always be like this. You'll always be as in love with each other as you are now.'

It doesn't sound so bad when she says it like that.

That should be enough, I know, but it's not because no, we may not be special, but I believe in her. I believe in us. I believe that we're bigger than all of this. And it's more than just attraction. More than lust and adolescent impatience. It's something underneath it all. Something that makes me want to live. And I know I can't – not now – but she can. She can still be here even if intervening means that I won't be allowed to.

So let Charon come get me. Better that than watch Poppy die when I could have stopped it. I can't watch her get on that boat and go somewhere I'll never find her. That doesn't need to happen for all the things, the things Esen just said, to be true. Even if she lives until she's ninety, I'll never disappoint her. It will always be like this. We'll always be as in love with each other as we are now.

I will always be the girl who saved her life.

I really want to be that girl.

Esen must know that, because she shakes her head again. 'I can't stop you. I can't even lie and say that I wouldn't do the same thing because it's the grand romantic gesture, isn't it? Saving Poppy so she can live the life that you never will. Just promise me you'll think about it. If you do this, it – *she* – better be worth the risk.'

I don't even need to think about it.

Of course she is.

TWENTY

Deborah calls Esen with a reap near Tarner Park so she tells me to check in with her later and with that, she's gone. As soon as the front door closes behind her, I hear Poppy call out my name, asking me to come upstairs. When I get to her, I see that she's fully dressed and all in black, like me. Black skinny jeans. Black socks. An oversized black jumper. Her skin is pink from the shower and she looks so cosy that I want to reach out and hug her, feel the scratch of her wool jumper against my fingers, but then I realise that we're finally alone.

I don't think Poppy's thinking the same thing, though, because she hands me a green plastic box. I look down to find that it's a first aid kit and when I look up again, she sticks out her chin and raises her palms.

'Do you think I should do something with these? Do I need a plaster or something?'

I lean closer to peer at cuts she got when she fell in the graveyard. 'They've stopped bleeding, so it's probably best to let them dry out. But let's clean them in case you got shampoo in them when you were showering.'

She turns and walks into the bathroom. I follow, joining her at the sink. The mirror over it is steamed up so I can't see our reflections as I open the first aid kit and rest it on the edge of the sink. I find a sachet of clear liquid then check that it's saline before cutting the corner off with the small pair of scissors that's at the bottom of the box, among the plasters and a roll of bandages.

'Lean forward,' I tell her, pouring some of it over her chin when she does, watching it spill off and splash into the sink below. She winces as I do and I stop. 'Does it sting?'

She shakes her head. 'It's just cold.'

I do the same thing with her hands and when I'm done, I reach for the towel on the rail next to the sink and carefully pat her hands dry. That makes her wince again and I apologise, but she reaches for my wrist, curling her fingers around it so tightly that her silver rings dig into me, and I stop, scared that I'm hurting her.

But she lifts her eyelashes to look at me. 'I missed you so much, Ash.'

'I missed you, too,' I say back immediately, not letting even a second pass.

Her eyes flutter shut and before I get a chance to hope it will happen, she tilts her head and presses her mouth to mine. Then there's no space between us at all and I daren't move, clutching on to the towel so I have something to hold on to because this can't be real. I'm having one of those dreams you have when you're sick, when you dream about being trapped in a house that's on fire and you can't get out.

Except I don't want to get out.

I want to stay here for ever.

But then she steps back and looks at me – her eyes are black now except for the finest line of blue around the edges.

She licks her lips, then takes the towel out of my hand, tossing it in the sink before pulling me to her again. I didn't think we could get any closer, but here she is, her chest pressed to mine, one hand on the small of my back, the fingers of the other curled around the back of my neck and I wait for it. Wait to feel what I did under the bridge the first time she kissed me. But it's not the same. I can feel the heat of her mouth and the slow turn of her tongue, but it doesn't set me alight like it did that night. Still, there's something – a stir somewhere far, far away – and I think about what Dev said. About how we can't feel these things any more, but we can still remember, if we let ourselves.

So I let myself remember how she held me under the bridge and I know this is different. And it's different to how she kissed me goodbye on New Year's Eve. Then, she kissed me like she knew there would be another – and another and another and another – but now she's kissing me like she knows there might not be, like this is all we might get. So I let myself reach for her, cling to her and hope she knows that I have no intention of letting go, either.

Finally, she steps back, her whole body shivering. She brings her hands up to my face and looks at me – really looks at me – as though she is trying to relearn everything about me. The colour of my eyes. My nose ring. The mole on the bridge of my nose. I reach up and curl my fingers around her wrists, like she just did to me, so tightly that I can feel her pulse. It's too fast and I should be concerned, but how can I be?

I did that to her.

I did that.

We kiss and keep kissing until she goes limp in my arms, her head falling on to my shoulder.

'Come on,' she says into my neck, reaching for my hand and leading me out of the bathroom. When we stop at her bedroom door, I hesitate and she looks back at me with a groggy smile. 'Don't worry. I'm not going to jump on you. I just want to lie down for a minute before my parents get home. It's been a long night.'

'It's not that. It's just that grim reapers don't sleep, do we?'

'I don't want to sleep. I just need to be still for a while.'

That's probably a good idea, I think, letting her tug me into her big pink room.

'Don't let me fall asleep, OK?' she tells me as she checks her phone, which is charging on one of the bedside tables, before throwing herself on to the bed with a long sigh. I sit on the edge, unlacing my DMs and toeing them off before lying next to her. She immediately curls into me, slinging her arm across my stomach.

'Don't let me fall asleep, OK?' she says again. 'I don't want to miss anything.'

I nod.

'Promise?'

I hear her breathing slow and when I realise that she's falling asleep, I almost stop her. Almost nudge her awake, make her tell me everything. All her secrets, in case this is it and that's the last thing we say to each other. But she sounds so content, the steady rise and fall of her chest almost enough to lull me to sleep as well (if I still could, of course) that I let her give into it. And while I'm loath to break my promise, she must need it, so I lie there as she falls asleep in my arms, counting each breath against my neck, then waiting for the next – one, two, three, four – as I look at the tall, wide windows and will the sun to come up.

TWENTY-ONE

Poppy wakes with a start then jumps back when she finds me lying next to her, our heads on the same pillow. We stare at one another for a moment, and again, I know I shouldn't, but I feel unspeakably lucky because that's another thing I never thought I'd know about her. The way she looks when she wakes up. Her heavy eyes and soft mouth, the fine creases on her cheek from the pillowcase, her hair a mess, but still perfect somehow. All of these secret things only a few people know about her. Now I'm one of them.

She blinks at me, clearly unsure if I'm really there or the lingering after-effect of the dream she was having. She reaches out, gingerly pressing her fingers to my lips and waits, as if expecting me to disappear as soon as she touches me. When I don't, her whole face changes and I see her shudder as it all comes back to her. The cemetery. Me. Esen. Dev. Not wanting to die on that fucking bench.

Her shoulders sink and I sit up, unsure what to do. How to make it better. Do I reach out and clasp her shoulder? Pull her to me? Lie to her and tell her that everything is going to be OK.

Before I can do any of that, she slaps me on the arm. 'You promised you wouldn't let me fall asleep!'

For a moment, I think that she's genuinely furious with me, but then she smiles.

'Morning,' she says, and I've never been so pleased to hear that word: morning.

'Morning.'

We made it.

I'm wondering if she's thinking the same thing as she leans in and kisses me on the mouth. It's so gentle – barely there – like the way she just touched my lips with her fingers, and I'm glad. Glad that she doesn't grab me and shove her tongue down my throat. She leans back and looks at me again, hands cupping my face, and I wonder if this is how it feels to be certain. To look at someone and know – really *know* – that they feel for you what you feel for them. That they're not going to ignore you the next day at school or kiss the first boy that will kiss them back just to prove that it meant nothing. And by it, I mean me, of course. It certainly feels that way when she looks at me and it makes me think about the world and how big it is. How far away everything is. How short my life is. How short hers is supposed to be. Yet we're both here, at the same time, on this same scrap of earth.

Do you know how impossible that is?

I think about it sometimes, about what would have happened if we hadn't met that day on the boat. If our class had gone on the following one or hers had gone on the one before or Mr Moreno wasn't as enthused about the wonders of renewable energy as he was and made us read a book about it instead. It's not just that Poppy and I would never have met, but that I'd have gone to Donna Niven's New Year's Eve party instead, got drunk and kissed someone I shouldn't have at midnight while Poppy sat on the beach, no doubt kissing someone else, before we went home and fell asleep in our make-up, not knowing what we'd missed.

That we'd missed this.

Us.

Here.

Now.

We sit in silence for a while, letting the stillness settle around us.

Eventually, she turns to me with a small smile. 'Come on. I have to get out of here. I can't breathe.'

I watch as she walks over to the wardrobe and opens it, taking out a black coat I've never seen and slipping it on before going over to the chest of drawers and pulling the bottom one. She tugs out a yellow tartan scarf that I've never seen before, either, wrapping it around her neck, then reaching for some black wool gloves.

She grabs a pair of boots that are on the floor by the bed then stops to glance around the room like she's looking at it for the last time. She suddenly looks very sad. So sad that I take a step towards her.

'What's wrong, Pops? Do you want to wait until your parents get home so you can say goodbye?'

'It's not that.' She shakes her head. 'It's funny. I thought this is where I wanted to be, but I still have this feeling.'

'What feeling?'

'This need to go home.' She looks around the room again. 'But I already am, aren't I?'

TWENTY-TWO

Poppy can't leave it like this. I know she has a weird relationship with her parents – especially her father – but she has to say goodbye to them.

Some time away will help, I think as I follow her out into the street, pulling the door closed behind us. It will give her a minute to compose herself and decide what she's going to say when I persuade her to come back later.

But, for now, she has other things on her mind.

'Where are Esen and Dev?'

I shrug. 'No idea.'

'Can you call them?'

'Why?'

She tugs on her gloves. 'I want to play mini golf and it'll be more fun with four.'

Esen and Dev arrive to find Poppy and I sitting at one of the picnic benches on the roof of the café at the beach, looking out at the sea. It's surprisingly sunny for January. Still, it's almost ten o'clock on a Sunday morning so we're the only ones there. Just us and an exhausted-looking woman who is sitting in the playground beneath, pushing a buggy back and forth as she sips on what I can only assume is a very strong coffee.

Poppy gets an oat milk latte, which she is finishing when Esen and Dev find us.

'You're here!' she squeals, throwing her hands up when she sees them.

Esen isn't a throw-your-hands-up-and-squeal type of person at the best of times, but given the state Poppy was in the last time she saw her, she's understandably concerned.

'Is she OK?' she asks as Poppy tells us to come on and heads for the stairs down to the café.

'What do you think?'

I hear her mutter something as I follow Poppy, then mutter something else when Dev tells her to stop being so grumpy and a few seconds later, I can hear them behind me on the stairs. The woman is still there, still sipping the coffee and pushing the buggy back and forth as the seagulls peck at the empty playground, no doubt looking for stray crisp crumbs or a discarded rice cake.

Poppy is standing by the counter of the café, practically vibrating with excitement.

Or maybe it's all the caffeine she's just consumed.

'Yay, mini golf!' She claps her hands wildly.

Esen shoots a look at me, her gaze narrowing. 'Mini *what* now?'

I didn't tell her that's what we were doing – for obvious reasons – and hold a finger up to her, lowering my voice to a sharp whisper. 'I would just like to remind you that Poppy might die at any moment so if she wants to play mini golf with us, then we are going to play mini golf.'

'Absolutely not,' Esen says out of the corner of her mouth.

'Come on, Ess!' Dev says, clapping as well. 'I haven't played mini golf for years.'

'Four, please!' Poppy practically sings at the man behind the counter of the café.

He looks at her like he hasn't heard her properly. 'It's January.'

'I know.'

'Why do you want to play mini golf in January? It's freezing.'

Esen looks at me then raises her hand to him as if to say, *See? Listen to the man.*

Poppy is unfazed, though. 'We'll warm up when we start playing.'

'But it's so windy.'

'It's Brighton. It's always windy. Plus, it will test my finely honed golfing skills.'

He doesn't look any less convinced that she isn't utterly insane, but obviously can't be arsed to persuade her that it's a bad idea, disappearing and returning with four putters and a couple of golf balls.

'Two teams, I assume?' he says, handing them to her.

Poppy takes them with a huge smile. 'Yes, two teams. One winning team and one losing one.'

She turns to Esen and Dev, sticking her tongue out.

'You owe me,' Esen mutters as Poppy raises her arm, directing us to the course. 'You owe me big.'

I nod, slightly concerned what the penance for making her play mini golf will be.

I know I shouldn't be surprised, but Poppy is fiercely competitive. When she suggested this, I thought it would be lots of giggling and flirting and Poppy standing behind me, showing me how to hit the ball. But she's too focused for flirting, separating us into two teams and explaining the rules. I didn't even know there were rules, but apparently there are. Lots of them. Rules that I'm almost certain Esen is ignoring as she looks at me like she's going to clobber me with the putter that she's swinging back and forth in her hand.

'Let's do this,' Poppy grins, tossing one of the golf balls to Dev.

'I just want to make it clear, before we start. So there's no confusion,' Esen says and I tense, unsure what she's about to say. 'I know this is like a plot from an arthouse film; the girl who's about to die challenging three grim reapers to a game of chess for her soul. Or mini golf, in this case. But if you win this game, Poppy Morgan' – she points the putter at her and shakes her head – 'that doesn't change anything, OK?'

We're the only ones there, but I still look around, hoping no one heard. Poppy just laughs, though – that wild, bright laugh that it feels like I haven't heard for years – and I no longer care because she's happy.

Look how happy she is.

I've never played golf – mini or otherwise – so I'm relieved to find that it isn't that hard, even with the wind. The first couple of strokes are actually pretty easy, but by the time we reach the bridge, we begin to realise that Esen is just as competitive as Poppy is. Maybe more so.

'This is too hard!' she roars when the ball rolls back towards her a moment after she hits it. She tries again and when it does the same thing, she pounds the fake grass with the putter, her hair everywhere.

I'm not going to lie, if she wasn't so pissed off and holding a golf club, I'd laugh.

Dev goes to help, telling her to calm down before we get kicked out. Esen does for a second, then they immediately start bickering about the logistics of putting the ball around the trunk of a fake palm tree.

'It's rigged!' Esen hisses. 'Like the 2p machines at the Pier. There's magnets or something!'

'There are no magnets, Ess.' Dev rolls her eyes. 'You're just shit.'

Esen thumps the fake grass with her putter again and I don't know if it's frustration or an attempt to dislodge the magnets preventing her from getting the ball over the bridge, but it makes Poppy laugh.

'So, mini golf,' I say, watching Esen as she bends down to snatch the golf ball and threatens to lob it into the sea. 'Of all the things you could have done today, why mini golf?'

'I don't know.' She shrugs, smiling to herself as she watches Dev and Esen. 'I was thinking about the last time I was happy.' She turns her cheek, smiling at me this time. 'New Year's Eve, with you.' She wrinkles her nose and kisses me quickly on the mouth. 'Then before that the last time I was happy, really happy, was my eleventh birthday.'

'Yeah?'

'My dad and I got the little train from Black Rock station.' She stops to thumb over her shoulder then points ahead. 'To the Pier. We played on all the 2p machines, the ones with the magnets, then spent our winnings on candyfloss and ice cream then got the train here and played mini golf. It was the best day. Honestly. I had so much fun.'

She sighs sadly and I know now why she wanted to come here.

This is how she's going to say goodbye to her father.

'Sounds nice,' I say, reaching for her hand, and I swear I shiver when our palms touch.

Or maybe that's her.

'It was.' Her smile isn't as bright as she looks back at Dev and Esen. 'They sent me to Wycombe Abbey a few weeks later. I don't know what I did.' She shrugs. 'Why I suddenly became so difficult to love.'

Before I can say anything, she's gone, bounding over to take her shot now that Dev has grappled the ball off Esen. Poppy hits it perfectly and Dev swallows a gasp, covering her mouth with her hand.

'This is bullshit!' Esen spits, throwing down her putter. It bounces twice then lands on the fake grass as she stomps off to sulk by a wooden tiki head with an expression that perfectly matches her own.

Dev gets called away to a reap so without her there to keep Esen calm, I suggest we call it a draw. I half expect Poppy to object, but she doesn't seem to care, clearly amused by the whole thing as she tries to explain why Esen's putter is bent when she returns it to the guy behind the counter at the café.

'What do you want to do now?' I ask Poppy as we head towards Duke's Mound.

She considers it for a moment and I wonder if she's made a list of all the things she wants to do before . . . well. Then I think about the lists we made on New Year's Eve. I didn't get to do any of the things I wanted to do, but maybe we can do some of hers. There must be something else she wants to do other than play mini golf.

'I want toast,' she announces as we get back on to the road.

OK.

We can definitely do toast.

'Shall we head back to yours, then?' I ask, nodding across the street her house.

'My parents don't have a toaster.' She looks horrified. 'Or bread. No,' She stops, waiting for a bus to pass before crossing the road. 'There's a place up here that does the *best* vegan breakfast.'

Esen points at her. 'The blue café on the corner opposite St Mary's Hall?'

'Yes!' Poppy points back at her. 'Have you been?'

'Nah. It wasn't there before I, *you know*. But whenever I pass it's always *really* busy.'

Poppy doesn't even look at her house, just keeps heading up Lewes Crescent. As we pass the Kemptown Enclosures, my instinct is to ask Poppy if she has her key so we can go in and see if my father's in there. *We're near the hospital as well, aren't we?* A couple of days ago, I would have engineered it so we walked that way back to the bookshop and I could linger outside in the hopes of catching a glimpse of my mother. But after seeing Poppy, I don't dare, terrified of what will happen if I do. Poppy must know what I'm thinking, because she reaches for my hand and squeezes it and when I look at her, she nudges me with her hip.

'There it is,' she says when we get to the top of Sussex Square, pointing at a café. It's exactly where Esen said it would be – on the corner, opposite St Mary's Hall – and as busy, the queue snaking out the door on to the pavement. We're joining the end of it when I hear my phone and take it out of the back pocket of my jeans to find it's Deborah.

'Shit,' I mutter as I answer it. 'Hello?'

She doesn't say it back. 'Ash, you're with Esen, aren't you?'

'Yeah.' I frown, unsure how she knows that.

Maybe Esen told her that she was coming to meet me.

'You're near St Mary's Hall?'

OK. Deborah can't know *that*.

I look around, suspiciously. 'Yeah.'

'Good. We've got a stabbing near there and I'd rather there were two of you.'

'A stabbing?'

I try not to say it too loudly as I look at Poppy, but she's not listening, too distracted by two pugs that waddle past. Esen is, though, her brow furrowing, and I wonder if she's thinking the same thing.

Don't say Poppy Morgan.

Don't say Poppy Morgan.

Don't say Poppy Morgan.

'Yes.' Deborah stops and it feels like an eternity before she finally says, 'Alfie Fuller.'

I shake my head at Esen. Not that I need to – I'm so relieved it must be obvious.

'Where?' I ask.

'The Manor. Do you know it?'

'Yeah.' My cousin used to play football there on Saturday mornings. 'When?'

'Soon. 12:13.'

'OK. We're heading there now.'

'Who was that?' Poppy asks when I hang up.

'Deborah,' I tell her, then look at Esen. 'How did she know that I was here, with you?'

She just rolls her eyes. 'It's Deborah. She's a witch.'

'Or she's tracking you on your phones,' Poppy says, adjusting her bobble hat.

I look down at the phone in my hand then up at Esen, who looks equally horrified.

'What?' I hold it up. 'On this piece of shit? It doesn't even have the internet.'

I haven't been around long enough to earn an iPhone like Dev and Esen.

Poppy just shrugs. 'Tracking devices are tiny. They fit pretty much anywhere.'

I look at Esen again and wonder if she's also considering throwing the phone into the street.

But she just tips her chin at me. 'Where we going?'

'Stabbing.' I nod up the road towards the Manor. 'It's not far.'

'OK.' Poppy takes her gloves out of her coat pocket and tugs them on. 'Toast can wait.'

'No way,' I tell her, holding my hand up. 'You stay here. We'll come get you when we're done.'

'How am I any safer here?' she asks with a furious frown. 'What if it happens and you're not here?'

'She's right,' Esen agrees. When I glare at her, she shrugs. 'You can't leave her on her own.'

'Fine,' I concede with a huff. 'Just stay back, OK? Don't get involved.'

Poppy nods obediently.

We arrive at the Manor at exactly 12:13 to find a body spread-eagled in the middle of the field. It must have just happened, because two blokes are running hell for leather towards the flats on the other side. Esen watches them go, then turns to me. 'Must have been them who stabbed him.'

'Them?' Poppy frowns. 'There's only one.'

It takes us a moment longer than it should, but when we realise that Poppy wouldn't be able to see Alfie Fuller – only we can – Esen and I look at one another and say, 'Shit!' at the same time.

Why do these things only happen when I'm with Esen?

Esen starts running. 'Stay with Poppy!' she calls out over her shoulder, then looks back and asks, 'Which one is he?' when she realises that she doesn't know which of them is Alfie Fuller.

I look down at the body at my feet. 'The one with the fur-lined hood!'

She catches up to him, reaching out for the hood and yanking him back. He stumbles, landing on his back on the grass. She helps him up and he's so concerned with trying to shrug her off, that he must not notice his body lying in the middle of the field because he doesn't seem to be freaking out about it. By the time they get back to us, I can hear Esen telling him, 'Yes, I know he stabbed you, but you need to come with me.'

'What are you lot?' He spits, looking at Esen then at me and Poppy. 'The police?'

'You wish,' Esen says, taking him by the elbow and leading him towards the gates.

The last time I was at this end of the beach was for the reaper party. It's empty now, but I still insist that Poppy and I hide behind one of the coaches parked up on the road while Esen escorts Alfie Fuller across to Charon. If I had my way, we wouldn't even be this close, but Poppy was determined to watch.

'I can't see anything from here,' she says with a pout, poking her head out from behind the coach.

'You can't see anything, though, can you?' I remind her,

tugging her back by her sleeve. 'I told you, only Esen and I can see Alfie. How do you think we can escort them down here without anyone noticing?'

Poppy looks genuinely disappointed. 'I thought maybe.'

I hope maybe never, I think as Esen strides back to us, curls bobbing.

'All good?' I ask when she finds us behind the coach.

'Won him over in the end, didn't I?'

'How is it that I've done over a dozen reaps with Dev and no one has ever done a runner?'

Esen just smiles and turns up the collar of her coat.

We agree to go back to the bookshop, deciding that I should show my face before Deborah gets too suspicious. Poppy must be tired, because she suggests we take the bus back into town, but when we tell her that we prefer to walk as we're less likely to draw attention to ourselves, she books a cab on her phone. I'm not entirely convinced that's much better, but the driver is so embroiled in a heated discussion on his hands-free when he pulls up at Duke's Mound that he barely looks at us as we clamber into the back seat.

When he drops us on North Road, Esen offers to stay with Poppy, who's decided that she wants to try all the teas at Bird & Blend. Unless she chokes on a dried rose petal, she'll be fine so, content that she's safe with Esen, I head to the bookshop. As soon as I'm through the door, I say hello to Dev, who is lying on the sofa reading a book, a pair of chunky boots I've never seen her wearing resting on the arm. I turn to greet Deborah, but when I see that she isn't behind the counter, I hesitate, looking around the bookshop to find that it's just Dev and me. Deborah is always here – *always* – but before I can ask Dev where she is, she emerges from one of the stacks holding a feather duster.

'Miss Persaud.'

She's changed again, this time into a fitted white shirt that's tucked into a pair of black cropped trousers and glossy brogues, and is very Audrey Hepburn.

'How was the Manor?' she asks, leaning against one of the bookshelves. 'Any problems?'

'Of course. It's Esen,' I say, throwing myself into one of the armchairs.

I recount the story of Alfie Fuller doing a runner with great glee, which is enough to make Deborah smile wide enough to reveal a gap between her front teeth I didn't know was there.

'Only Esen,' she says under her breath, shaking her head.

She resumes dusting the books so Dev indulges me in idle chatter about her birthday party, which, after everything that has happened with Poppy, I'd forgotten was tonight. After about ten minutes, I decide that I've done enough to convince Deborah that everything's OK so I can leave.

Before I do, I glance at the framed print on the wall by the door. I must have passed it dozens of times, never really looking at it and assuming it was just an abstract painting of a black circle on a cream background, but as I stop in front of it, I see that in the centre of the circle there's a series of dots and lines with a title over it.

'Carte Céleste,' I read aloud, unsure I've pronounced it right.

I must have, because Deborah doesn't correct me and merely says, 'Heavenly card'. When I turn on my heel to face her, she's watching me over her glasses from behind the sofa. 'It's a map of the stars.'

I look back at the print, following each line to the dot it meets then up another line and another, trying to find a pattern. But there doesn't seem to be one, some of the lines longer than others, making each shape slightly different. The squares aren't completely square and each of the triangles is a different size. Some of the shapes I couldn't even name, *but I'm sure Rosh could*, I think, as I stare at it.

'Ash,' Deborah says when I get to the door, and I brace myself as I turn to her with what I hope is an easy smile. 'I know it's Dev's party tonight, but make sure you listen out for your phone, OK?'

I nod and she nods back, disappearing between the stacks again.

Poppy's still in Bird & Blend, sipping tea while Esen lingers by the doorway, clearly bored.

'All good?' Esen asks when she sees me.

'I don't think Deborah suspects anything.' I cross my fingers and hold them up. 'Is Poppy OK?'

'Yeah. Her mum called.'

'She did?' I say, suddenly buoyed by that. 'When?'

'Just now. While Poppy was trying to persuade me to try

something called Rockabye Raspberry.' She stops to glare at the woman approaching with a jug of what looks like pot pourri stewing in water. She takes the hint and veers the other way. 'I didn't want to intrude so I don't know what was said, but she seems much happier.'

As if on cue, Poppy sees me by the doorway, talking to Esen, and bounds towards us, bobble hat bobbing.

'What's that?' I ask, nodding at the paper cup in her hand.

'Banana-bread chai tea!' She grins, holding it out to me.

'First of all,' I tell her sternly, taking the cup from her, 'chai means tea so you just said *tea tea*.' She sticks her tongue out as I remove the lid and grimace at the contents before handing it back. 'That's not chai.'

She just shrugs, putting the lid back on and taking a sip as we head out into the street. 'Well, I like it.'

'Listen.' Esen stops, nodding towards North Street. 'I'm going to help set up for Dev's party tonight.'

Poppy's eyes light up. 'Dev's party?'

'You can't come,' Esen tells her, making no attempt to be diplomatic about it. 'It's reapers only.'

Poppy pouts. 'But I'm reaper adjacent.'

'Not the same.'

'Hey!' She points the cup of *tea tea* at her. 'I helped earlier. Alfie Fuller would have run off if I wasn't there.'

'That's true,' I tell Esen, nodding slowly.

'Besides,' Poppy adds, 'how will anyone know I'm not a reaper? You can't *all* know each other.'

'We don't,' Esen concedes, slipping her hands into the pockets of her coat. 'I'm not taking the risk, though.'

'If anyone asks, I can say that I'm from Hastings or something,' Poppy insists.

'And if *they're* from Hastings? Do you know how much shit we'll be in?'

Of course she doesn't.

'What?' Poppy asks when she catches me mouthing *Shut up* at Esen.

'Nothing.' I smile sweetly. 'It's fine.'

'It's not *fine*,' Esen spits, her voice noticeably louder. So loud that the shock of it makes Poppy and me jump.

When I turn to look at her, she's suddenly furious, her whole face hardening as she glares at us.

'How is any of this *fine*, Ash? The pair of you are deluded.' Esen takes her hand out of the pocket of her coat to jab her temple with her finger. 'You're running around playing mini golf and drinking tea like it's *nothing*.'

I'm so stunned, I don't know what to say and just stare at her. I had no idea she was so stressed out about this. She didn't seem bothered an hour ago when she was telling me that I couldn't leave Poppy on her own while we went to reap Alfie Fuller in case she choked on her toast.

When I don't say anything, it seems to piss her off even more, and she turns to Poppy. 'And *you*.' Esen jabs her finger in Poppy's direction this time. 'You're not supposed to know about us and what we do. And you're certainly not supposed to be coming on reaps with us. Do you know what Deborah would do to us if she found out?'

Poppy takes a step back, her eyes wet, and I don't even think about it, I'm between them.

'First of all. Don't you dare yell at her! I'll kill you again!'

I don't know where it comes from – this roar – but it feels like I could punch a hole in the sky.

If Esen's surprised, she doesn't show it, licking her lips at the challenge.

But before she can say anything else, I take another step towards her and it's my turn to jab my finger. 'It's not Poppy's fault. She's going to die and she doesn't know how or when so cut her some slack! If you want to yell at someone, Esen, yell at me.' I slap my chest with my hand. 'I'm the one who dragged you into this.'

'Yes, you did,' she reminds me with a sour smirk. 'And now we're all fucked.'

I throw my arms out. 'How?'

'If you want to do this,' Esen gestures at Poppy, '*fine*. You know what you're getting yourself into. But if Deborah finds out that Dev and I knew about this, that we went along with it, we're *fucked*, Ash!'

'She won't,' I insist, but even as I say it out loud, I don't believe it.

It's Deborah.

'I'll tell her that you didn't know,' I promise, because that's all I can do. 'That it was all me.'

'Don't be so naïve, Ash. I'm guessing this is above Deborah's pay grade. They probably already know.'

That hadn't even occurred to me.

I finally get what she's saying and I'm suddenly very, very scared.

'It's OK.' I hold my hands up and I don't know whether I'm

saying that for her or for me. 'It'll be OK.'

'Whatever.' She shakes her head and takes a step back. 'Do what you want, Ash. You will anyway.'

'That's not fair, Esen!' I call after her as she turns and walks away.

But she doesn't look back, and is swiftly swallowed up by the crowd of tourists and Sunday shoppers who are too absorbed with sniffing incense and taking photos of the red-and-white-striped legs kicking up from the Komedia to even notice that we're there, let alone what we're arguing about.

When I turn back to Poppy she's staring at me, her whole face red now.

'What is she talking about, Ash?'

TWENTY-THREE

I just look at her, my hands in the pockets of my leather jacket, because I don't know what to say. I don't even know what I'm risking, do I? Not for sure, anyway. Just that whatever it is has to be worth it.

Poppy isn't having it, though.

'Ash?' she pushes, taking a step towards me.

I take my hand out of my pocket and press it to my forehead. 'I don't want you worrying about this.'

'Worrying about what?'

'Whatever happens after, *you know*.' I can't look at her. 'I just want you to focus on now.'

'How can I when you won't tell me what's going on?'

'Because it doesn't matter, Poppy. The only thing that matters is what you want to do today.'

'What? So you can worry about me, but I can't worry about you? That's not how this works, Ash.' She gestures at the space between us. 'I can't believe you didn't tell me that this would get you into trouble.'

'Only if Deborah finds out and she won't find out. I'll make sure of it.'

Poppy raises her arm to point in the direction Esen just stomped off. 'What if Esen's right? What if she, they, whoever *they* are, already know?'

'If they did, I'd know about it,' I reassure her and I really do believe that.

'And if they do find out? Are they going to punish you for this? For being with me?'

'I guess.'

'You guess?' she chuckles tartly. 'How?'

'I don't know.'

'You do, Ash. You might not know for sure, but you have an idea.'

'I'll be banished,' I admit, stuffing my hands into the pockets of my leather jacket. 'Whatever that means.'

'What do you think it means?'

'That I won't be here or there, wherever you go when you get on the boat with Charon.'

'Where will you be, then?'

'Nowhere.'

'What?' Poppy blinks at me. 'Like purgatory or something?'

'I guess so. I asked Dev once and she said that she heard that it was like falling through darkness. Just falling and falling and falling forever, but never landing.'

She thinks about it, then the crease between her eyebrows deepens. 'How do we stop that happening?'

It's my turn to think about it, and when I do, for the first time since I decided to intervene, I hesitate as I ask myself if Esen's right, if it's worth the risk. But then I look at her, standing in front of me, the January afternoon sunshine settling in her hair so I could count each strand of gold if I wanted to, and I can see it – I can't actually *see* it – *life*, burning out of her, right through her clothes. It feels like New Year's Eve, when we were sitting on the beach, our future rolling out from our feet like a red carpet, and this can't be it.

It can't be.

'We can't stop it,' I tell her. 'Maybe if I told Deborah straight away, but it's too late now.'

'No.' She takes another step towards me, so close the toes of our boots are touching. 'You're not doing this, Ash. I'm not letting you do this. I'm not letting you get banished to purgatory for *me*.'

'I told you, that will only happen if Deborah finds out and she won't.'

'But what if she does?'

'Well, if she does, then she does.' I shrug again. 'It's done. There's nothing I can do about it now. We're both beyond the looking glass. You know who – what – I am and you know what's going to happen to you. You shouldn't, I shouldn't have told you, but I did, and now you know and I can't take it back. And I don't *want* to take it back because if I tell Deborah the truth, she'll send you to Charon and that would mean that we wouldn't have this.'

'What?'

'*Us*. Together again.'

'Yeah, but what's the point?' She takes another step back, turning to toss her paper cup into the bin on the kerb next to her. 'What's the point of being together if we can't stay together? It's cruel.'

She won't look at me but I can see how angry she is, her whole body tense and her cheeks burning.

Poppy turns and starts to walk away, but before I can follow, she stops and turns to face me again.

'I'm scared, Ash,' she says. 'I've been trying to hold it together, but I don't want to fucking die.'

'I know.' I charge towards her, closing the gap between us. 'I know.'

When I reach for her hand, raising it so I can press my mouth to it, she lifts her heavy eyelids to look at me. 'Ash, what are we going to do?'

'Listen, Pop,' I say softly. 'I don't know what's going to happen, but I do know this: I believe in this, in us.'

A tear tumbles down her cheek. 'You do?'

'I do.'

It's the only thing I do know for sure.

TWENTY-FOUR

We decide to go to the café – our café – and just be still for a while, but as we're walking there, we pass Snoopers Paradise and she pulls me in. The last time we were in here was last year when we were trying on hats for some costume party she was going to. It's exactly as I remember – a mess – everything on top of each other, clustered together randomly. We pass a cream teapot with brown leaves perched on a stack of battered biscuit tins, next to a clowder of china cats, the tips of their ears chipped. Under them is an old leather suitcase full of other people's photographs and I wonder who'd buy them. Someone else's memories.

The aisles are so cluttered that only one of us can walk down them at a time. It's much busier than the bookshop, which doesn't help, a mix of tourists taking photos of the china plates propped on the Welsh dresser and locals flipping through old records, trying to find a classic Otis Redding 45. Poppy is somewhere between the two, her eyes wide as she opens rusting tobacco tins to see what's inside and takes a scuffed Rolleiflex camera off one of the shelves, pretending to take my photo before putting it back. As she does, she almost knocks a glass box off the shelf and when I see that it contains a single doll's leg, I grimace at her.

'Do you think it's cursed?' she asks as I pull her away.

'Let's not find out, OK?'

She stops and points at another glass box, this one containing a taxidermy crow. 'Look at this guy.'

'I'd rather not.'

'What's his name, do you think?'

'Edgar,' I suggest.

'As in Allan Poe?' When I nod, she laughs. 'I like it.'

We head around the corner and when she stops again, I wonder what she's going to point out next, but she tells me to stay there. She promises she'll only be a second, but I'd still rather not let her out of my sight. She's so excited, though, so I let her go, watching her disappear as I calculate all the ways a person can die in a shop like this. Death by taxidermy crow.

What a way to go.

Mercifully, she returns a few moments later and reaches for my hand.

'Come on,' she says with a wicked smile.

'Where are we going?'

'You'll see,' she says, tugging me around the corner and there it is.

The Photomatic booth.

She remembered.

She remembered the list I made on New Year's Eve.

'I needed change,' she explains, letting go of my hand to reach into the pocket of her coat. She takes out some pound coins and inserts them into the slot then grabs my hand again and pulls me inside. I sit beside her on the bench and as we wait for the flash to go off, I suddenly feel very safe.

Like nothing can happen to us here.

The first flash catches us by surprise, but we recover quickly, doing a series of silly poses that concludes with Poppy grabbing me so suddenly, her hands on my face, that I laugh into her open mouth as she kisses me. It makes her laugh too and we stay like that for a few moments, laughing and kissing. It feels so real and for the first time since I found her in the cemetery, Poppy isn't this fleeting, fragile thing. A bird that will fly away if I don't hold on to her with both hands. She's there – right there – warm and solid and utterly fearless, like nothing can break her. And if we can just stay here, I think, right here in this photo booth, nothing ever will.

But we can't, I know, so I pull the curtain back, taking her hand and leading her out, the pair of us giggling as we wait for the photos to be printed. When they are, she snatches them out of the slot, but her face falls when she sees them. I take the square of glossy paper from her, wondering what's wrong – if they didn't come out or I've ruined them by pulling an ugly face – but then I see.

It's not me.

It is, but it's not the me that she can see now, it's the me she looked past outside the Dome.

She doesn't look like her, either, her red hair tamed in black and white, losing a little of its magic.

So we leave the photos there, tucking them among the other ones people left behind that are stuck to the front of the booth. I take her hand and we walk out in silence, no longer amused by the taxidermy crow.

It's beginning to get dark and before I can ask her what she wants to do now, Poppy is distracted by the jewellery stall outside the shop. With that, the photos are forgotten as she tries on rings and holds up a pair of hoops so big I'm sure I could get my whole fist through and asks me what I think. I smile and she puts them down, reaching for a necklace with a round pendant engraved with a tree. I'm distracted by a ring centred with a piece of amber so big it looks like the entire universe is trapped inside it and when I look up, I see Poppy handing the man behind the stall a £20 note. I ask her what she's doing and she takes my hand, pulling me in front of a shop window.

'Give me your necklace,' she says and I frown at her.

'My necklace?'

'Your scythe.'

I'd forgotten about that.

I reach up to unclasp it and when I hand it to her, she threads something on to it and tells me to turn round. She stands behind me, refastening it then taking me by the shoulders and turning me so that I'm facing her again.

'There,' she says with a slow smile.

I look down, lifting the pendant with my fingers to find a silver bumblebee.

'Pop.' I look up at her again and she's grinning so much I can see her teeth.

'Bumblebees are the best.' She presses her finger to it. 'Not only do they symbolise good luck, but they protect you. It's said that if you follow a bumblebee, it will lead you to a new destination.'

She leans across, pressing a kiss to my mouth, then looks at me again with another huge smile, obviously waiting for me to say something, to thank her, to tell her that I love it, promise that I'll never take it off. But I can't speak as I cup her face in my hands and kiss her this time, hoping it's enough because all I can think about is what a shame it is that wherever she's going and wherever I'm going, isn't the same place.

TWENTY-FIVE

We finally make it to the café. Our table is free – the one in the corner by the window – and I think about the last time we were here together. We talked about what we were doing for Christmas, the pair of us trying to work out when we'd next see each other. She'd said that the only thing she was looking forward to was hanging out with her grandmother on Christmas Day. They have this tradition where they go for a walk along the beach after lunch, but her grandmother is in a wheelchair now so she wasn't sure if they'd able to do it this year.

I get a tea in case it looks weird that I'm not drinking anything and Poppy gets an oat milk latte – a normal one, much to her annoyance, because they've stopped doing the gingerbread ones. She pairs it with a vegan bun the size of her head that's dripping with white icing and dotted with pieces of pistachio. She hasn't even taken a bite out of it before my phone rings and I sigh heavily, wondering how Deborah knows that we've only just sat down.

But it's not Deborah, it's Esen, and I hesitate, in no mood for another bollocking. So I consider letting it go to voicemail, but I've had enough arguments like that with my mother over the years. Those furious, feral arguments where I couldn't even remember what she said to make me so mad, just that I was, the anger so real it felt like there was someone else in the room, standing beside me, egging me on. So I tell myself to answer, knowing full well that the longer I leave it, the harder it will be to go back to how it was before, and the space between us will just get wider and wider until it's impassable. But as I stare at her name on the screen, I wonder if what I'm really trying to avoid isn't another argument, it's having to admit that she's right. I am being selfish. I've been so concerned about Poppy that I didn't even think about the position I was putting her and Dev in.

'Hello?' I answer, wincing as I wait to be yelled at again.

'Come to the party,' Esen says with a huff.

That's all she says and I pause, wondering if Dev's put her up to it.

'It's OK. Poppy says that she wants to try the vegan hot dogs at the Hope & Ruin.'

It occurs to me then that most of what Poppy wants to do revolves around eating. There are no friends that she wants to see, even though I've told her that she should, and she doesn't want to run away to Paris like I thought she would. She just wants to walk around like we did when we first got together and it felt like we were discovering Brighton for the first time. The street art we'd never seen. That second-hand place with the taxidermy rats in top hats. That weird vegan shoe shop opposite the bookshop. She wants to pet every dog and find all the lost cats and listen to every busker we pass. Except she's not looking at everything as though she's seeing it for the first time.

She's saying goodbye.

And I get that, but I'm worried that she thinks that she has time to do the other stuff, when she doesn't.

'First of all, they're disgusting,' Esen tells me, pulling me back. 'I don't even need to have tried a vegan hot dog to know that. Second of all, stop sulking and come to the party.'

'I'm not sulking,' I say, but it kind of sounds like I am.

'Come, then.'

'Why the sudden change of heart?'

She huffs again. 'Dev heard us yelling in the street.'

'Did Deborah hear?' I ask, sitting a little straighter.

'No. She was busy with a customer, thankfully.'

'A customer?' I blink, unsure if I heard her correctly.

'I know,' Esen says with a chuckle. 'He wanted some random book and we actually had it, can you believe?'

'I cannot.'

'Anyway, she didn't hear, but Dev did and ripped me a new one.'

'Oh.' I nod, even though she can't see me. 'So that's why you suddenly want us to come.'

'No,' Esen says defensively. 'I mean, it might have given me the kick up the arse I needed to realise that I was being an asshole—'

'So, you concede that you were being an asshole?' I interrupt with a smug smile.

'Yes,' she says and even down the phone, I can tell that she's saying it through her teeth. 'I can admit that. I can also admit that none of this would have happened if I hadn't taken you to the cemetery.'

'I'm glad you did,' I say as I watch Poppy picking the pistachios off her bun and popping them into her mouth.

'And I can admit that I've forgotten.'

'Forgotten what?'

'What it was like to feel that way about someone.' She pauses to sigh tenderly. 'It's been so long.'

I nod again.

'Anyway, come to the party,' she says, more softly this time. 'Dev wants you here. I want you here.'

'What about Poppy?'

'Don't worry,' she says and she sounds much calmer than the last time we spoke about this. 'It's only the second week in January. No one's met *all* the new reapers yet. It could work.'

'You think?' I ask, glancing at Poppy again, who is licking icing from her fingers.

'Yeah, we'll try the Hastings thing. I doubt there'll be anyone here from Hastings.'

I hear the *we* and smile. 'Well, if you think it will work.'

'It will if you just be cool and don't do anything to draw attention to yourselves.'

'OK,' I promise. 'We're leaving now.'

Esen hangs up without saying goodbye and when I look at Poppy, she's grinning at me.

'Are we going to the party?'

'Yes,' I say, but before she gets too excited, I hold up my finger. 'On one condition.'

She eyes me suspiciously. 'What?'

'Call your dad.'

'No.' She shakes her head. 'Absolutely not.'

'Poppy,' I say with the tone I used to use with Rosh when she was little and refused to hold my hand when we crossed the road. 'You need to call him.'

'Do I?'

I tilt my head at her. 'You know you do.'

'Fine.' She flicks her hair. 'I'll talk to him when I get home tonight.'

I use *the tone* again. 'Poppy.'

'What do I even say to him?' She throws her hands up. 'How the fuck do I say goodbye over the phone?'

'What did you say to your mum earlier?'

'Nothing.' She won't look at me. 'Just that I love her.'

I pick her phone off the table and hand it to her. 'Say that, then.'

'Fine.'

She takes it with a petulant huff then unlocks it and taps at the screen, making a show of huffing again as she presses it to her ear. I wonder if she's hoping he won't answer because she seems startled when he does.

'Hey, Dad.' She grimaces and sticks her tongue our at me. 'Yeah, I'm good. Did you get back OK?'

She makes all the right noises but clearly isn't listening as she plucks another pistachio from her bun.

'How was Paris? Did you have a good birthday?'

She pops the piece of pistachio into her mouth and pretends to be riveted by whatever he's telling her.

'That's nice. Where are you now?' She frowns. 'How come you're back in Cambridge already?' Then nods. 'OK. I'll let you go.' I don't know what he says, but her whole face softens and she blinks a few times, the corners of her mouth twitching. Then I see her chin shiver as she says, 'I love you, too, Daddy.'

She smiles to herself as she hangs up, then catches herself and scowls at me. 'Happy?'

Very.

Poppy gets the woman behind the counter at the café to put her coffee in a takeaway cup so she can take it with her. As I watch her merrily downing the last of her latte, I decide to remind her of the rules.

'If we're going to pass you off as a reaper,' I tell her, lowering my voice even though we're the only ones on the street – us and some blokes across the road, smoking outside a pub. 'There can be none of this.'

'Don't worry.' She shakes the empty paper cup at me. 'I'm done.'

'OK.' I clap my hands together. 'So the plan is: if anyone asks, you're a new reaper from Hastings.'

'That was my plan, actually,' she reminds me.

'You're a new reaper from Hastings and let's say that you've been assigned to adolescent sudden deaths as well because you know the deal with that, right? Plus, there can't be many of those every day in Hastings so it would explain why you're at the party.' I think about it and start to doubt myself. 'I don't know. Hastings is *miles* away. How would you even get back there if you had a reap?'

'You're overthinking it,' she says, pointing what remains of her bun at me. 'No one gives a shit.'

'True.' I tilt my head from side to side. 'In fact, it's probably best that you just try to avoid talking to anyone at all, but if you can't, don't volunteer any information until they specifically ask you.'

She nods.

'That's the secret to a good lie,' I tell her, glad that I finally have a chance to put all those years of lying to my parents to good use. 'Keep it simple. Don't say too much. Just keep your answers short and as closed as possible. *Having fun tonight? Yes. I haven't seen you before, are you from around here? No.* Or, if that fails, answer their question with a question. *I haven't seen you before, either, where are you from?* Got it?'

'Do you think I should have a fake name? Like Cressida Montgomery? Cressida Montgomery,' she says theatrically, eyes narrowing. 'She's tough, but deep down, she has a heart of gold.'

She's going to blow it, I conclude with a heavy sigh.

She's going to blow her cover within about three minutes of arriving.

If I'd known we were going to the party, I wouldn't have let her have all that caffeine and sugar.

'Don't worry,' she says, taking a huge bite out of her bun. 'I go to Roedean, remember? We invented lying.'

'Did they teach you to talk with your mouth full at Roedean as well?'

She opens her mouth to show me the contents and I recoil so violently, she laughs.

339

We hear the music before we turn on to Bristol Gardens and Poppy is suddenly so excited that I have to stop her running down the street towards it. As we get nearer, I can hear it's something slow and creepy, the sort of song that should be on a Halloween playlist, which is perfect for a reaper party, now I think about it.

'The Cure!' Poppy grins as we walk up the path towards the front door.

I have no idea who The Cure are, but she seems thrilled.

When we get inside, Poppy turns to smile at me. I know this is exactly how she imagined a reaper party: everyone dressed in black and the house dark except for clusters of church candles on every surface – the floor, the table by the front door, one on each of the stairs – so everything looks slightly golden, like on a still autumn afternoon.

We peer through the first open door to find it's a living room. The curtains are drawn and all the furniture has been pushed back, the rug that must have been in the middle of the floor now rolled up and propped in the corner by the window like a massive cigar. It's cluttered with candles of all sizes and colours as well, their flames flickering steadily against the walls, weeping wax on to the mismatched saucers they're sitting on.

A group of people I don't recognise is gathered in the middle of the room. They're dancing, or trying to – this song not cheerful enough – and I can tell that Poppy is itching to join them, as she takes my hand and leads me in. When she does, we see that whoever lives there has knocked through so the living room opens straight into the kitchen. That's just as dark apart from more church candles that have been grouped into three and put on dinner plates that are dotted around the kitchen surfaces and the small square dining table.

Poppy tugs my hand, gesturing at Esen and Dev who are by the fridge, bickering in that way Rosh and I used to when my side of the room was a mess or she didn't want to turn out the light because she was reading. That way only siblings can when they despise each other one moment then are laughing at an episode of *The Fresh Prince of Bel-Air* the next. It suddenly makes me miss Rosh very much. When Esen steps out of the way to snatch her phone off the kitchen counter, I get a flash of pink sequins and the shock of it is enough to make me gasp.

'Dev!' Poppy squeals, letting go of my hand to run towards her. 'You look amazing!'

She literally *jumps* on Dev, the pair of them laughing and swaying side to side, almost losing their balance as they hug with such ferocity, I can't help but wonder when they got so close. I don't know whether it was the mini golf or the whole Poppy dying thing, but they seem genuinely pleased to see one each other.

'Is that the dress you were looking at in Primark?' I ask when they finally let go of one another.

'Yes!' Dev puts her hands on her hips and lifts her chin to grin at me.

She gives me a twirl and she looks so happy, all glowing and glittery and giddy like a normal teenager.

Even if, technically, she's twenty-five as of today.

'She shoplifted it,' Esen tells me, her dark eyebrows raised.

Dev ignores her. 'I begged Deborah.' Her eyes widen. '*Begged*.' 'You look great.'

'Thanks, Ash!' she gushes, hugging me this time.

She steps back and looks between Poppy and I. 'Thanks for coming, guys.'

'Thanks for having us.' Poppy smiles back, tugging off her bobble hat.

'Sorry about the music. We,' she stops to glare at Esen, 'agreed that *I'd* pick a song and *she'd* pick a song, which is why it sounds like we're at a tragic goth disco right now.'

'Um, excuse you,' Esen pipes up, clearly unamused. 'The Cure are not tragic.'

I take it that's what they were bickering about when we arrived.

'Right?' Poppy says, unwinding her yellow tartan scarf. '"Lullaby" is one of my favourite songs.'

Esen points at her as if to say, *See?* but Dev waves her hand at her. 'I mean, it's fine for lying on your bed, wallowing in the weight of your existential dread, but you can't really dance to it, can you?'

Esen looks like she's going to have a stroke so I change the subject.

'Happy birthday, Dev.'

The music stops then, so she doesn't respond, holding her hands up with an excited smile as she waits for her song choice to come on. There's a beat of silence, then I hear the familiar *ding ding ding ding* of 'Bad Girls' by M.I.A. and she starts bouncing up and down, her white-blonde bob swinging back and forth.

'Yes!' Poppy hisses, ripping off her coat and throwing it on the kitchen counter with such force it snuffs two of the candles out. Dev, clearly grateful to find someone who wants to dance with her, takes Poppy's hand and leads her into the middle of the living room.

'OK. Bye, then,' Esen calls after them, as we watch everyone shuffle out of the way to make room as they start singing along to M.I.A. and dancing gleefully.

'Live fast. Die young,' Esen says, shaking her head.

You couldn't make it up.

'Who lives here, by the way?' I ask, looking around at the kitchen. Even in the candlelight, I can tell it's too nice to be an abandoned house Dev is 'borrowing' for the night. There's a pile of post on top of the microwave and a patchwork of postcards secured to the fridge by plastic fruit magnets. 'I didn't think reapers could have houses.'

'I think it used to belong to someone Erik reaped.' She points at a guy standing on the other side of the living room talking to a girl in a black hijab and I turn back to stare at Esen. I must look as horrified as I feel because she frowns then shrugs. 'What? They're not using it any more, are they? Don't worry.' She waves her hand at me. 'We'll leave it exactly as we found it. It's not like anyone's gonna get wasted and puke in a pot plant, is it?'

I give her a look that tells her she'd better, but she doesn't seem bothered. 'Where else could we go? We can't have *another* party on the beach.'

I suppose so, but it still creeps me out as I look back at Poppy and Dev who are now laughing and jumping up and down in the middle of the living room, pretending to brush their shoulders off.

'What are you doing?' I hear Esen ask.

I don't look at her, though, too concerned with whether or not Poppy is talking to anyone.

Is she talking to that guy next to her?

I hope she's not.

'Ash.'

I don't look at her. 'What?'

'What are you doing?'

'You mean, other than judging you for using a dead person's house for a party?'

'I mean, apart from that, what are you doing?'

'Huh?' It must be obvious that I'm not listening, because she nudges me. 'What?'

'Why are you here, Ash?'

I blink at her, confused. 'You told me to come.'

'No, I mean, why are you *here*.' She points to the floor. 'In the kitchen, with me?'

What is she on about?

'Where am I supposed to be, Esen?'

I frown at her and this time she points to where Poppy and Dev are dancing. 'You're missing it.'

'Missing *what*?' I ask, but before she can tell me, a Radiohead song comes on and everyone stops dancing and turns towards the kitchen, their thumbs turned down as they boo at Esen.

'Oh *all right*,' she sneers, muttering something about no one being able to appreciate decent music any more as she snatches her phone off the kitchen counter and puts a Missy Elliott song on instead. 'There? Happy?'

They clearly are as they cheer and start dancing again,

Poppy and Dev in the middle of it all.

'Missing *what*?' I ask again, when she puts the phone back on the counter.

'It. *This*. Being at a party with your girl.' She gestures at the living room again and I turn to look at Poppy who is jumping up and down on the spot, red hair everywhere. 'You're so worried about looking out for big holes and falling pianos that you're missing everything. I mean, I know my outburst earlier didn't help.'

When I turn to look at her again, she looks embarrassed.

Actually embarrassed.

I know it's at herself, not at me, but I still feel the urge to apologise.

'Listen. I'm sorry,' I say before she can continue. 'You were right. I'm being selfish.'

'You're not being selfish.' She shakes her head. 'You want to be with Poppy and I get that.'

'Yeah, but I shouldn't have dragged you into it.'

'You didn't drag me into it. It was my idea to go to the cemetery, remember?' She stops to shake her head again. 'None of this is your fault, Ash. Besides, I'm not exactly backwards in coming forwards, am I? I could have said no at any point. It's just . . .' She presses her lips together and I tense, slipping my hands into the back pockets of my jeans as I realise that she's trying to stop herself from saying something. She can't ignore it, though, and lets out a frustrated sigh then spits it out. 'You're a pain in the ass, Ash, but I've got used to having you around.'

Oh.

I giggle with relief but she suddenly looks solemn again.

'I don't want anything to happen to you, Ash.'

I smile clumsily, startled by the rare moment of affection. 'I don't want anything to happen to me, either.'

'That's why I didn't tell you.'

'Tell me what, Esen?'

She won't look at me and it feels like I'm back on the boat, the whole kitchen tipping back and forth.

She huffs out a sigh then says, 'We've always been three.'

'Who?'

'It's always been me, Dev and someone else.'

'OK?' I say, unsure where she's going with this.

'Before you there was a guy called Joseph.'

'Yeah?'

'But he left us on New Year's Eve.'

'OK.' I frown as I remember the girl Dev introduced me to at the reaper party on New Year's Day – what was her name? Danica? The one who told me that she reaps children with cancer. 'What did he get promoted to? Reaping puppies that have been run over?'

'He didn't get promoted,' Esen says, but she still won't look at me. 'He left.'

I'm frowning so hard it should be making my head hurt. 'Left to go where?'

She hesitates and I want to reach for her and shake her.

'I can't. Deborah will kill me again if I tell you.'

I take a step towards her. 'Tell me, Esen.'

My voice quivers as I say it and she must hear it as well because she finally looks at me.

'You're not supposed to know until New Year's Eve.'

Just tell me, I want to yell, but nothing comes out as I stare at her.

'He got on the boat,' she finally spits out then closes her eyes and lets go of a defeated sigh.

'What boat?' It takes me a moment to get what she's saying, then when I do, I almost lose my balance as the kitchen seems to turn so suddenly it feels like I'm suspended upside down on a rollercoaster. 'Charon's boat?'

She nods and I'm light-headed as I try to decipher what that means.

'Where did he go, Esen?' I ask again, my voice far steadier than I feel.

'I don't know.' She just shrugs. 'Wherever it is that they go. Every New Year's Eve we get a new reaper so one of us can go. Me and Dev didn't want to this year so Joseph did.'

I stare at her as my brain tries to grasp what she's saying then slips.

Grasps.

Slips.

Grasps.

Slips.

'So.' She shrugs when she realises that I'm not getting it. 'I mean, *technically*.' She shrugs again, putting her hand in her hair and fisting it. 'You can get on the boat next New Year's Eve if Dev and I decide not to.'

I should be furious – I thought this was it, for eternity – but there it is, at last.

Hope.

Bright, beautiful hope.

'And find Poppy,' I say, the words sparking off my tongue and exploding around us like fireworks.

Esen shrugs again. 'Not necessarily—'

'You said,' I interrupt, taking my hand out of the back pocket of my jeans. I see it shaking as I point at her, but I don't try to stop it. 'You said that we go wherever we believe is beyond the sea.'

She doesn't say anything, but she doesn't need to.

'So, if Poppy and I believe that we're going to the same place then we'll go to the same place.'

She chuckles sourly. 'What the fuck do I know, though?'

I ignore her, spinning round to face the living room where Poppy is dancing wildly. 'I have to tell her.'

'No.' She reaches for my arm. When I turn back she's frowning. 'Don't get her hopes up. It's cruel.'

'I have to give her *something*, Esen.'

How can I not tell her?

This is more than we had a few minutes ago.

'Just leave her be. Let her have this.' She nods towards where Poppy and Dev are dancing. 'Let her enjoy the party and whatever else she wants to do. Let her leave on her own terms, then if you find her on New Year's Eve, great, but if you don't, at least you've said goodbye and she won't spend eternity waiting for you.'

I hesitate at that, imagining Poppy waiting on some shore somewhere for a boat that isn't coming.

'Go,' Esen tells me. 'You don't know how long you've got, so just go dance with your girl.'

So I go to Poppy, sliding between everyone on the makeshift

dance floor until I find her in the middle. She throws her arms around my neck when she sees me, peppering my face with kisses. I tell her to get off, but I don't want her to, because she's never looked so alive. Her cheeks pink and her hairline glistening with sweat, the energy burning off her almost enough to kick start my long-dead heart.

'This is all I want,' she says into my ear, holding me tighter.

TWENTY-SIX

I don't know what time it is, but when I look up from the corner Poppy and I have retreated to, the living room is almost empty. Esen left to do a reap a while ago and when Dev approaches, her pink sequinned dress gone in favour of what she was wearing when I saw her in the bookshop earlier, I know that she has to leave to do the same.

So Poppy and I decide to go as well, hugging Dev goodbye as we part on the pavement outside the house.

'What time is it?' Poppy asks as she winds her yellow tartan scarf around her neck.

'Shit,' I mutter when I check my phone. 'It's almost half-three.'

Everything will be closed now, even in Brighton.

As I'm about to put it back in my jacket pocket, I get a message and say a little prayer that it's not Deborah.

Luckily, it's Esen.

If you get a reap, tell me and I'll do it – E

I don't even pretend to protest, replying immediately to thank her, then turning to Poppy.

'You tired, babe? Do you want to head home?'

'No.' She shakes her head furiously as she tugs on her bobble hat like a toddler refusing to go to bed.

'What do you want to do, then?'

'Everything,' she says, suddenly breathless, her eyes bright.

'Like what?'

She thinks about it for a moment and I already know what she's going to say.

'Let's go to the beach,' she says, reaching for my hand. 'Say goodnight to the moon.'

I don't think about it until we get there, but it's kind of nice, bookending the day with the beach. We have it to ourselves, the sea rushing up to greet us like an eager puppy as Poppy picks a spot that's close enough to hear it – rather than the cars on the road behind us – but still far enough away that I don't need to worry that it's going to reach out and snatch us off the beach. I shoo away a seagull that pads over as if expecting to join us, then shrug off my jacket and lay it on the pebbles, gesturing for her to sit down first before I join her. She rests her head on her shoulder as soon as I do, then looks up at the sky, the moon hanging over us like a naked light bulb in an empty room.

'There she is,' she says with a blissful sigh.

When she tilts her face up towards it, the moonlight catches on her face. Her cheekbones. Her eyebrows. Down the smooth sweep of her nose, pooling at the tip in a dot that reminds me of the star map back at the bookshop.

351

She sighs again. 'Say it, then.'

'Say what?'

'Say goodnight to the moon.' She nudges me. 'Didn't you read that book as a kid?'

'Of course.'

It was Rosh's favourite.

'My mum used to read it to me as a kid,' Poppy says, reaching for my hand and squeezing it.

When she goes quiet, I know I should leave it, but there's one more person she needs to speak to.

'Speaking of your mum, you've spoken to her today, and your dad,' I say carefully, hoping not to disturb the soap bubble around us. 'But what about your grandmother? Have you spoken to her yet?'

Her face changes then and with that, the soap bubble bursts.

She doesn't look at me. 'She died.'

'What?' I pull away, frowning at her as I wait for her to look at me. 'When?'

'A couple days after you did.'

'Poppy.' Her hand is still in mine and I squeeze it tightly. 'No.'

She looks away again, picking up a pebble with her other hand and sweeping her thumb over it.

'I'm so sorry, Pop. I know you adored her.'

She nods sadly. 'I did.'

'Are you OK?'

'It was just a lot, you know? I'd only just got the message from Adara on Insta telling me what had happened to you.'

So that's how she found out.

352

I've been aching to ask her, but I didn't want to make her think about it.

About how people are going to find out when she dies.

'I had to go for a walk after she told me because I didn't want my parents to know how upset I was. I went and sat in the Enclosures for a while and when I got back, Mum said that Dad was in his study, on the phone to the home my grandmother was in. I could hear him crying and I knew.'

'Oh, Poppy.' I bring her hand to my mouth and kiss it. 'I'm so sorry.'

'I've never been to a funeral.' She laughs again, but it's just as hollow. Like canned laugher. 'Then I went to two funerals in a week.'

'Poppy, I'm sorry.' I kiss her hand again.

'I'm OK. Really.' She waits for me to look at her, then nods at me with a brave smile. 'I loved my grandmother. She was *amazing*. She was seventy-two and she did it all. Everything. She trekked through Nepal and saw Hendrix at Woodstock and was a member of Greenpeace. I mean, she walked from London to Paris when she was pregnant with my dad to protest nuclear testing in France. She had this long, incredible life, you know?'

I don't, actually.

'I thought it was so cruel when she was diagnosed with MS and had to use a wheelchair, but how can I be now?' Her smile is a little more honest this time. 'She's so lucky, Ash. She did all of that stuff, everything she ever wanted to do, and now she's with my grandfather, where she belongs.'

I bring her hand up to my mouth and kiss it again.

'Hey,' she says when I do. 'Can I play you a song?'

'Sure,' I say as she takes her phone out of her coat pocket and holds it up.

'They played it at her funeral. It was the first song my grandparents danced to at their wedding, but it reminded me of you.'

'Me?'

'Yeah. I started bawling as soon as I heard it because it made me think of us, on New Year's Eve. Hang on,' she says, unlocking her phone. She has a string of messages that she ignores, opening a playlist. She scrolls through it and smiles when she finds the song that she's looking for, then looks up at me, waiting for my reaction as it starts playing.

I vaguely recognise it.

It sounds like something from an old movie.

'Do you know it?' she asks. '"The Way You Look Tonight" by Frank Sinatra.'

'Yeah.'

It's the song Chris and Lorelai danced to in *Gilmore Girls*.

Her smile fades as quickly as it came and I wonder what she's thinking.

If she's realising that she'll never have that.

Never have a first dance.

I don't even think about it, just clamber to my feet and hold my hand out.

'What?' she asks, her cheeks pink as she looks at my hand.

'May I have this dance, Miss Morgan?'

'It would be an honour, Miss Persaud,' she grins, almost stumbling in her haste to get up and take my hand.

We don't so much dance as sway, which is all we can manage on the pebbles. We slip a couple of times, almost losing our balance, which isn't quite as romantic as I'd imagined, but I don't care as she throws her head back and laughs up at the moon. And oh, it's such a shame. Such a shame that she'll never get to do this in a long white dress that swishes behind her like peacock feathers. There's no time now. No time to do any of the things on the list she made on New Year's Eve. No time to fly to Bali. No time to surf and eat Nasi Goreng in a tiny café on the beach with sand between her toes. No time to learn to speak Mandarin or how to make the perfect grilled cheese sandwich. No time to decide what university to go to then get wasted during Freshers' Week and miss her first lecture because she's so hungover. There will be no first car. No first flat to paint. No first garden to plant tulips in. No golden retriever. No rowdy Christmas dinners with everyone talking at once.

I won't have any of that stuff, either, but for the first time since I woke up on the sofa in the bookshop on New Year's Eve, I don't care. Sixteen years is nowhere near long enough to live a whole life, a life like Poppy's grandmother's, but it's enough to have learned this: don't worry about dying, because while you're worrying about that, you won't notice the thousand tiny ways that you die every day.

Every time someone tells you to grow up.

Each time someone tells you to be realistic.

Every time someone tells you that you're too much and not enough, all at once.

Don't listen to them.

You don't need to be better than anyone else, you just need to be better than who you used to be.

It doesn't feel like it now, but one day you'll be scared of becoming the person you are today.

Actually, you'll be scared that you never stopped being that person.

People come and go. Some are just cigarette breaks and others are wild fires.

Some people take more than they give. They take it and they never give it back and it doesn't matter how tightly they hold you or how often they kiss you, it will never be enough to replace what they took.

Don't let them.

If they want to leave, let them.

You can miss someone, but not want them back.

You can want to know why, but still ignore your phone when they call.

But never regret something you once wanted.

Because if you let it, like Dev says, it will grow and grow until there's no room for anything else.

For anyone else.

There's a difference between those people and the ones who love you, even if you question it because they don't say it in the way you need to hear it. Not everyone knows how to say *I love you* so learn to hear the different ways they tell you. They say it all the time. Even if it's just, 'Don't forget your gloves' or, 'Have you eaten anything today?'

Make sure you're listening.

It's OK to take the songs you skip off your playlist.

It's OK not to finish the book if it feels like a closed door, not a window.

It's OK not to get married, if you don't want to.

It's OK not to have kids, if you don't want them.

It's OK not to know all of this yet.

'What are you thinking?' Poppy asks and I almost laugh because what do I even begin to say that?

In the end, I don't have to think about it, all of it shuffling out of the way until I am left with a single, ringing thought. 'I feel like I've loved you for a really long time, but it still isn't enough.'

That's another thing I've learned: if you love someone, tell them.

If you already have, tell them again.

Poppy presses her cheek to mine. 'I almost want to die now so that's the last thing I ever hear.'

TWENTY-SEVEN

We sit there for a while, her head on my shoulder as we look out at the big black sea and play each other songs on her phone until the battery dies. She skips 'Born to Die' by Lana Del Rey, for obvious reasons, but plays me that Death Cab for Cutie song I listened to on the bus home after our first date – the one about following someone into the dark – and it's like hearing it for the first time all over again as I hold her closer.

For a moment, I think she's falling asleep. I wouldn't blame her if she was, she must be exhausted, but then she turns to me and smiles, all loose and a bit groggy, and I know exactly what she's thinking, because I'm thinking the same thing.

We made it.

We get one more day.

She sits up suddenly. So suddenly that it makes me jump.

'Let's go for a swim,' she says, her eyes bright, bright blue again.

I laugh, assuming she can't be serious. It's January. The sea is freezing at the best of times, but it must be heart-stoppingly cold tonight. But then Poppy is on her feet, the pebbles shifting grumpily as she regains her balance. I hear a crackle of static, strands of her hair flying up and staying there for a moment as she pulls off her bobble hat and drops it. Then she's unwinding her yellow tartan scarf, letting that fall, too, and holy shit, she's serious.

'Poppy.' I blink at her as I watch her unbutton her coat. 'What are you doing?'

'What does it look like?' she says with a mischievous grin.

'You're joking, right? You're not going for a swim now? It's *freezing*!'

She shrugs off her coat, not bothering to catch it as it slides off her shoulders, change spilling out of her pockets, disappearing between the pebbles as the coat pools around her feet.

'Poppy, wait,' I say as she bends down to unzip her boots then kicks them off.

They land with a splash – one, two – on the pebbles between us.

'For what, Ash?' she asks, hooking her finger into her socks and tugging them off as well. But before I can tell her, she gestures at me to get up. 'Come on. Before I chicken out and change my mind!'

I don't move, though, just look up from where I'm sitting.

'What's wrong?' she asks with a frown and she genuinely doesn't understand why I don't want to do this.

All I can do is laugh. 'Pops, this is mad.'

'Please, Ash. Indulge me.' She holds her hand out, beckoning me with her fingers to take it. 'I've always wanted to go for a swim at night.'

'Do it in July, then.'

I realise what I've said and I want the whole beach to swallow me up.

'I'm sorry, Pop. I—'

'It's OK,' she interrupts, shaking her head.

It's not, though.

If it's true – she has always wanted to go for a swim at night – then this is it, isn't it?

When else is she going to do it?

So I get to my feet. She cheers as I do, clapping happily as I bend down to unlace my DMs.

'We'll only go in for a minute,' she promises as she watches me take off my socks and tuck them into my boots. 'Plus, I'm five minutes from home. It's right there.' She points up at the road. 'We'll go in, see what the moon looks like from underneath, then I'll go straight home and jump in the shower, I promise.'

I must not look convinced, but she takes my hand and squeezes it. 'I know you're scared of open water, but you can swim, right? You've swum in the sea before, haven't you?'

'Only a couple of times.'

When I was a kid.

When I was fearless.

Unbreakable.

My bones made of rubber, my heart a ball that always bounced back, no matter who I threw it to.

'What are you scared of, then?' she asks, her frown reappearing.

She doesn't say it – *You're already dead* – but as I turn my cheek to look out at the sea, I notice that it's as still as bathwater now, the waves just a whisper against the shore, so there's nothing to be scared of, is there?

But then I realise that it's not me I'm scared for.

It's her.

'You're here, right?' she says, squeezing my hand again. 'Nothing's going to happen to me.'

What if it does, though?

What if it does and I can't save her?

'We'll be in and out, I promise, Ash.'

When I turn my cheek to look at her again, she's smiling hopefully.

If this is what she wants to do, how can I say no?

Plus, I'm kind of curious to find out what the moon looks like from underneath as well.

'OK,' I hear myself say before I can stop myself, squeezing her hand.

She thanks me, giving me a quick kiss on the cheek, then I let her lead me towards the shore. The pebbles must be cold, because she's giggling and hopping from foot to foot. I'm aware of it, but it doesn't bother me in the same way as I watch her, hair ablaze in the moonlight as she gets to the edge of the sea.

'Ready?' she asks.

But before I can tell her that I'm not, the sea reaches out to touch our bare toes. She squeals, holding my hand tighter as she goes to step into it. I don't move, though, unable to look away from the horizon as I wonder what's out there, beneath the surface. But then I see the red flashing lights of the wind farm – all 116 of them – and I look at her, wondering what my life would have been if I hadn't met her. If I'd be at home right now, swaddled in my duvet, my back to the radiator as I silently mourn some girl who hasn't messaged me back, the pain enough to break my bones, smash them to dust so the universe can reclaim them.

Turn them back into stars.

I might have never known that someone's smile could set me alight like this.

That their hand in mine would be enough to fan the flames, enough to keep them alight for years.

Years and years.

So I nod and we step forward together.

The pebbles are more slippery than I expected. I don't think she did, either, because she loses her balance and I catch her by the elbow before she falls, arse first, into the water. She laughs wildly as I do, stopping for a moment to catch her breath, letting me know when she's ready to take another step forward. We're more careful this time, the water lapping around our ankles now as we stop, regain our balance then keep going. Step. Stop. Step. Stop. Step. Stop. Until the water is up to our knees and she's shivering, her mouth open so wide that I can see the pink of her tongue.

This is probably far enough, but she looks so happy, looking out at the sea like she's found a secret room in her house, a door that opens up to a grand ballroom she didn't know was there. Because how can it be? It's the same sea she grew up with. The same sea she looked out of her bedroom window at when she was a kid, watching the boats go by. The same sea she must gaze out on every day, from her window at Roedean, watching it go from blue to bluer to black, until it's hard to see where it ends and the sky begins. The sea she's swum in so many times, but much like how the sky is a different colour at 4 a.m., now she knows that the sea at 4 a.m. is completely different.

Something not everyone knows about.

Now she does.

We take a few more steps and I feel a bit steadier, wondering how much further the pebbles go out, if we can walk for miles and miles – walk all the way to France, like her grandmother did – and they'll always be there. But just as I think it, I feel them begin to slope down – down, down – until it becomes harder for my toes to find them. Then they're gone and I start kicking wildly, the water whipping up around me.

'Ash,' Poppy says softly. 'It's OK.'

It's not.

It's in my eyes.

My mouth.

But then she's there, her arms around my waist and her chest to mine. The water is up to my chin now and I tip my head back before it swallows me up.

'Don't,' she says, a hand cupping the back of my head to bring it back up. 'Just stay still.'

But I can't.

I can feel the water circling my neck.

'It's OK,' she says again. 'It's OK. It's salt water. You'll float.'

No.

It's devouring me, I can feel it.

'I'm going to let go now, Ash.'

'No!' I gasp, kicking as hard as I can.

I kick something and *oh God*. There's something there. Under the water. Then I'm flailing, losing control of my arms and legs, as though they're no longer under my command, my body surrendering to it.

Letting it pull me under.

'Ash, it's me,' she says and I can tell that she's trying not to laugh. 'You're kicking me.'

'Oh, shit. Sorry,' I gasp, water getting in my mouth as I do.

Then her hands are on my waist, lifting me so my shoulders break the surface and I gasp again.

'Bend your knees,' she tells me. When I do, she says, 'Now kick your legs. Slowly. *Slowly*.'

I do as she says, smaller kicks that don't make the water splash around us so much.

'Now move your arms.'

'How?' I ask desperately.

I've only just mastered kicking.

'Side to side. That's it,' she says when I start doing it. 'Slowly. Slowly.'

Slowly.

Slowly.

'There,' she says with a proud smile. 'You're doing it.'

'Am I?' I laugh. 'Am I swimming?'

'Well,' she says, her nose wrinkling. 'You're not drowning.'

I laugh again, watching as her arms gently swish from side to side, copying her.

It's only then that I realise that she's not holding on to me any more.

'Shit,' I gasp, almost going under again, but then she points up.

I lift my chin, and there it is: the moon, flat against the

midnight sky. The sky suddenly clear – no clouds, no seagulls, nothing – as if to give us an uninterrupted view. I blink the water from my eyelashes so I can get a better look, and while we can't see the underneath of it, this is as close to it as I've ever been.

Suddenly, everything is still and we stay like that for a while, faces tilted up.

Then I feel her hands on my face as she reaches for me. 'Thank you.'

She presses her mouth to mine and when she pulls back to look at me, I can't feel my heart, but I can feel something else. Something deep, deep in my bones that makes me wonder if some part of me has always known her.

Always loved her.

If we're made of the same star stuff, like Carl Sagan says.

'Is it what you expected?' I ask as she tips her head back and looks up at the moon with a slow smile.

'It's better.'

I want to tell her what Esen said at the party, tell her to wait for me, that I'll find her, but before I can, she's gone, tipping forward and disappearing so suddenly that I wonder if something has yanked her under. I open my mouth to scream, but nothing comes out as I stare at the surface of the water, waiting for it to part and for her to reappear, but she doesn't. So I blindly reach down, grasping at nothing. Again and again until I grab a fistful of her jumper, yanking her back up. She breaks the surface with a squeal and a gasp, clearly thrilled.

'Poppy, what the fuck?' I bark as she smooths her hair back with her hands.

She just laughs.

'It's not funny!' I tell her, kicking my legs furiously, trying to keep afloat.

She smiles at me the way she did the afternoon we met on the boat, in that slow, mischievous way that makes me forgive her immediately. Before I can kiss her and tell her not to do it again, her whole body jerks. I reach for her, wondering if she's been stung by a jellyfish, or something, or if a piece of seaweed is grabbing at her ankle, but then she's gone, her eyes closed and her mouth open as the sea pulls her back under.

'Poppy!' I plunge my hand into the water, but my fingers grasp at nothing. I find something – her hair, I think – but then it's gone and my hand is empty. A second becomes a few seconds which becomes a minute and I'm frantic. She's going to drown. But then I find the collar of her jumper and drag her up.

She bursts from the water with a wild laugh.

I slap her on the arm this time. 'Poppy! Don't do that!'

She laughs, clearly unrepentant.

'Right,' I say through my teeth and I sound like my mother. 'We're going back.'

To my surprise, she does as she's told, which is good because I need her help. After all, staying in the same spot without drowning is one thing, finding my way back to the shore is quite another. I don't dare take my eyes off her, my hand still fisted in her jumper as she leads us back, terrified that I'm going to lose her again. She's looking at me as well, giggling and apologising for scaring me, telling me that she's always wondered what it's like to be a mermaid.

I glance at the shore and I'm relieved to find that we're closer than I thought. I can see everything begin to take shape again – the pale-green arches of the terrace, the biscuit-coloured pebbles, our clothes in a hasty heap, the yellow of her scarf the only thread of colour among them – and I see something else.

Charon.

TWENTY-EIGHT

I look at Charon then at his boat as it bobs gently in front of him.

No.

She can't be.

How?

Where's her body?

I look back over my shoulder, but there's nothing there, just the quiet push and pull of the waves behind us.

I turn my head back to the shore, wondering if I imagined it, but he's there.

He's definitely there.

Charon.

'It's OK,' Poppy says, kissing my cheek, but all I can think is how?

When?

Somewhere in the desperate blur of panic, something begins to take focus and I remember. Poppy's body jerking before she sank beneath the surface the second time. I thought she was teasing me, but whatever happened must have happened then. Her body went under, but her soul came back up.

No.

I was supposed to stop it.

I was supposed to save her.

I didn't save her.

There's a fierce growl of thunder followed by a strike of lightning so loud I'm sure the sky is splitting in two, as if it knows. I wait for the seagulls to start squealing, but there's nothing, just this aching stretch of silence before it starts raining – quick and hard – like bullets puncturing the water around us as my feet finally find the pebbles.

'I'm sorry,' she tells me, frantically kissing my cheek. 'It's OK. It's OK.'

I'm supposed to be telling her that.

But she keeps saying it – keeps kissing my cheek – as we walk up the slope towards him.

That's when I see them. Dev and Esen, standing a few feet to his right, Dev's hair the same colour as the moon watching over us and Esen's curls as dark as the sea calling Poppy back. They begin walking towards us as we approach, reaching out to help us as our feet slip on the pebbles. Esen holds unto my arm with such urgency that I lift my chin to stare at her. She's looking at me in a way she never has before, with this maddening mixture of sorrow and pity that would make me fall into her arms if I wasn't so scared to let go of Poppy.

Dev is the first to say it, though. 'I'm so sorry.'

'We didn't know that you were already at the beach,' Esen says then, raising her voice, loud enough for Charon to hear. 'Otherwise we wouldn't have bothered coming and left this one for you.'

So that's our story, is it?

'It's OK, Poppy,' Dev says with a smile that doesn't register in her eyes. 'Come with us.'

'Come where?' she asks fiercely, so fiercely that I wonder if she's putting it on or if she really doesn't know.

Esen gestures at Charon who is still by his boat, watching us carefully.

Poppy looks at him then at me and she goes limp in my arms as we realise that we can't say goodbye. She can't kiss me or tell me that she loves me. I can't tell her to wait for me, that I'll find her on New Year's Eve. All I can do is watch as she takes the few steps towards Charon, her hair roaring red in the moonlight.

'Am I dead?' she asks when he reaches for her hand.

He nods.

'How?'

'Aneurysm.'

I've never heard him speak before. I thought his voice would be as deep as a roll of thunder, but it's light.

Almost gentle.

She turns and runs back to me and for one mad moment I think that she's going to refuse to go with him, that she's going to cling to me and beg to stay. But she stops in front of me and slips the ring from her thumb – the silver one with the red heart-shaped stone with a dagger going through it – and presses it into my palm.

'You said that you weren't going anywhere,' she whispers and I remember the promise I made to her in the back of the cab that afternoon, before the driver kicked us out. 'And you didn't.'

Never, I think, curling my hand around her ring.

She smiles at me one last time and I want to tell her, tell her to wait for me, that I'll find her, but Esen's right.

It's not fair to give her hope.

But at least I have enough for the both of us.

That's when I realise that the rain has stopped and everything is still again as I think about Poppy's aneurysm. This bright red dot on the limitless cosmic canvas of her brain that we didn't even know was there until it popped.

She sneaks another look at me as she gets in the boat, and when she sits down, she looks like the woman in that John William Waterhouse painting she likes so much. *The Lady of Shalott*, I think it was called. She's sitting in the same way, her back straight and her chin up looking out towards the horizon, her hair quivering in the breeze as Charon gets in and the curved wooden boat begins moving towards the moon.

I watch until she's gone.

Eleven Months Later

Veronica Price is exactly where Deborah said she would be, on the bridge overlooking the motorway, watching the cars pass beneath. She's not what I expected, but then they never are. I can only see her profile, her smooth, round face and rich golden-brown skin that looks more gold than brown under the street lights, her sweet button nose dotted with a diamond stud that, from here, looks like a single star. She has more hair than Esen, which I didn't think was possible, a thick heart-shaped afro, parted in the middle, that bobs gently in the breeze and glistens like crow feathers.

After spending much of today – the last eleven months and two weeks, actually, not that I've been counting – fretting that where Poppy is and where I'm going, isn't the same place, it's a relief to see Veronica because I can finally find out. I've been repeating it like a mantra – *Just believe that we're going to the same place* – over and over. After each reap. Between each step. Every time the bell rings over the door to the bookshop and someone comes in.

Just believe that we're going to the same place.

The thought makes me so giddy it's all I can do not to run over to Veronica and reach for her, but in my eagerness to get here on time, I'm early. So I hang back in case she sees me and changes her mind.

I don't want my last act as a reaper to be intervening in someone's death.

Can you imagine?

When Deborah held up the Post-it note and said, 'We have our new reaper,' Esen suggested I do it, saying that I'd never done one on New Year's Eve. Deborah had eyed her suspiciously, no doubt wondering why she didn't want to do it herself after losing out to Dev last year. And I suppose it's fitting, me reaping my replacement, even if Deborah doesn't know that Veronica is going to be my replacement yet.

Esen wished me luck as I left and Dev just smiled. I could tell that she had to stop herself from hugging me, in case she aroused Deborah's suspicions further, so I just smiled back and told them that I'd see them soon.

Now, here I am, waiting for Veronica to fall.

When Deborah handed me the Post-it note and I read:

Veronica Price

Fall

Bridge over A23

23:59

I wondered if she had got it wrong and it was a suicide because how do you fall off a bridge?

Deborah was right, of course, because there's Veronica, leaning over the edge, one hand on the railing and a can of spray paint in her other as she writes something on the side of the bridge. I can't see what it is from here, but I can't help but wonder if she's the one that wrote *JUST KISS HER* under the bridge by the station.

The one Poppy and I had our first kiss under.

She's on her tiptoes now, so far over the railing that I have to stop myself charging forward to grab her waist as she lifts her right foot off the ground. Then she's gone, arms first, then her feet, like an Olympic diver ready to pierce the pool beneath. There's a beat, then another, and finally, I hear it, the shrill shriek of metal hitting metal, of something hitting something it shouldn't, followed by the snap of breaking glass as the cars beneath the bridge screech to a halt. Then car alarms and someone pumping on their horn – and then, finally, there it is.

POP.

The first firework of the year.

I know I should be relieved because this is what I wanted, right? For her to stay so I could go. But as Veronica looks up at the fireworks fizzing over our heads, scattering shards of coloured light across the sky, she looks like a little kid. She's in utter awe of them, her mouth smoothing to a smile so big, I suddenly feel unreasonably, unreachably sad because how can I be happy about her dying like this?

It's such a waste.

Finally, she turns, and when she sees me, she takes a step back.

'Veronica Price?'

The crease between her eyebrows deepens. 'How do you know my name?'

'I'm Ash.'

She stares at me, so I nod at her. It takes her a moment, but when she realises that I'm gesturing at her to look over the railing, she does, but she doesn't let out a wail, like Alice

377

Anderson did, she just turns to face me again.

'Are you—' She stops to eye me suspiciously. 'Are you an angel?'

'Not quite,' I tell her as I reach my hand out to her. 'Come on. There's some people I'd like you to meet.'

We walk in silence, Veronica as woozy and compliant as all the others, and I wonder if I was like this with Dev.

If I just followed her without question.

When we get to the bookshop I linger on the pavement, looking at the scene through the window. Deborah behind the counter, stooped over whatever she's writing. Dev is in the middle of the shop, pacing back and forth like an expectant father in a maternity ward. She's talking to Esen, who is slouched in the armchair with a sharp smirk, her long legs slung over the arm as she twirls one of her curls around her finger, clearly taking the piss out of her.

My family.

It's enough to make me hesitate, but then I think of Poppy, leaving on Charon's boat, her hair ablaze in the moonlight, and I get that sudden, maddening itch I feel every time I think about seeing her again.

So I push the door, the bell over it heralding my return. They each look up. First at me, then at Veronica, who follows me in, there but not there, her steps heavy – almost tender – as I lead her by the elbow to the sofa. She doesn't fight me on it, just lies down, and by the time I've covered her with the tartan blanket, she's gone.

Where, I don't know, but she'll be back soon.

'So this is Veronica Price,' Esen says, head tilted as she looks down at her, curled up on the sofa.

I nod, crossing my arms with a sigh. 'This is Veronica Price.'

'I'm going to call her Ronnie.'

'What if she doesn't like Ronnie?'

'I'm going to call her Ronnie.'

'What's she like?' Dev asks, at my other side.

'She didn't say much.' I shrug. 'She didn't say anything, actually. Just asked if I was an angel.'

Esen scoffs at that and I elbow her.

'Come on,' Deborah says from behind the counter and when I look over at her, she's gesturing at us to join her. 'Leave Veronica to rest for a minute. I need to speak with you ladies.'

This is it, I think, looking between Dev and Esen who nod at me in turn.

We do as we're told for once, heading over to the counter and waiting as Deborah takes her glasses off.

'OK,' she says with a light sigh, curling her fingers around them. 'So now we have our new reaper, ladies, we have an important decision to make.'

I pretend to look confused. 'What sort of decision?'

'Dev and Esen are familiar with this, but I know you aren't, Ash,' she concedes with a nod. 'You must forgive me for not telling you about this earlier, but I hope that you understand when I do.'

'Tell me about what?' I ask, making a show of frowning.

'When we get a new reaper, an existing one can leave.'

'Leave? Leave and go where?'

She tugs on her earlobe with her fingers, avoiding my gaze. 'On the boat with Charon.'

'Charon?' I gasp theatrically. 'So we don't have to do this for ever?'

Deborah shakes her head then raises a finger to me. 'However,' she warns, looking me in the eye this time. 'The offer is made in order of seniority. So Esen first, then Dev and if they want to stay, you will be asked, Ash.'

'OK.' I look from side to side at Dev and Esen, making the groove between my eyebrows deeper.

'So . . .' Deborah pauses and I don't know if it's for dramatic effect or if she genuinely needs a moment before she asks the question, but she waits a second or two before she turns her cheek to Esen and asks, 'Miss Budak. Would you like to stay with us or would you like to continue on your journey?'

Esen pretends to think about it then says, 'What? And miss out on all of this?'

When she holds her arms out, turning to gesture at the bookshop, Deborah doesn't flinch, obviously expecting that response, as she turns to Dev.

'Miss Devlin. Would you like to stay with us or would you like to continue on your journey?'

Dev shakes her head. 'I want to stay.'

'Very well.' Deborah turns to me and if my heart still worked, it would be hammering hard enough against my ribs to splinter them. 'Miss Persaud. Would you like to stay with us or would you like to continue on your journey?'

'I don't know,' I lie, tucking my hands into the pockets of my leather jacket and biting down on my bottom lip. 'Where would I go if I get on the boat with Charon?'

For one dizzying moment, I think that she's going to tell me, that by being a reaper, I've earned the answer to the great, unanswered question – the meaning of life and what's beyond the sea. She doesn't, of course, giving me the same safe, neat answer we give everyone. 'Wherever it is that you would like to go, Miss Persaud.'

I pretend to think about it for a moment longer, then nod. 'Yes.' I nod again. 'Yes, I want to get on the boat.'

'Very well,' she says, nodding back. If she's surprised by my decision, she doesn't show it. 'We'll miss you, Miss Persaud,' she tells me and I believe her. 'But I hope that you find whoever it is that you are hoping to find.'

She lifts her chin to look at me with a smooth smile that makes me wonder if she knows.

'I need to go somewhere first,' I tell Dev and Esen as soon as we head out of the bookshop. 'It won't take long.'

They don't object, walking either side of me as we head out of town towards the sea. I think Esen knows where I want to go, but Dev is obviously confused as we walk past the beach. I don't dare look over the railing in case Charon is down there, waiting for me, slowing as we pass Poppy's house. I turn to glance at it. The lights are on, but the one in her bedroom isn't, so I turn my face away, walking a little faster as we approach Marine Gate.

Before we get to it, we turn left on to Whitehawk Road and as the houses get smaller and closer together, I think Dev knows where we're going. It's weird because I used to be embarrassed about where I lived. I always wished that we lived on Marine Parade, in a grand, wedding-cake white one with wide windows that look out on to the sea, like Poppy's, but I feel a sudden flush of pride as I walk past the procession of houses.

Each one may look the same, this unbroken row of red-bricks that stretches from here to my estate, each one with the same neat square windows – two up, one down – the same front door and the same rectangle of grass separating it from the pavement, but people live here. Really *live* here. Not like Poppy's parents, who drift from house to house, hotel to hotel, country to country, never putting roots down anywhere.

Each door is painted a different colour and while some of the gardens are tidier than others, most are well-kept and have been carefully planted with rose bushes and hydrangeas that, come summer, will bloom pink and peach and blue.

They're not houses, they're homes. There's some comfort in that. In knowing that they're either someone's first or last house, and in each one there are people. People who, like me, have lived here all their lives. Who learnt to ride their bike here and ran after the ice-cream truck. People who just got married and are saving for a new kitchen. People who came home from hospital, cradling babies who'll sleep in freshly painted nurseries under mobiles with giraffes and elephants that are just out of reach. People who, right now, are asleep on the sofa, open-mouthed, a half-drunk glass of wine beside them, who'll call their grandmother in the morning to wish her a Happy New Year.

I can hear the sluggish DUM DUM DUM from a party winding down as we approach Kingfisher Court.

'You don't want to go in, do you?' Dev asks, her eyes wide.

'Of course not,' I tell her, leading her to the playground. When her shoulders relax, I realise why she doesn't want me to go up there and chuckle. 'You're not still scared of Dorito, are you?'

'You weren't there, Ash!' she says, suddenly furious. 'It was like he was possessed!'

That makes Esen chuckle as well as we sit on the bench, me in the middle.

'Is this the slide you fell off when you were six?' Dev asks, pointing at it.

'Yeah.' I instinctively reach up to stroke the scar under my chin with my knuckle.

'Which one is it?' Dev asks, gesturing at the block of flats towering over us.

'Sixth one up.' I point to it. 'Third one along.'

I've wanted to come back here so many times since New Year's Eve, to just sit on this bench and know that they're up there. Rosh in our room, her nose in a book. My mother at her sewing machine while my father dozes on the sofa, the remote in his hand, because he won't go to bed without her. Now – after what happened with Poppy – I'm so glad I didn't come back because if I'd seen one of them, I don't think I would have been able to stop myself from running to them and falling into their arms, no doubt scaring the life out of them.

If you pardon the pun.

The kitchen light is on and I smile to myself as I realise that my father actually made it to midnight this year. Before I look away to tell Dev and Esen about his mysterious headaches that only seem to strike when he's doing something he doesn't want to do, my mother appears in the window and my whole body stiffens. If they see her as well, they don't say anything, and sit quietly next to me as I gaze up at her. I'm too far away to see her in any detail, but I know it's her and I swear she's looking right at me, as if she knows I'm there.

I don't dare move, my head spinning as a rush of something that I haven't felt in such a long time floods through me, starting at my scalp and spilling down to my toes. We stay like that for a while, before she finally turns away from the window. As she does, I see her swipe her cheek with her fingers and I know then that I can go.

That she knows I'm OK.

When we get to the beach, Charon is waiting for me, the moonlight picking out his wooden boat as it bobs gently on the suddenly still sea. I look at it, saying it again – *Just believe that we're going to the same place* – as I turn to Dev and Esen.

Dev doesn't hesitate, just throws her arms around me and holds me to her for a beat longer than usual before letting me go. When she steps back, she puts her hands on my shoulders and squeezes.

'I really hope you find her,' she says, then kisses me on the cheek.

'Me too,' Esen nods, hands in the pockets of her heavy wool coat.

As I step back from her, she reaches for me, and holds me to her, like Dev just did, kissing the top of my head.

'You'll find her,' she whispers, tucking the words between the strands of my hair. 'You found each other in life and you found each other in death and you'll find each other in whatever's beyond the sea.'

I hug her back – cling to her – the pair of us staying like that for a moment before she eventually lets go.

'Have a safe journey,' she says, reaching for her scythe pendant and pressing it between her finger and thumb.

I take mine out of my hoodie and press my lips to it.

When Esen steps back, I nod, my gaze darting between her and Dev.

I don't know what to say, hoping some wise parting words will come, but they don't.

So I nod again, then start walking towards Charon, who holds out his hand to me as I mouth Esen's words over and over, thinking about Poppy, her hair everywhere, waiting for me on a shore somewhere.

We found each other in life.

And we found each other in death.

So I will find you now, whatever's beyond the sea.

ACKNOWLEDGEMENTS

My mother passed away the day my third book was published. It was painful in so many ways, ways I'm sure I don't need to recount if you've been through it yourself, but losing someone after a prolonged illness is particularly cruel. Not that there's a 'right' way to lose someone you love, of course. Loss is loss. However it happens. The pain is just as keen and the space they leave behind just as unfillable.

But losing someone in pieces is a loss unlike any other. One day my mother could feed herself, and the next she couldn't. One day she could sit up, and the next she couldn't. One day she could lift her head, and the next she couldn't. She went piece by piece until, finally, her heart gave way and that was it.

It's a pain not everyone knows. Your world divides into Before and After and you become a member of a club that you had no desire to join. I had been a long-time member of that club after losing my father to cancer at sixteen so to do it all again twenty two years later was, frankly, too much.

Afterwards, it felt like there was nothing left. I was burnt out, like if you cut me open, all that would come out was smoke. I stopped reading, unable to focus on a book for more than few pages before my mind wandered somewhere else and didn't come back. Then I stopped reaching for my notebook, stopped scribbling down the snatches of conversation I overheard on the top deck of the bus or a sentence that, when I put the words in the right order, suddenly sang. And just like that, I stopped writing.

So I waited. I adopted a dog. Moved somewhere I could see the sea. Got a job, served tea and cake to people who wouldn't look me in the eye. A year passed. Then two and still, nothing.

All I wanted was for someone to tell me that everything was going to be okay, but then it occurred to me that, as a writer, that's what I do. Or I should. I should put into words the things that are too big – too awful – to articulate. The things most people cannot. If I do my job properly, you'll finish one of my books feeling seen and, I hope, knowing that you'll get through this, no matter how insurmountable *this* is.

I hadn't realised how lucky I was that I could do that until I couldn't anymore. Writing was how I made sense of the world, so not being able to do it was a different kind of loss, but it was equally unfillable.

So I stopped waiting, told myself that it didn't matter if I didn't write again. That was before. This is After and After involves walking my dog along the beach every morning and serving tea and cake to people who won't look me in the eye and that's okay because at least I made it through the fire.

But some people did wait. Malorie Blackman. Nikesh Shukla. Catherine Johnson. Sara Barnard. Holly Bourne. Eleanor Wood. Juno Dawson. They each sat with me while I cried and told them that I'd never write again knowing full well that I would, that once the smoke had cleared After would feel less like a room I'd wandered into and couldn't find my way out of and more like somewhere I wanted to be.

Jan Kofi-Tsekpo at The Arts Council, who, when that finally happened, gave me the time to write, otherwise I would not have had the space or the confidence to finish telling this story. Polly Lyall-Grant at Hachette Children's Group who saw something in it when I did and her team – Halimah, Emily, Aash, Alice and the copy editor and proofreader and typesetter – who turned it into the book that you are holding now. Including Sarah Maxwell who illustrated the *stunning* cover that made me scream the first time I saw it.

The smart, funny, *brilliant* women who got me through the last five years without even knowing. Sunny Singh. Bim Adewunmi. Bolu Babalola. Daniellé Dash. Charlotte Abotsi. Melissa Cox. Laura Dockrill. Bethany Rutter. Alice Slater. Keris Stainton. Thank you. I wish nothing but the best for you all.

My dear friends, Val, H and Alan, who literally held me together after my mother passed away, and Angela, Suzi, Catherine, Hannah, Tracy, Duncan, Ian and Lucy, who have made Brighton feel like home. Not to forget, Scoot, Kelly, Fiona and Jade who knew me Before and know me After and every version of me inbetween.

My sweet baby angel nephews, Jacob and Nathan, who honestly couldn't care less how many books Aunty Tanya writes, as long as we go to the Aquarium and pick shells on the beach and wrestle to Kung Fu Fighting. (Them not me.) And my brother for bringing them to see me so that we can go to the Aquarium and pick shells on the beach and wrestle to Kung

Fu Fighting. I love you all so very much.

My darling dog, Frida, who I had thought I was rescuing, but ended up saving me.

Finally, Claire Wilson, who has been so kind and so patient and would not give up on me when most agents would have cut me loose for not making them any money for five years. She knew that I would write again and, as always, she was right. (Frame this, Wilson. I'll never say that again.) I don't even know how to begin to thank her for that, but these few sentences will have to suffice until I find a way.

So. There you go. If you've read Ash's story and you're glad I told it, these are the people that made it possible. Without them, Ash would never have found her first – and last – love and I am forever grateful.